TRADE-OFFS

'Paula, do you ever wonder what will happen when we get old? I mean really old?'

'Wonder isn't the operative word,' said Paula wryly. 'Worry, that's it. Sometimes I wake up in the middle of the night and wonder who will bury me.'

Cass wrinkled her nose. 'Somehow, we never get it out of our heads that Mr Right will show up and buy us the rest of our lives, do we?'

'Nope,' said Paula. 'Complete with house, kids, white picket fence and . . .'

'And meanwhile, we fritter away our money, if we have any. Which we do. I mean, you and I earn more in a year than our fathers earned in five. And we never consider what's going to happen to us if the prince doesn't show up.'

'Some of us do,' said Paula.

TRADE-OFFS

Jane Adams

A STAR BOOK
published by
the Paperback Division of
W. H. ALLEN & Co. PLC

A Star Book
Published in 1984
by the Paperback Division of
W. H. Allen & Co. PLC
44 Hill Street, London W1X 8LB

First published in the United States of America
by William Morrow and Company, Inc., 1983

Printed and bound in Great Britain by
Anchor Brendon Ltd, Tiptree, Essex

ISBN 0 352 315229

ONE

First there was the money and then the house. Someone commented that the timing was lucky but not essential; if events had been reversed—even if the money hadn't come along when it did, like an unexpected legacy—Cass still would have found a way to buy the brownstone on Twelfth Street.

Cass was chagrined when she heard that; she didn't perceive herself as the agent of her own life. As she told Paula, sometimes things just happened right for her.

'Really?' Paula asked. 'Don't you think you make them happen?' She never should have repeated that remark; now Cass would fret over it for days.

'Who said that?' Cass wanted to know, but Paula made a vague gesture and evaded the issue. As a matter of fact, it was Nick who said it; Cass would make him pay for that, Paula knew, insist on knowing exactly what he meant by it. She would not take it as a compliment, or even as a harmless observation. Cass always looked for hidden meanings in what was said about her.

'It sounds so manipulative,' she complained, putting invisible quotation marks around the word. She made a short jabbing motion with her hand, spilling a few drops of champagne on the sable coat of a woman manoeuvring through the crush of people who filled the library bar at the Palace that night.

Paula shook her head; her wiry curls sprang away from her face. 'So? Why is that word so loaded for you?'

Cass sighed. 'Because it's such a stereotype.

Dominating, power-crazed, ball-breaking, unfeminine—that's a big one. . . . Amelia says it all comes down to one thing: how do we get to be like them without being like them?'

'Men, you mean?'

'Mmmm. When all it means is getting things done. Like you, for instance. You focus on what matters—a case, a political issue, a job—and you go for it. But you don't jerk people around, manipulate them. You don't do that.'

'No?' Paula was amused; how had things gotten around to her? The topic at hand, after all, was Cass—as usual.

'No,' replied Cass firmly. 'You're not manipulative, Paula, just ambitious. Goal-orientated. You don't have to apologize for that.' She patted her friend's hand.

'I'm not,' Paula said drily. 'And you don't need to, either.'

Cass did that often; she projected her own uncertainties onto Paula at a distance which was to her no distance at all, merely an extension of her self. It did not bother Paula; in a way, she was flattered by it.

'Well, this time things *did* happen right for you,' she said, to mollify Cass and divert her from prying into the source of the comment. 'For us,' she added.

'Uh huh,' Cass agreed happily. 'It all just fell into place, the money and the house.' She squeezed Paula's hand. 'And you, of course.'

The house was the brownstone on Twelfth Street, which Cass found in the most unlikely way, and which she bought with Paula late that autumn. Which Ellin moved into, with Paula and Cass, the following winter—into the brownstone's small attic apartment, with the eaves that peaked the ceiling, and the windows that flooded the space with light.

But Ellin didn't even know about the house then, that night at the hotel bar, when Cass and Paula toasted their venture into Real Life. That's what Paula called it. 'Holy shit, we're grown-ups!' She laughed tipsily as they finished off the bottle of champagne. 'We just bought ourselves a fucking house!'

She ignored Cass's involuntary wince. And Cass leaned over the small table to peck Paula on the cheek, reflecting for the hundredth time in their durable friendship that, though she was thirty-four and already a grown-up, some things about Paula were just never going to change.

TWO

Cass saw the house for the first time right after she heard about the money. She was outside on the terrace of Amelia Jordan's apartment, a duplex whose interior, filled with French and English antiques, had been photographed so often by so many design magazines that even Cass, who cared a great deal about things—particularly fine, old, expensive things—took it for granted.

Cass was a lively streak of colour that evening in a red chiffon gown that clung to her body as she moved gracefully through the elegant mauve rooms, where flowers bloomed year round in Meissen bowls and silk-draped lamps suffused everyone with a soft glow. She had been smiling at Amelia's clients and friends for hours; her face felt stiff, and she wanted some air.

She stood on the terrace, above the motley cluster of buildings that give the West Village its charm, watching the swirling flakes of the season's first snowfall dust everything into a blurred harmony. The clock steeple of the Jefferson Market loomed in the distance; directly across the courtyard, she saw a square of golden light streaming out from the top floor of the building that faced the terrace.

She could not see very far into the room, but in what she was able to make out there was a sense of transition. There were canvases stacked against packing boxes, and shelves empty of books. In the centre of the room rested a large, paper-covered bundle that might have been a rug removed from or perhaps destined for storage.

A man sat at a desk behind the french doors to his own terrace. His head was cradled in his arms so she could not see his face, but she thought he was an old man; he lifted himself upright with great effort, as if it required all of his remaining strength to do so.

He turned away from her and motioned with short, stabbing gestures. Following the movement with her eyes to where the light seemed brighter, she realized that he held a poker in his hand. It was the fireplace that did it, she said later; suddenly she missed her own fireplace, with a deep longing. And that was where it all began.

As she watched him, she was overwhelmed by homesickness. It was a feeling familiar since childhood. No matter how glowingly her father praised their new quarters, in whatever city the Navy sent them to, it engulfed her as they drove away—the sadness of leaving, and the fear that no one would remember her if she ever, or never, returned.

Her apartment in New York didn't feel like home, despite her efforts to personalize the depressing, boxy and overpriced three rooms on the Upper East Side. The cottage in Seattle did, but strangers lived there now, except for August. In August Cass went back to clean and scrape and paint and putter, readying things for the next renters. In August she went home to the cottage on the Sound, where the nights were so quiet she could hear a gull land on the edge of a wave. Nights she would sit up suddenly in bed and wonder how, and why, she could ever leave.

But each September she did and came back to the city. Back to her job at Amelia Jordan, Incorporated, her expensive and characterless apartment, and her on-again, off-again affair with Nick Pappas.

She stood on the terrace, watching the man across the courtyard, until he looked up and noticed her. Embarrassed, she turned away.

'Everyone in New York watches everyone else,' said a man who materialized, unnoticed, at her side. 'It's an occupational hazard of vertical living, or a reward, depending on what you see.'

Cass turned and smiled automatically. She noted his thick, bulky body, and the crisp reddish hair that fell over sandy brows, from beneath which his clear blue eyes appraised and engaged her. He looked like the kind of man who dictates memos in the first-class section, and always gets off at O'Hare.

'What do you see from your window?' she asked him.

'Street theatre,' he responded, offering her a cigarette from a slim gold case. 'Sometimes it's participatory, whether you like it or not. For instance, somebody threw a rock through my window last week, and I'm on the fourth floor.'

'Did it hit anything important?'

'Like me, you mean?'

She chuckled. She quickened to style, and she liked his. He knew it, and was enjoying it.

'No, but it just missed. I'm Grey Tucker. I don't think we've met.'

'I'm Cass Campbell,' she told him. 'Was it routine vandalism, or an angry stockholder?'

He smiled back at her, acknowledging that she knew who he was. He had been the subject of a recent profile in *The Wall Street Journal.* But even before that, his clips were in the file compiled when the first Amagansett account landed in the agency. Grey Tucker was the chief executive officer of Amagansett Industries, described in Standard & Poor in terms Amelia had required Cass to memorize the day the first piece of A1 business went onto the agency's client roster.

The Company and its subsidiaries are mainly engaged in manufacturing, wholesaling and retailing speciality women's and children's apparel, footwear, cosmetics, leather goods and accessories. It also operates retail footwear, speciality and variety stores. The Company and its subsidiaries operate over 100 plants and warehouses and 300 retail stores and leased departments in the US and Canada. Output is sold to independent merchants, mail order houses, chain stores, speciality stores, and through the Company's own chain of retail stores and leased departments. The Company also owns Amagansett Financial Corporation, textile mills, and oil and gas holdings in the South-west (Scottsdale Energy Ltd), California (Golden West Natural Gas) and Canada (Prairie Oil). These are principal operating subsidiaries, partly or wholly owned.

For years, Amagansett consisted of several small companies in the rag trade, and a chain of stores in the South-west which sold dry goods and apparel, plus Blythe's, a venerated old department store that had stood on its upper Fifth Avenue corner since the turn of the century. Tucker had been brought in to revitalize the Company; his first step was to sell off the dry goods chain. With new capital, he embarked on an ambitious buying spree: a parfumerie in France, a leather firm in Israel, shoe companies in South America, swimwear factories in South Africa. AI grew quickly and profitably, and Tucker's reputation as a wunderkind grew with it.

'Why do I know your name, Cass Campbell?' Tucker asked. 'Are you a client of Amelia's, or a client's wife?'

'Neither,' she told him. 'I'm the vice president of Amelia Jordan.'

She said it proudly; Amelia's was one of the city's most successful advertising agencies, and Cass's title was important. Everyone knew of Amelia—she was colourful, flamboyant, and her name was on the agency's front door. But nearly as many—those who knew anything at all about Madison Avenue—knew Cass's name, too.

'Of course,' Tucker apologized, 'I should have remembered. I've admired your work for us, particularly that last marketing analysis.' Cass was ready to hear more; she liked to have her accomplishments praised. But Tucker deftly changed the subject. 'Tell me,' he said, 'why does Amelia always have her Christmas party the night before Thanksgiving?'

'Because I like to go to other peoples' parties,' said Amelia, who walked up to them on the terrace. 'This way, I get my do over with in time to rest up for theirs.' She turned to Tucker. 'I'm delighted to see you, Grey.'

'I'm delighted to be here.' Tucker gave a slight, old-fashioned bow. 'But where have you been hiding Cass Campbell?'

'Oh, Cassandra is usually clever enough to avoid state occasions,' answered Amelia, and Cass coloured slightly.

'Not on purpose,' she explained. 'But this is the first time I've been in the city for Thanksgiving in years.'

The previous year Cass had spent the holiday in East Hampton with Nick and the staff members of *Apple*. While they laid out the January issue on the rough pine table in the dining room, Cass basted a twenty-pound turkey to golden crispness. Occasionally someone drifted into the kitchen, offering her a drag on a joint or sampling the extra dressing packed into a greased casserole dish, awaiting its turn in the oven. But mostly Cass cooked and tasted, humming to herself as she worked, and read an Agatha Christie mystery inattentively while the voices from the other room rose and fell in argument and agreement. After dinner, Nick built a bonfire on the beach, and they sipped brandy from paper cups to cut the chill of the Atlantic wind.

On other Thanksgivings, she'd gone to Hartford with Paula. But not that year.

'Are you sure you don't want to come?' Paula asked her that morning. 'With Nick gone, you'll be all alone.'

But Cass begged off. 'You're the one who cries when she's alone on Groundhog Day, not me,' she told Paula. 'I plan to sleep until noon and drop in on a few parties. I'll be fine. Every married couple in New York wants me, to reassure themselves that single isn't necessarily blessed.'

Nick was in California again, so Cass was alone that evening. She rather thought Grey Tucker might be coming on to her, and it was a tempting thought, but full of potential problems; he was a client, after all. No, Cass thought, she'd stick with her original plan; there was a new P. D. James paperback on her night table, at home on Sixty-third Street. Still, he was an interesting man, this Tucker.

Amelia steered them gently back to the living room. 'I'm delighted you two have finally met,' she told Grey.

'Not nearly as pleased as I am,' he said, smiling over her head at Cass. Then he saw someone else he knew, and moved away, nodding to the women. 'I'm sure we'll meet again,' he murmured to Cass, who watched him thread his way smoothly through the knot of guests. Women smiled at him as he passed, and men moved back to give him room.

'A fascinating man,' commented Amelia. 'Smart as a bee sting. Eligible as well.'

Cass knew precisely what Amelia meant. She was not trying to matchmake—she was too intelligent for that. She was simply reminding Cass, in her own way, that it would not hurt the agency to have Grey Tucker think highly of its vice president. Amelia knew exactly where the line should be drawn between being charming and using what she called, in a slightly anachronistic way, 'feminine wiles.' Even without the wiles, she often told Cass, a woman might capitalize on her assets without compromising herself or her professionalism. Business, like everything else, was a matter of relationships, and how well one did in any company depended upon how much others wanted to do business with her. On how comfortable they were in her presence. It was a truth Amelia had long since mastered, and she urged her wisdom on Cass. 'Don't ever discount charm, my dear. Or beauty, either.'

Cass learned a great deal from Amelia, but not that. She was gracious, which is by definition charming, and she was a good listener. She paid intense attention to people, who were flattered by her interest. No one ever had to tell Cass that charm and beauty were useful; she seemed to have been born knowing it.

Cass was not beautiful, although she often looked that way. She had high cheekbones and a wide, generous mouth. Her eyes were that particular shade of grey which picks up light and reflects it; they were fringed with long, smoky lashes. Her skin was creamy and smooth, and her dark-blond hair, streaked with gold, fell thick and straight to her shoulders. A man she once dated told her that every time he kissed her he thought of Greta Garbo. It was a compliment she loved, although Paula hooted when she heard it. 'You're the *shiksa* of Barry Levin's dreams—his wet dreams,' she told Cass. 'There's something about blondes that reminds all Jewish men of Garbo. Don't be hurt, I'm just jealous. You look the way I always wanted to, but I was born with the wrong genes.'

Cass was appeased. She never took for granted her looks, or her luck, or anything others found to praise in her. She accepted that she was a pretty woman, although, on a bad day, a glimpse of herself in a mirror or store window was cause for despair. Cass was vain, but not unpleasantly so. She was stylish, but not slavish. She fitted in well at Amelia Jordan, especially because one of the beliefs she shared with Amelia was that it was not necessary to pass as a man in order to be taken seriously as an executive. Certainly Amelia had never tried to pass; from the beginning, she made business take her on her own terms. Cass was enchanted and awed by Amelia from the start. She knew there was a daughter somewhere, about her own age, from whom Amelia was said to be estranged; if Amelia sublimated her frustrated maternalism by helping Cass manage her own life and career, it was an excellent bargain for both of them.

But Cass wasn't thinking about Amelia, or Grey Tucker, as she left the party, or even later, when she brushed her teeth and made faces at her reflection in the mirror. She was thinking about the old man in the window. She was placing her jade Buddha on a low fruitwood table in front of the window, settling her small green velvet couch in front of the fireplace. In her mind's eye, she was furnishing his room with her things, moving her books onto his empty shelves, putting her family photographs in their antique frames on his mantel. By then she knew that she wanted his house. And she knew that she would have it.

THREE

The Monday after Thanksgiving, Cass met Paula for lunch, and told her about the money. They sat at a table by the window at the Charcuterie, watching the traffic on Fifty-seventh Street.

She pushed John McKay's letter across to Paula.

Proving as we have both always known that you are right more often than not, I am delighted to inform you that we have an offer on the cottage which I, of course, told you not to buy. It is for a hundred grand; some smart developer has found a way around the shorelines management act, and plans to put up a luxury condominium on the bluff. And I am equally pleased to wipe the egg off my face and tell you that decrepit shack is going to make you a rich woman.

Cass and John had found the Seattle cottage together one rainy Saturday soon after Cass's mother died. The tiny house was old and needed work, but she liked the way it perched on the bluff above the Sound, arrogantly daring the winds that blew down from the straits to tumble it into the sea. The bluff was thickly treed, and the cottage looked like an abandoned doll's house, nestled between the expansive estates on either side. There was a faded, peeling For Sale sign, and Cass wrote down the estate agent's name.

'You really want to be landed gentry, huh, Cass?' John enquired, when she tucked the slip of paper into her jeans pocket.

'You of all people ought to know how we Navy brats

long for roots,' she replied. She and John had grown up together, their families posted to many of the same duty stations over the years.

'Yeah, I know.' John smiled. 'And I know that inheritance from your mum is burning holes in your jeans. I understand that, too. If you want a house, buy a house. But not this one. Look at it . . . it's falling apart.'

At her insistence, they climbed in through an unlocked window and explored the small rooms. Later, they sat together in an old glider that swung, rusted and creaky, from the roof of the porch. They smoked a joint and considered the cottage.

'Notice the cracks in the ceiling?' John asked. 'It's that madrona tree over there. Every time there's a storm, the tree shakes, and with the roots going under the cottage, you get cracks. Cost you a few hundred to get rid of the tree and kill the roots.'

'But I love that tree,' Cass protested. 'It's marvellous. I bet the leaves make wonderful sounds in a storm.'

'The roof's almost gone, too,' John warned. 'And the wiring looks like it hasn't been touched in years. Probably old fuse boxes. Put a penny in one night and boom, you go up in smoke.' He laughed. 'You'd look funny all charred. Not great for the complexion.'

She punched him lightly. 'Even I know better than to put a penny in a fuse box, dummy. So it's not Versailles. But I like it. I'm going to make an offer.'

She did, and it was accepted.

She had returned to Seattle after graduate school; her mother was ill with cancer. With her credentials—a B.A. from Smith, and an M.B.A. from Harvard—she had no trouble locating a good job with a speciality apparel store. She moved into the cottage, and lived there until she moved to New York. She had changed jobs once already, for a better post at the advertising agency which handled the store's account. It was an Amagansett store, and when Cass, on a visit east to see Paula, was offered a spot at Amelia Jordan, which already handled several

Amagansett accounts, she took it. She could not hope to rise much higher at the agency, nor did she think she would earn much more money. She had some lovers in Seattle, but none who mattered. And some friends, but only John McKay really counted.

He was the one man she trusted completely; he had a place in her life as solid and enduring as Paula's. He adored her totally, and without reservation, even though she was sometimes rude to him, often careless of his feelings, and frequently critical of his life-style. He was almost impervious to her disfavour, coolness, or slights. Sometimes she prodded him intentionally, hoping for a reaction of some kind to her words or behaviour. But she received none, and after a time she gave up. She thought he was insensitive; finally she realized he was merely self-absorbed, in a different way from her.

John had rolled her her first joint, taken her through her first acid trip, and been there when her mother died. Cass attributed their friendship to its duration—and to the fact that in all those years, they had never been to bed together.

Men washed up against Cass like water on rocks —ceaselessly and rhythmically. Sometimes she was engulfed; more often their ardour only lapped at her edges. She liked the feel of it. It soothed her, like their attention, which was never enough until it was too much. And then she wanted none of it.

John was different, yet she thought hardly at all about how he might feel when she decided to accept the job with Amelia Jordan, Inc. She asked John to let the cottage for her, and look after it, and she left Seattle. Each time she returned, the cottage seemed less her own, less who she was becoming; by the time she received his letter about the offer, it seemed irrelevant to her life. She had all but abandoned it, except for Augusts.

'What are you going to do with the money?' asked Paula,

and Cass pointed to a woman stepping out of a limousine on the street below them.

'Maybe I'll buy a red fox like that one,' she replied. 'I finally decided fur coats aren't political anymore, they're practical.'

Paula buttered a roll. 'After all, you didn't shoot it, right?'

'Right,' said Cass, giving Paula a meaningful look. Paula put down the roll.

'I don't know why you and I love each other. I hate thin women, except you. I'd give my fucking eyesight for Gentile thighs. Thighs without handles.'

'For the *zaftig* type, you look fine,' Cass reassured her. Compliments from Cass were always edged, like a cake knife.

Paula changed the subject. 'Seriously, Cass, what are you going to do with the money from the cottage? If you hold onto it, you'll get eaten alive by taxes.'

'I think I'll buy a house.'

Paula laughed out loud. 'In Manhattan? You've got to be kidding. Only Richard Nixon buys a house in Manhattan. Or a rich Arab, or an Argentine. Or an Italian who's afraid of kidnappers in his own country.'

'That's almost what John McKay told me,' Cass replied. 'Look, somebody in this city owns a house, right? Lots of people. Why not me?'

'An apartment maybe, or a loft,' said Paula. 'But a whole house? You're nuts.'

'No, I'm not,' said Cass stubbornly. 'An apartment doesn't feel like a house. All yours.'

'That's exactly what's nice about it,' Paula countered. 'No old wiring you have to replace. No leaky plumbing the super can't fix. You don't need a house, Cass, you don't need that aggravation. Look for a loft. In SoHo, or maybe TriBeCa. I have a client who's a developer, he has property over there. He'll have something. I'll call him.'

Cass wasn't listening. 'Wouldn't it be funny if that house behind Amelia's is available?'

'Highly unlikely,' Paula replied. 'Unless the tooth fairy is real. Besides, a brownstone in the West Village? That has to be at least a half-million dollars.'

'We'll see,' said Cass.

'Sure. Maybe that nice old man you saw will be dying to give it to you. He'll fall in love with you and beg you to take it off his hands for a hundred thousand.'

'I hate it when you assume men fall in love with me like that.' Miffed, Cass pushed the bread basket away from Paula. 'I met a man at Amelia's last Wednesday night who didn't seem the slightest bit interested. As a matter of fact, I spent nearly an hour with him and he didn't make one move.'

'He's blind,' said Paula. 'Or married. Or gay. Probably all of the above.'

'Not true. He's very good-looking, his eyes were open, he's single and he's straight. Also a client.'

Paula nodded, and Cass knew she understood. Clients were off limits for a professional woman. Come to think of it, women clients ought to be off limits for professional men. Some lawyers bedded their divorcees, brokers romanced wealthy women, a few shrinks took sexual advantage of their patients. Cass didn't like it, but there it was. She didn't mix her business and personal lives, although Grey Tucker was compelling; she had thought about him several times since Amelia's party. And, she told Paula, it seemed that Nick had been out of town forever.

'Contrary to public opinion, the hornies are not terminal,' Paula said. Cass frowned at her. 'Says who?' she asked.

Cass didn't miss sex as much as she missed what came with it—strong arms around her, someone to smile at her in the morning, a loving man to snuggle with, the feeling of being cherished. Things she was used to getting from Nick, who had been trying to launch a West-Coast version of his slick New York magazine, *Apple*, for several months. They'd had one long weekend in East Hampton over

Fourth of July, and a Labour Day holiday togeth... in California, plus a hurried overnight visit three weeks ago. It wasn't enough for Cass.

Cass was accustomed to the attention of a man. It made her skin glow; she thrived on it. And she was beginning to resent Nick's prolonged absences. Maybe that's why Grey Tucker looked so good to me, she thought, and said as much to Paula.

But Paula was disapproving. 'There are hundreds of men in New York if all you want is to get laid,' she said, and Cass strived to control the snapping together of her teeth. Paula was too earthy, in public and sometimes even privately, for her.

Besides, she didn't want to talk about men. 'You ought to think about investing in something yourself,' she told Paula. 'You want all your money to keep fuelling the war machine?'

'All your money' was a comfortable income of close to seventy thousand dollars a year. Paula still did not feel rich, but she was growing accustomed to feeling secure. She had grown up in a family of modest means; she worked her way through college and law school with part-time jobs and scholarships. Early in her career, she worked in government-supported law practices; when she moved to Washington to be Chris Carey's committee counsel, she increased her earnings substantially. Enough, Cass thought, so she could eschew cheap apartments and jug-wine potlucks and thrift-shop clothes. But Paula had not given up her East Village apartment, only sublet it, and when she moved back to New York, to the even more lucrative practice as an associate in a thriving, profit-making law firm, she did not noticeably improve her standard of living. She was slated to make partner that Christmas; she'd already been promised, when she brought her Washington credentials and growing national reputation to the firm's plush offices on Park Avenue and Forty-eighth Street.

Cass was right; it rankled Paula that she paid so much

in taxes to support the policies of an administration she thought hopelessly benighted.

Paula did not think about money very often, except when it was a symbol for something else. She was spending much of her time on the abortion case, and even the most liberal of the partners at her law firm were beginning to voice their displeasure; all her unbillable hours were costing the firm the fees she might otherwise be generating. She had all but dropped her other *pro bono* cases; she could no longer afford to take them. But the abortion case and its outcome would make a bigger difference in the lives of most poor people than all the other ones—the tenants' rights group, the prostitutes' union, the native American liberationists. She was being paid her high salary to bring lucrative business into the firm, not to reinterpret the Constitution, her seniors reminded her.

'My taxes wouldn't gas up one army tank to roll over some peasant in El Salvador, don't worry,' she told Cass.

'Okay, okay.' Cass backed down. 'I think I'm going to look at houses today. Want to come?'

'Can't. I have a divorce hearing this afternoon, a deposition to take after that, and a meeting tonight with Chris's staff. He's going to try for the nomination, and they're putting campaign committees together.'

'Are you going to work for him?' It was Chris Carey who'd taken Paula to Washington with him, soon after he was elected to the Senate.

'Not full time. Campaigns are crazy, they take over your life. And now that mine is finally in some kind of order, I don't want to fuck it up. But I'll talk to the guys—I owe Chris that. Your turn to buy or mine?'

'Yours.'

Paula counted out some bills. They took the glass elevator down to the first floor, and Paula stopped to finger a sweater on the sale rack.

'You don't need another sweater, you need a tax write-off,' Cass said, pulling her away.

'You go to your *shul,* and I'll go to mine,' Paula replied.

'Go buy a house, *bubbela*. If you find any bargains, buy two.'

'Don't cry when I don't invite you to toast marshmallows in my fireplace.' Cass smiled. 'I love you. Talk to you later.'

FOUR

Cass hailed a cab and gave the driver Amelia's address. She leaned back against the cracked leather seat. She didn't like the idea of Paula getting mixed up with Chris again. The junior Senator from Massachusetts was a clever politician. He might even have a chance at wresting the nomination away from the incumbent, if the President continued to drop in the polls. Chris Carey had made a big name for himself in his first term in the Senate—the Harvard Law School professor who came to Washington and uncovered the biggest scandal since Watergate. He was Paula's teacher and mentor—they had in common an unshakeable belief in the Constitution, and under his direction she wrote a con-law paper that propelled her right to *Law Review*. She was living with Jake Stern then, but later, when Jake skipped town after being indicted for his role in the Cambridge bombing, Paula turned to Chris for solace.

Chris was married, but he wanted Paula Gabriel, and he did not demand that she love him as she had loved Jake; in fact, Paula knew, he preferred that she did not. Some years later, Paula went to Washington, and became chief counsel for Chris's subcommittee on government ethics. Her role in the hearings—she was on television daily, for weeks—enhanced her already growing professional reputation. And her affair with Chris continued, intermittently, in her Georgetown apartment.

Cass watched Paula on the news regularly then. And

when she called to talk to her, often she could tell from Paula's whisper that she was not alone.

'It can't go anywhere,' she warned Paula. 'He's an opportunist, and you're part of his game plan. Once he gets where he's going, he'll drop you.'

'I know that,' Paula replied. 'But he's not there yet. And it's not as if anyone else was begging to marry me.'

'No chance anyone could get your attention,' Cass said. 'He's just stringing you along.'

Cass was sometimes uncomfortably direct. If she thought Paula should know something, she told her. She was critical rather than supportive. She never waited for her opinion to be solicited, she simply offered it. When she told Paula Chris was no good, it was not because Paula had asked her; she was incapable of not saying what she thought, regardless of whether Paula wanted to hear it. She felt her directness was a sign of friendship; other people often thought it was only rude.

She was concerned about Paula and Chris, who had not really ended the affair when Paula left Washington; there were times when the Senator showed up at Paula's West Side apartment, late at night, often with his aide waiting in the limo. 'What do you need with him?' Cass asked Paula. 'You're a big-shot lawyer, earning tons of money, with plenty of men dying to marry you. And there he is, with a wife who's a drunk but absolutely essential to his career, and an occasional yen for a roll in the hay with you.'

'Those plenty of men aren't dying to marry me, they're dying to fuck me,' Paula said. 'And it's very occasional with Chris. A few times when Maribeth's drying out at Silver Hill, and some passionate phone calls now and again.' She sighed. 'Sometimes I have this itch to tell my mother about Chris. Maybe that would convince her there's hope for me yet.'

'Somehow I don't think that would calm her mind any,' said Cass. 'What would is for you to *schlep* a nice Jewish guy to Hartford, complete with ring and licence. She wouldn't even care if you were pregnant.'

'Fat chance,' said Paula. 'Although sometimes I'm tempted to prick a few holes in my diaphragm, just to see if I could. All these years, and never a scare, not since the abortion. Maybe that made me sterile.'

'I doubt it. Getting knocked up would certainly solve the problem of Chris Carey.'

'It sure would. Well, in the fullness of time it will all work out the way it's supposed to. If Chris gets the nomination, it will take care of that, anyway. Knowing there's a Secret Service man at the foot of the bed might curb my passion.'

'Or at least bring you to your senses,' said Cass.

Paula was luminous; she glowed with feeling, even when she was still, bent over a book or a project. The projects were all around her—in her office, in her rooms, on her body, in the gifts and possessions her friends prized most. A brilliant parrot embroidered on a shirt. A mobile made of bits of shiny paper and cloth, hanging on invisible filament, fastened to a bit of dowelling. An elaborate Halloween costume, all sequins and glitter. She was generous with presents she made; Cass, and all of Paula's other friends, looked forward to birthdays and Christmases.

Paula could not pass a thrift shop or a rummage pile without stopping; her clothes were often unlikely combinations of the discarded pieces of other lives. Even when she could afford to shop in expensive stores, she preferred to remake something old. 'You have no sense of history,' she told Cass once, who wrinkled her nose when Paula dragged a tattered velvet dress off a sidewalk rack.

The air around Paula was always charged with her energy. She was not a remarkable-looking woman, just memorable in a certain way. With dark, frizzy hair and olive skin, enormous eyes in a Semitic face, she looked like every other thirtyish Jewish woman in Manhattan; people always thought they had met her before.

She was carelessly attractive, free with her affections, casual in a way that nearly hid the intensity of her beliefs and the perseverance, even the dedication, with which she pursued her career. She was an only child; her father had emigrated from Germany, and before Paula was born, he changed his name from Gaberowsky to Gabriel. The most important of his possessions were his citizenship papers and a worn red copy of the Constitution, which he thought was the greatest document ever written—greater even than the Talmud. 'This is what separates us, human beings, from them, the animals,' he told Paula often. 'If Germany had had this, we would still be there.'

His hopes rested on Paula, who did not want to disappoint him; she revered her father, a taciturn man who rarely touched her, except when he came in to say good night, and found her bent over her schoolbooks. Then he might stroke her hair gently. '*Shana* Paula,' he would say. Beautiful Paula—to Isaac she was that, and more. She brought him honour and *nachas*, and grew up with the same abiding faith in the Constitution that Isaac had, and she always knew she would have a career in the law. There was not much money for extras —Isaac's halting efforts in a new language kept him from advancement, despite his excellent training—but she worked every summer, and won a full scholarship to college.

Cass and Paula were an unlikely match. Paula was ethnic, earthy, and sharp-tongued, although she was always kind, and even when she and Cass gossiped about other women, she was careful to point out their good qualities. Paula was firm in her loyalties; she didn't need the sisterhood that was thrust on women in the sixties to reinforce them. She was competent and capable; she thought if she followed the directions, she could figure anything out. She believed in the power of intellect, not its complexity but its simplicity. Her humour was broad, bawdy, and rarely dependent on nuance or sophistication; the word 'fart' could always make her giggle.

Both she and Cass were surprised that they chose each other as friends; it must have been a mistake, they thought, when they were assigned to room together at Smith. Even then they were clearly different types. Cass had taste and Paula had style. Each secretly wished she was a bit more like the other—not a great deal more, just a touch. But what each felt about the other, even to preferences in clothes, was closer to admiration than envy. 'You always put yourself together and then add one more ridiculous thing,' Cass told Paula, 'and somehow it works.'

'You do it the same way, except you take something off,' Paula replied. 'We're the lady and the tramp.'

'I prefer to think of us as the peacock and the swan,' Cass countered.

At eighteen, Cass already gravitated toward the brightest, most attractive and popular of her peers. She had long since decided that she would someday make a brilliant marriage and in that way assure her own status and success. She was conscious of the gradations of rank early; her father was an officer, which she felt made her more privileged than her classmates. But she also knew that in the larger world beyond the cyclone fence that set the Navy bases apart from the towns in which she rarely settled for more than a few years, other things counted more than military rank. So she sought them in her friends, a habit of which she was occasionally ashamed. She did not like feeling insincere, but she wanted acceptance in another, better world, which she could sense only dimly.

Smith represented that world to Cass. It was not a wholly inappropriate choice; although her father was just a Navy captain, she had good Boston connections on her mother's side.

Paula, being Jewish, had an even slighter claim than Cass's to the social privileges of an elite college, and cared nothing for them anyway. Cass, who was never entirely secure about her social status, was bothered by any hint of exclusion. A Muffy or a Buffy or a Sissy could pass her on campus without speaking and ruin her day. That may have been why she and Paula loved each other from the beginning. No experience or feeling or idea was ever too insignificant to share; even when they were apart, their connection remained strong and alive. The bond between Cass and Paula was palpable, like a living thing. They were committed to each other in a way that could not be understood—only accepted. No one could intrude on their closeness, and after a time, no one tried—not families or other friends or even lovers. What was between them was just there, like a birth-mark, indelible and unchanging. It did not exclude others; it simply had nothing to do with them.

FIVE

'How busy are you today?' Cass demanded.

'I haven't even taken my coat off yet, how do I know?' Paula juggled the phone under her chin while she proceeded to do so. Her secretary brought in her daybook with the coffee. 'What's the big emergency? Did you find out that nice old man is dying to give you his house?'

'Not exactly,' said Cass. 'But it is for sale, and the broker is showing it to me today. Please, Paula?'

'I'm swamped today, Cassie, appointments up the kazoo, today and most of the week. Anyway, the house will turn out to cost a million dollars or be full of termites. You just let me know when you find the right one, and I'll come with the bread and salt and honey. I'm sorry, love, but this week's out.'

'Except Thursday, we have a date then, don't we?'

'Oh, shit, yes—we do.'

Cass was miffed. 'Well, shit to you, too.'

'Come on, Cassie, that's not what I meant, don't get sensitive. I have to go to Washington Thursday—I promised Chris I'd at least talk to him about the campaign. But I'll get the eight o'clock shuttle, and then I'll come to your apartment and we'll talk, okay?'

'No, but it'll have to do. I'll have the doorman let you in if I go out for dinner.'

'Unbridled desire driving you out into the streets, or is Nick back?'

'No. He wants me to go out there for Christmas. Is it worth four hundred dollars to go?'

Paula laughed. 'Listen, I'd pay four hundred dollars to get laid by that gorgeous Greek, and so would any other woman in this city of faggots and losers and married men.' Sometimes Paula's forthrightness shocked Cass, but it always made her laugh.

'Speaking of which,' Paula went on, 'there's an ACLU fundraiser tonight. Maybe there'll be a man there who likes Jewish thighs. Want to come?'

'No,' said Cass. 'I'm going to see the place late today. The house will be impossible, or expensive, I'm sure, but I'd just as soon get this fantasy out of the way now, so I can forget it and start looking somewhere else.'

'Okay,' said Paula, 'you know best. Happy house-hunting. And good luck with your Amagansett meeting today. Knock them on their ass.'

'Will do,' Cass replied. 'Bye, sweetie.'

'Bye, love.'

Her secretary came in with the morning mail and a sheaf of memos handwritten on Amelia's own distinctive ecru stationery. Cass winced.

'When I left here last night, the presentation was all wrapped up.' She groaned. 'What did she do, sleep here?'

'She sent them over by messenger this morning,' Clio said. 'She'll be in at eleven. She said she had some preparations to make.'

Which means she's at Kenneth's, pulling herself together, Cass translated. Amelia maintained her youthful good looks with the same dedication she gave her clients, and Cass approved; her employer had a fine-boned, patrician elegance Cass herself hoped one day to acquire, or grow into.

Amelia had sent Cass to her own hairdresser soon after naming Cass an agency vice president. 'Take your face to Amy, and your eyebrows to Ann, and your hair to Angela,' she'd suggested, writing down the name and address of the salon. Cass was not offended, and even Paula thought the results becoming. 'You look polished,' she told Cass after her makeover. 'I adore the makeup, and I like your hair that way, all sculptured around your face. You look very.'

'Very what?'

'Just very,' Paula replied.

'Very, but not too much?' Cass worried.

'Not too much. Simply very.' And Cass was satisfied. Paula was always honest with her, but only if she was asked. And even then, she was quite sensitive to just how much truth, for Cass, was enough.

Cass settled down with Amelia's memos, and called the account team into her office for a final run-through of the presentation. Soon Amelia swept into the room, trailing clouds of perfume and an air of excitement.

'You look wonderful,' Cass told her. A tiny blonde woman with porcelain prettiness and an unlined face, Amelia was dressed in a handsome cranberry wool suit by an English designer she had discovered before anyone else. Twice a year Amelia went abroad to choose her clothes, even before the buyers from Bergdorf's and Bendel's saw them. The wardrobe Amelia selected was exclusively hers, a gift from the grateful designer. 'You'll knock Grey Tucker out.'

'That's what I wanted to tell you, Cassandra.' Amelia always used Cass's full name; it had, she said, dignity and stature. 'I can't be here for the presentation today, so you'll make it yourself, you and the team. I wouldn't dream of missing the meeting, except that you're perfectly capable of running it. It was your idea, anyway. And we've gone over every word and every story board. It can't be improved —not if you made the changes I suggested. Tony will handle the materials, you'll keep things moving and do the wrap-up. Superbly, I'm sure. After all, I trained you, didn't I?'

'Well, yes,' Cass began, 'but—'

Amelia interrupted her. 'Of course you can. I never hire an executive who cannot do my job at least as well as I can—otherwise, why bother? You'll do it beautifully.' Her face brightened. 'I have a very important luncheon engagement.'

She saw the question in Cass's eyes, and smiled. 'No, not a man; I wouldn't miss this meeting just for a man. It's Natalie. She's flown in from Paris, and wants to see me. Apparently she has a young man with her, and she wants us to meet.'

Amelia reached for the heavy silver coffeepot and poured the steaming liquid into a delicate bone-china cup. She sipped her drink slowly, and dismissed the others in the room with a casual wave of her hand.

'I haven't seen my daughter for nearly four years,' she confided to Cass. 'I'd heard that she was working for *Paris Match,* but apparently she's taken a new job at *Elle.* She said she sent an announcement, but I never received it.'

Cass understood Amelia's separation from Natalie on an intellectual level, but she could not accept it emotionally. She had been very close to her own mother; the years in which her father was so often away had brought them close; closer than most mothers and daughters, she thought when she heard her friends discussing their own mothers in disparaging terms. She had not needed a lot of girl friends when she was growing up; she had her mother. Even during Cass's adolescence they were close; when she needed to strike out at someone, in those rebellious years, it was her father who bore the brunt of her anger and rejection, such as it was. Neither of her parents told Cass about Kathryn's illness until several months after it was diagnosed; when Cass saw how shrivelled and tiny her mother looked in the big brass four-poster, that Christmas vacation from business school, she was horrified, and furious with her father and brothers. 'How could you?' she demanded, tears staining her face, after her mother, tired from the exertions of Cass's homecoming, had retired for the night. 'How could you have known and not told me?'

Her father looked at her sadly. 'What could we have said, Cass? What could you have done? Believe me, we've done everything. And she wouldn't let us tell you, anyway. She wants this for you—she wants you to live your own life. She wouldn't tell you now, if she didn't have to.'

She couldn't believe it. Her lively, busy, energetic, beautiful mother—Kathryn, who always had time for a hug, a chat, an afternoon to shop and talk, and, especially, listen. Who was capable and strong—hadn't she raised three children practically alone, all over the world, in strange cities and countries? Hadn't she headed every Mothers' March, every zoning committee, every bake sale, every Navy Wives club in every place they'd lived? And sewn Cass's first party dress by hand, and wallpapered every bedroom in each new house, and been there whenever Cass, or her father, or her brothers, needed her? And now she was so sick, so wracked with pain, from the cancer that was eating her from the inside out, pinching her mouth with tiny, deep-edged lines, drawing the colour from her skin, shrinking her day by day until it seemed there would be nothing left, except the papery fragrance of her hand lotion, and the soft flannel of her nightgowns, and her tiny reflection in the polished glow of the huge, ornate bedstead.

'Stop, Cass,' her father said. 'She's been looking forward to this vacation for months—looking forward to seeing you. I won't have you spoil it for her. She's determined to beat this; she won't have you sitting a deathwatch for her. Get your crying done now, and don't let her see it.'

'All right, but I'm not going back to Cambridge after vacation,' she told her father.

'You most certainly are,' he said. 'I insist, and so does she. She's showing some improvement from the chemotherapy; the side effects, that's why she looks so frail. But she's getting stronger every day, and if you give up on her, she'll give up, too. You'll go back. If you need to be here before the year is finished, I'll send you a ticket.'

Cass could almost always get her way with her father,

but this time, she knew, she could not. He was a soft-spoken man, but he loved his wife, silently and intensely, and he would not indulge Cass if it would alarm Kathryn. So Cass got through the few weeks, treasuring each hour that Kathryn Campbell was strong enough to spend with her, doing the Christmas chores that were traditional in their family, from unpacking the fragile old gingerbread house to popping the corn that her mother's suddenly translucent hands could barely string on silver cord.

Cass stored up memories of her mother against a time when she would need them; she did not cry again, not until she kissed her mother good-bye soon after the New Year, and Kathryn smoothed her hair. 'Don't worry, doll baby, I'll be here when you come back,' she said. 'I promise I'll be here.'

Cass held back her tears, and tried not to crush her mother in her embrace.

Kathryn had been there—by dint of will, the doctors said. When Cass came back to Seattle in June, Kathryn was in remission; not strong enough to join Cass and her brothers on the golf course, or sailing or hiking, but sure enough of her own time to insist that they go, and welcome them home with a cold pitcher of drinks and sit happily in the big wing chair by the fireplace while they told her about their day.

Cass knew her mother's time was measured in months, so she took a job in Seattle and continued to live at home. 'Every other daughter I know is chafing to get out of her mother's house,' Kathryn said. 'I'm not pushing you, darling, but you really don't have to live here, you know. I'll stake you to an apartment, or help with a down payment if you want to buy a place of your own.' Kathryn was a wealthy woman in her own right; she had married the big, handsome Navy ensign against the wishes of her Elitist father, who warned that James Campbell, while solid enough, would amount to little in his lifetime. 'He's an order taker, not an order giver,' he'd told her, and Kathryn knew her father was right, and didn't mind it a bit. She used her own money sparingly; it was a sore spot between her and James. She spent it on the very best medical attention when Cass's brother contracted polio, on the best education when Cass wanted to go to Smith, on the small but elegant things that made Navy quarters a home. And she offered it to Cass, who declined it.

'Are you trying to push me out of the nest?' she asked. 'Well, tough luck, because I like it here.' Kathryn smiled, because she knew that she was dying, and that her daughter did not want to miss a precious moment of their time together.

Between Natalie and Amelia there was no such binding affection. Cass could not imagine what it would be like to be as alienated from her family as her employer and her daughter were from one another. Kathryn had been dead for over twelve years, and Cass still missed her with an ache that hardly eased in the ensuing years. She knew the gossip about Amelia's only child, a troubled girl who moved from school to school, seemingly willing herself to fail at each one. Finally, Natalie had run away from Madeira and gone off to live in an Oregon commune. According to the office grapevine—to which Cass listened intently, though she did not often participate—the girl was on drugs for many years, and nearly died from an overdose. Amelia had had her committed to Menninger's, but Natalie ran away from there, too, surfacing a few years later in Europe. Amelia kept track of her with the aid of private detectives; Cass had once seen the invoices for their services. 'They have to make their own mistakes,' Amelia said once. 'You can't shield them from life forever. I don't think Natalie has ever forgiven me for leaving her father, or, worse, becoming successful in business. She wanted me to be the kind of mother who was home baking cookies when she returned from school. I was always terrible at cookies.' She shrugged. 'Of course, if I hadn't kept working, we'd have starved to death. But they don't understand that; they only remember how you've wronged them.'

Cass didn't know how to respond to Amelia's occasional confidences. 'I'm sure you'll love this man, whoever he is,' she reassured Amelia. 'In any case, he'll certainly love you. After all, you're Natalie's mother.'

'That makes no sense at all.' Amelia smiled. 'As Natalie used to tell me whenever she found the opportunity, we're nothing at all alike.'

'We're all much more like our mothers than we care to believe,' said Cass. 'Sometimes we just don't want to admit it.'

'Perhaps,' said Amelia. 'Look, Cassandra, go over the pitch one more time with me. Call Tony and the account team back in for a full run-through. And then it's up to you.'

Cass thought the presentation went well. Grey Tucker said little; she watched him closely, paying particular attention when he scribbled notes on a small pad in a Mark Cross leather cover. She made some notes of her own when he did. 'Pete Marks is the one we need to convince,' Amelia had told her. 'Marks, and Tucker, of course, although he probably won't show up. Play to Marks without being too obvious.'

Amelia herself had done the groundwork—the party where Cass met Tucker had been an opportunity to woo the wives of key clients. 'These women have greater influence than you might think,' she told Cass. 'And they have a rather distorted image of me; they all think I'm a siren on the prowl for their men. A party helps dispel that.' Cass had watched in amusement as Amelia devoted herself to cultivating the women, even as she found time for private talks with their husbands.

Amelia returned to the office just as Cass was preparing to leave. 'How did it go?'

'Quite well, I think. Tucker was there, after all. He was a stone face, except when we showed him the comp of the catalogue, and the layout for the *Time* ads. He liked them; he thought the new logo for all the divisions, underneath their own sigs, was an excellent idea. He asked for copies of everything, including the market research reports. Marks said we'd hear from them sometime next week. How was your lunch with Natalie and her friend?'

'Wonderful.' Amelia brightened. 'Natalie looks healthy and content, and was quite effervescent. Almost loving. We're dining together tomorrow evening.'

'Is she staying with you?'

'No. She didn't ask, so I didn't offer. I think perhaps it's time we tried to relate as adults, rather than mother and daughter. I was never terrific at the mother bit, anyway.'

'I think you underrate yourself,' said Cass, more boldly than she intended. 'I'm sure you were wonderful as a mother. Natalie just wasn't very good as a daughter, that's all.' It was probably not easy, being Amelia's daughter, especially in the early, hard-scratching days, Cass thought, but still she could imagine no grievance severe enough to account for such a rift. Although Amelia seemed to have come to terms with her daughter's apparent disregard for her, sometimes Cass sensed her deep, hidden unhappiness. It left its mark on Amelia, despite the excellent care she lavished on herself.

'You are a dear to put it that way,' Amelia told her. 'I can always count on you to give me the benefit of the doubt, Cassandra. Your loyalty touches me—no, don't blush, although it's rather appealing, I mean it. Are you off for a rendezvous with that handsome young publisher of yours?'

'No, Nick's still in California. I'm going to look at a house I might buy. It's in your neighbourhood, as a matter of fact.'

'What an excellent idea!' Amelia beamed. 'Well, do give a call if you're not busy afterward. Perhaps if Natalie and her fellow come by for drinks, you'll join us.'

'Perhaps. Thank you, Amelia. And . . . I'm glad about Natalie.'

She left the office. It pained her to see how vulnerable Amelia was to that ungrateful brat of hers; she was not sure, in any case, that she could bring herself to be civil to Natalie. Amelia was not by nature a soft person; she couldn't be and have risen as high as she had. But she had never neglected Natalie; she had given her the best, not only of material things, but of time, and caring, and her own strong values. Cass had gleaned that, in Amelia's infrequent periods of sharing; perhaps Natalie had not understood that Amelia only wanted for her daughter what she herself had not been privileged to have.

In the cab on the way to the Village, Cass thought about Amelia. She remembered their first meeting, when Amelia fixed her gaze on her and asked, 'How hard are you willing to work, Cassandra?' Before Cass could reply, Amelia told her how hard that might be.

'To be successful in a man's world—and don't think otherwise, that's exactly what it is, despite all this talk of feminism—means that you get up very early in the morning, and go to bed quite late at night. Alone. In between, you do very little except work, in a demanding, draining, high-pressure environment in which you are fuelled only by your ambition, which is even more important than your ability.'

More important than your daughter? Cass wondered, for she had done her homework on Amelia; she had heard the stories.

Amelia continued. 'You must need to achieve, to win, to be first. You must need that the way others need to breathe. And every day you deal with some people who assume that because you are a woman, you are somehow second-rate. Or worse, that you slept your way to whatever position you hold.'

Had there been rumours like that about Amelia? Perhaps at first, but not for a long time now. Did Natalie think that of her mother? Cass wondered.

'You will scrap your friends, your social life, your interest in Shakespeare or theatre or needlepoint. You won't spend late nights at Elaine's, or take vacations when normal people do.'

When children do? Cass mused. Did Amelia and Natalie ever take vacations together?

'You can't,' Amelia continued, 'because you have to be on a six a.m. plane to Atlanta, or Duluth, or even Pocatello. And that's not the worst of it. Your work will often be overlooked because it was done by a woman. You will never pass as a man, or get into the brotherhood; even if you own your own business, they will exclude you.'

Had they excluded Amelia? Was there a bitterness eating in her, that corroded even her love for Natalie? Cass shuddered inwardly, but she went on listening.

'There are times when you need a different persona—times when you'll have to be Mr Campbell, not Ms Campbell. When you are, they'll call you all the names men have to demean and degrade you, to make you less than you are. And if they don't call you by those names, other women will.'

Then why bother? Cass thought. What is the payoff, after all? But even before Amelia answered her unspoken question, she knew the answer.

Amelia leaned back in the pale rattan chair. She was a small woman in a sleek, uncluttered office, perfumed by yellow roses that stood in silver vases everywhere, and by her own scent, Amelia, named for her by an appreciative client. She looked Cass directly in the eyes.

'On the plus side,' she said, a smile softening her face, 'you will be taken seriously here, compensated in direct proportion to your contribution, and, most of the time, you'll think it's worth it.'

Then, Cass didn't know what or where Elaine's was. She went to the theatre infrequently, had no interest in needlepoint, no family and few friends, except Paula, in New York. But she was fascinated by Amelia. Amelia Jordan was an extremely successful businesswoman, whom Cass had expected to find cold, bitter, and unhappy. Instead, she was charmed by her; if Amelia was any of those things, she hid them well. Cass accepted the position, and the bargain was sealed. She never regretted it; and she came to know that Amelia, while saddened by her estrangement from her daughter, and tough in the ways a businesswoman must be, was a kind and caring woman.

For the first few years, it was much as Amelia said it would be. Amelia tested her often, and Cass welcomed the challenge.

'Do you mind?' Amelia would ask, tossing a half-finished proposal on Cass's desk on a Friday afternoon, 'Is there anything on your calendar you can't reschedule?'

'No, nothing important, Amelia,' Cass would reply; as soon as the door closed behind her employer, she telephoned her date for dinner and cancelled. 'Can you make a meeting tomorrow?' Amelia might ask, and Cass would nod her head, even when she knew Nick had just closed that month's *Apple* issue and would want to celebrate late into the night. 'Of course, Amelia, I'll handle it,' she said, and she did.

Cass didn't mind. She thought she might be one of the women who would make it, and when she did, there would be plenty of time for dates and trips and other, private pleasures. Amelia rewarded her efforts, with promotions and salary increases; five years after she joined the agency, Cass was named vice president. She earned eighty thousand dollars a year, more than enough for her needs. She admired and respected her boss, and enjoyed the people at the agency; some of her colleagues were men, and some women, and the competition was equally intense from both. It was healthy, and tough, but not bitter—Amelia saw to that. She sponsored Cass for the Women's Forum, a professional network that included the most powerful and accomplished women in New York. Cass fulfilled Amelia's expectations, and her own. She had her job, and Paula, and Nick, when he was around, and that was enough. What she did not have was a house of her own, but she planned to remedy that as soon as possible.

'If I have any regrets,' Amelia told Cass once, 'it's that I never thought I could have it all. I wanted my independence, and money, too. I thought that meant I had to give up the rest of it, so perhaps I did. But you don't have to, today. Not if you're smart.'

Cass was smart, and she wanted it all, too, whatever all was, even if some things had to wait. She had worked hard for several years, and she was beginning to take more time for herself. Amelia approved. 'Go to a museum, or to the country tomorrow,' she would say occasionally. 'Or go find that nice man and have a long, romantic lunch. There's no reason for you to stay around this weekend. No one's watching your time sheets.' Still, on nights Cass worked late, Amelia would pop into her office and nod her approval. 'It's all a matter of priorities,' she said. 'That's the secret, knowing what the priorities are.'

Amelia herself had married young, and divorced a few years thereafter. 'He wanted me to have a job, not a career,' she explained in a moment of self-revelation, of which there were increasingly more since Cass's elevation to vice president. It was Amelia showing Cass, a little at a time, the turning points in her own life; whether as goad or warning, Cass wasn't quite certain. 'I think when I started the agency, it was just too much for my husband. Bill supported me, pushed me to do it, and when I did, it broke us apart in a way I still don't quite understand. All of a sudden, there wasn't any marriage there.'

Amelia was an almost mythic figure on Madison Avenue; when younger women in the business talked about role models, they had her in mind. She was one of the city's small handful of women agency principals, and how she accomplished that had been a favourite subject of rumour and gossip for decades, occasioning at least one novel, which enjoyed a brief flurry of publicity before

Cass joined the agency. In the book, the heroine blackmailed her lover into financing her agency with his account. The truth in Amelia's case was less colourful, though Cass thought it much more interesting.

Amelia, at twenty-six, was frustrated by her job as a writer at a mediocre agency whose biggest account, a cosmetics company, was steadily losing ground in the market. It remained at the agency only because its president was a close personal friend of Amelia's employer. The two men were roommates at Choate and Yale, best men at each other's wedding, and godfathers to their friend's children. The account was unprofitable for the client, but old-boy ties, Amelia realized, were stronger than balance sheets, more intimate than market shares.

The agency was falling apart, and most of Amelia's colleagues spent their lunch hours looking for other jobs. With no one noticing, Amelia mastered every aspect of both the cosmetics business and the agency responsibilities. She didn't look for a better job; instead, she armed herself with skills and information. Meanwhile, her employer himself took longer and longer lunches, returning, if at all, unsteady on his feet and reeking of liquor. And Bill, her husband, tended their young daughter.

Her boss was drying out at Silver Hill when Amelia made her extraordinary proposal to his friend, the client. It was an audacious and brilliant move; a year later, when she opened Amelia Jordan, Inc., the client told the *Times*, 'Amelia simply wouldn't take no for an answer.'

She found a talented young designer whose sexy, avant-garde clothes were just beginning to be noticed. His ideas worked as well in jars and boxes as they did in lavish silks and soft woollens, and his newly repackaged line of the client's products was a hit with young, affluent customers. Amelia recruited a dozen bright models from Ford and Wilhelmina, and dressed them in Marc's smart clothes. Marc designed the interior of the blue-and-silver jet that flew the girls around the country for beauty clinics and personal appearances in all the major markets. The company, and Amelia Jordan, Inc., flourished.

Amelia dealt with the rumours by ignoring them. In fact, she told Cass, she found them useful. 'Never say never, rarely say yes, and always say maybe,' she advised Cass. 'Some people may be able to mix sex and business, but I could not.' She explained, 'The problem is that you can never be sure of the basis on which judgements of you are being made. And there's much too much at stake: even a little of the usual man-woman hysteria can cost you a client as well as a lover.'

Cass smiled at Amelia's advice; it sounded rather quaint. She heeded it, but not purposefully; few men she met through the agency appealed to her. She did not need them. She was popular from the time she arrived in New York; she was a woman men loved to escort, to take to parties. They could trust her to be charming and pretty and vivacious; her presence on a man's arm announced to the world that he was someone to be reckoned with.

Cass was the kind of woman lovers remembered long after the affair was over. They sent her gifts on holidays thereafter, souvenirs of what they had shared with her. Someone she met in the wine country in France sent her a case of Beaujolais Nouveau every Christmas. On Valentine's Day a man with whom she had once climbed a mountain sent her a down jacket. A hippie she picked up hitchhiking in the desert mailed her a book on meditation—pressed between the pages she found peyote buds. She spent a few months with a photographer she met at the Cedar Bar soon after she came to the city; for weeks afterward, each mail delivery brought something from him—letters, cards, pictures.

Even after she took up with Nick, she saw other men from time to time. Her relationship with him was largely unarticulated, which suited her. When she met Grey Tucker, and felt the strong pull between them, she dismissed it, not out of loyalty to Nick, but because Amelia's words were strong in her mind. Amelia was her mentor—more important to Cass, she was her friend. When other women criticized Amelia, or people gossiped cruelly about her, Cass defended her. And thought in passing that her daughter Natalie was certainly a graceless bitch.

SIX

'Three floors, with a floor-through on each one and a flat in the basement that was probably the maid's room. They want three hundred and twenty-five thousand.'

Cass could hardly contain her excitement about the brownstone, though it was Paula who was moving, pacing up and down the length of Cass's living room.

'Terrific,' she said. 'But are you ready to be a landlady? That's a lot of aggravation.'

'Maybe,' said Cass thoughtfully. 'Paula, do you ever wonder what will happen when we get old? I mean really old?'

'Wonder isn't the operative word,' said Paula wryly. 'Worry, that's it. Sometimes I wake up in the middle of the night and wonder who will bury me.'

Cass wrinkled her nose. 'Somehow, we never get it out of our heads that Mr Right will show up and buy us the rest of our lives, do we?'

'Nope,' said Paula. 'Complete with house, kids, white picket fence, and a Purple Cross plan.'

'And meanwhile, we fritter away our money, if we have any. Which we do. I mean, you and I earn more in a year that our fathers earned in five. And we never consider what's going to happen to us if the prince doesn't show up.'

'Some of us don't,' said Paula. She went into Cass's tiny kitchen and opened the refrigerator door.

'Hungry?' asked Cass.

'Uh uh. Just grazing. You know, I ran into Maggie Kerr

in Washington today. Bumped into her at the bar at the Watergate—I was waiting for Chris. Remember her, that woman in my study group at law school?' Cass nodded; she remembered Maggie, but not as well as she remembered Tom, Maggie's ex-fiancé. Cass and Tom had had a brief fling when they were both in Cambridge, and that was the end of Maggie's engagement.

'Well, she's working at Justice now. She has a kid.'

'Really?' Cass raised her eyebrows. 'Did she marry Tom after all?'

'You know very well she didn't.' Paula shook her curls and snorted audibly. 'No, she met this fellow from the civil rights division a year ago, married him six weeks later, and left him a month after the baby was born. She's living in a nice apartment, has a beautiful little boy, and a good job. Everything she always wanted. She practically told me she got married just to have the baby.'

'Would you do something like that?'

'I might,' Paula admitted. She came back to the living room and flounced into a deep tub chair. 'I really want a kid. It would be more honest to do it alone, I think; artificial insemination or something. Pick out a stranger in the night. It's probably a moot point now, anyway. I bet my eggs are all dried up.'

'Doubtful,' said Cass. 'I know several women who didn't even have their first child until they were forty.'

'Yeah, and where are they now, Bellevue?' Paula got up from the chair and wandered around the room, picking up Cass's objects, touching and replacing them. 'It's not the age, it's the stage that kills you. Who has the stamina to chase a toddler around at forty? And what happens to the rest of your life?'

Cass wondered that, too. What did happen? To one's work, and friends, and all the things that mattered to her now? Did they just suddenly become unimportant? Did you miss them—did a child, or a husband, make up for all of them? For her, she thought, it might not; for Paula, perhaps it could. 'Are you ready to make that kind of commitment?' she asked.

'To a child, maybe. To a man, not now.' Paula could not sit still —she was up and down, sitting and pacing; like a child herself, Cass thought. 'I'm a lot readier to commit to a child than to anyone I know now. There are times my body just screams to fill up with a baby.'

Cass wasn't interested in talk about babies, not then. 'Babies or not, Paula, there's always the possibility, far-fetched as it may seem, that we'll have to provide for our own old age. I really liked that brownstone, and I may never have a chunk of money like this again. I'm too chicken to put it into the market, and I don't think municipal bonds are very sexy. They don't keep you warm at night, or give you a feeling of belonging.'

Paula came over to Cass and ruffled her hair. 'Neither does a house,' she said, 'but I get your point.'

'Do you, Paula?' Cass asked earnestly. 'Do you really?'

'I understand that you want me to buy it with you.' Paula grinned. 'When do I see it?'

Cass jumped up and hugged her friend. 'Saturday,' she told Paula happily. 'I told the broker you'd see it with me on Saturday!'

Paula was not surprised. She and Cass had talked about living together before. She bought the house with Cass because it made good financial sense, and because she loved Cass. And because it meant she could postpone any decisions about her career.

Chris was pressing her to come back to Washington. He had been doing so since she left him two years before. 'What about our work?' he pleaded with her. 'We've just begun. We haven't even started on the ties between the oil companies and the Oklahoma Congressmen. The evidence is there, just waiting for us to dig it up, on the offshore oil leases, the bribes. You can't leave now, Paula.'

She had been firm. 'Chris, I don't care anymore. It's that simple. There's a lying, stealing Congressman under every rock in Washington. Let somebody else find them and prosecute them. I want to do other things. We've won a lot of the abortion battles, but that doesn't mean the fight is over. We're going to see a backlash soon. And the administration's going to backpedal fast when it comes, once the right-to-lifers get geared up for a constitutional amendment banning abortion. We're celebrating now, but wait a few years. Women can lose it all, and when that happens, I don't want to be hounding sleazy politicians who are lining their pockets with Arab money. Frankly, I want to tend my own garden. I want my life back. It's time to go home.'

'Time to be a rich lady lawyer, you mean,' said Chris.

She flared. 'That's easy for you to say; you never had to worry about money, but I did. I went to college on scholarship, and I only finished paying off my law school loans a year ago. My parents aren't rich—my mother's entitled to spend her winters in Florida if I can help. Yes, money's an issue, I never said it wasn't. But that's not the real reason.'

'Then what is?'

They were in bed in her apartment in Georgetown. She got up and stood at the window, looking down at the slowly moving twilight traffic on M Street.

'You and me and Maribeth,' she told him. 'That's part of it, too.' He began to protest, but she hushed him. 'You're not going to divorce Maribeth, Chris, not now and not later. And you shouldn't. She's given you everything, and what's she got now? A bottle and an empty bed. I don't know which came first, but it doesn't matter. There isn't a new face in the liberal wing of the party except yours, and you don't get to the White House by dumping your wife. That's where you're going—not now, but soon. So that's a reason, too. But that's still not all of it.'

'What is?'

She paced the room. 'It's this place, it's politics, it's

power. Before, when I didn't have any power, I was an anarchist—'

'Like Jake Stern?' Chris interrupted. Jake, like Paula, had been Chris's student at law school. Like Paula, Chris was captivated by Jake's intelligence, his brilliance, and his politics. Until he went too far—until the bombing. But that was long ago; Paula would not be diverted.

'Like Jake,' she admitted. 'But then I got sucked in, by the chance to find out how power really operates. I came to Washington. I saw what power does to people. I hate it. I see what it does to me, too. I don't like the way it skews me, the way I look at people now, like so many obstacles to be removed from my path.'

'So what are you going to do? You can't just pack up your principles and float out there alone with them. That's a waste of your talents.'

'Oh, I won't,' Paula said blithely. 'I'll find a way to work for the things I believe in, but not here. This town is corrosive. You start believing your press clippings, and then you're hooked by them . . . by power. I'm going to work on an abortion case for the Centre, and maybe I'll join a firm.'

'Didn't you always tell me your father thinks you'll be the first woman justice on the Court?' he asked innocently, and Paula laughed.

'You're not going to bribe me with anything that blatant, are you?' She came back to the bed and ran her fingers lightly over his chest. 'I hope someone's taping this conversation,' she teased. 'It will look great in Anderson's column . . . Presidential hopeful woos lady lawyer with Supreme Court bid.' She moved her hands down to his belly. 'I wish you the best, Chris. I'll campaign for you, I'll raise money in New York, I might even doorbell in Brooklyn. But that's a long way off, and right now I'm getting chilly.'

She climbed on top of him. She licked his closed eyelids gently, then more insistently, but he did not open his eyes. She guided him into her centre and raised his hands to her breasts, covering them with her own. She moved on him slowly, grinding herself into him. She was ready in seconds; the heat spread through the backs of her legs and into her belly as the shuddering started deep inside her, at the exact spot where their bodies were joined. Caught by her own rhythm, she heard his words dimly, as if from a long distance; he did not open his eyes as he raised her above him, but she did. Looking down, between them, she watched the beads of moisture drip from her onto his thin, hard, blue-veined cock. And then he said, 'You always have to be on top, don't you?'

SEVEN

'It looks like the set for a movie musical,' Cass told Nick as he braked the rented Mercedes and stopped in the courtyard motor entrance of the Beverly Wilshire. Countless tiny Christmas lights flickered in flower-laden mimosa branches.

'They light it like this even when it's not the season,' Nick told her, giving the bellman keys to the luggage trunk. Cass uncoiled her body from the car and stretched gratefully. 'I'm sorry about the hotel—I thought I had a house lined up in Laurel Canyon, but it fell through.'

'I don't care,' said Cass. 'I love hotels. They make me feel illicit. And room service . . . I might just hang out in bed for a week.'

Nick smiled down at her. He was a big man, over six feet tall, and his body was wiry but powerful. He looks good, Cass thought as he led her to the elevator. She noticed a familiar-looking and extraordinarily attractive man coming out of Hernando's, the hotel bar, and recognised him: Warren Beatty, she thought, my God. She was annoyed at her reaction; she had become enough of a New Yorker to pride herself on remaining unaffected by celebrities.

'Wish I could hang out there with you, but I've got meetings all day tomorrow,' Nick said. They were alone in the elevator; he took her in his arms and she fit herself against him, enjoying his familiar feel after so many weeks.

'But not tonight, I hope?' she said as the elevator stopped.

'Not tonight,' he said with a wink, and she followed him down the corridor.

The lavish suite included a well-stocked bar, and Nick poured them both drinks while Cass unpacked her clothes. She was in the shower when she heard the phone ring; a few moments later, Nick came into the bathroom, handing her a glass of champagne. She stepped out of the shower and took it, wrapping herself in a thick towel from the heated rack. Nick eyed her appreciatively.

'I missed you, Cass,' he said, embracing her. His hands roamed over her body. 'I missed this, too.'

'Me, too,' she said happily. 'It's been six long weeks. But we'll remedy that in just one hot New York second.'

He stepped back. 'Uh . . . Cass, what about one hot second and sixty minutes?'

'What do you mean?' she asked, frowning.

'That was Bob Treat calling. He's the guy with the bucks—the one who's going to help me get *Orange* launched right. He's downstairs.'

'Downstairs?' she asked, incredulous.

'Yeah . . . he's going out of town for the holidays, and he says he needs to see me just for a few minutes—one drink—before he leaves. Look, I know you're pissed off, but it'll only be an hour, I promise. He's a very important person . . . Cass, I *need* this guy!' He followed her into the bedroom. 'Why don't you finish unpacking, lie down, relax, I'll be up as soon as I shake him loose. He said it wasn't a big hang-up, but it was a hang-up. He's supposed to come in; he's supposed to okay the bread before he leaves.'

Cass sighed. 'You are possessed, Pappas, you know that?'

'You mean obsessed, don't you?' he said, grinning.

'No, I mean possessed,' she replied. 'Totally owned by that rag of yours.'

'Soon to be those two rags of mine,' he said. 'If Treat comes in.'

'All right, go already,' she told him good-naturedly. 'But if you're not back in an hour, I'm going to go pick up Warren Beatty or somebody.'

'You're the broad that can do it,' he said, kissing her. 'All indications to the contrary, I'm very glad you're here.'

He left then, and Cass stretched out on the bed. Nick's things were scattered all over the suite; even in his absence, there was a sense of urgency and impatience about the space he inhabited. He was an enthusiastic man; Cass liked his passion for living. It was not confined to his magazine; it imbued everything he did with a zest that made most other men pallid in comparison. She had met Nick nearly three years before, at a Doubleday press party for a book written by a friend; Nick's magazine was excerpting the book. He was everywhere in *Apple*'s early days; at parties, benefits, dinners, prizefights, in the clubs, at the openings, and in the columns.

They had stood in a corner together, sipping their wine, while Nick identified celebrities in the city's literary and publishing worlds. 'They're not talking books; they're probably talking about how hard it is to find a good apartment in New York. Everybody in New York wants the same thing: a better apartment, a better job, and a better lover,' he said.

'Do you?' she asked the big man with the curly black hair and snapping eyes.

He laughed. 'I've got a great apartment, right over the store. And the best job in the world.'

She went to his apartment with him that night; it was, as he had told her, the top floor of the East Side town house owned by *Apple*. The bedroom was austere and sybaritic at once. A daybed approached via a small platform intercepted the view of First Avenue and the Fifty-ninth Street Bridge. An elevated window-seat bridged the floor-to-ceiling windows; it was upholstered in the same dark-grey flannel that covered the bed and floors. A massive seventeenth-century armoire was a commanding presence in the room.

He was right, she told him later; he already had a better apartment.

'And now I've got a better lover, too,' he said, nuzzling her comfortably.

Within a few weeks, it was clear to his friends, at least, that she was Nick Pappas's girl. She spent two or three nights each week at Nick's, but refused to move in with him. 'I moved my curlers to a man's apartment once, and that was enough,' she told him. Frequently, she brought her own work with her; Nick would leave a stormy late-night editorial meeting in the *Apple* offices below, and come upstairs until the others decided to do it his way, disturbing the careful order she'd made of her reports and memos as he stretched out on the daybed and pulled her close for a kiss. 'Hey, I'm working,' she'd tell him. 'So am I,' he'd reply. Later, after he went back downstairs, she'd stuff her work back into her briefcase, reaching over to set the alarm on the rosewood-and-quartz Cartier clock on the night table. When Nick came to bed, hours later, she'd hear him turn off the alarm; he could not sleep, he told her, when he knew he would be awakened by a shrill bell, or even a muted buzz. 'I'll get it as soon as it goes off,' she said, and learned to awaken shortly before it was set to ring, clicking the button before it disturbed Nick.

'If you know you'll wake up before it goes off, why do you bother to set the damn thing?' he asked her repeatedly.

'Because knowing it will go off if I don't gets me up,' she replied. 'And I have to get up. I don't own the agency, love; I can't wander downstairs and have it start when I'm ready to work, you know.'

'Neither do I,' Nick answered, but they both knew the actual ownership of *Apple* did not detract in the least from the fact that the magazine was, indeed, Nick Pappas's own. He'd started it with borrowed money, and expanded ownership to keep pace with his expanding vision for the new publication so that he owned less than a controlling interest. But with his hand-selected staff, Nick controlled a majority of the voting stock. At first, the other backers had few disagreements with Nick. They liked what he had created—a readable, gossipy, slick city magazine, which made money and earned them profits less than three years after the charter issue.

But Nick soon grew bored with his creation, and he had little tolerance for boredom. 'Now I know how God felt on the eighth day,' he told Cass, only half joking. He had not only created a magazine, he had invented himself—a poor Greek immigrant's son who breakfasted with the mayor of New York, dined with the merchant bankers of Wall Street, and danced all night with the society girls, models, and hangers-on of the jet set. He filled in the gaps in his own education; he learned to dress and talk and taste the difference between good wines and bad, know the rich and famous and, more important, have them know him. He made himself an expert on art, fashion, and theatre; he soaked up knowledge like a sponge, Cass thought. The sweet-faced girl he met and married while in the Navy had long since returned to Pensacola, where he had found her, taking with her their son, Peter, who spent infrequent vacations with his father. Cass had met Peter only once; she would not have if she had not insisted. He was a quiet, well-mannered boy, who seemed happiest, that whole week, when she and Nick took him to the airport for his return home. And Nick seemed happy, too, when the plane departed. He dropped Cass off at her apartment, and she did not see him for three days; she learned later that he had gone on what he described as 'a major bender', and when she tried to draw him out about it, he rebuffed her efforts. 'Look, you're just feeling guilty about Pete,' she began, and he cut her off angrily.

'How in the name of Christ do you know what I'm feeling?' he snapped, and she retreated; he was as close to out of control as Cass had ever seen him. He might turn on her, and she was not prepared for that. Cass thought her way through most situations before she allowed them to happen to her.

Later Nick was apologetic, and the fabric of their relationship closed over the rip, leaving almost nothing to mark it. She understood how much Nick loved Peter, how the boy's coolness upset him. But she did not bring up the subject again, and simply coped with Nick's moods when he returned from his infrequent trips to Florida to see his son.

Cass could understand Nick's eagerness to see the man who might help him out of his dilemma; in his place, she would have done the same thing, she reflected, as she waited for him in the hotel suite.

'They're a pack of fucking accountants, assholes,' he'd said on the drive in from the airport, pounding his fist on the wheel. 'No idea what it takes to make your mark out here—nobody understands understatement in Lotus Land. They only know about extravaganzas.'

He defended the exorbitant amount he'd paid for serial rights to a new book. 'We outbid *Esquire* and *Atlantic* for it,' he told Cass proudly, 'and we'll run it simultaneously in *Apple* and the opening issue of *Orange*. This is the most important writer in California—she's chic, she's hot, she's one of theirs. My board—my stupid board —can't understand it.'

'But they understand money,' said Cass. 'Can't you make a splash without spending so much on the first issue party?'

'Jesus, you sound like Miles,' Nick said, and Cass tried to soothe him; the freeway traffic was bad enough without Nick's temper.

'They'll come around,' she assured him. 'Just don't back them to the wall. Decide what you want to fight about—the book excerpt or the party. Maybe you can't get it all.'

Nick made a rude gesture to the driver who cut sharply in front of their car. 'Goddamn right I can get it all,' he fumed. 'If it weren't for me, there wouldn't be any all—there wouldn't be anything. Christ, Miles Aldrich has so much money he can't count it. He pisses away more than you or I will ever see. And he's been making money on *Apple* since I let him buy in.'

'How about Charlie?' Cass asked. 'He has as many shares in *Apple* as Miles does. Can you persuade him to go along?'

'Charlie thought the world began and ended in Upper Montclair before he came on the *Apple* board,' Nick answered. 'Now he's got a fancy place in Sag Harbor, and his wife has our restaurant critic eating her lasagne and our music critic hearing her genius kid play the piano and our business manager taking her to opening nights, and suddenly that bozo's telling me how to run a magazine! Jesus fucking Christ, do you have to be stupid in order to be rich, or does it just help?'

'When did Pete take Alma to what opening?' Cass asked, trying to divert him.

'It was a preview for some new experimental play she backed, so far off Broadway it was in New Jersey,' Nick told her. 'She wanted the theatre critic, but he had his secretary tell her he had the clap, so she got Charlie to call Pete. Charlie's so pussy-whipped he'd call Jimmy Carter if Alma told him to bring him home for dinner.'

'With all the money Charlie gave the Carter campaign, he'd probably come,' mused Cass, 'with Rosalynn and Amy and Miz Lillian.'

'I guess,' Nick said, turning onto Wilshire. 'I told them to give me a call when they decided who they wanted to run their magazine. Christ, I get tired of dealing with the money boys. A nice Greek kid like me should be running a deli somewhere, not this circus.'

Later, when Nick returned to the suite, he continued his tirade against his backers. 'It would all be so much easier if I just had fuck-you money,' he sighed. 'How come you were born smart instead of rich?'

'What, not beautiful?' she pouted playfully.

'Gorgeous,' he said, kissing her neck. 'Smart, too. But Mama always told me it was just as easy to marry a smart, gorgeous rich broad as it was to marry a smart, gorgeous poor one.'

She kissed him lightly, unbuttoning his shirt. 'I bet she didn't say broad,' she said. 'And marry—who said marry?'

'I don't know, somebody said it,' Nick pulled the sheet away and took her breast in his hand. He rubbed the nipple lightly until it reddened and hardened, and then took it in his mouth. Cass moaned with pleasure. She lifted her body up off the bed and Nick enclosed her in his arms, licking her body, blowing on the golden hairs that darkened and were thicker below her navel. He kissed the insides of her thighs, and the warmth of his lips fanned the flickers of her desire into a steady, burning heat that radiated out from her centre. He brought her to a quick, shuddering orgasm, and then he brought his mouth to her wetness, lapping at her in long, slow strokes.

'I want you inside me,' she whispered, 'again, please,' but he kept licking her, faster and faster, until she could stand it no longer and pulled him up to her, tasting her own saltiness on his tongue.

'I think we should do it in the spring,' she heard, and then he entered her again, huge and insistent, cutting through her wet smoothness and dissolving her walls, nerves and tissues in rolling waves of pleasure.

They did not speak for a long while; there was no sound in the room except the air conditioner's low hum, and their own noises, his deep groan and her soft cries.

He buried his face in her neck. 'Just before the first issue. Maybe the day of the party.'

Cass moved, in surprise, and he slipped out of her, rolling onto his back. He put his arm around her, and she lay with her head on his chest, feeling the harsh pounding of his heart ease into a slower, steady beat.

'We can borrow Bob Treat's boat for a honeymoon.'

Cass sat up in bed. Nick reached into a drawer in the night table and brought out a joint. He lit it and passed it to Cass, stretched out on his side, leaning on his elbow and looking up at her.

She did not know what to say. After a while, she asked, 'Treat? The moneyman?'

Nick nodded.

'Just who is he, anyway?'

'Some people think he's the great white hope of Orange County. His father's the Treat of Treat Industries, a one-man multinational. Treat's involved in oil and computers and tankers and agribusiness. Companies in nineteen countries. Bob's the wonder boy, going to inherit a lot of stock one of these days. They're grooming him for politics—sort of the young Kennedy of the Right. Except he's discovered show biz. He's producing a movie with his own money; he wrote it, packaged it, is directing it. No kidding—he wants to be Woody Allen. Once they've discovered Hollywood, you can't keep them down in the boardroom, I guess. Or even the Republican ladies' luncheons. He's too nice a guy—he'll never make it in politics. Too nice to make it in the movies, too.'

'What's his picture about?'

'It's a movie with a message—some allegory about prison. The old man's having a fit; Bobby's spending too much time at the Polo Lounge and Ma Maison, and not enough in Pasadena. The candidate's wife is getting to be an afternoon lush. I met the old man once. Crusty old bastard. Looks ruthless, like a titan of industry should. Terrible bigot.'

Cass took a long drag on the joint, 'We've never talked about marriage before,' she said. 'The night we met, you told me you tried it once and didn't like it. You said the trouble with women is that they turn into wives when you marry them.'

Nick stroked her belly in lazy circles. 'Did I say that?'

'Mmm hmm,' she replied.

'Maybe I was wrong. I don't think you'd turn into a wife.'

'What makes you so sure?'

'You're not the type. You've got a life of your own—you don't need me to give it purpose. You have a career. You wouldn't be expecting me to come home and explain the world to you every night; you're out there in it, and you'd be just as tired as I am.'

'What about children?'

'Do you want them?'

'I don't know,' said Cass. 'Sometimes I do. And sometimes I think it's a terrible idea.'

'If you wanted a kid . . . it's up to you. I'm not such a terrific father to the one I've got.'

'That's true, sort of. But it's not your fault. Shirley doesn't make it easy for you to spend time with Pete.'

'Maybe she would if we got married. Would you mind that?'

Cass stubbed out the joint. She felt light-headed; she couldn't believe they were talking about marriage. From the beginning, their relationship had been marked by an easy, bantering lightness. She was never certain of Nick's feeling for her; he kept her always slightly off-balance. At first, both of them had continued to see other people; for nearly a year, she had not slept with any other man, however, and neither, to her knowledge, had Nick had another woman. She felt that, but she was not sure; she never asked, and he never did, either. There had been words of love spoken between them, but not of commitment.

She had not thought there would be. She did not worry about their relationship; she thought it would endure until it ended, as others had, because it no longer worked. Her previous affairs had not worked for a variety of reasons; most often, because she was tired of the man, but sometimes because he did not do the things which, to her, meant that she was loved. The things could be trivial, like paying too much attention to another woman at a party, or important, such as being insensitive to her needs. She kept a mental list of what she thought to be the properties of love; when enough were present, the relationship worked, and when they disappeared, so did it.

'No. I think Pete's a nice kid. Nick, if you don't care that much about having a child, why do you want to get married?'

'I don't want to get married,' he said. 'I want to marry you. That's different.'

'But why?'

He shook his head in exasperation. 'Because you are one of the world's great broads. Because I love you. You love me, too. We make a good team.'

'You know I just bought this house with Paula.'

'So? We'll live in it, if you want to. The magazine needs more space, they can take the apartment and use it for offices. Your floor in the house is bigger anyway. I like Paula. It'd be nice to have her upstairs. Hell, you never get to choose your neighbours in New York. What a break.'

'But you're always in California.'

'So you'll come out here with me for a few months. Once *Orange* gets going, I'll be back in the city. I'll come out here once a month or so; I've got a good managing editor, he doesn't need me breathing down his neck.'

'I can't just leave Amelia. I wouldn't anyway.'

'Take a leave of absence for a while,' Nick suggested.

'Could you take a leave of absence from *Apple*? Or *Orange*?' she asked.

'That's not the point,' he replied.

'Of course it is. You want to marry me because I'm independent, because I've got a career—a purpose, you said. So then you want me to walk out on it. No wonder you think women turn into wives when you marry them. That's exactly what you're asking me to do. To become.'

'Yeah, maybe you're right,' he admitted. 'So we get

married, take a little trip, and then we commute for a while. It won't be forever.'

'Oh, the romance of it all,' she teased. 'The man marries, and leaves the little woman while he seeks his fortune in the West.'

Nick laughed, and they kissed. 'I love you,' he said.

'Me too you.' They nuzzled happily for a few minutes. 'I'm surprised, that's all,' she said. 'And flattered. I need to think about it.'

'No hurry,' he told her lazily. 'The offer doesn't expire at midnight. I'm not going anywhere else for a while.' He looked at her quizzically. 'Are you?'

'No,' she said, snuggling into his arms. 'Not for a while.'

EIGHT

Cass was meeting a friend of Paula's for brunch. 'I want you to look up Ellin Barnett when you're in LA,' Paula had told her. 'I think she might be a good tenant for the top floor. Or a potential third partner, if she decides to stay in New York.'

'But you said she's in LA. Isn't she the one who did that book on the Movement women?'

Paula nodded. 'She has a contract for another book. And she's taking what she calls a sabbatical on the East Coast. Trying it out to see if she likes it.'

'Didn't you tell me she has a kid?' Cass frowned. 'I'm not crazy about crayons on the walls and trikes in the front hall.'

'Lara's not a kid, she's fourteen. But she's not coming, anyway, she's going to live with her father, Ellin's ex. She'll just be around during school vacations. Ellin's a fabulous woman, you'll love her. She's one of those people you meet and think you've known each other all your lives. Like you and me.'

'Except we have known each other practically that long.' Cass felt vaguely threatened; she was possessive about Paula. Usually Paula liked that, but in this case it was an irritant. We have to find another tenant, she thought; the brownstone was going to be a bigger financial strain than she'd expected. Cass was spending money recklessly on things Paula thought unimportant. Like sandblasting the exterior—though it would be a lovely rosy colour when it was done, she knew—and repainting all the trim, and that new front door with the stained glass inset. She would be grateful for Ellin's rent, if things worked out. And she wanted them to work. She liked Ellin a great deal. But she sensed Cass's ambivalence.

'Look, just go meet her, will you? I know you'll think she's great, and it would be a lot easier not to have to deal with a stranger upstairs, wouldn't it?'

'I guess,' said Cass. Maybe Paula was right. She didn't have time—neither of them did—to screen tenants. Maybe Ellin would work out perfectly. Perhaps she would want to buy into the house. There was a provision for taking in a third partner in her agreement with Paula. 'Not only would it save us money, it would make it easier to buy each other out if we had to, with a third share,' Paula had said.

'You mean in case one of us gets married?' Only a husband, Cass thought, could be reason enough for them to dissolve their partnership; Paula, who had a lawyer's more sceptical view of contracts, could think of several others.

'Or something,' she told Cass, who did not hear her reply.

Cass did call Ellin, and they arranged to meet. She dressed carefully for the encounter. Not that it matters, she told herself, she's probably an old hippie, stuck in the sixties, sort of like Paula. Or like Paula used to be. Really, she thought, it's time Paula started dressing like a grown-up.

Cass was pleasantly surprised by Ellin, and revised her estimate. She was a big, well-fleshed woman, with smooth skin and an intelligent face. She was high-breasted and had good legs, evident even under the tailored trousers, which she wore with a pale-lemon-coloured shirt and a raw silk jacket. They ordered Bloody Marys and gave the waiter their order; Joe's Shack, on the Santa Monica pier, was relatively uncrowded that early afternoon just before Christmas. The day was breezy, and the wind ruffled Ellin's short, curly hair.

'How did you and Paula meet? She told me once, but I've forgotten,' Cass said.

Ellin grinned. 'At a NOW meeting, if you can believe it. I'd heard about her; when I was doing research for a book, her name kept coming up.'

'In connection with Jake Stern, probably,' Cass commented. Ellin nodded. The women in the Movement had thoroughly disliked Jake, not because of the bombing that sent him underground—many of them approved of his action—but because he treated women with a kind of sneering disdain, unless, of course, they could be of use to him. 'Jake Stern really fucked Paula Gabriel over,' someone Ellin interviewed told her. 'Gossip says she was pregnant when he took off. He always was one of the biggest pigs in SDS.'

The Paula Ellin met in the early seventies was not, she thought, someone to be pitied. She was a brilliant and impassioned speaker, and her arguments were as carefully reasoned as her fervour was strong. Ellin was dazzled by her words, and her energy.

'That's right,' Ellin replied to Cass. 'Paula lit my fire.'

When she met Paula, Ellin wasn't much of a feminist. That movement seemed barely relevant to her life; she was liberated because she had no choice, she used to say. She attended the meeting in connection with a newspaper assignment. Paula's persuasiveness had an effect on her; she was caught up by a new possibility. If she had been asked to put it into words, she might have said that Paula made her see that feminism was not, as she had thought, a distinct political ideology; rather, it was the set of assumptions inherent in one's world view, the assumptions of possibilities open or closed to someone simply because of her sex. After she met Paula, she was less interested in writing the kind of articles at which she had been successful for several years—how to spend money with style, where to find the best massage in

Orange County, where the trendy shops were in West Los Angeles. She began to shift her focus a bit—'somewhere between the bra burners and the bubbleheads,' she told Cass.

'Paula's very good at making people re-examine their priorities,' Cass agreed, though in fact her efforts to do just that with Cass fell on mostly deaf ears. 'She's always after me to donate something to her causes.' That was how Cass responded to Paula's nudges—with a cheque. 'Just tell me how much you want,' she'd say, 'just spare me the violin strings.'

The more Ellin talked, the more Cass began to see the possibilities Paula had suggested. At first, she brought up the subject of the brownstone cautiously, even indirectly.

'Have you been planning this move for a while?' she asked.

'Oh, it's been a long-standing fantasy, until Lara's father decided to settle in California. He rented a cottage a few miles from where we live. On the beach, which suits Lara perfectly—she lives for surfing.'

'Was that so he could be closer to her?'

'Not exactly. Tony's an actor; he's doing a film here. When Lara was little, he moved to London. Since then, they haven't spent much time together. Now they've discovered each other, and it's love at second sight. He's thrilled with his beautiful teenage daughter, and she's delirious over her handsome, sophisticated daddy. So she decided to live with him.'

Ellin felt both relief and regret at the prospect. At fourteen, Lara was often angry, sullen, hostile, and rebellious. Adolescence is nature's own psychosis, said the psychiatrist mother and daughter had been seeing together for nearly a year; some kids outgrow it, and some don't.

Lara probably would, but Ellin wasn't sure if she would live through it. Before Tony came back to California, Lara had not mentioned him for several years, but Ellin knew she thought about her father frequently. If she didn't know it intuitively, she could have tracked it by Lara's frequent references to being 'practically an orphan', by the defiance with which she met Ellin's simple rules, by the accusation in Lara's eyes when Ellin brought a man home, which she did less and less often lately. It was different when Lara was small; then, she threw herself into the arms and onto the laps of Ellin's dates, asking each of them, silently and aloud, if he would be her daddy. On her own initiative, Lara had written to Tony, and the letter she showed Ellin made her heart ache. 'I am growing up and want to know something about my oragens,' the still-childish writing read. 'I would like to meet you, and get to know you, if it wouldn't be too much trouble. I am not bitter about the divorce, I just want to know who my father is.'

Ellin knew that Lara blamed her for Tony's departure, though it had been wholly his own idea. In his absence, he had grown to mythic proportions in Lara's eyes, as fathers will when they leave before the reality of life teaches children that parents are, alas, human and fallible.

'You must be thrilled about that,' Cass said. 'Without a child, you can really live your own life.' She couldn't imagine herself tied to a smaller, dependent being. And she had been thinking about that quite a bit since Nick's proposal. Peter was one thing—he was practically grown. But a baby was another matter entirely. She was glad Nick had no strong feelings about starting a new family. In time, she might change her own mind, she thought, but that was a distant speck on her personal horizon.

'I've had some thoughts along that line,' Ellin said. 'I'm ready to be a vacation mummy. I've done it full time for a lot of years.'

The waiter brought their omelettes. Paula's right, I do like her, Cass thought. She's more than just a woman with a kid and a half-assed career. Cass did not know many women with children; women who simply stayed at home and raised their families. For them she felt a dismissive awe; how could they stand it? she wondered. But Ellin was a professional; Cass had read some of her work, a few articles, her book, and admired them. She did that, and brought up a child, too, she thought; it can't have been easy.

'I've been feeling stale here for a while,' Ellin said. 'Ready to change my life a little. I have a contract for a new book, a novel, and New York sounds like a good place to write it. There's a kind of energy there you don't find here.'

'Have you thought about where you'll live? Apartments are impossible to find in the city.'

'I know,' Ellin said, 'I grew up there. I moved here when I got married, and stuck around. It seemed like a good place to bring up Lara. I tried New York once when she was tiny—it was too tough for me. Maybe I'm ready for it now.'

She was twenty-six then, and Lara was a little over a year old. It was the first time she left Tony. He left her, actually—he spent so many nights away from the tidy two-bedroom apartment in Santa Monica that he finally formalized his liaison with a set designer in Westwood and moved in with her. He had started coming home late at night when Ellin was pregnant. She didn't know it yet; when she did, and told Tony, the late nights stopped. They began again when Lara was a few months old, and the morning after her first birthday, he didn't show up until nearly noon.

Ellin was not dressed; she was sitting at the kitchen table, watching helplessly as Lara tossed string beans and pieces of hamburger in all directions from her high chair. Ellin was wearing a dirty old chenille bathrobe; she had not slept.

'Hi,' said Tony cheerfully, coming upon them. He bent down to kiss his daughter, who cooed at him and poured her Tipsy Tumbler of apple juice over her head.

He brushed past Ellin, and she heard him in the shower. When Lara was finished eating, Ellin changed her and put her down for a nap. Then she went into their bedroom.

Tony was dressing; she knew he had an audition at four.

'Well?' she said.

He did not turn from the mirror, where he was adjusting a scarf.

'Well?' he said, echoing, not mocking her; he was not unkind.

'Is this going to continue?'

He did not insult her by asking what 'this' was, or by lying.

'Probably,' he replied.

It continued for a few months; often Tony didn't come home for days. She knew who the other woman was; word got around in the film community. One night she called him there.

'I'm leaving,' she told him.

'When?'

'On Saturday, the noon plane.'

'I'll come by Friday night.'

He came and played with Lara, who gurgled when he hugged her and told her to have a good time in New York with Sophie and Papa, and kissed her a great deal.

'What are you going to do?' he asked after Ellin put the baby down.

'I don't know. Get a job. Find an apartment.'

They said nothing about a divorce. 'Let me know when you get settled,' he said. 'If I have any bread, I'll send you some.'

'Sure,' she answered.

She was going to do just what she told Tony. But Lara got sick with the flu and strep throat and constant ear infections; she screamed all night long. Ellin's father, Lou, was awake with Lara's first thin cry of pain. 'I'll walk her,' he told Ellin, 'go back to bed. She'll sleep for me. Where are the ear drops?'

Ellin was eager to get into her own place—you can go home again, she thought, but who wants to? Even marriage to Tony was better than being a girl again in her mother's house, though this time she had a baby of her own. There were some compensations; she never had to worry about babysitters, which would have been fine if she had had anywhere to go. The maid washed the baby's clothes, and cooked and served dinner, and Lou left money on Ellin's bureau as unobtrusively as he could. It was a cocoon, but there was a cost involved; Ellin lived with her mother's unspoken accusations—how could a daughter of hers have failed at something as simple as marriage, even though Tony was not a *mensch,* like Lou?—and felt like the failure Sophie thought she was.

Finally she found a job writing budget-floor advertising copy for a department store. She spent a third of her salary on a one-bedroom apartment on the Lower East Side. It was a four-flight walk-up in a run-down brownstone; Ellin dragged herself and Lara and groceries and nappies up and down the narrow steps with the threadbare carpeting several times a day. The elderly lady in the apartment below charged her a hundred dollars a month to watch Lara while Ellin worked, but by winter the apartment was intolerable. Often there was no heat; just as often, the fumes from the broken chimney swept through the building and nauseated Ellin. When she plugged in a space heater, all the fuses in the apartment blew out.

She never brought anyone there; she had no social life at all. She hated the apartment, the city, her meaningless job. She was very close to a nervous breakdown.

Tony came to New York and appeared without notice at her office, an airless cubicle in the bowels of a crumbling old store. He carried a dozen roses. That night, she packed her things and Lara's, Tony made arrangements for a removers to the Coast, and they headed back to California together.

For six months, it was falling in love all over again. They bought a beach house in Malibu—Tony had landed a regular role in a television series with a twenty-six-week guarantee. And then the late nights began again, and the early mornings, and eventually the weekends, and then there was the divorce.

'Would you live with your family?' Cass asked, bringing Ellin sharply back to the present. She hadn't thought much about that other time in New York, or even about Tony, until he reappeared in her life again. 'We have something in common now—Lara,' he had told her a few weeks before. We always did, she thought, but without bitterness. Tony's timing erased the residue of that. She needed him in a way she had not for many years—she needed him for Lara. She needed him for herself, too—to reclaim her own life. Bitterness was futile.

'Oh, until I get settled,' Ellin replied to Cass. 'But not for long. No, I'll find something.'

'Renting or buying?'

'Renting at first. If it turns out to be a good move, if Lara stays with Tony, if I do a decent job on the novel, if I can sell the beach house . . . there are several ifs. I might buy in the future; Lara has three more years until college, and then I can do whatever I like. There's no compelling reason to come back here then; once you're over eighteen in LA, you're over the hill. It would be nice to live somewhere where the lines in your face are attributed to character, not character deficiency. As if you'd let the whole culture down by giving up.'

Cass laughed. 'I don't think I could stand the pressure of having to look perfect all the time.'

Ellin eyed her narrowly. 'I don't think you'd find it hard.' Ellin didn't always deal with her age as well as she would have liked. She did not look like a young woman; she looked forty, which she was. She had a mobile face with interesting features and lively brown eyes, framed by a crop of soft curls in which the first strands of grey were beginning to appear. She left them unretouched in a gesture of defiance to the California greed for youthfulness. 'I don't have that much angst about getting older,'

Ellin said, 'except sometimes I feel as though I ought to file an environmental impact statement just to exist here.'

She was giving Cass the opening she sought, and Cass took it. 'Paula's told you about the house we've bought, hasn't she?' she said, and Ellin nodded.

'There's an apartment available in it,' Cass said. 'We haven't started looking for a tenant yet; we don't close until the first of January. Paula thought—and I agree—that it might be a good deal for all of us if you considered taking the apartment. Rent it at first—then maybe buy in if you're interested.'

Ellin chose her words carefully. 'I really appreciate the offer,' she said. 'I know I'm too old to live with Lou and Sophie—I might be too old for dormitory living, too. I need to be able to close my door when I'm working, or want to be alone. And there's Lara as well—she'll be spending vacations with me.'

'That's the beauty of this,' said Cass persuasively. 'We each have our own apartment—our own floor. Yours is the smallest, with only one bedroom. But the living room is huge—you could do something with a sleeper couch for Lara's vacations. It's quite a special house. And the Village—that's where all the writers in New York live.'

Ellin didn't think of herself as a writer; that was just the way she earned a living for herself and Lara. Piece-work, she called it. Until the book. When it was published, she had a professional identity, and the longer she owned it, the more comfortable she began to feel in it. She was not a competitive woman; she didn't, then, yearn for anything more than the chance to be as good as she could be, however good that was. Of course, publishers were in New York—and agents and editors and, as Cass pointed out, writers. Ellin could write anywhere; she was not moving east to pursue her career, she told Cass, just to live in a different way—in a different life.

'Well, but that happens,' Cass said. 'You meet other writers, you get around more, you start comparing your work to theirs—if you're not careful, you catch the New York disease.'

'The New York disease?'

'Oh, sure, you get it by osmosis. I know a lot of writers. They want to get in on the action, to hang out at Elaine's, get taken to the Four Seasons by their editors, get their name in the *Post,* go to literary parties . . . mostly it's harmless.'

'And when it's not?'

Cass shook her blond head. 'Then it's tough. Every time someone else succeeds, you feel like you've failed. You're not satisfied with what you have, or do—you want more, bigger, splashier, better. Like that.' She patted Ellin's arm. 'But that won't happen to you. A lot of Nick's writers have it—you know, the people at *Apple.* They're miserable if a Hollywood studio doesn't option a two-thousand-word article for a major picture, or Elaine seats them in the back room. You're too mature for that.'

Ellin grimaced inwardly. Too mature. The way Cass said it, it was a compliment, but she wasn't sure. Cass was, after all, an unknown quantity. True, she was Paula's friend, and Ellin loved Paula dearly. The night they met, after the NOW meeting, Ellin had offered to drive Paula to the airport. Her plane was delayed for several hours, and they sat in the bar, sharing the intimate details of their lives as some women will with strangers encountered unexpectedly and existentially. By the time Paula's flight was called, they knew they would be in each other's lives for a long time. That was six years before, and their friendship had endured. When Paula came to California, she stayed with Ellin. She remembered Lara's birthday with cards and gifts, and she and Ellin spoke on the telephone regularly. Ellin had no qualms about living with Paula.

Cass, though . . . she was different. In some ways, she was like the women Ellin knew in LA—those Ellin thought of as, simply, women with careers. Women who were, or wanted to be, network vice presidents, feature producers, studio executives. Women who talked about strategies and options and trade-offs. Women who wore what the magazines Ellin wrote for called 'power clothes'. Women who generally made Ellin tired.

There was more than a touch of them in Cass. She was obviously smart and successful; she was also very beautiful, and young—Paula had said thirty-four, but Cass looked barely thirty. Perhaps, Ellin thought, I'm judging her too quickly. She can't help having brains and looks and a fabulous job and plenty of money—she must have, to buy that brownstone—and one of the city's most attractive men for a lover. Ellin knew about Nick Pappas from Paula, and also from people in LA. He was making a big splash on the coast—taking a big gamble, some said. So Cass has him, and everything else—Ellin, she told herself, you're just jealous. Don't let that screw this up for you—it could be the solution to your problems.

Still, she had doubts. 'We might be the odd couple—or the odd trio. I'm compulsive sometimes. And other times I'm a compulsive slob.' Given sufficient justification, Ellin could live in semi-squalor. Tony's treatment after Lara was born had provided that justification; she punished him with dishes left piled in the sink until they crusted over, and stacks of nappies that mildewed in the bathroom. She didn't lose the weight she'd gained with Lara, either, which maddened Tony more than anything else. His anger made Ellin even more stubborn. He didn't want to be there with her and the baby, and she wanted him to want to, so she drove him away. Or thus, after a year of analysis, she reasoned.

'You can live any way you please.' Cass dismissed Ellin's objections airily. 'Nobody's as compulsive as I am, and nobody's more of a slob than Paula.'

'Let me think about it,' Ellin said. 'I won't be coming east until mid-January. Will you be moved in by then?'

'Hopefully,' said Cass. 'Paula's still drawing up our contract.'

'Contract? Isn't that odd, considering how close you two are?'

'Paula thinks it's important . . . oh, there's Nick.' She half rose from her chair, waving at a man who approached them.

He's almost too pretty, Ellin thought as he joined them. Ellin did not care for handsome men; she had married one, and avoided them since. Tony once told her his good looks were a disadvantage, personally if not professionally; other men didn't trust him and neither did women. With good reason, Ellin thought, although she did not feel too sorry for him. She didn't think beautiful women had difficulties, either—at least, few that beauty could not smooth over. For most of Ellin's life she had felt clumsy and graceless and unattractive; given a choice, she would have traded places in an instant with her prettier women friends.

Nick did not seem to notice her reticence; he was friendly and gregarious. He complimented her on her book; he suggested she meet the managing editor at *Orange*. 'We might look into publishing you in the new magazine,' he said. 'I liked that last piece you did for *Los Angeles*.'

In spite of herself, she was charmed. 'It would be nice to write for *Orange*,' she said. 'I could cultivate my California readers, if I have any, so I can come back if New York doesn't work out.'

'You won't have any problems,' he said reassuringly. 'The natives are mostly friendly.'

'Are you one of them?'

'Now I am,' he said. 'My father ran a grocery store in Bridgeport, which I escaped by joining the Navy. And they sent me to college on the GI bill, but my wife worked to help me through.'

'Oh, were you married?'

Nick laughed. 'Wasn't everyone?'

She laughed, too, while Cass watched the interaction between them. Was Nick flirting with Ellin? Relax, she told herself, he's being nice because he knows you want her in the brownstone. She's not his type at all—you're acting like a wife already. Still she broke into the conversation, turning her attention to Nick, linking her arm possessively through his.

'What took you so long to get here?' she asked.

'Oh, this kid came into the magazine office this morning, a big husky surfer type with a locked briefcase under one arm and a skateboard under the other. He was trying to peddle a story—claimed he had the secret list of all the mantras in the world, straight from the maharishi himself. He says there are thirteen different ones, and he wanted a thousand for each.'

They laughed, and he regaled them with more stories; he was an excellent raconteur, and Ellin was enjoying herself immensely. They talked about Bob Treat, Nick's hoped-for backer.

'If he gets his movie together, does that mean he won't buy into *Orange*?' Cass wanted to know.

'Hell, no, he's got enough money to make twenty movies and still give us what we need. In fact, he wrote me a cheque an hour ago. So let's have some champagne and celebrate!'

'And I suppose you've already spent it?' said Cass.

'Ah, baby, you nag like a wife already.' Nick turned to Ellin. 'Did Cass tell you we're getting married?'

'Not exactly,' Cass replied for her. 'Didn't you just tell me the offer didn't expire yet?'

Ellin listened to them sparring and parrying. Nick was complaining that Cass had to leave the next Monday.

'This guy, Grey Tucker, is he making a move on you?' he asked Cass. 'That's all I've heard since you got here. And now he calls and you rush back to New York. Should I be getting worried?'

Cass explained to Ellin. 'He's the most important client in my agency, and we've just been awarded a big chunk of his business. He's taking a personal interest in my new campaign; he seems to think I have to be there to dot every *i* and cross every *t*. Which isn't true at all, of course,' she added with what Ellin thought was false modesty—whether it was or not, Cass clearly enjoyed feeling indispensable. 'If he wants me back for a meeting on Monday, then back I go.'

That gave Ellin an opening; she extricated herself from the conversation, which was beginning to lose its lightness, with the classic LA excuse.

'And I have a meeting this afternoon,' she said, pulling back her chair. 'Cass, thank you. You've given me a lot to think about. Let's be in touch when I get to New York, okay?'

'Okay,' said Cass happily. 'It's going to be wonderful, Ellin. You and me and Paula and the brownstone. I can hardly wait!'

'You women settle everything so quickly,' said Nick fondly, rising as Ellin did; he has wonderful manners, she thought idly. 'You take it for granted that things work out, and they do.'

Perhaps that was why Cass succeeded—there was no reason why she shouldn't. Paula, by contrast, knew from the beginning what she would do with her life. Not Ellin. Ellin drifted into a career, and, in much the same way, into Cass and Paula's lives and into their house. As Cass said, sometimes things just happened right.

Ellin found a ticket on her windshield, and when she got home she discovered that a neighbour's dog had knocked over her garbage cans, scattering trash everywhere for the umpteenth time. As she retrieved the smelly litter, she composed a mental list, and titled it, too: What I'm Looking Forward To in New York. Not having dogs for neighbours. Getting rid of my car. Calling a super when something doesn't work. Being a human being first and a mother second. In the kitchen, she noted that Lara had stopped by and helped herself to a snack while Ellin was out—she still had her key to the house. Having the only key to my apartment, she added.

Ellin was intrigued by the offer from Cass and Paula. Her vague plan about New York—her fantasy—was suddenly more than possible. It was fully formed—probable. Exciting. Scary.

Ellin had made a life for herself in LA. She had a few close friends, people she had grown to love. She had constructed an identity and a place out of the leftovers of her marriage—a marriage that should never have happened, considering the vast differences between Tony and her. She married him because they had tried everything else, and then there were five years of waiting for the unsuitable, unworkable fever to burn out so they could get on with their individual lives. She had never really expected that the marriage would last; she thought from the first that he would tire of her soon . . . handsome, charming, glamorous, talented Tony. So she welcomed each major event—having a child, buying the beach house—as one more brick in a structure she knew must collapse, for it was built on sand.

Her life here and now was safe—predictable, and not unpleasant. There were some people she could call in the dark middle of the night if she needed to. They nurtured and encouraged her, but they inhibited her, too; she felt unable to change without separating herself from them. And she knew she was changing; there was a need to sort out who she had been, and who she was, and who she might become. Without them, and Lara, she thought she might discover that.

She no longer saw life through the eyes of a girl, or even a young woman—in that way, she was different from Cass and Paula. More of her life stretched out behind her, probably, than ahead. She could not remember a time she had been innocent, had believed that things happen for the best. That was not to say she did not look forward to being surprised by joy, or success, or even love. She knew that some and perhaps all of those might yet unfold for her; just as she knew that friends would die, her child might disappoint her, and some of her fantasies would never be realized. Life to Ellin seemed to be random, despite her efforts to bring order to it. As soon as she had dammed up those she loved against hurt or danger, one sprang a leak somewhere else. No sooner did she recover from one near mishap than another reminded her how unpredictable and unfair life could be.

There had been no love affairs in several years, not since Robert, her first lover after Tony. With him, she was open, vulnerable, hopeful; she thought that she might make a life with someone else again. She was a woman of the last generation to grow up expecting that a man would take care of her; she was not cynical about the way things had turned out, just rueful. She grew up understanding the trade-offs involved in being a woman, and she was prepared to accept them. Feminism caught her unawares; it took many years to accept it as central to her life.

After Robert, the men were less and less appropriate. At a party she met a man who, on learning that she had been divorced for several years, enquired whether she had mated in the interim. She thought it was a funny phrase; probably, he had sifted carefully through the available choices and selected that one as least likely to offend, and most certain to connote his meaning. It made her imagine pairs of animals—rutting moose and patient lady moose, dogs coupling in a pile of sawdust, even neutrons and electrons bumping into each other and having a go at it. And then she was sad, when she realized she had not been in a plausible relationship, really, since Robert.

She half wanted one, and thought that in New York the men might be more capable, more grown up; what she really meant was that they might want in a woman something more than a flattering manner and a body without stretch marks. She was not counting on finding such a man; it was just there, a possibility inherent in the move, like the electricity that hangs in the air before a storm.

NINE

'I hate New York, I wish I'd never come. Why didn't you stop me?' Ellin was on the phone to Kate, her best friend from California.

'Because you didn't want to be stopped,' Kate replied. They had that exchange frequently, at great expense, during Ellin's first weeks in the city. She had to talk to Kate, for she knew no one well in New York except Paula, who was in Washington when Ellin arrived on the East Coast. Cass, who had been so enthusiastic about Ellin's plans only a few weeks before, was out of town, too, touring Amagansett plants around the country with Grey Tucker.

Ellin rattled around alone in the empty rooms overlooking Central Park—Sophie and Lou were in Florida for the month—wondering why she had come. She was stern with herself: this is ridiculous, stop it, she thought when she felt the tears well up, as they did so often in the beginning. This is what you wanted, where you wanted to be—this is the fantasy you dreamed up during all those empty nights in California.

She had not expected a difficult transition—certainly not this constant state of tension. But this was not like her previous visits, either. Then, she had packed everything into the too short days and nights—breakfasts with editors, lunch with agents, afternoons on assignments and evenings at theatres or jazz clubs or elegant restaurants. Now time was elongated, stretched out; she woke up in the morning wondering how she could fill the day, instead of planning how she might spend the precious hours until she had to pack and leave.

This time she was not leaving. This time she was overwhelmed by the city—by its noise and traffic, its tall buildings that shut out the sky, its crowds of people who pushed by her, unnoticing, ignoring, pressing into and around her as if she did not exist except as an obstacle to be gotten by.

Since she could not inspect the brownstone on Twelfth Street yet, she made half-hearted attempts to find her own apartment. She read the Sunday real-estate ads as soon as the *Times* hit the stands on Saturday; she called everyone she thought might have a lead or even an invitation that would fill her empty hours. People were not as gracious to her as they had been when she was only an occasional visitor; then they had made time for her, found room on their busy schedules to accommodate her, since she would be leaving shortly to return to California. 'Oh, now that you're going to be living here, we'll get together for lunch,' one acquaintance said, but without specifying when or where. There was no urgency, and she was uncomfortable about pinning anyone down; she was not sure where assertive left off and aggressive began, and she feared being thought of as pushy.

Every apartment she saw seemed smaller, dirtier and more costly than the previous one. She thought longingly of her own house, but she had turned that over to tenants—who were undoubtedly ruining the finish on her floors, being careless with her furnishings, disturbing neighbours with their noise, she decided. When she spoke to Lara, her daughter was abrupt and distant; she did not need Ellin now, she had Tony, Ellin thought jealously.

She had uprooted herself—she felt like a transient, with no address, no connections, no sense of place or even, now, purpose. She stopped reading the rental ads, stopped calling people. She immersed herself in trashy novels and read for long stretches of time. Occasionally she would look up from her book and notice that the day had become night, and then she went out, to a movie or a restaurant. Once she spent an entire evening at the movies, three different theatres, one show after another.

When Paula finally called to make a date to meet at the brownstone, Ellin woke up from her fortnight of somnolence. She arrived at Twelfth Street an hour before Cass and Paula were due; she walked around the neighbourhood, noting the landmarks, getting a feel of the area. She liked the tree-shaded street and the well-dressed people strolling purposefully along it. She stopped to pet a friendly dog, and to help a woman laden with bundles fold herself into a taxi. I could live here, she thought, her spirits lifting. I could be happy here.

She wanted to see her apartment at once—she was already thinking of it as hers—but acquiesced when Cass and Paula insisted on showing her through the rest of the house first. She was cheered by their obvious pleasure at seeing her; for the first time since she'd come to New York, she felt welcome and wanted, and she was optimistic as she walked through the brownstone's freshly painted dusty-pink front door.

There were ladders, cans, and boxes crowding the foyer; the smell of paint thinner and wood stripper was strong and sharp. Cass led her proudly through the elaborate mahogany drawing-room doors into the first-floor apartment. The living room was long and narrow, with tall windows facing the street. The room was sparsely furnished, but each piece was of obvious quality. The banded oak floors had been finished to a high gloss; on them, a handsome Savonnerie carpet, deep blue-green with cabbage roses sculptured in ivory, stretched nearly the length of the room. A pair of soft green-velvet love seats flanked the fireplace, which had an ornate marble mantel and was set with deep-green tiles. A low glass coffee table between the sofas held neatly arranged magazines and a cut-crystal ashtray.

The walls of the room were a rosy terracotta, accented

by clean, creamy white at the mouldings and baseboards. There was a six-panel Coromandel screen against the far wall, and a pair of inlaid Chinese cabinets that served as end tables; on them rested French country baskets filled with hyacinths and chrysanthemums. A carved gilt mirror hung above the fireplace, reflecting the blues and greens of the screen.

Cass preceded Ellin into the dining room. Its walls were painted in the same colours as the living room, and the crystal chandelier that hung over the polished Sheraton table gave the room a diffused, elegant glow. Around the table were Chippendale side chairs upholstered in a striped, velvet fabric. 'My mother's,' Cass said. 'I had some things shipped out from Seattle.'

Cass's bedroom was spare and uncluttered; this room looked not unlived-in, but expectant. It needed her to breathe life into it, despite the heavy brass bedstead and the pine pastry tables that flanked it, as nightstands. The leaded glass windows through which late-afternoon sun poured were draped in heavy Belgian linen; the walls were a pale green, the colour of the jade Buddha that sat, inscrutable, on an ornately carved Chinese chest beneath the window.

There were flowers everywhere; on the mirrored makeup table, porcelain jars held freesias and violets as well as tubes and brushes. Cass opened the closet doors; inside, her clothes were neatly arranged in double-hung rows, her shoes aligned tidily on shelves, her sweaters encased in plastic bags.

In the kitchen, everything was carefully ordered; there were no dishes in the sink, not even a coffee cup. Swedish ivy cascaded from wire baskets hung from a French baker's rack; the copper pots and pans were burnished brightly enough so that Ellin could see her reflection in them.

'Is that it?' she asked Cass, who shook her head.

'There's another bedroom, and the library, but they're not done yet. I hate looking at unfinished rooms. Take my advice and get everything done in your apartment before you move in—that's the way to do it.'

Paula giggled. 'In that case, I'd still be in the East Village,' she told Ellin. 'Compared to this, my place looks like a disaster area.'

'Compared to anything, it looks that way,' Cass said, and Paula smiled at Ellin.

'Some of us are perfect, others have to try harder,' she said. 'Come on upstairs.'

There were tendrils of old wallpaper hanging from the upper half of the stairwell; below it, the mahogany wainscoting had been stripped and refinished. Paula's front door was painted bright orange; Cass wrinkled her nose in disgust, which Paula ignored.

Inside, clothes and books and half-empty suitcases were strewn everywhere. Over Paula's fireplace hung a silly-looking reindeer, made of a fuzzy brown fabric that looked vaguely familiar to Ellin. 'Didn't you used to have a jacket like that?' she asked, and Paula nodded.

'It looks much better on Rudolph,' she said. Bits of Paula's projects were everywhere. A papier-mâché balloon hung from the ceiling, covered with snapshots of people, some of whom Ellin recognized. There were plants made of fabric and wire; 'You don't have to water them,' Paula said. She led Ellin through the mess into the kitchen, which was impossibly bright. The walls were cherry red, the floors painted a glossy black, and the cabinets lacquered royal blue. A gaily striped kite swooped across the ceiling, and colourful Toulouse-Lautrec posters covered the walls.

Cass sniffed again. 'Paula, how can you face this room in the morning? The colours give me a migraine.'

'*Chacun à son gout*,' said Paula blithely. 'I like a cheerful room.' She showed Ellin through the apartment, a virtual twin of Cass's, in size and shape. There were clothes and fabric and shoes and books and clutter everywhere, almost obscuring the few pieces of furniture: a pair of wicker chairs which Paula announced she had found in a skip on Fourteenth Street, a chesterfield sofa Ellin remembered from Paula's other apartment, and in the dining room, a table made from a purple door that rested on a set of painted sawhorses. 'I found these on the Lower East Side,' Paula said, and Cass sniffed again.

'Cheerful,' she allowed. 'Disgustingly cheerful.'

Only Paula's library looked habitable. Her law books were ordered neatly in pine-and-brick bookcases set up beneath the windows, and a scarred, battered old oak rolltop desk held a typewriter, long yellow legal pads, and a half-dozen manilla file folders. There was an equally ancient leather couch in one corner of the room. 'I've been sleeping in here until I find a bed,' Paula said, 'or at least clean out one of the bedrooms enough to unroll a sleeping bag.'

To Ellin, Cass commented, 'Paula thinks it's politically incorrect to buy a new piece of furniture, you know. If it doesn't come from the streets, it's not acceptable.' She wrinkled her nose in distaste, and Paula hugged her.

'Come on, Cassie, you'll make a consumer of me yet, I promise. Didn't you just talk me into buying a house, for God's sake?'

'Buying it, yes—cleaning and furnishing it, that's another matter.' She turned to Ellin. 'I hope you'll be a good influence on Paula. She's constitutionally opposed to being a grown-up.'

'With a Macy's charge card and my very own interior decorator, you're right,' Paula allowed. 'But I'll let you two convince me. Maybe.'

Out of nowhere, a scrawny calico cat appeared, darting between Ellin's legs. She gasped. 'That's Cat Stevens,' said Paula. 'Steve, meet Ellin.'

The cat was completely uninterested; it leapt away from the women and settled on a stack of newspapers stacked haphazardly in a corner, regarding them balefully from its perch. 'He came with the house,' Paula said. 'Absolutely refused to leave. So I said okay, what's one more warm body with all this space?'

'It was either Steve or a whole family Paula wants to save from eviction,' Cass commented. 'But he messes in the hall. Maybe they wouldn't have.'

Paula frowned, then picked up the cat. She rubbed it under its chin, and it tolerated her, but seemed not to take any pleasure from the contact. 'He's just getting used to us,' Paula said. 'He'll learn to use a box soon, won't you, Steve?' In answer, the cat jumped out of Paula's arms and returned to his newspapers.

'If he doesn't, he's getting put out with the rest of this garbage,' Cass said, eyeing the mess in Paula's rooms meaningfully. 'Paula, there's a fabulous man in my office, he's not really a decorator, he's a designer, actually, but he has terrific taste, and he'd be glad to help you—'

Paula shook her head. 'I told you, to each his own. It's okay, Cass, I promise I'll keep the doors shut, no one will ever know.' She said to Ellin, 'Cass thinks of my interiors as Early Borrowed Relative, not her favourite period at all.'

'More like late My Sister Eileen,' Cass said. 'Oh, you'll get yours one of these days, Paula Gabriel. Just wait, you'll fall in love with an architect, a purist, one of those men who lives for white walls, and worships minimalism. Then you'll change.'

'Fat chance,' Paula said. 'Well, come on. Ellin, let's show you your little corner of the universe.'

'Little is right,' Cass said, as they climbed upstairs to the third floor. The stairs narrowed slightly as they ascended; if she stood straight up, Ellin could barely keep her head from touching the ceiling. Once inside, however, there was more room; the ceilings were not as high as in the lower floors, but they were more than adequate.

The apartment was doll-like; for a moment, Ellin felt too big for it, clumsy and out of scale. 'It was probably the maid's quarters, once upon a time,' Cass said. 'But it has a wonderful view, and this marvellous terrace, too.' She pulled back the dusty, heavy old draperies that covered the sliding glass doors to the terrace. Ellin caught her breath; it was nearly dusk, and from where she stood, in the middle of the living room, she could see the lights of lower Manhattan twinkle on. 'You really have a fabulous view, you've no idea,' Cass said, somewhat enviously. 'It makes up for the size, doesn't it?' Without waiting for Ellin's reply, which would, in any case, have been yes, she went on. 'That's Amelia's house across the way,' she said. 'That's how I found this place to begin with.' And she told Ellin the story of the first time she'd seen the brownstone.

Ellin loved the apartment on first sight. She said so, they agreed on a rental price, and it was done. Paula jumped up and down in delight, and Cass smiled and hugged Ellin. 'It's settled,' she cried. 'It's all settled. Oh, Ellin, I'm just thrilled! Paula, isn't it great? Ellin's going to live with us.' She beamed with happiness, and Ellin, feeling welcomed and content for the first time since she had arrived in New York, beamed back. Finally, gratefully, she felt at home.

TEN

Paula jumped out of the cab and dashed for the front door of the house, trying to shield herself from the violent rainstorm that had hit the city at rush hour. Shit, she thought, I'll have a Jewish afro by tonight if I don't do something about my hair. And I'm supposed to meet Max in an hour.

Once inside she dumped her things on a newspaper-strewn chaise and dialled Max's number. He kept an apartment in the city, although these days he was rarely there. Max was an entertainment lawyer, with a bicoastal pratice; he had followed the movie and television action out to California when the industry moved west. He was in town for a Broadway opening; one of his clients was starring in a new play.

'Listen, Max,' said Paula after she said hello, 'would you mind if I met you at the theatre? I had an impossible day and I just got home; I'll never get a cab in this weather, and I may not make the curtain.'

'No problem,' said Max. 'In fact, we can skip the play. I saw the preview, and it's going to be the biggest theatrical disaster since Booth shot Lincoln. I just have to show up at the party after—or the wake, which is more likely. Why don't we have dinner together?'

'Oh, you're a lifesaver,' said Paula, and they settled on Frère Jacques, a small French restaurant near the theatre district.

She drew a hot bath. Settled comfortably in the tub,

she considered Max Morton, and smiled inwardly at the thought of seeing him.

They'd met a few years before; he was newly divorced, still raw from the breakup. And he was on the couch five days a week as well; the combination was too much for Paula. 'Why do I have the feeling that everything that happens between us is dissected by you and Himmelfarb at eight o'clock the next morning?' she asked him. 'I like you, Max, but I don't have the energy you require. Let's just be pals, okay?' She offered to sleep with him—despite his problems, he was a very nice man, and not unattractive to Paula—but he declined. It was not that kind of nurturing he wanted.

'I think you're wonderful, and I'm very turned on by you, but I just don't want to be one among many right now,' he said.

Paula was not offended; her own sexual style was casual, even promiscuous—according to Cass— and she had not been in a monogamous relationship since Jake. She knew Max wasn't judging her; therapy had taught him to ask for what he wanted, and refuse what he could not handle, and she approved of that.

Besides, she had no time for a love affair then. She had finally broken off—nearly—with Chris Carey. She had quit one job and started another, and she was engrossed in trying to put a solid professional life together. It demanded most of her energy and a great deal of her time; it was hard work. Max needed more than leftovers, which were all she had to give him.

Still, they grew genuinely fond of each other, and continued to spend time together when they could manage it. Then Max moved west, but he kept in touch, which was Paula's way, too—she never let go of anyone who mattered. Max sent her silly postcards and newspaper clippings. He had a dry sense of humour, and a taste for the ironic and bizarre. In return, she phoned him—she was not much of a letter writer. She had not seen him for three months, and was looking forward to the evening.

She soaped herself idly, wondering about Max. There was something going on in his life—she had that feeling. Perhaps he was in love.

She felt a tiny stab of jealousy at the prospect, and chided herself for it. It would be good for Max to find a nice woman and get married, she thought. He was ready. 'One thing I learned from the divorce was that marriage isn't a trophy you put on the shelf and dust off once a year on your anniversary,' he told her once. 'I learned that a career isn't the only thing in life.' His marriage had foundered on those shoals; his ex-wife married a man who had inherited wealth, and had no need or burning ambition to make his own name for himself, as Max had.

Most of the men Paula dated cared more about their careers than about their relationships, if they had any. Their concept of intimacy was much narrower than women's, even women who were equally caught up in getting ahead. By the time most men were professionally secure, they were long-since married to women who were satisfied with the trade-off—security in exchange for whatever leftovers of time and energy were offered. They got married right out of college or graduate school because they needed a wife, and a base—one place where they could let down, feel, be vulnerable.

The ones who were not married were still struggling up the ladder and would have no time for the distractions of love until they made it, or gave up. The others were men who had achieved success and paid its price. They were close to divorce when Paula met them—near it, in it, or newly through it, like Max.

Some had learned nothing from the experience, and seemed not to feel any pain. They wanted carbon copies of their first wives, if they were looking at all—Stepford wives, Cass called them. Or they said they wanted independent women, but were not satisfied until they made those women dependent. We cooperate in our own oppression, Paula thought. She knew many women who, after a few years in the jungle—and it was all a jungle, whether it was Wall Street or the university, the corporation or the courtroom—were glad to trade in their ambitions, and fit themselves into the corners of men's lives.

Max was different. He didn't want a woman who had no life of her own, who counted on him to make up for what she'd given up, or never had. He didn't want to dominate a woman. And he wasn't so busy seeking achievement—the cornerstone of his identity as a man—that he couldn't let himself feel, or care, or consider the quality of his life.

All in all, Paula thought, Max Morton was an extraordinary man. And as soon as she realized it, she began having her own self-doubts.

What was it Max had said the last time they were together? He said it just before he kissed her good night. It had been a real kiss, gentle, exploring, questioning; not the let's-fuck-now, quick-tongue-in-the-mouth kind of kiss, and not the brisk, tight-lipped kiss of a man who's not at all interested. He'd said it about a woman they both knew who'd got to the top and discarded a husband and two children *en route:* 'I wonder how long it'll be until she realizes that a career isn't everything—or even the only thing?'

Paula had wondered, then, if Max was telling her something. She wasn't certain. Did he think she was concentrating too hard on her own career? Or was he telling her he wanted more . . . that perhaps he wanted her?

She still wasn't sure. But since Max's postcard which announced his impending visit—a funny picture of Dick, Pat, Tricia, and Julie in happier times—and the phone call making the date, Paula had been just a little excited. She was more relaxed about her own career now, too. It was moving along on target, with an important case, her case, headed for the Supreme Court. If it got there—and if Paula handled it well—her reputation would be firmly established. A new goal would become clear, and time to pursue it at more leisure. Then she could begin to think about the rest of her life. About a man, a relationship, a child. Maybe Max, she thought, as she towelled herself dry and dotted her pulse points and the curve of her breasts with a musky scent. Maybe even Max.

Over the *coq au vin* she cross-examined him. 'Tell me everything,' she demanded, 'Every single thing, and no leaving out the details.'

'Well, they gave me my own parking spot in the garage,' he said, 'and I made partner last week.' His was a big firm, the biggest in Los Angeles. Partnership was the summit; at forty-one, he was young for it, but he had worked hard. And, Paula thought, made plenty of sacrifices.

'You look wonderful,' she told him. 'Success agrees with you. Also LA—I love your tan. Oh, I wish you could all be California boys!'

He laughed, his teeth white and even in his copper-coloured face. He was attractive in a boyish way, rumpled and healthy-looking, despite the grey at his temples. He was wearing his hair longer than she remembered, and there were other signs of change as well. He looked looser, more relaxed, happier. Of course, that hand-painted tie he was wearing with his British-tailored suit was ridiculous, even by Paula's standards, but she guessed it was the California influence. He'd grown a beard since the last time she saw him. It was tidy and presentable, but it definitely looked like LA, not New York.

They finished their meal and left for the party. 'I'm going to have to nurse my client through the first few reviews, and when he's suitably tanked, we can leave,' Max told her as they entered Sardi's.

The waiters were pouring drinks quickly and liberally. They seemed to sense an imminent disaster, and were coping with it the best way they knew how, anaesthetizing the principals for what was in store.

'Actually, it wasn't as bad as I thought it would be,'

Max told her as they headed downtown afterward. 'At least my guy wasn't singled out for sole responsibility.'

'Contributory negligence, I'd call it,' Paula replied. 'He got off easy compared to the writer and the leading lady.'

She led Max inside the brownstone. 'Welcome to Casita Rosita,' she said, 'our humble home.'

'Oh, the pink door and window boxes, huh?' said Max, and she nodded. 'That's what Trini, Cass's cleaning woman, calls it, and the name stuck.'

She poured brandy for them, and gave him a complete tour of the apartment. They lingered for a few minutes in the bedroom, and Paula thought she felt a sexual buzz from Max. If he asks me, I will, she decided. Maybe he's ready for me now. Maybe I'm ready for him. Not that sex had that much to do with it; for Paula, sex and relationships rarely had much to do with each other.

Back in the living room, though, Max seemed ill at ease. Paula felt it, but didn't understand. It's just Max and Paula, the same as always, she thought. Or was it? Maybe the sexual buzz wasn't there. Or maybe it wasn't for her.

'So you have the house, and your case is moving along, huh?' he said when they sat down on the couch.

Paula nodded.

'That's the big one, isn't it?'

'Mmm.'

'And then what? Still Paula the party girl?'

She didn't take offence; she knew what Max meant. It was an assessment she assented to; she did not apologize for it. It meant no ties, no strings, no hurts; it meant going out often, sleeping with men when she desired them or they wanted her, and knowing when to leave—before they demanded that they come first.

'Sort of,' Paula answered Max. 'Maybe nobody's made me a better offer.'

'When you're ready, the right person will,' Max said firmly.

'You think so?' She smiled. Was there a message there—for her? 'How come you're so certain?'

Suddenly a thought occurred to her. 'Hey, Max, you're holding out on me, aren't you?' He flushed beneath his tan, and she noted that. 'Well, tell me, for Christ's sake,' she said. 'Is it true love, or just a passing fancy?' It had probably been a bad idea to start with, she thought, her and Max. The wrong timing for sure, the wrong couple, maybe. I hope she's not another tight-assed bitch like the last one.

'Not a passing fancy—more like a fantasy,' he said. 'True love? Who knows? Only children and virgins believe in true love.'

'Who is she?' Okay, Paula, you're not going to fuck Max tonight, you might as well hear about her—Max is your friend, and he's dying to tell you. Maybe she'll turn out to be your friend, too.

But with Max's description—halting at first, then hurriedly, the words tumbling out of his mouth—she knew that was not to be.

'Her name is Susan,' he told her. 'Susan . . . uh . . . Starflower.'

'Starflower?' Paula hooted; she couldn't help herself. 'Is she an Indian, or a hippie?'

Max shifted uncomfortably. 'She's . . . well, she's different, that's all. Rather mystical, you know?'

Paula thought she probably did. 'How old is this woman?'

'In her twenties.'

'What part of her twenties?'

'What does it matter?' he countered defensively.

'It doesn't matter much, if you love her,' Paula said gently.

'Love? I don't know about that,' said Max. 'It's just that she makes me feel . . . look, I can't describe it, I can just feel it.'

'Is that what Himmelfarb says to do, just feel it?'

'I haven't seen Himmelfarb in two years,' Max said. 'You know that. I finished with him. I got what I went for.'

'Which was?'

'Oh, who knows . . . permission to be happy, maybe.'

'Then you got a good deal,' Paula replied. 'For a while there, I wondered . . . it seemed to be making you suffer so.'

'It did,' Max said simply. 'I needed that, too.'

Paula was sceptical; nobody needed to suffer, there was plenty around without looking for it. But she didn't push it. 'Tell me more about Sunflower,' she said.

'Starflower,' Max corrected her, 'Susan Starflower. It used to be Finkelsomething . . . she doesn't talk much about her past.'

'How much of a past can a twenty-something-year-old have?'

'Look, you want to listen or talk?' asked Max, not disputatiously. 'So it's a cliché, like buying a Porsche after you get divorced. I never bought one. But she's very intelligent. She's a deep thinker. She lives in the now.'

Oh, Max, you poor baby, Paula thought. This one will hurt you, I know it. Living in the now—that was all very nice in theory. All that Fritz Perls bullshit—you do your thing and I do mine, and if by chance we meet, terrific, but if you get hurt it's not my fault. Oh, Max.

'Does Flower—does this Susan work?' Paula asked.

'She's an artist . . . textiles, tie dyes, she sells things at craft fairs. She made this tie for me.'

Paula could see the scenario, and it worried her. She knew what would happen; the girl would use Max for a time, and then dump him because he was not a frivolous man. He had his moments, but few of them were playful ones, and even those might not be considered fun by someone twenty years younger. Max was witty, clever, ironic, intelligent—all the things Paula loved him for—but he was a thoughtful man who took himself, and life, seriously. Like most men, he had a romantic streak, and this girl had clearly found it. What do I say now? Paula wondered.

From the beginning, Paula always told Max the truth,

though with him, as with Cass, she softened it with tact and timing. Max was more direct with Paula, though he was never needlessly, heedlessly candid, as Cass habitually was. Paula was careful about how she responded to Max's description of his new love affair; he did not often expose his feelings, and she was conscious of his vulnerability, and careful with it. So she listened as he described Susan, how she looked and what she thought and the way she lived. With every phrase, she grew more concerned; why was it that when men *did* try, *were* willing to take risks with their emotions, they did it with the wrong women? Oh, my dear, don't let her fuck you over too badly, she hoped silently, and for a minute she felt violent rage at someone she didn't even know. Max, as usual, knew his affair for what it was—a cliché. But that wouldn't make it hurt any less when it ended; more, probably.

Finally he ran out of things to say about Susan, or perhaps he knew by Paula's unaccustomed silence what she was thinking. Of course he did; nothing escaped Max. She was grateful when he changed the subject; she wanted to be happy for him, but she knew this relationship would not, ultimately, make him happy at all. He put his arm around her in a friendly fashion, and she snuggled into him, stroking his face, ruffling his hair. I bet I could make him stay, she considered—well, maybe I could. And maybe Sunflower won't look so hot when he goes back. Max had wanted Paula before, even if he hadn't followed through; Paula always knew when a man desired her. She was sensitive to sexual nuances; she filtered them out of the densest miasmas of casual chatter and touch and body language.

She resisted the temptation, barely considering the possibility that Max would reject her. It would not be fair of her; she would be playing dirty, not just with his feelings but with What's-her-name. Paula was rigid about avoiding men who were involved with other women. She had learned that from her affair with Chris, and not since then had she even dated a married man, or seen more than once someone she learned was already involved. It was not just to avoid her own pain; she would not do that to another woman.

Of course, she didn't even know Susan. Cass, Paula thought, would have said she owed the little hippie nothing. In fact, that was exactly what Cass said when Paula told her about it the next day. 'You would have done him a favour by distracting him,' Cass asserted.

But Paula only sighed. 'It's no favour if he loves her,' she said. 'And it's no favour to her on the slight chance that maybe she loves him, too.'

'It sure sounds like she's going to take him for a ride,' said Cass.

'Well, he's getting on with his eyes open,' Paula replied. 'You know, it's all a matter of timing, isn't it?'

'Isn't what?' Cass enquired.

'Oh, nothing. Hey, you want to go to a movie tonight?'

ELEVEN

Ellin was sorting the day's mail when Cass manoeuvred her way through the front door, pushing a large box in front of her.

'I waited for a cab in front of Korvette's for half an hour, and I finally got on a subway and lugged this thing all the way downtown,' she said. 'God, it must be ten degrees below out there. I'm sick of winter.'

In fact, Cass was tanned to a deep golden hue; she'd been spending much of the past few weeks in the Southwest and in Florida with Grey Tucker. Since their meeting, and her presentation, he'd taken a particular interest in her; he seemed to want her opinion on every facet of Amagansett's operations, especially marketing. She could not understand it; when she mentioned it to Amelia, the older woman nodded her head approvingly. 'He must have something in mind for you,' she told Cass. 'He's mentioned to me several times that you have a very impressive presentation yourself—that was his word.' Cass frowned, and Amelia shook her head. 'No, my dear, I don't think it's that at all; that's not Tucker's style. He simply said that you have a very good mind, and a fresh approach. He likes that. He may be thinking of offering you a job with his company.'

Cass laughed nervously. 'I'd never do that, Amelia,' she said. 'I don't want you to think that I'd—'

Amelia interrupted her. 'Of course I don't think that, Cassandra. Nothing of the sort. I think that Grey Tucker is surrounded with yes-men, and he finds you a refreshing change. He may be planning a major new department for his company; that wouldn't be unlike him at all. Trust Tucker to pick the best brains around. You should be flattered that he thinks you have them. Don't worry. He's a most important client, and if he thinks it necessary for you to learn everything about AI's operations, then I suggest you do just that. I don't see any problems, unless . . .' She hesitated. 'He *is* behaving like a gentleman, isn't he?'

'Absolutely,' Cass assured her. 'I could almost understand if that's what he had in mind.' At first, she had thought it might be. She waited for him to make his move, planning how she would fend it off without alienating him. But the opportunity did not present itself; he treated her, she thought, like a man.

Which was probably all to the good, she mused, although it only underscored her longing for Nick. He was in California for weeks at a time; she could live without him for a while, but why should she have to? she wondered crankily. Cass missed the feel of a man's arms around her, missed the warmth of approval, the heat of desire. But she was too busy to dwell on it. Between her responsibilities at the agency and Tucker's increasing demands on her time—which were surely professional, but cut into the hours she was used to thinking of as her own—she kept her loneliness at bay.

Grey Tucker she found pleasing, and interesting; he was gravely polite, respectful, and challenged her. Often at night, in a hotel room, during their frequent business trips together, after they had dined and retired to their separate rooms, she thought about him—how he would look without his carefully tailored suits, how he would touch her, if he did, what sounds he would make in the act of love, how he would taste and feel and smell. And then, usually, she called Nick in California, and complained about his absences. And took a small yellow Valium so she could sleep without thinking of Nick, or of Tucker—already dreamlessly asleep, she assumed, in the room next door to her own.

'Well then, there's nothing to worry about,' said Amelia, 'Is there?' And that, for the moment, was that.

'What's in the box?' asked Ellin.

'A slide projector. I'm going to sort out my pictures and set this up in the library with the stereo and TV. I thought I'd order in Chinese food and put that room together tonight. Want me to order for you, too? We'll look at slides together.'

'Sure,' Ellin said, 'that sounds good.' She was finding, to her surprise, that she liked the easy camaraderie of the brownstone. She liked living with Paula and Cass. There was usually company when she wanted it, someone to share the details of the day, a feeling that was somewhere between roommates and neighbours. The other women were close, but not on top of her. She wasn't responsible for them, nor they for her, but they counted on each other. That the city was beginning to feel like home to Ellin had a great deal to do with being settled in the brownstone. With living in a house, not just an apartment; for while the women respected each other's doors when they were closed, at other times they had the run of the entire building. Ellin never felt isolated; she was only alone when she wanted or needed to be.

She liked Cass, too; her initial wariness had worn off, and Cass was proving to be a good friend, reliable and loyal, and very considerate of her. 'You're getting the rush,' Paula told her. 'When Cass shines her light on you, you can't help loving her.'

It wasn't love, not yet, but Ellin was warming to Cass. She enjoyed her intelligence, her astute observations about people, her enthusiasm for the brownstone.

'Is Paula home yet?' Cass asked her.

'There's no noise from the second floor, and I haven't seen her, so I guess not. Cass, here, let me unlock the door for you, your hands are full.'

'Oh, it's all right, it's not locked.'

Ellin was shocked. 'You don't lock your doors?'

'Not this one. Nobody can make it past the street, not with the Fichet that Vic installed on the front door. I must say, I feel safer with him in the house . . . it's not very liberated, but it's true. They tell you to learn karate and carry hatpins, but the heck with the militants, I just feel more secure with a man around.'

Vic was Ellin's contribution to Casita Rosita. She met him at the Lion's Head, a comfortable saloon near the brownstone; he was a relief bartender who told her he was trying to write a book, and looking for another part-time job. His rent had gone up, and he was also looking for an apartment.

He was, she learned, a skilled carpenter and handyman: exactly what the women were looking for, a good candidate for the little flat in the basement of the house. She introduced him to her housemates, who agreed that he was perfect. Cass, of course, checked his references. 'He's a Viet Nam veteran, he has a couple of degrees, he used to be in banking, he had a couple of short stories published, he doesn't have a criminal record,' she told Paula and Ellin.

'I never thought he had,' Ellin marvelled. 'How did you find all that out?'

'Oh, through Nick. A lot of his writers hang out at the Lion.' Cass giggled. 'He's quite hunky-looking, don't you think? If Nick doesn't come home soon, I might just go knocking at Vic's door one of these nights.' They knew she didn't mean it; starving bartenders weren't Cass's cup of tea. But Paula warned her anyway.

'Whatever you do, don't screw this up,' she told her. 'Do you know how hard it is to find a handyman in this city?'

'Uh huh,' said Cass. 'My definition of a renaissance man has changed since we bought this place. Now it's someone with Nick's brains and sex appeal, and the skills of a plumber.'

'Cass didn't really mean that, did she? About Vic, I mean,' Ellin asked Paula later.

'Hardly,' Paula replied. 'Vic's not for Cassie—she's a power fucker.'

Ellin was surprised. 'How can you say such a thing?' she demanded.

'Because it's true.' Paula was nonchalant. 'Cass gets off only on successful men. Men who have more of whatever matters to her at the time than other men do—more money, more status, more everything. She's always been like that.'

Cass almost knew that Paula's observation was accurate, although she would have denied it if Paula ever said it to her face. Cass carefully chose the bits of self-knowledge she would accept—those that fitted neatly into her image of herself. It was true, she might concede, that she liked a man to be stronger than she was. She liked him superior to her in some important way—not just to her, but to other men as well. She wanted her man to dominate her, Paula said, and Cass did not disagree. Sometimes the power was simply the edge of not being loved as much as she wanted to be; once she was, once the balance of power was redressed in her favour, the edge was gone. And often, so was the man.

Cass and Ellin were spooning lemon chicken out of little white boxes when Cass's secretary phoned.

'Who? He did? What did he want? Yes, I'll call him . . . give me the number,' Cass said, scribbling on a pad near the phone.

'It's Grey Tucker,' she told Ellin, 'he's been trying to reach me.' Ellin went to the kitchen to get a beer from the refrigerator, and when she returned, Cass was replacing the receiver.

'Tucker wants to see me for breakfast tomorrow. Odd, isn't it? He said it was important, but not what it was. I hope there's nothing wrong with the new campaigns—we have them all ready to go, and now this!' She fretted while they finished dinner, and while she set up the slide projector. Ellin, who was hopeless when it came to mechanical things, prowled the library. Bookshelves gleamed with the lustre of mahogany, and a leather couch was soft and pliable with the patina of age. It was flanked by a pair of old-fashioned wing chairs, and there was a leather-topped writing desk set in a corner. A claret-hued Ushak carpet from the cottage glowed on the polished floors.

'It looks wonderful in here,' Ellin said. 'Like you've lived in it for a long time.'

'It's like my grandfather's library in Boston,' Cass said. She was pleased. 'I always dreamed of a room like this one.'

She shuffled through slides, holding them up to the light, squinting at them. The first group was of Paula and Cass, in college and afterward. Cass commented on each slide as it clicked on.

'That's me in London, when Paula and I went to Europe. There we are at the Pitti Palace, with that gorgeous driver Paula picked up . . . Look, there's Paula on the beach in Greece.'

'Who's that?' A handsome, grizzled man in a ski parka flashed by.

'Peter somebody—I had a thing with him once in Vail. . . . Look, here's Curt, the fellow who made me that backpack, we climbed Rainier one summer. . . . Here's David, I almost lived with him.'

'He's quite pretty,' Ellin said as Cass flashed another slide, of a fair-haired man at the tiller of a sailboat. 'Who's he?'

'Matt, at Newport, he was crewing one of the Cup boats then. Oh, here's Todd, he and I had a thing for a while.'

'What happened to him?'

'Oh, I don't know. He got tiresome, and possessive. I took an account away from his agency, he couldn't deal with it.'

'Is that Matt again?'

'Uh huh, at St Barts, we went there one year.'
'Did he get tiresome, too?'
'As I recall. I hate men who think you owe them an explanation for everything you do. Or don't do.'
'Does Nick?'
'Only when he notices I'm not around . . . right after he puts the magazine to bed. He's quite driven. Ambition is a raging disease with him.'
She continued sorting the slides, identifying them for Ellin.
'There are more men in those pictures than I've met in forty years,' Ellin commented. 'How come none of them worked out?'
'What does work out mean?' Cass shrugged. 'They were there for a while, and then they weren't.'
'Are you going to marry Nick?'
'Maybe. Probably. Sometime. I don't know.' Cass wasn't sure how she felt about Nick; they hadn't been together for so long that the strongest emotion she felt was resentment. 'Oh, there's the door, that's probably Paula,' she said. 'I'll go see if she wants some lemon chicken. Except I thought she was seeing Max tonight. Well, there's plenty for both of them.'
A few moments later, she returned to the library. Her face was drained of colour, and Ellin's heart jumped in alarm.
'It wasn't Paula? Who was it? My Lord, Cass, you look like you've seen a ghost!'
'I think I did,' Cass replied slowly. 'Yes, that was Paula. There was a man with her.'
'Max?'
'Uh uh.'
'So what? She's brought other men around before. Good for her.'
'Not very,' said Cass. 'It was—it is—Jake Stern.'

TWELVE

Paula finished the appellate brief that was due in the circuit court on Monday. The word processors could have it now, clean up her amended draft and process it to arrive in the right place at the right time. She glanced at her watch; she was to meet Max in less than an hour.

Poor Max. The little hippie had dumped him. She'd called him a few nights before, just checking on things. Or was she missing him a bit, needing to hear his warm, dry voice, wondering what was happening with the Sunflower?

'Funny you should ask,' Max said, with an edge to his voice that was nearly, but not quite, a tremble.

'What does that mean?' she demanded with concern.

'Well, it's kind of like being back in Kansas, only without Aunt Em. And Toto's not here, either.' He laughed emptily. 'I know, I know, it was a cliché. Predictable, a man in midlife crisis. All those things. But Christ, it hurts.'

Max never said it hurts. He had a way of turning everything into an ironic aside on the human condition; he deflected pain that way. That was how he handled it, despite his analysis, or maybe because of it—he made suffering into an intellectual exercise, at least when he acknowledged it. Only this time he wasn't doing that, and Paula felt his grief.

'Oh, sweetie, I'm so sorry,' she told him. 'What can I do? Do you want company? Shall I come out?'

'Don't be silly, I'm not bleeding,' said Max. 'Nowhere

you'd notice, anyway. I'll be fine. I'm only wallowing because it's slow time at work—the directors' strike, the writers' strike, nothing's happening.'

'Okay,' said Paula, not really believing him. 'If you're sure. But I'm here if you need me.'

She was right not to believe him. He'd called her that morning, early—it must have been four in the morning, California time. She didn't like the slur in his voice; he'd been drinking, maybe, or taking something. 'He sounds like a man who hasn't shaved for a week,' she told Cass.

'Listen, you still want to lend a shoulder to a friend?' he'd said, as she struggled awake. God, it was still dark out.

'I'm ready anytime,' she replied sleepily. 'You coming here?'

'Yes. Catching a noon plane. See you at my place around nine?'

'Absolutely,' she said, now fully awake. 'Max, fly safe.'

She and Cass shared a cab uptown that morning, and she told Cass about the phone call. 'Are you sure you want to play the sympathetic old buddy?' Cass asked her. 'I thought you were interested in him. Let him cry on some other woman's shoulder, and when he gets it out of his system, when he's ready, make your move. You know perfectly well most men never stay with the woman who helps them get over the last one.'

'Jesus, Cass, do you see everything as a matter of strategy?' Paula replied. Of course she did—Paula knew that. 'Max is my friend, he needs me. You think I'm going to play games at a time like this?'

'I think you should,' said Cass coolly. 'There aren't a lot of Maxes around, you know.' That was Cass. She measured affection in careful quantities, usually giving less than she received. She knew the power of withholding. It seemed to work for her, but it was not Paula's way.

She was about to leave the office when the phone rang in the silent room. Hold on, Max, I'm coming, she said to herself. He was one of the few people who knew her private number—Max, Cass and Ellin, and her father. But it was not Max, or any of them, whose voice she heard and recognized instantly when she picked up the phone.

'Paula? This is someone from a long time ago . . . remember?' She began to tremble; slowly, she lowered herself back into her chair, forcing herself to take deep breaths.

'Yes, I remember,' she said evenly. She grasped the receiver tightly to stop her hands from shaking. 'Where did you get this number, Jake?'

'I have friends,' he said calmly in the same rich baritone; his voice had been one of Jake's greatest assets, even when amplified and distorted by a loudspeaker or bullhorn; he moved people to action with his voice as well as his words.

'What friends?' she asked, struggling to remain calm. Certainly not hers; Cass hated Jake with a passion, Max had never met him, her parents wouldn't have given it to him. Probably he had gotten it from one of the secretaries, she thought; Jake was always good at wheedling things out of women.

He didn't answer. 'Where are you?' she asked.

'In the neighbourhood,' he replied casually. 'Pretty fancy neighbourhood, too. Not like the old days at the clinic in Roxbury or the storefront in Cambridge.'

'Those days are gone,' she said quietly. 'What do you want, Jake?'

'I want to see you.'

'Impossible,' she replied curtly. 'I have nothing to say to you any more. Besides, you're an escaped felon. I'm an officer of the court. Get lost.'

'Not a felon,' he broke in. 'Bail jumper, yes. But I was never convicted.'

'You didn't stick around long enough to be,' she said.

'I know. I want to deal, Paula. Will you help me?'

'Help?' She laughed, close to hysteria. 'Help was never in your vocabulary, as I recall. You never wanted it before. Why the sudden change of heart?'

'A lot of reasons,' Jake said. 'Maybe I had to learn to ask you for it. Maybe you were always so damn strong I couldn't. I need you.'

She rummaged in her drawer and found a package of stale cigarettes; she'd given them up six months before. She lit one, and her lungs ached, but it felt good.

Ten years, she thought. I waited ten years for him to say he needs me. And now, when he has, it doesn't sound as good as I thought it would. Maybe I'm finally finished with him. Maybe it's finally over. Maybe.

'Come on, Paula,' he pleaded, and she recognized the tone, the softening of his voice when he wanted something.

'Thanks for the memory, Jake, but what have you done for me lately?'

'Not much,' he admitted, and a wave of tenderness swept over her, scaring her. Don't fall for it again, Paula, she warned herself. He's pulled that hurt, lost-little-boy number before. Not in those words—he never said, I need you—but in that voice. The Black Prince, Cass had called Jake; the spoiled only son of wealthy parents who had given in to his whims, adored him without reservation, and probably still tormented themselves with guilt, wondering what they had done wrong.

'I can't just walk in and say here I am,' he went on, as if he had not heard her; in that respect, he had not changed, Paula thought. 'They'd send me to the joint before I could even call a lawyer. And that may be just, but it sure as hell isn't fair.'

'The government might not see it quite that way,' she replied.

'Come on, Paula, talk sense,' he said impatiently. 'At least meet me somewhere, and let's talk. It's cold out here—literally and figuratively. I want to come in.'

'Aren't you romanticizing things a bit, Jake? It's not the sixties any more. Nobody cares. Nobody's doing time; they even parolled Armstrong last month.'

'Yeah, but he did seven years,' said Jake. 'That's not for me.'

'He was convicted of murder and arson,' she reminded him. 'You didn't kill anyone, and Harvard's not the University of Wisconsin. All the rest came in. I hear even Bernadine's going to. The worst that can happen to her is probation, and maybe a fine. You could handle that. Your parents would pay it.'

'And have a felony conviction follow me around for the rest of my life? No, thanks. Please, Paula, let's talk. Just for a few minutes.' His voice changed again, smoother, silkier, inviting. 'A day hasn't passed that I haven't thought about you. Missed you. Wanted you.'

She couldn't stop the shaking of her hands, but her voice was steady. 'No,' she answered. 'No, Jake. I sat *shiva* for you ten years ago. You're dead for me. You killed it when you left. Without one fucking word, not even goodbye. Nothing. Nada. No.'

'What was I supposed to do, take you with me?' he said hotly. 'Life underground isn't that much fun. And sticking around waiting for them to send me to Lewisburg, so you could come up once a month on visiting day—was that what you wanted?'

'Hardly anyone actually did time for what happened back then,' Paula said reasonably. 'All the conspiracy convictions were reversed later. Howard Levy did a couple of years, but he was in the Army—no surprise. The government never proved one conspiracy charge. Chicago, Gainesville, Harrisburg—not a single defendant went to jail.'

'The times were crazy then,' said Jake. 'I was stupid. Am I going to have to pay for the rest of my life?'

'That's up to you,' she said. 'What you do with your life always has been. Don't call me here again, Jake. I meant it. I don't want to talk to you or see you—not ever again.'

'I don't believe you, baby,' he replied. 'I don't believe

you can just walk away from what we had, not that easily.'

'Easily?' she asked with a thin laugh. 'Oh, now, maybe. But not then. What we had is history. Dead history. It was a long time ago, Jake; we were different people then. My life kept going when you split. And it's full now. Leave me alone.'

She replaced the phone, cutting off his words, and buried her face in her arms. A torrent of memories assaulted her; she was helpless to keep them at bay.

He was the first man she loved. Jake with the lean, lanky body and arrogant grin. A miasma of tear gas hung in the humid Chicago air. As he ran from the club-wielding police, he knocked her down in the street outside the convention centre. When he stopped to pick her up, her angry response dissipated in the suffocating night, and whatever he said to her—later, she couldn't remember his words—evaporated it.

A month later, she started law school. Cambridge was volatile, excited, angry. The city was in ferment. There was an antiwar demonstration the day she registered, and Jake Stern was leading it. He was a second-year law student; until that day, she had not even known his name.

When the first semester ended, they moved together to a flat on Brattle Street. He was temperamental, impetuous, and noisy—the flat was filled with activists, disaffected students, liberal professors, and hangers-on. And, always, worshipping young women; he was frequently unfaithful to her, and she knew from the beginning that he would make her cry. She could not stay angry at him for long; he was high-handed, cocky, inconsiderate, and she loved him anyway.

They argued constantly about tactics and strategy, how they could hinder or even halt the country's involvement in an unjust war. Chris Carey warned her about Jake. 'His militance is going to lead to violence, and he'll go to jail,' Chris told her.

'He's just noisy, he's not dangerous,' she assured him.

Jake disliked Carey from the start. 'He's just another fucking Establishment pimp, waving the goddamn Constitution around while his buddies in Washington napalm the hell out of southeast Asia!' he sneered.

But Paula's case was different. She was working at a women's health clinic in Roxbury, involved in the effort to overturn Massachusetts' archaic laws against contraception and abortion. Her friends from the clinic did not approve of her lover. 'He's a lousy chauvinist just like they all are, especially the SDS men,' they told her. 'And he treats you like shit, besides.'

She was on her way home from the Roxbury clinic when she heard the explosion. Chris was with her; he had taken an interest in Paula's project. 'Not because he gives a good goddamn about your cause, baby,' Jake had told her. 'It's your ass he's after.'

Police were directing traffic away from the site. 'Some stupid kids tried to blow up the computer centre,' a campus guard told them, and Paula felt the first stab of fear. Where was Jake?

When they arrived back at Brattle Street, he was there. His face was smeared with dirt; there were cuts dripping blood into his eyes, and his thick, long hair was singed and blackened. One arm hung limp in its torn sleeve, and his eyes streamed tears from the gas used by the police to break up the demonstration that followed the blast.

'Were you involved in the bombing, Stern?' Chris asked.

Jake laughed meanly. 'Oh, no, Carey, I'm telling you nothing. I won't say a word without a lawyer. And I don't see any lawyers around here—just a couple of fucking mealymouthed liberals, covering themselves with a Constitution that doesn't mean shit. Bombing? What bombing? Get out of my way, Carey, or I'll knock you on your pasty little Brahmin ass!' He pushed past Paula and Chris, standing on the steps of the Brattle Street house, as sirens preceded the fire engines that screamed through the narrow streets of Cambridge.

'You'd better get out of here, Chris,' Paula said distractedly. 'I have to go upstairs. Jake needs me.'

'Wait, Paula!' Chris grabbed her arm. 'Jake's in trouble. Get away from here. You've only got a few more weeks until the end of the term. Don't jeopardize your fine record here. Stern's uncontrollable. He can't see you—he's blinded by his own self-righteous fervour. Come with me. Maribeth and the kids are on the Cape; there's a housekeeper if you're worried about propriety.'

She pulled away from him angrily. 'Propriety? What are you talking about? I don't give a damn where Maribeth is. I'm not coming with you. Jake's hurt. I don't have time for you now.' She ran up the rickety steps. The door to the apartment was open; in the bedroom, Jake was throwing some things into a backpack one-handed.

'Where are you going?'

'Oh, somewhere, away from here, it doesn't matter. Are you coming?' He looked at her defiantly, and she moved towards him.

'Jake, you're hurt, let me see—'

He thrust her away roughly. 'I'm not hurt, I'm okay. Except there's fuzz all over, and I have to get out of here. I'm splitting. I'll go up to Vermont to Mac's cabin for a few days until things calm down. I'll be back to take my finals.'

She looked at him in disbelief. 'Finals? What finals? Jake, they'll know it was you, they'll arrest you. There won't be any finals.' She covered her face with her hands and began to cry.

He put his arm around her. 'Nobody saw me. Nobody at all, except Carey, and he won't say anything. Not as long as he has the hots for you, he won't.'

Paula shivered. She laughed—a strange, thin cackle that seemed to come from outside of her. 'So that's it,' she said. 'You want me to put out for him to save your ass!' A coldness invaded her; it began at her toes, and stopped midway up her body. 'Jake, what about us? What about you and me?' She began to cry.

Jake slammed his fist into the wall. 'Nobody's asking you to put out for that creep, or anyone else!' he stormed. 'Nobody's asking you to do a damn thing if you don't want to. Just shut up and pretend nothing happened. If anybody asks, tell them I had to go home—a family emergency. Tell them I left this afternoon. I gotta go. I'll call you in a few days.' And he ran past her, down the stairs, out the door, out to where the screech of sirens echoed in the warm spring night.

He was gone when they came for him. He did not go alone; two weeks later, a young woman went to the police. Paula knew her, she'd hung around the apartment all that spring. She told them Jake had come to borrow money from her that same night, and forced her to accompany him over the Canadian border. She said he had raped her, and the police added that to the list of charges against him, when they indicted him *in absentia*.

'He didn't do it,' Paula told Cass flatly. 'Jake never had to force a woman against her will. I think he conned her into helping him, and when he dumped her, she cried rape. It would never stand up in court.'

Finally, the memories ceased their assault on her. When the racking sobs stopped, she packed her briefcase and let herself out of the silent office. The custodian looked at her strangely as she passed him in the hall. I must look like a crazy woman, she thought, running her fingers through her tangled hair, touching the dried tears on her face. If I can just get myself into a cab and home, I'll be all right.

She remembered the Valium in her desk and ran back to get it before the elevator came. She rummaged through the drawers until she found the bottle, a three-year-old prescription. The last time I took this was because of Chris, she realized, swallowing the pill, washing it down with the dregs in her coffee cup. I hate it when men make me crazy. I hate, hate, hate it!

She made it into the elevator and through the lobby without further incident, though her legs felt unsteady and her head was throbbing. She saw a cab waiting in front of the building, and ran toward it.

'Oh, I'm sorry, I didn't see the light was off,' she said, already half inside the cab before she saw that it was occupied.

'It's okay, Paula, I'm waiting for you,' Jake said, pulling her inside. 'Why don't you just go across the Park, to the Upper West Side, driver?' The cabbie obliged, and pulled away from the kerb.

'You were waiting for me,' Paula said to Jake accusingly.

'Guilty,' Jake replied. He lifted her chin and looked into her eyes. 'You're still beautiful, Paula. Even more so. I always told you you would be. I was right.'

'Wrong, Jake,' she said. 'I am not beautiful. I am red-eyed and exhausted and furious and confused. I don't want to see you, I don't want to be here with you, I . . . I don't need you. We're finished. Driver, pull over at the next corner, please, I'm getting out.'

'No, she's not . . . hey, Paula, come on. I'm not going to attack you, for Christ's sake. All I want is to talk. Come on . . . for old times' sake. A few minutes can't hurt. I need a lawyer . . . here, I'm retaining you.' He thrust some crumpled bills at her.

'You don't have enough money to hire me, Jake. But I'll find someone for you, I'll do that much. Give me a number where I can reach you, I'll talk to Mike Tigar, or Kunstler, or Weinglass. Or some public defender, if you're down on your luck. It's a simple plea bargain; any law student could do it.'

'I don't want Tigar, or Bill, or Lenny, or a law student. I want you, Paula. I want my freedom back, not probation. Or the joint. I want to be able to walk the streets without jumping at shadows. I want to practise law.'

She laughed without humour. 'You want to practise? Just where, Jake? What bar would admit you? I'm good, but not that good. Nobody is. The best deal you could get might be a pass on the escape charge, but you'd have to do your time. Then probation, maybe. But no bar will ever admit you to practise. They wouldn't let Mitchell, or Haldeman, or Ehrlichman practise again . . . and none of them ever blew up a building.'

'Setting fire to half of Asia doesn't count, huh?' Jake answered bitterly. 'They let Egil Krogh in again.'

'He was just a briefcase carrier,' Paula argued. 'And he did his *mea culpas* . . . he paid for it. No, I don't think law's your calling any more, if it ever was.'

But it was, she thought sadly, oh how it was. She remembered the nights in the Brattle Street flat, arguing until the late hours about a fine point of the law. Jake had burned with a fierce light; passionately, he told her that the law could change the world, and he would help do it. But he had thrown that opportunity away ten years before, with a homemade bomb, a few kerosene-soaked rags and empty beer bottles.

'I don't think they'll forgive and forget, Jake,' she told him.

'They will if the famous and well-connected Paula Gabriel is on my side,' Jake countered. 'Especially if the junior Senator from Massachusetts seconds your efforts.'

Paula snorted. 'Fat chance,' she said. 'Chris hates you. He hates everything you stand for.'

'Stood for,' said Jake. 'What he hates isn't my politics, but the fact that you're my girl. He has the hots for you; he always did.'

'Was your girl.' Paula replied. 'Was. Not is. Not now, and not ever again. That's finished. Over.'

Jake smiled in a way that had made her heart race so long before. She noted objectively that he was still handsome. His body was thicker than it had been a decade ago, but well muscled and strong. His beard was neatly trimmed, and his eyes were warm and guileless above the straight, long nose. He wore an old suede jacket over a turtleneck sweater, and in the stuffy cab the smell of him was overpoweringly familiar, and achingly sweet. It was a smell that brought back two years of her life. He looked the way she had thought he would look at thirty-five: his hair was still thick and curly, but touches of grey dimmed the shine around his temples. She closed her eyes, and images of Jake naked, bending over her, came unbidden to her mind, and she felt herself soften and moisten. Traitor, she thought of her body.

'It'll never be over, Paula,' he said softly. 'Finished, maybe, but never over.'

She sat up and pulled her coat tightly around her. 'Driver, would you—'

Jake's hand covered her mouth, firmly but not roughly. 'Paula, wait. I'm sick of sitting on my ass out in the woods, watching the country go to hell and the rest of the world follow suit. I wasn't cut out for living underground, on the run. I hated every minute of it. I still do. I want to settle my accounts, get right with the courts, clean up my slate, and get on with my life. I'm not a kid any more. I've learned a lot these last few years. I worked with kids, youngsters, and I want . . . I want to do what I'm good at . . .'

'What's that?' Paula answered hotly. 'Bombing? Rape? Or just fucking over the people who love you? Is that what you want to do . . . again? Driver, pull over here, please.'

Before she could move, Jake pulled her into his arms. 'Paula, Paula, please . . . I loved you . . . I still love you. I never meant to hurt you, you know that. Please, baby . . . don't turn me away. I can't make it up to you, I know, but I'll try. It'll work. Please. I need you, Paula.'

'Hey, lady, you gettin' out or not?' The driver had taken them through the park, and stopped on the corner of Eighty-fifth Street. 'The meter's still goin', you know.'

'She doesn't want to get out here. Do you, Paula?' said Jake.

She sighed heavily. Her will seemed to have seeped out of her, disappeared in the warmth of Jake's arms. He took her sigh for assent, and gave the cabbie an address a few blocks away. She looked at him questioningly.

'It's a room . . . belongs to a friend. Not much, but it's warm,' he said innocently.

'Oh, Jake. For God's sake . . . driver, not there,' she said, and gave him the address of the brownstone. 'I'll make some coffee and we'll talk, okay?' she told Jake. 'No promises. I probably can't do anything. But we'll talk.' She pushed him away from her, gently, and sat up straight in the cab. 'We'll talk.'

THIRTEEN

Grey Tucker waited until Cass drank her orange juice before he explained the purpose of their meeting.

'I want you to come to work for me,' he told her.

The Edwardian Room was bustling that morning. It was not the Plaza's weekend languor; no young girls breakfasting with their divorced fathers, no honeymoon couples, only a few tourists preparing for a day of sight-seeing. There was an air of determination and purpose that blended with the steam from countless coffee cups. Men, and a few women in tailored suits, checked their calendars, scanned the newspapers, and made notes in daybooks or on documents that rustled when they were replaced in Italian leather attaché cases.

The same sense of resolve was evident in Tucker's direct, intense manner, and in his compact, powerful body, as he leaned forward.

'I want you to do for the corporation what you do for the accounts your agency handles for us. Give us an image, a style, an attitude—an identity that establishes who we are, how big and important we are in our markets, and ties all our apparel companies together in a word, an idea, a look—a kind of Gestalt, one that reflects who we are today, not who we were a decade ago.'

'Then what you want is for the agency to handle the accounts we don't have now, and our team to come up with a corporate identity programme for you,' Cass said. 'You don't want me, you want the agency.'

'No, I want you,' he said firmly. 'That's only part of

the job, although it's a big chunk. We're so diversified that there's no connection between any of our divisions. And I've always operated on the principle that the sum of something is bigger than its parts. We have someone to do the image polishing, and all the divisions have their own ad managers. Plus we've got marketing directors in each of the subsidiaries, and Pete Marks in the apparel and retail operations. He's a good marketing man, but he has the wrong perspective. I want someone who looks at every aspect of the Company from a different point of view—from the customer's angle. The one who buys our shoes, or our perfume, or cosmetics, or accessories, or shops in any of our stores. I want that customer to think not just about what she's buying, but about the Company behind it. I want her to understand what else we can do for her besides sell her perfume, for instance; how many other ways we can make her more attractive, more fashionable, give her what she wants.'

'You've got the agency for that, Grey,' Cass responded. 'Amelia's the biggest one, and the best, but the others—they're doing decent work for you.'

Tucker shook his head. 'Everyone else shows me product, Cass. You show me style. Even more, you show a sense of direction that's missing in most of my management group. Oh, they're smart individually, but they all wear blinders; their vision is only for their company, subsidiary, division, or responsibility. Even Pete Marks. But that's only part of the job.'

Cass said nothing; Grey Tucker would not have heard her then, she realized. He had prepared his pitch carefully; all right, let the man make it. She felt a growing sense of excitement, and waited for him to go on.

'The second part of it is even more important. We're embarking on a major corporate expansion. We've got money, and I want you to help me spend it. We need to broaden our lines in some markets—footwear, for instance. Do you know how many runners there are in this country? With all our shoe companies, there's not one that makes a shoe as good as Nike, or even Adidas. And our stores—they're losing customers every day. I want to keep those customers, and add new ones. I want to broaden our markets; I'm looking at some outfits that can help. There's a little company in Missouri that makes small appliances. Personal-care items—blow dryers, teeth cleaners, vibrators, even. It's ripe for picking up now. There's a fancy spa in California that looks promising, too—and our geologists from Golden West think there's gas underneath it. I want you to work on acquisitions—strategic planning. As well as looking at all those potential purchases with the same marketing perspective—the customer.'

He leaned back in his chair, satisfied.

'It's a big job, Cass—two big jobs, actually. I've been looking for the right person to fill them for a while, and I like what I see, hear, and know about you.'

'Why?' She was honestly confused, but she never turned down an opportunity to hear positive words spoken about her.

With his fingers, he ticked off his reasons. 'One, you're good. You have great taste and style, and common sense—an unusual combination in the fashion business. Two, you're smart. You don't go into things half-cocked—your work for us has been solid, well researched, carefully thought out. Not just fuzzy, pretty pictures and fancy words that add up to nothing and don't ask for the order. Three, you have a feeling for the bottom line—it's markedly absent in most ad people I've come across. Four, you work well with people; I've watched you at meetings. People seem to want to do their best for you, and that's what makes a good manager.'

Cass did interrupt him then. 'Corporate management is different from the agency, Grey. I had a staff of six when I worked in retailing, and not that many more before I came to New York. In spite of an MBA, I'm simply not that competent—not that way, anyway.'

He waved away her objections. 'It's not all that

complicated. We'll send you back to Harvard for a brushup if you like. Those are skills you can relearn. But your eye, your sense, your intelligence—if that's not there, all the fancy business schools in the world can't teach you anything. What I'm buying isn't what you know now, Cass, but what I think you can learn. How to assess risks and benefits—how to calculate a risk, take it, and make it pay off. In many ways, I want you to do just what you've been doing—on a bigger scale. Supervise, not just produce ads. Consult, not necessarily implement. Find talent, in the companies we buy, and the ones we own. Sort of a roving marketing director.'

'That might be the Peter principle at work,' Cass replied. 'Promoting me beyond the level of my competence. I like the ad business. I like the agency.' Then she added, 'I can do that job, at Amelia's, and still have some kind of personal life.'

He did not respond to that, but he dismissed her first objection. 'I have no doubts about your competence. Or your ability to do this job. I'll make you my personal assistant; I'll find some place for you on the organization chart after you're settled in.'

'A PA?' said Cass. 'I know titles aren't everything, but I have a good one now. Vice president.'

'There are dozens of vice presidents at AI,' Tucker told her. 'Too many for it to mean anything. You'll have greater access and authority as my assistant. If things work out as I expect, we'll make you an executive vice president—that's the one that counts. And eventually, perhaps, a seat on the AI board. Certainly, you'll be on the management committee to start.'

'And how do I fit into the corporate hierarchy now?' she enquired. 'I can see that more than a few feathers will be ruffled if I take the job. Pete Marks, for instance. A great deal of this sounds like it's part of his job.'

Tucker dismissed her concerns airily. 'I've already talked to Pete Marks about it. Frankly, he wasn't bowled over with enthusiasm. But he respects your ability, and he's concentrating on our other properties and operating divisions—the oil and gas holdings, the financials, the real estate. He knows we need you. He'll come around. You'll be working closely with him, so he'll have to. I have no doubt you can handle it.'

'I earn a good salary at Amelia's,' she said. 'I have some important benefits and incentives there as well—bonuses, profit sharing, stock options.'

'I know exactly what Amelia pays you, Cass,' he said, smiling disarmingly. 'In fact, I daresay I know more about you than almost anyone else. I don't go into something like this without the data. I know exactly what you've done, how well you've performed, in every job you ever had, including that summer you worked at a resort in Yosemite.'

'Glacier,' she corrected him.

'Yes, Glacier,' he amended. 'I know what you majored in at college, and concentrated on in business school, and the recommendations every employer has given you. I know where you live, and shop, and who . . . well, it doesn't matter.'

'Yes, it does,' said Cass emphatically. 'I don't know if I like that. You seem to have a distinct advantage over me.'

He relaxed. 'You've led an exemplary life, Cass Campbell, at least as far as the kind of executive search I undertook goes. If there are skeletons rattling around in your closet, they can't be very important ones. And of course I have the advantage.' He grinned, and his face looked momentarily boyish. 'Listen, the whole secret of success is very simple: get to the meeting five minutes early, and know the agenda. That's all I've done. Besides, you know as much about me, and AI, as you need to; I'm sure Amelia has a complete file on us. You want to look at our books?'

'I don't think that's necessary.' Cass smiled. Now she knew why Tucker had demanded so much of her time in the past several weeks, insisted that she accompany him on business trips, exposed her to so many facets of Amagansett's operations. He had been looking for someone to fill a particular role, and she must have met him just as he was beginning his search. Paula was right; so much had to do with timing.

She confronted Tucker across the table. 'I do want to know what's in it for me,' she said. 'There's no title, no line of authority—what there is seems more derivative than organizational.'

'Derivative to start with,' he agreed. 'It comes from me. But we'll be working hand in glove. I don't think you'll have any trouble setting your own procedures, your policies, once you've been at AI for a while. We'll work out a compensation package. The salary will be generous—forty thousand more than you're earning now. All the fringes, plus some frills Amelia doesn't offer.'

'But what about my function?' she questioned him.

'Sort of a policy planner . . . you can call on whoever you need for research, development, support. You'll have complete access—and access is power, Cass, don't forget that.'

He leaned toward her, his face only inches from her own; she wondered idly how he had acquired the tiny scar that ran from the end of his brow to below the corner of his eye. 'Sometimes you have to take risks, Cass. That's how I've gotten where I am, being willing to stick my neck out. Too many women don't make it because they're only willing to take the same, pat, proven way. This isn't any affirmative action job, you know. Acquisitions and strategic planning are mostly male territory. We don't have a woman executive vice president—not yet. You could be the first, in time.'

'Why do you want one? Why there?'

'Because what AI needs is a complete, thorough picture of the person on the other end of so much of our business—the customer. Mostly that customer is female. It makes excellent sense to have a woman in this job, and there are very few who are capable of handling it. I should know—I've been looking at one hell of a lot of résumés the past few months. What do you say?'

Cass thought quickly. She remembered Amelia's words: 'Grey Tucker has a knack for finding the right people for the right tasks.' And despite his cool, businesslike attitude toward her, a camaraderie had sprung up between them recently, a shared appreciation of each other's intelligence and skills. They complemented one another; she noticed details, while he was quick to see the larger picture. She had the kind of efficient, everything-accounted-for style that could make his grand plans workable. And she was beginning, herself, to think on his wider-ranging level. Her mind kept up with his now, though she had to stretch for it. They were, she realized, a good team. He trusted her judgement; he said often that it was her strongest point, that she had, intuitively, the same kind of imagination he had himself, that he looked for in his key people. 'You think like a man,' he told her and she was pleased when he did. Still, she hesitated.

'Don't give me an answer now—take some time,' he urged. 'Call me tomorrow.'

'I'll need more time, Grey. First of all, I can't just walk out on Amelia. And I want to think about it, play with it some, see how I fit into that tidy picture you've drawn. Of course, I'm flattered, and excited; it would be an enormous challenge, and an opportunity. Give me a few weeks; I'll let you know by the end of the month. Meanwhile . . .'

'Meanwhile we'll keep this between us,' Tucker assured her. 'I presume you'll discuss it with Amelia?'

'Before anyone else,' Cass said. 'I owe her a great deal, you know.'

'Of course you do, and I admire your loyalty. But even Amelia would agree that this move is in your best interests. Perhaps not hers, but she's a wise old bird; she'll give you good counsel despite the disruption your absence would cause at the agency. Loyalty is important; I like my people to have it. But it isn't the end-all and be-all.' He picked up his coffee cup and drank from it. 'That's another problem typical of businesswomen: too many of them stay in the same place too long, because they're afraid they'll let their company down if they leave. They ought to remember that loyalty is rarely rewarded commensurately with its worth.'

'Don't you want your employees to be loyal?'

He signalled for the cheque. 'If I can't get it by paying them well, making their work challenging and interesting, and letting them go as high as they're capable of, I don't deserve it. Self-interest is a helluva better incentive than saluting the company flag, I think.'

He consulted his pocket calendar. 'I'm out of the office until the twenty-seventh; there are some prospective acquisitions I want to take a look at. The kind of thing you could be doing for me . . . will be doing. Let me know by then?'

'The day you get back,' she promised.

'Good.' Their business done, he was impatient to leave. 'Come on, I'll have my chauffeur drop you at your office.'

The limousine drew up in front of the agency on West Fifty-fourth Street. Cass was about to step out when Tucker offered her some parting words.

'You'll have an important place at AI, Cass. And in the business world, too. If you don't sit on our board, you will somewhere else. Women like you are in demand for corporate seats; there aren't enough talented ones around to meet all our equal access needs. But that's not why I'm offering you this. It's no token job, believe me. But it is a fantastic opportunity for someone your age, man or woman. This is where the action is, Cass. It's a job women almost never get a shot at. Think it over carefully.'

Cass considered his words as she entered her office. It was pretty and practical, all a mellow rose shade, from the lacquered soft-edged desk to the matching storage-and-display wall unit. There were low cabinets covered in hand-painted silk fabric that matched the pillows on the couch that faced her desk, and the two tub chairs. Boston ferns flourished under the windows, and two Georgia O'Keeffe prints, framed in chrome, hung over the sofa—desert, sand, and sky streaked with tones of pink.

Clio followed her into her office, with the heavy silver coffee pot. 'Shall I start placing your calls?' she asked.

'Not yet, Clio. Just let me have a few minutes alone in here before anyone knows I'm in, okay? And then we'll get this day started before it's over with.'

She dialled Paula's office and reached her secretary. 'I'm sorry, Miss Campbell, but Miss Gabriel isn't in. She left a message at the switchboard asking me to cancel her appointments today, that's all I know.'

She tried Paula at home; there was no answer. Then she called Ellin. 'Did you see Paula this morning?' she demanded. 'She's not at work today, and I'm a little worried.'

'As a matter of fact, I did,' Ellin told her. 'She was with that fellow—Jake? I went down to check the mail, and she was leaving with him. She had an overnight bag; she said she was going out of town for a few days. That's all she said.'

'Shit,' muttered Cass. 'Did she leave a message for me?'

'Not that I know of,' Ellin replied. 'Why? Did you two have plans together?'

'No, not really,' said Cass. 'We were going to look at carpeting for the hall and stairs, remember?'

'Sort of. Well, let's talk about it tonight; maybe you and I can handle it. Don't worry about Paula, though—she's a big girl, she can take care of herself.'

'Not where that son of a bitch is concerned,' Cass said bitterly. 'I hope she's not starting up with him again. He's nothing but trouble, looking for a place to happen. But it's not like her to just take off without telling me first.'

'Dormitory living,' sighed Ellin. 'I told you. Look, don't

make a big deal out of it. She hasn't seen him in what, ten years? Maybe she's just curious.'

'You don't know Paula like I do. She never really got over him before. He has a strange kind of power over her . . . it's quite weird.'

'Did have, maybe,' Ellin said. 'Ten years is a long time. A lot has happened to Paula since then.'

'Maybe.' But Cass was unconvinced. 'Well, we'll see. But I wanted to talk to her. Grey Tucker just made me an extraordinary offer.'

'Of a scandalous nature, I hope?'

'Oh, no, nothing like that. More's the pity. But Nick's coming back in a few days, so I guess I can live until then. Listen, if you happen to hear from Paula, tell her to call me, okay?'

'Okay,' said Ellin. 'But I'm sure she'll call you, not me. Look, Lara's coming in; she's on spring vacation. We're going to Sophie's for dinner, but we'll be home early. Come on up and visit after. She's dying to see you; she says she's going to have a career just like you and Paula when she grows up.'

'What about like her own mother? Does she think you sit home and clip recipes all day?'

'Oh, you know, a prophet without honour, and all that. You don't understand; her mother works, but her mother's friends Cass and Paula have careers.'

'Well, we'll show the kid where she's gone wrong,' said Cass. 'I've got to go. . . . Remember, if Paula calls, tell her—'

'She won't call, Cass, not me. If she calls you, tell her I love her.'

Paula telephoned as Ellin was leaving for the airport to meet her daughter's flight. 'I just wanted to tell you not to worry,' she said. 'I'm with Jake—it's okay. I'll be away for a few days. Tell Cass I'm fine.'

'Why don't you tell her yourself?' Ellin enquired. 'She's very worried.'

'That's why not,' Paula replied. 'I can't deal with a lecture from Cass about Jake just now. Pass on the message, okay?'

'Okay,' said Ellin doubtfully. 'But she'll be mad.'

'She'll get over it,' Paula said. 'She'll have to.'

It was not until very, very late the previous night that Paula had remembered her promise to meet Max. She and Jake were in bed in her apartment when the telephone rang, and she reached for it sleepily. She was exhausted; Jake's sudden reappearance was a shock, and the emotional roller coaster on which she had spent the hours since his telephone call made her forget everything else, blotted out her work, her friends, even Max. As soon as she heard his voice, she felt sick to her stomach; she pushed Jake's hand away from her breast and sat up in bed.

'Paula, what happened? You didn't show up—I've been very worried. Are you all right?'

'Yes, I'm fine, Max, don't worry,' she said. Jake's hands were insistent; she couldn't think clearly when he touched her. 'Look, Max, something's come up, I can't explain, it's really important—'

'A family emergency?' Dear Max—he was helping her make excuses.

'Uh . . . sort of,' she said. 'It's complicated . . . look, I have to go away for a couple of days, I can't help it, can you stay in town over the weekend? I think I'll be back on Monday, and we can—'

'Shit, Paula, tell him to get lost and get off the phone!' Jake said loudly, and Paula covered the receiver with her hand, but it was too late. Max had heard every word.

'I see,' he said bitterly, 'something has come up, is that it?'

'Oh, Max, you don't understand, it's not what you think,' Paula began, but it was too late: Max hung up on her. Oh, God, she thought, what have I done to him? How could I let him down like that? She tried to call him back, but instead of Max, she got a busy signal. She got it again when she tried in five minutes, and in ten, and in twenty, but when she called the intercept operator, she was told that the telephone seemed to have been taken off the hook. 'We'll report that in the morning,' the operator said, and Paula thanked her, and hung up. In the morning, she thought, as she gave herself up to Jake again, I'll call him in the morning.

The next day, Max's phone was working again, but instead of Max she got the impersonal voice of his answering service. 'I'm sorry, Mr Morton has returned to California. I can give you his number there, if you like.'

'No, thanks, I have it,' said Paula wearily. 'No message, I'll call him there on Monday.' Max must have left early that morning, angry and disappointed. Would he ever forgive her? She had forgiven Jake for sins of vastly greater magnitude, hadn't she? Yes, she thought, but I'm not Max, and he may not feel that way. First the starchild fucks him over, and then I fail him, too . . . oh, God, Paula, how could you?

She knew how she could have, and had, and the answer was standing with his hands in his pockets, waiting for her to finish her business so they could leave, to hang up the telephone and follow him out the door . . . where? To what? She didn't know. She didn't know what she was going toward, with Jake, and what she was walking away from, with Max. She only knew that she was moving, with the direction and ultimate destination unknown.

FOURTEEN

'Is that a police car behind us?'

Paula glanced in the rearview mirror; behind them, the Woods Hole harbour was framed like an ektachrome postcard. The masts of the fishing boats grew smaller, then disappeared entirely as she drove up the winding hill and away from the village. Although it was still slushy late March in New York, the leaves here were just beginning to show signs of spring; a fuzzy green enveloped the receding hills of the village, and the smell of new growth, and salt air, blew in from the open window. The morning sun felt good on her bare arm; on Cape Cod, her favourite season had begun.

The only car behind them was a dark late-model sedan, and as she turned the car onto Route 6, she saw that the driver was an elderly man. Jake's concern annoyed her; she felt replete and full from a weekend of sex and love, and old memories overlaid with new smells and tastes and sounds. She did not want to think about what lay ahead, not yet, and she was irritated by Jake's paranoia.

She had agreed to help, to use whatever connections she had to try to clear him. 'For old times' sake,' she said. He made love to her that night for the first time in ten years, sex that was bittersweet, achingly familiar in all the old ways. So she stilled the nagging doubt in her mind, and ignored the reasons why she had shut him out of her heart. For two nights and three days she managed to pretend that the intervening decade had not happened. She chose Woods Hole because it was a special place to them, special from the time before. But it was Monday now, and the present intruded, rudely, on her reverie.

'Relax, Jake,' she told him. 'No one's following us. This isn't *Bonnie and Clyde*. You're old news to most people. By the way, that was a dumb stunt at the motel, registering as Mr and Mrs Philip Nolan, for God's sake. Why'd you do it?'

'Sometimes I feel like a man without a country,' Jake answered. She felt a twinge of pity for him. Perhaps he has changed, maybe he has learned something in all these years, she thought. 'Besides, any motel that insists on cash in advance doesn't look closely at the register. Why did you pay in cash instead of a credit card?'

'Habit, I guess. Practising law too long, listening to clients tell me about their dumb mistakes, like leaving trails behind them that any simpleton could pick up. One weekend with you and I'm beginning to think like a criminal.' She reached for his hand and squeezed it to take the sting out of her words.

He didn't want sympathy. 'Teach you understanding,' he remarked. 'I thought you weren't doing much criminal work these days.'

'I'm not,' Paula said.

'Not major league enough, huh?' said Jake, and Paula's hands tightened on the wheel. 'No money in it, either, I guess.'

'Watch it, Jake,' she warned, pulling out to pass another car so suddenly that he was thrown against the dash-board. 'It's not a matter of big or expensive. I'm carrying a full load at the office, and trying to prepare a brief for a big case—an abortion case.'

'And working for Chris Carey, too, I guess,' said Jake. 'Is he going to make you the first lady Supreme if he makes it to the White House?'

'I doubt it,' she replied. 'Christ, Jake, I don't have to defend myself to you—not my practice or my politics.'

'Relax,' he said, putting his arm around her shoulders. 'You do plenty of good, and if you also do well, that's great. Isn't money the long hair of the eighties? Everybody's got a hustle—selling stocks and bonds, fronting for gurus, picking up big bucks for books about life underground . . . it ain't what it used to be.'

'No, it's not,' Paula said. 'Jake, are you really sure this is what you want to come back to?'

'What I want is to go back to the motel and make love to you for the next twenty years or so, baby, but that won't do me much good in the long run. Or anyone else, either.'

'What anyone?' asked Paula. 'All the old lefties talk about is the price of real estate. The whole country's swinging to the right. It's not your direction; they're not your kind of radicals.'

'Then why are you working for Carey? You really think he can get the nomination, and if he gets it, win an election?'

'Probably not,' said Paula. 'But I owe him.'

'You owe him shit,' Jake said. 'He used you, he got where he wanted to go. You were always too loyal, that was your problem.'

Paula saw an exit a few yards ahead, and took it. After a few feet, she stopped the car.

'Jake, you're exactly right,' she said. 'I'm too loyal, that's my problem. That's why I'm here with you, in this car, on my way to Boston to try to get you out of a jam you were stupid enough to get into. It was a great weekend, thanks for some fantastic sex and a few kind words, and get the hell out of this car and find some other loyal *shmuck* to help you, okay?' She buried her face in her hands, trying not to cry.

Jake held her close. 'Paula, Paula, I'm sorry, so sorry,' he said. 'I didn't mean it . . . about your loyalty, I mean. I guess I'm just jealous of Carey—Christ, he always had a thing for you, he used to look at you in class like he wanted to be screwing you instead of teaching us, and I hated him for that, always have. And this weekend . . . it was more than sex, at least for me. Wasn't it for you?'

She relaxed in his arms, tired of the struggle. 'You know it was, Jake. You know it. I just can't fight two battles at once, fighting you and fighting myself. I can't do it unless you let up on me, I can't do it when you cut me up like this.'

'If Carey gets elected, would you go back and work for him?' Jake seemed concerned; Paula was moved by his evident jealousy. Moved, and a little scared; was Jake this vulnerable, this frightened of losing her again? She didn't want to think about that; it was too great a responsibility. She couldn't think of anything except what she had to try to do in the next few days; if she succeeded, there would be time to figure out the place she wanted Jake to have in her life.

'I don't think so,' she told him. 'I had enough of Washington. You don't own your own soul there.'

'If the conservatives get in, there'll be plenty to do just to keep them from repealing the Bill of Rights,' Jake added. 'That's why I want to come back.'

Could she believe him? She wasn't sure. He sounded sincere, but he'd sounded that way before, and still abandoned her. She didn't know, but she had come this far, and it seemed stupid to pull out now. She sighed, restarted the car and headed toward Boston. Toward an old law school friend who might help Jake, and who, perhaps, might not.

As they drove, Jake talked about his life since leaving Cambridge. He chose his words carefully; she listened intently, sifting through the names and places and anecdotes, wondering who had been there for him, in whose arms he had lain during the long nights away from her, what secrets he had shared, what connections he had made, what obligations and promises. She looked for clues that he had missed her, ached, like her, for what they had had together, and there were some, but not enough to erase her nagging doubts, her fears that he was using her; that when he had what he had come for, he would again abandon her.

'It wasn't really a farm,' Jake was saying as they drove into Boston. 'Just a big old broken-down house on a few acres of land. We had a couple of pigs and some chickens and a pair of goats.'

'How did you live?' she asked. 'I mean, what did you do to earn money?'

'Most of the folks worked in town, in Burnaby or Vancouver. Cliff fixed cars—he was a draft dodger, a lot of the ones who came through Canada were. Matt was a short order cook. Claire was a midwife, self-taught; she'd been at medical school for a while, couldn't hack it, and split, ran into Cliff somewhere and founded the farm with him. Sharon and Beth taught at a free school in the village, and so did I.'

'You? Teaching school?' She smiled at the thought of Jake with little children, gruff Jake with the deep voice and the fiery temper; he must have scared the lessons into them.

'Damn right,' said Jake, with pride. 'I was good, too. I had a few other jobs: picked fruit in the Okanogan for a few seasons, worked at a cannery in Vancouver. And I did some men's rap groups there, at a centre we started.'

'You?' Paula grinned. 'Men's rap groups? Did you tell them how all the women in your life pussy-whipped you?' It was Jake's own phrase, for any woman who would not let him have his way, for his mother, his girl friends, his teachers, even Paula herself.

'Ease up,' Jake said. 'People change, you know?'

'Objection sustained,' Paula said. She wanted to believe that; fiercely, she wanted to believe that he had changed. But she remembered Jake from the old days, from the Movement, where women were never allowed in the leadership, were always second-class citizens. For that reason, she had opted out of it, chosen to work with other women on an issue that was wholly theirs: abortion. She had watched the Movement women; as she'd told Ellin, long before, when Ellin was writing her book about those very same people, they were slaves, and willing ones, at that.

'Besides,' Jake went on, 'who said we only talked about women? You think we had nothing else bugging us?'

'I don't know what you think these days, Jake,' said Paula seriously. 'Tell me about the women, though. Which one was yours?' She made the question as light as she could; be casual, she told herself, don't make a thing out of it. After all, it's not like you haven't had a few men since then yourself. And Jake never knew about the baby, she reminded her inner voice; when he left, after the bombing, she hadn't been able to tell him that she was eight weeks pregnant with his child. Would it have made a difference? If he had known, would he have stayed? Would she have had the baby? She wasn't ready to tell him yet; first, she needed to know more about who he had become.

'Nobody was mine, as you put it,' Jake said. 'I . . . uh, had a thing for a while with Beth.'

Paula said nothing, and after a while Jake continued. 'She left the farm a few months ago. She lives with Sharon in California now.'

Had she left Jake for a woman? Paula knew that Jake would not tell her if it was so; his pride was too great for that. A man they had known at law school was abandoned by his wife for just that reason; Jake had been quite cruel about it. 'What kind of asshole jerk lets his woman leave him for some cunt?' he asked Paula. Many kinds of men, she'd thought then—many, many kinds. But she had not said it, nor would she probe any deeper about Beth now.

'Is there anyone from Vancouver who would give you character references?' she asked. 'Anyone you worked for, any solid citizens who might vouch for you? Or any of your housemates?'

'Probably not. When we lost the lease, everyone split. But there's a minister in Vancouver who offered to help me; I did the men's group through his church.'

'No trouble with the law in Canada?' she asked. 'No dope busts or traffic tickets?'

'Clean, completely clean,' Jake replied. 'Believe me, I didn't go looking for trouble. Say, do you want me to drive for a while?'

'You just said you weren't looking for trouble. We're just about there, anyway.'

She manoeuvred the car through the traffic, seeking a parking place in the crowded streets near the Quincy Markets. She found one; she got out and stretched her legs gratefully. 'Want to get the bags?' she asked, and Jake complied.

He followed her into the lobby of a high-rise apartment building overlooking the Boston harbour, waited while she asked the doorman for a key left for her by the apartment's owner. Then he followed her into the elevator, wincing under the security guard's careful scrutiny.

'Pretty fancy,' he said as she unlocked the door and let them inside. 'What does your friend who owns this place do, rob banks?'

'She's a television producer,' Paula said. 'I was on her show a few times, and we got to be friends. She's away for a few days, said I could use the apartment. I thought it would be better than a hotel.'

Jake stood at the windows, taking in the view. 'Boston's sure changed in ten years. Look what they've done to Faneuil Hall down there. Looks like a shopping centre.'

'It is,' Paula told him. 'But Cambridge is still pretty much the same.'

Jake ran his hands over her body. 'Does this fancy apartment have a bed?'

She sighed. 'Is that all you can think about, Stern?' she asked.

'Not entirely,' he said. 'I'm nervous, that's all. When I'm nervous, sex soothes me.'

'Any sex in a storm, huh?' She pushed his hands away.

'Aw, Paula, you know I don't mean that,' he said, 'You know how long I've wanted you? How many weeks, months, years it's been?'

'About twelve hours, by my calculations,' she said. 'Let

me make a phone call, then we'll . . .' But his hands had trapped her again, caught her with their skilful magic, and she felt the trembling begin in her legs once more, and the words die in her throat.

Later, she made a phone call to her former classmate. 'Tom? It's Paula Gabriel. Yes, I just got in. Are we still on for dinner? Sure, I'm buying . . . if I were hitting you up for the alumni fund, we'd go to McDonald's.' She laughed. 'No, I'll tell you when I see you. Locke-Ober's is fine . . . at six-thirty? Good, I'll make a reservation . . . yes, I'm looking forward to seeing you, too.'

She hung up the phone, and Jake, lying next to her on the bed, snorted. 'Locke-Ober's? Pretty fancy setting for a plea bargain. But Tom Jeffries always had a taste for fancy living, didn't he? I thought he'd be with a State Street firm by now, with all his connections. Didn't he marry that fat little Lowell woman while we were still in school?'

'Mmm hmm,' said Paula. 'They had a kid—I meant to send a present. Didn't know I'd be needing him. If he wants to eat fancy, okay, I'm the one asking for the favour. And he's my only connection in the US Attorney's office. I have to start somewhere.'

'Not a bad place to begin,' Jake answered, fingering the rich satin of the bedcovers. They watched the ships move in and out of the harbour, silently. Then Jake spoke.

'You women are really raking it in these days, aren't you?' She shot him a baleful look, and he backed down. 'Cool it, I'm just asking. You, Cass, that other woman in your house, the writer, the broad who owns this apartment—the women's movement did a lot for you, didn't it?'

She didn't know whether he was envious, or derisive.

'Some of us were in the right place at the right time, that's all,' she said. 'Most of us still earn sixty cents for every dollar a man earns, and there are . . .' She broke off. 'What is it about you that gets me up on my soapbox, anyway?'

'Force of habit,' he told her, holding out his arms. She leaned into them gratefully, relaxing as his strong fingers kneaded the tired muscles in her back and shoulders. 'Except in the old days, we were usually on the same side.'

'Are we still?'

'I hope so,' said Jake. 'You're a lot touchier than you used to be.' He tilted her face away from his own. 'I've been away for a long time, Paula. All I know is what I've read in the papers. Most of the people I knew have sold out. I'm not judging them, or you; you do what you have to do to survive, I've learned that. So don't jump on me for everything I say, okay?'

'Okay.' She was touched by his quiet, reasonable tone of voice. 'Sometimes you say things that trigger a lot of old stuff in me. It's not politics, it's . . . us.' I keep listening for words I don't hear, she thought. I keep wondering who you are now, and whether you still love me. I don't really care about your politics or your pig farm or anything else except that you're here. And in two hours I have to go make whatever deal I can to clear you, and then wonder, after I've done all that, if you'll want me, in whatever life you make afterwards, and whether I'll ever belong in it again.

'I know,' said Jake, stroking her hair. 'I'm sorry, Paula. That's all I can say about what happened then . . . I'm sorry.'

Jake was pacing up and down the apartment when she let herself in after dinner with Tom Jeffries. She saw the foil-wrapped remains of a Big Mac and felt slightly guilty; she had stuffed herself on shrimp and lobster and chocolate mousse.

'What happened? Can he do anything? Did you tell him I'm here?'

'No, not really,' she said. 'I told Tom I was representing

a party who wanted to make a deal, and he knew immediately I meant you —he kept starting his sentences with "Somebody like Jake Stern, that is." ' She took out her pocket diary and looked at the words she'd jotted down during dinner.

'First of all, Tom has very little power in this situation. He's only an assistant, and he works mostly in the civil area. He's been working on some complicated computer scam lately.'

'I don't care what that prick is doing, what did he say?'

Paula sighed. 'Are you going to let me tell it my way, or what?'

Jake grinned in that little-boy way she remembered from long ago. 'Sorry, Paula, just anxious. Take your time. Just don't leave anything out.'

'Essentially, any deal will have to be passed by his boss, a man named Maloney, who's the chief US attorney. Tom said the first step is to get the felony for the bombing reduced to a misdemeanour, and that's possible; there's a charge that could apply, nonfelonious injury or mischief to government property. That's what the computer installation you trashed was, under federal contract to Harvard. If Harvard will drop its charges, they might be able to do that. You'd have to make restitution, but probably not do any time; maybe a brief probation, *mea culpas*, all that. If there's no felony and you can get someone to back you on a bar admissions committee, you might be able to get admitted. You'd also have to make a deal with the law school to let you take your last semester over, or your exams. Nobody will promise anything about getting you past the bar committee; that's up to you. But you have to get the felony reduced to a misdemeanour; if you don't do that, it's all academic.'

'All right,' said Jake, rubbing his hands together, 'so that's the way we go. Will Jeffries' boss agree to the deal?'

Paula shrugged her shoulders. 'That's the sticky point. The guy is basically a hack, but an ambitious one. He wants to be a district court judge. Which he needs a Senator's blessing to get.'

'You mean Chris Carey?' Jake frowned. 'You need Carey to get the guy that job?'

Paula spoke evenly. 'I don't need Chris Carey, Jake. You do.'

He snorted in disgust. 'Then I might as well go back to Canada,' he said. 'Chris Carey wouldn't give me the sweat off his balls.'

Paula agreed. 'He certainly won't just because you ask him nicely. On the other hand, there are plenty of people in the party who owe Maloney a few favours. They might put some pressure on Chris, and he needs them—especially if Ted Kennedy really means it about staying out of the race for the nomination.'

'Carey needs you, too,' said Jake.

'Oh, no, you don't,' she replied quickly, thinking about what Jake had said about going back to Canada. Please, no, she prayed, no; don't let him go again, just when I've found him. But she kept her voice even and free of emotion as she responded to Jake's question.

'He liked and respected you once, Jake,' she told him. 'He might listen to you. Then again, he might not. Because after you split, he and I . . .' She didn't finish the sentence, but Jake did, nodding grimly.

'I figured,' he said. 'He was just too conveniently there with the tea and sympathy. And he always had the hots for you. I couldn't blame him. That uptight wife of his, he needed somebody like you.'

He was being too nice about it, she thought. She remembered the weeks after Jake left, the kindness Chris had shown her, the help he had provided. And her old anger at Jake returned.

'What about what *I* needed, Jake?' she asked him. 'Where were you then? Off with that little groupie hiding out in the woods, while I was pregnant with your baby? Who do you think found me a doctor and loaned me money for an abortion?' It had been Chris; Cass was in Seattle, where her mother was dying.

She was mollified by the heat of his reaction to her words. 'Abortion? What are you talking about? Why didn't you tell me, for chrissake?'

She warmed to her words. 'What was I supposed to do, put an ad in the underground papers? "Jake, come home, Paula is pregnant"?' She laughed bitterly; despite the words of love and the old closeness that had come back over the weekend, she remembered the feelings of abandonment, of fear, when Jake went away, leaving her alone except for the child growing within her. 'I was going to tell you about it, that night, the night of the bombing. But you never gave me a chance. And then you didn't come back, you didn't call or write, and I . . . I . . .' Her voice broke then, her anger dissipated in the heat of an old hurt, the scar uncovered again, bleeding, leaving her raw.

Jake was oblivious to her pain, to everything except his own shock.

'Why the hell didn't you tell me, somehow find me?' he shouted. 'Jesus, if I'd known, I'd never have left, no matter what.' He hung his head in his hands. 'Jesus, I never dreamed . . . We'd have gotten married, had the kid. God, he'd be almost ten now, wouldn't he?'

Paula nodded, crying, and she and Jake comforted each other. The hurt was fading a bit now; now that she had told him, now that he knew, perhaps it would heal for good. She had carried it within her for so long, a sore that would not go away, an ache that never left her. She rocked back and forth in Jake's arms, feeling the grief leave her, recede back into the edges of her mind.

'That girl . . . Paula, she didn't mean anything to me,' Jake said. 'She was just . . . there. You know I never raped her; hell, she handed it to me on a silver platter. She changed her story when I wouldn't take her west with me.'

'They dropped the rape charges anyway.' Paula sniffed.

'There was a nice Harvard boy who wanted to marry her, and didn't want the publicity, so she withdrew her statement.' She wiped her eyes. 'It wasn't her, Jake,' she said, 'it was you. All those weeks, and nothing. I couldn't go through with it. I couldn't have the baby alone. Chris was there. He was kind, he helped me. He was all I had.'

Jake paced the floor restlessly. He turned to her. 'Paula, the abortion, Carey . . . it changes things. I won't ask you to intervene with him for me, not now. I mean, I know he never liked me, but this—'

She interrupted him. 'That's not true, Jake, he thought you were brilliant, he told me so. Just, toward the end, he thought you went overboard. He admired your courage.' That was true; a few days after the bombing, before Paula told Chris she was pregnant. 'What a waste of an incredible mind,' he'd said, 'what misguided courage he had.' And then, 'What stupidity.' But she didn't tell Jake that. And why was she rushing to comfort him, anyway? She was the one who was hurt, who had lost everything.

'There goes it all,' he said, as if echoing her thoughts, 'the whole thing. My career, my life . . . that kills it.'

His career, his life . . . at least she'd had that. Correction, she had that. She'd lost . . . what? A baby, not even a baby yet, just some tissue and nerves and . . . Stop it, Paula! she told herself. You let that go a long time ago. Think like a lawyer. Think how you can convince Chris to help Jake.

'I thought—he helped a few others, didn't he? I heard he did. He was a pretty fair guy; we had some arguments about means, but our ends were similar, he wanted us out of Viet Nam—'

'That's right, he did,' Paula said.

'Look, maybe I could talk to him, do you think?'

'You might,' she said cautiously. 'You might be able to convince him—' As you've convinced me? she thought fleetingly. Then she had a cynical thought. She looked at Jake sharply. 'Look, you're not thinking about trying to blackmail him about our affair, his and mine, are you? Because if that's what you have in mind—' He hadn't seemed all that surprised to have the affair confirmed; it was almost as if he had known it all along. She was furious—again. Oh, God, was this what manic depressives went through? Up one minute, down the next? She thought she could not take any more. Images flashed in and out of her mind: making love with Jake the first time, in Chicago, and the last time, hours before. The abortion: the kitchen in Malden, the feel of the icy instrument stretching her wide, hurting her; in the clinic, in Roxbury, they always heated the speculums, she thought before the real pain overwhelmed her and she bit her lip to keep from crying out. The sight of Jake, in the cab, the feel of him, just a few days before. Would it never end?

Get hold of yourself, Paula. Forget the past, forget the baby, the abortion—you've finished that. What mattered now was whether Jake thought he could use her affair with Chris to help himself.

'Don't be ridiculous,' said Jake. 'What do you take me for? Besides, it wouldn't work—' He saw her face whiten with anger and pulled her into his arms. 'I mean, I'd never involve you in anything that would hurt you, and blackmail is wrong.'

Much later she would remember that; funny, how his words had echoed Nixon's—it would be wrong. But then she did not, she let her doubts be swept away in the warmth of him, exhausted from the emotional seesaw, one minute crying, helpless with love, the next angry, bitter, suspicious. Only Jake could make her crazy that way, no one else. Not before, or since. Of course Jake wouldn't try to blackmail Chris into helping him; it would be morally wrong. Think like a lawyer, Paula.

'You know, you're right, Jake, Chris has helped a lot of the others. And he did admire you, he thought the law lost when you did what you did . . . maybe he'd help you. I could try to set up a meeting. . . .'

Jake was immediately grateful. 'Would you, Paula?

After I—after you and he—would you really? God, that would be terrific, maybe I could reason with him, maybe—'

Paula looked at him intently. 'You promise you're not going to threaten him about our affair? It's over with him, you know.'

'I promise,' Jake said earnestly. He smiled sweetly at her. 'Over? You never were a door closer, Paula. You're not sleeping with Chris, but it's not over. Any more than it was over with us ten years ago.'

'That's always been my problem,' she said tiredly, 'hasn't it? I never can throw anything out.'

He ran his fingers through her hair, and held her face in his hands, kissing her gently. 'A saver,' he said. 'That's what you are, a saver. Old clothes, old causes, old souls.'

She pushed him away, but not harshly. 'Don't, Jake,' she said. 'You don't know me anymore. People change. This weekend, us . . . it was probably a bad idea. I'll help, because . . . well, because we were connected in a special way a long time ago. And because maybe you've changed, too. Maybe you can make a difference; God knows, someone has to. I owe it to the profession. But you and me . . . I don't need you in my life. You make me crazy. You make me exhausted.' Not like Max, she thought fleetingly—oh, God, Max.

'You're saying after this is cleared up, that's it?' he asked. 'I don't believe that. I still love you, Paula. I never stopped. I don't plan this as an ending. Just a different beginning for me and you.'

'You believe that now, Jake,' she replied. 'I also think you think it's what I want to hear. So relax and stop selling. I said I'd help you and I will. You don't need to drag out the hearts and flowers. It's a little late for doing the honourable thing.' Or was it? Not the honourable thing, but the right thing . . . the thing that would make all the pain, and the hurt, and the disappointment worth it. Was it too late? she wondered.

'Oh, Paula, stop being so tough and hard-ass,' Jake

said. 'I don't buy it. I know why you're doing it, but I don't buy it, not now, not from you. I know you, remember? I was stupid, I hurt you, you have every reason to twist it in a little. I can take it. I expected it. Enjoy. And then shut up.' He covered her body with his own, and as his fingers touched her cool skin and found the hot, moist centre of her, she accepted the truth of his words, and gave herself up to him again. Oh, Paula, you are such a dummy, she told herself, don't you ever learn?

When she awoke, the lights of the harbour beacons were twinkling in a dark sky. She looked at her watch; it was close to midnight. She pulled on a robe, left Jake asleep in the big bed, and went into the living room. She phoned Cass.

'Where the hell are you?' Cass demanded, and Paula spoke quietly, whispering in the empty room.

'In Boston, at Sonya's. I spent the weekend on the Cape.'

'Are you with Jake?'

'Yes,' said Paula, and she heard Cass's intake of breath, and rushed to fill it. 'Cass, it's all too complicated to explain right now. I'm all right, really I am. Just taking care of some unfinished business.'

'You make sure that unfinished business doesn't finish you,' Cass warned. 'Why are you whispering?'

'Jake's asleep, I don't want to wake him. I . . . look, Cass, I didn't want you to worry, that's why I called.'

'To tell me you're back at the scene of the crime, this time with the criminal, and that's not supposed to worry me?' Cass was practically shouting; that was unlike her. She lowered her voice and spoke more rationally. 'Paula, you can't afford to get mixed up with Jake Stern again. Think about your career. Think about your father. Think about what Jake did to you. Think about . . . oh, God, Paula, think about the abortion if you can't think about anything else!' She was nearly crying. 'Paula, think about the people who love you,' she wailed.

Paula was trying not to cry too. 'I am, Cassie, I am,' she said. 'Honest. Look, I'm being careful. I'm not going to get hurt again. I need to stay here and take care of some things. I'll be home in a few days, and we'll talk then. Don't make any judgments till we do, okay?'

'I don't have any choice, do I?' Cass was resigned. 'Paula, I need to talk to you, besides. Grey Tucker made me an incredible offer, Nick isn't here, Ellin and I have been so worried about you . . .'

'You don't need to be, I'm fine, honestly,' Paula said. 'I want to hear all about Tucker, and I will, I'll be back as soon as I can.'

Cass was mildly annoyed. Paula could have shown a little more enthusiasm. Of course, all she had on her mind now was Jake Stern. That bastard. She'd never liked him, even before he messed Paula up. He was so arrogant. Cocky. Full of himself. Not nearly good enough for Paula. That couldn't have changed.

'I'll call you, when I know when I'll be home, okay? Take care, Cass.'

'Oh, don't worry, I will. But you . . . Paula, you take care. I love you.'

'I love you, too, Cassie,' she said, and hung up the phone.

She had called Max at the office earlier that day. 'Mr Morton is on vacation for two weeks,' his secretary told her. 'But he may be calling in; may I take a message?'

She debated it for a moment, and then left her name. 'Tell him to call me when he gets back . . . tell him I'm writing him a letter . . . no, never mind, just leave word that I called and will call again,' she said. But just in case he wasn't really away, she tried him once more at home. She let the telephone ring and ring, but there was no answer, and finally she gave up. Then she re-joined Jake in bed, and fell asleep almost immediately. It had been a very long day.

Paula reached Chris Carey the next morning and learned

that he would be in Massachusetts at the end of the week. 'I need an hour or so of your time,' she told him, 'and I can't tell you much more than that.'

He did not enquire further, but suggested they meet for a drink when he got to Boston..

'It's private, Chris,' she said. 'About a client. I'm at Sonya's. Can you come here?'

'Around ten on Friday night? I'm due back in the capital the next day.'

They made a date; she gave him Sonya's address. 'Just you, Chris,' she added. 'Come alone, okay?'

'You must really want something.' It was a statement, not a question.

'A favour for a favour. I ran into some fuzzy-headed liberals with more money than brains, and one of them might be induced to serve as your New York treasurer.'

'You don't have to bribe me, Paula. If you say alone, then alone it will be. Friday night.'

Her responsibilities met, she considered the time ahead, and woke Jake. 'There's no sense hanging around here until Friday,' she said, 'let's get out of town. Nobody will recognize you, and we can just pretend it's a vacation, huh?'

'Sounds fine to me,' Jake said.

The weather was mild and sunny, so they headed north, away from the city. The days inevitably brought back memories of earlier times.

'Remember when we found that duck limping around the shore at Ipswich, and brought it home?' Paula said, and Jake nodded as they walked on the beach at Cape Ann.

'Remember that funny-looking waiter at Joseph's, the one with the beard with the white streak down the middle?' Jake asked, when they encountered a man who looked like him in the scrimshaw room at the Peabody Museum in Salem.

They strolled through Hammond Castle near

Gloucester, and remembered an acid trip when the sprinklers over the castle pool turned a drizzle into a magical rainstorm. They stayed the night in Rockport, but avoided the nearby hills at Andover, where Jake had gone to school.

They recalled their private jokes, and familiar habits; they were shy with one another only when something like the drive past Phillips Academy brought them back to the present.

Jake told Paula about his years in Canada, with nostalgia that touched Paula, reminding her that he had lived a decade of his life without her. And that, until that night when fire streaked the sky above the Harvard Yard, she had known everything about him.

Their lovemaking was an occasionally strained blend of the new and the familiar. Jake was Paula's first lover; what was missing now was that quality of innocence, virginity even, that was there in their first years together. Paula noticed it more than Jake did, although it did not escape him.

'You've been practising,' he murmured into her hair one evening as she licked gently at the soft, fleshy nipple on his furry chest and rolled it around with her tongue. She felt sexually powerful; equal, she realized, when she thought about it. She had not felt that way in the old days. And if Jake was uncomfortable with the subtle shift in roles, he said nothing to indicate it.

He talked nostalgically of the children he knew in Canada, especially Jeremy, for whose birth, he said proudly, he had been a labour coach. He came back over and over again to the subject of Paula's abortion, sadly and regretfully. At first, she was warmed by his concern; after a while, she began to resent it. 'I settled that a long time ago,' she said. 'Please, let's not talk about it, okay?'

Caught up as she was in the joy of being with Jake again, she noticed the changes in him. He has softened, she thought; and then, haven't we all? Then, she had not thought of relationships between men and women as having much to do with power—then, Jake had had all the power. They seemed more evenly matched now, and she liked it.

He was deft in ways she noticed. Her car kept stalling unexpectedly, and Jake spent a moment under the hood, and a few more at an auto-parts store. In fifteen minutes, he had fixed things. He enjoyed her surprise. She had called him a Jewish prince in the old days, and he had agreed, insisting that he lacked the genes for fixing mechanical objects: he had told her years ago that it was passed only from Gentile fathers to sons. His new competence pleased him. 'I built a house in Canada,' he told her proudly. 'Two, actually. One as a grunt—a carpenter's assistant—and the other as head of a construction crew. And I worked on the tractor and truck at the farm. Taught myself how from a book. It's no big deal.' But she knew that for Jake it was, and she liked it.

She wondered if he found her different, too, and asked him. 'In bed, a little,' he said, but he did not elaborate. 'You're fancier, more prosperous-looking. Prettier, too.' She was disappointed; she felt that she had matured, and she wanted his validation.

His habits seeped back into her consciousness, and so did her responses to him. Her present life she pushed away; when it intruded on the fringes of her mind, she ignored it. She gave herself happily up to him, and when he mentioned someone or some event that had happened to him in the interim, she wondered who the person was, and what she had been doing at the same time. Too soon it was Friday night, and she was stirring honey into her tea and waiting nervously for Chris Carey to arrive.

Jake went out at nine-thirty: soon after, the buzzer sounded. 'There's a gentleman here to see you,' said the security guard over the intercom, 'a Mr . . .' His voice trailed off questioningly.

Paula regretted that she had forgotten about the security precautions in the building and said hurriedly,

'That's all right, I'm expecting him,' and told him to send Chris upstairs.

'He didn't seem to recognize me,' Chris told her when he came in. 'You sounded so furtive on the phone that I didn't bother introducing myself. He's probably a Republican, anyway.' He handed her his coat and hat. 'This sneaking around, it's a little like the old days, isn't it?'

'I suppose.'

He raised an eyebrow. 'Somehow, I don't have the impression that this is a romantic assignation,' he told her.

'No, it's not.' She put his things away. 'Would you like some wine, or a drink?'

'A brandy would be nice, if you have it,' he said. 'Where's Sonya?'

'Out of town for the week. I'm just staying here.'

'Alone?'

She hesitated, then poured his drink and handed it to him. 'Chris, do you remember Jake Stern?'

He spluttered, spilling a few drops of his brandy. 'Rather a difficult young man to forget, wouldn't you say?' He looked at her carefully. 'Not so young anymore, I imagine . . . but then, none of us is, right?'

'Jake wants to come back and get straight with the law,' she told him.

Chris didn't seem surprised. 'And with you, too?'

She flushed. 'No, that has very little to do with it. He thinks the country is in trouble. He wants to do something with his life . . . remember, you always thought he would. You said he was brilliant.'

'And misguided. And stupid,' Chris said. 'Most of them were. What does he want from me, a word with the proper authorities?'

Paula went on as if she hadn't heard the question. 'He thinks the Right is taking over. That all the social programmes are going to suffer, and the people—and justice—along with them.'

'He has a point,' said Chris calmly. 'That's what I've

been telling whoever would listen, anyway.' He put down his drink. 'I'm not going to ask why you've gotten yourself mixed up with Stern again . . . that's your affair. Again, what does he want from me, and why does he think I should give it to him?'

'He wants to talk to you, Chris. He thinks he can convince you to help him.'

'He might at that,' Chris said. Paula was surprised. She had expected a lecture, a warning, a refusal to get involved. It was almost as if Chris was expecting this, she thought.

'You could, if the US Attorney would drop the felony charges and let Jake plead to a misdemeanour.'

'Why? He probably wouldn't have to serve any sentence now. No one was hurt, and it was a long time ago. He'd only get probation. Maloney has nothing to gain by dragging that up again.'

'Nothing to gain by letting Jake plead to a lesser charge, either. Except maybe an appointment to the district bench.'

Chris picked up his drink and sipped it slowly, rolling the brandy around in his mouth, savouring its flavour.

'I see,' he said. 'You don't think Jake's going to threaten to reveal our relationship, yours and mine, do you? Because that won't convince me to help him, you know.'

'Absolutely not,' Paula said. 'I asked him that. He said it would be wrong.'

'Interesting choice of words,' Chris observed. 'So you don't think he has extortion in mind, do you?'

She shook her head. 'He said not.' She thought Chris was remarkably self-possessed.

'And you believe him?'

'Yes, I do.'

'You always did,' said Carey drily. 'And I don't. But I'll talk to him.'

'You will?' She was elated; she had not expected it to be this easy.

'Yes. I don't suppose he's lurking around here, waiting

to pop out of a closet, is he?' Chris asked, looking around the room.

'No.' said Paula, 'he's out. He said he'd be back at ten. I think it might be better if I left the two of you alone.'

'Don't want to be an accessory, is that it?' Chris chuckled. 'You know better, Paula. Didn't you learn anything in crim. law? You're supposed to know everything your client knows.'

'I do,' she said earnestly.

'I hope so,' Chris said sincerely. 'For a naïve little girl who thought power was wicked, you certainly learned how to use it, didn't you?'

'Power? What power? I'm just presuming on an old friendship,' Paula replied. 'Besides, you said it was power if you didn't have it, leverage if you did.'

'That's right, I said that, didn't I?' He sighed. 'You'd better leave now, my dear.'

She went to a late movie, wondering how the meeting between Jake and Chris was progressing. When she returned to the apartment, Jake was alone.

'How did it go?' she asked.

'The way I planned—hoped,' he told her. 'He's going to help me, Paula. Help us,' he added.

She hugged him. 'That's wonderful, Jake! I was hoping . . . I didn't know if you'd be able to convince him!' Above her head, Jake allowed a wide smile to crease his face.

'All I needed was the chance to try,' he said. 'And thanks to you, I got it.'

FIFTEEN

'Why do we have to go to Sophie's tonight?' Lara complained to Ellin. 'It's so boring there. Boring, boring, boring.'

'Because she and Papa are leaving on a trip tomorrow,' she told her daughter. 'You won't see them until August. That's months away.'

'What a pity,' Lara said with sarcasm, and Ellin felt the tightness begin at her temples.

'Look, Lara, you don't have to like it, you just have to do it,' she said. 'Please be civil, and we'll get in and out of there in a couple of hours. You can go in the den and watch television until dinner's ready.'

'Terrific. What a thrilling evening. That's what I flew three thousand miles for? I thought we were going to go see some shows, and go shopping, and stuff like that.'

'We will,' Ellin promised, 'but not tonight. I can't fight on two fronts, you and Sophie both. Give me a break. Besides, Cass is going to come up when we get home.'

'That's nice,' said Lara. 'Maybe she'll help me fix my hair. I just love the way she does hers.' She studied her mother critically. 'You know, Ma, you ought to fix yourself up a little. You could be really pretty if you tried.'

'Thanks a whole bunch,' Ellin replied. 'Maybe if you spent more time—'

'I *know*, Mother, if I spent more time on my homework and less time in front of the mirror, I'd be better off. How boring.'

Ellin sighed apologetically. 'I'm sorry, babe. I wasn't planning to nag you on vacation.'

'That's what mothers are for, I guess,' Lara said philosophically. She put her arms around Ellin. 'I'm sorry, too. Let's go see the wicked witch. I'll behave, promise.'

'Okay,' said Ellin. She hugged Lara back. 'I really love you, y'know?'

'Now don't get all mushy, Ma,' Lara said. 'Let's just go get it over with.'

Sarah, Sophie's maid, let them into the apartment in the San Remo. 'Miz Sophie's on the phone in the bedroom,' said the tiny black woman who had worked for Sophie Barnett ever since Ellin could remember. 'Mr B is in the den with Walter Cronkite.' She gave Lara an affectionate tweak. 'And there's a whole plate of them stuffed shrimp you love in there, too, with your name wrote all over 'em.'

'My two favourite girls,' Lou Barnett said happily, rising from the overstuffed leather chair his wife could not convince him to discard. 'In that room, that perfect room—twelve thousand dollars it cost me, that room, and your father refuses to give up that old piece of junk,' Sophie had complained to Ellin—monthly, for at least five years, she calculated.

'Don't get up, Dad, it's okay,' said Ellin. She kissed his cheek. 'All ready to go tomorrow?'

'Ready? What's to get ready? Your mother says we go, so we go. I could stand to be in the sun a little, play some golf. It's not like they're calling me every day, Lou, come fix up a second act.'

Ellin thought her father looked a little pale. He had retired officially a few years before, at Sophie's insistence. 'You're not a young man anymore, Lou, you can't sit in draughty theatres or crummy hotel rooms, with the smoke and the noise and the crazy hours. We have enough money, let someone else do it.' Yet Sophie was not as pleased as she thought she would be when Lou stopped working. He had been a playwright for a few years, but his real success came later, as a craftsman who could tighten an act here, change a character there, doctor a script or a play in danger of folding out of town, or faltering in previews. Sophie nagged him about taking time to travel, to garden at their house in the country, to join a club at the condominium in Boca Raton, and he did, but he seemed lost, without purpose.

'I married him for better or for worse, but not for lunch,' she told Ellin, only half joking, when Lou closed his office on Broadway and let his secretary of twenty-eight years go. 'All these years, suddenly he's underfoot all the time, I don't know how I stand it.'

Ellin, for her part, didn't know how her father stood it. She loved and pitied him, this patient, soft-spoken man, gentle and genial, who seemed to exist in his wife's shadow. He raised his voice infrequently, and rarely interfered with Sophie's decisions about where and how they should live, how Ellin should be raised. 'I take care of the little things, whether we should buy a country house or send Ellin away to school, and Lou worries about the important things, like whether we should admit China to the UN.' That was one of Sophie's often repeated phrases during Ellin's girlhood, and it was true; certainly, her mother was a more significant figure in her life than her father, she told the analyst she began seeing after her own divorce. 'It's simply impossible that you have no unfinished business with him,' the doctor told Ellin. 'You're blocking it. Subconsciously you hate him for not protecting you from Sophie. You just won't face it.'

God knew, she tried. She pounded the stuffing out of countless pillows with tennis rackets, trying to contact the anger she was supposed to feel. 'If it's there, it's buried so deep that I'll never get in touch with it,' she told the analyst. 'On the other hand, I have a lot of anger at Sophie. Why don't we work on that?'

Sophie came into the room, scowling. She had the look of a woman who had always known that life would be a struggle, and stubbornly engaged each battle. Ellin thought her mother lived from crisis to crisis, creating one if it did not occur in the unfolding of her days. She was a tall, statuesque woman, dramatically dressed that evening in a long caftan striped in bold colours. Her black hair, greying becomingly at her brows and temples, was carefully coiffed in a thick chignon.

'You look terrible,' she told Ellin after embracing her. 'Where did you get that *shmata*, Klein's?' Ellin didn't answer her; some day, she thought, Sophie will say hello before she tells me how awful I look.

'Lara, baby, no kiss for your old grandmother?' Lara got up dutifully and complied. 'That's better,' Sophie said. 'Here, let me look at you. My God, you've grown a foot since September.' She turned to her daughter. 'Ellin, why don't you buy the child some clothes? Look at her in those raggedy jeans—it's a crime, she's so beautiful, she should dress like that.'

'These are perfectly good—' Lara began defensively, and Ellin shot her a warning look.

'What's the matter, her father the fancy actor can't buy her new jeans?' demanded Sophie. 'And you can't spare a day from your life to take her to Saks?'

'Sophie, the kid looks beautiful, leave her alone,' Lou said, but Sophie ignored him.

'Here, I'll give you my charge card, you'll take her shopping.'

'I don't need your charge card, Sophie, I can afford it. And don't talk about Tony that way, he's her father,' she added, as Lara settled back in front of the television set. 'She just got in from California, after all, we haven't had time to go shopping. I'll do it next week; I have to pick up a cheque at my agent's.'

'Agents, ridiculous, what you do, those silly columns, the book—well, not so silly, but not very steady. If you can't find yourself a rich man, you should at least look for a job. You should have gone to medical school, I always told you that.'

'I never got over a C in maths,' Ellin reminded her.

'That's because you didn't try.' It was a familiar litany; they both knew it by heart.

'I hated the sight of blood. And besides, I have a job. A contract. An advance. Leave me alone.'

'Are you two still arguing about med school?' Lara asked. 'Jesus, that was twenty years ago!'

'Don't swear, it's not nice,' said Sophie and Ellin simultaneously, and they both smiled, acknowledging the bond between them, despite the ever-present strain. Lou and Lara grinned, too, and then Sarah came in to announce that dinner was ready.

Ellin was in the bathroom when she heard Sophie scream. She ran into the dining room; her father, all the colour drained from his face, was slumped over, clutching his chest.

'Lou, Lou, what is it, is it your heart? Lou, talk to me!' Sophie screamed.

'Oh, God . . . Lara, call the police, call an ambulance, get the operator on the phone—hurry!' Ellin pulled her mother away from Lou. 'Sophie, get him down on the floor, get some blankets, get his angina pills, find the doctor's number . . . get away, let him breathe!'

'She's too hysterical to go in the ambulance. Get a cab and follow us,' the attendant told her as two white-suited men lifted her father carefully onto a stretcher. Another wound a blood-pressure cuff around his arm, which hung strangely lifeless. His hand trailed on the thick carpeting as they carried him.

Strangely, Sophie did not protest; she numbly accepted the coat that Ellin held out to her, and in the taxi she clenched her hands together until the knuckles showed white and talked to no one in particular in a rambling monotone which stopped only when she broke into sobs that racked her whole body. Then, Ellin put her arms around her and held her until the sobs stopped.

'Oh, Lou, Lou . . . I'll kill you if you die on me, not now, oh, not now. . . . I told him he didn't look good, I said, Lou, why don't you call Czernak before we go, just have a little checkup. . . . Ellin, did you get Czernak, is he going to be there at the hospital—'

'I called Dr Czernak, Mom,' Lara told her. 'His service said he was off duty or something but they'd try to reach him and I asked who was taking his calls and they said Dr Burton so I got him and he said he'd try to get Czernak, too, but he'd meet Papa at the hospital, and I said Sophie would want a heart doctor, too, and he said he'd get a carryologist—'

'Cardiologist,' Ellin corrected automatically, 'Lara, that was wonderful, that was exactly what you should have done, that was really terrific, thank you.'

Even Sophie looked up in surprise. 'How did you know I'd want a cardiologist?' she asked her granddaughter, startled.

'Because you always want the specialists, the big shots, Sophie,' Lara said, and both women laughed. 'Remember when you took me to get my ears pierced when I came in the fall, and you wouldn't let the lady at Bloomingdale's do it? You took me to that plastic surgeon guy on Park Avenue?'

Ellin chuckled. 'You never told me that, Sophie,' and her mother dismissed it with a wave of her hand—which Ellin took and held, feeling its coldness.

'For my baby's ears, the best,' she said. 'She can't get used to it too early. Oh, Ellin.' She broke into tears again. 'What am I going to do?'

'He's going to be all right, Mama,' she said into her mother's hair. 'You're going to be fine.'

'You'll be okay if he dies,' her mother said in an oddly accusing tone as they waited outside the intensive care unit. 'Your life won't change much, or Lara's. But mine . . .' Her voice trailed off.

Yes, it will, Ellin corrected silently. I won't be anybody's baby anymore. I will be finally, irrevocably, grown up. When he dies, and when you die. She felt a strange sense of déjà vu; she had rehearsed this scene often, often in the early hours of the morning when sleep wouldn't come, and as soon as she saw the opening scene roll into her mind, had banished it. In her scenario, though, it had always been a telephone call; Ellin, your father, or your mother, is dead. And the thought she had banished, quickly, before it had taken root, burrowed into her mind: how will I survive?

The doctor came in then, composed, even smiling. 'You can see him now,' he told Sophie, 'but only for a minute. He's stable. We're pretty certain he had a myocardial infarct, but his signs are good, he's awake. Don't tire him, only stay a few minutes. We've given him medication, he's drowsy.'

Sophie went into the coronary unit, and Ellin remained behind; the doctor gestured her to stay. 'Your father has had a major heart attack,' he told her. 'He's holding his own, but the next forty-eight hours will tell. Dr Czernak is out of town, but I called Ted Burton, he's an excellent heart man. He'll talk to you in a few minutes. I think you should take your mother home, calm her down. Do you have any Valium?'

Ellin nodded. 'Sophie has a whole cabinet of tranquillizers,' she told him.

She talked with Dr Burton, who was encouraging and answered all of her questions. 'You can see him before you leave,' he told her, 'when your mother comes out.'

Sophie returned minutes later, looking somewhat more composed. 'He talked to me,' she told Ellin, 'he told me don't worry, it was only indigestion, he'll be home in a couple of days. What did the cardiologist say?' Ellin started to tell her, but she interrupted. 'I knew it wasn't angina, he's had that before, I knew it was serious.' Why is it always so important that you be right? Ellin thought angrily, and checked herself.

'I'm going to go tell Daddy good night,' she said. 'I'll take Lara in with me for a second.'

'She's a baby,' Sophie complained, 'She doesn't need this.'

'She's not a baby, Sophie, she's doing beautifully. She loves him—she's got a right.' Lara gave her a grateful look, and they went through the swinging doors that opened silently at their approach, into the circular room with the beds arranged, spokelike, around the hub of the nursing station. Her father seemed somehow shrunken, frail and small against the glaring white of the bed and the room. Above him, an invisible stylus told his life in graphs and numbers. That is not who he is, Ellin thought. And a rush of feeling came over her, sharp and sweet.

They spent the weekend at Sophie's and at the hospital, where her father was improving steadily. By Sunday night the doctor pronounced him out of danger. Sophie clung to Ellin, accepting her reports from the doctors, thanking her absently for dealing with the phone calls from her friends. No, there's nothing you can do, she told most of them, though to a few she said, Come to the hospital and sit in the waiting room with her, or, Stop by later tonight for a drink, she needs diversion. Ellin busied herself with small errands, stopping at the brownstone to change her clothes and pick up some things. Upstairs, in her apartment, she picked up a reference book and leafed through it. Shakespeare, she remembered finally, and found the quotation: 'I am all the daughters of my father's house.' The ackowledgement she had sought so long from her mother—the recognition that she was no longer a child—was finally hers, but she did not want it. The taste was bitter; she did not want to be a grown-up, not then—or there, not in her mother's home, in her mother's eyes. But she did it; she listened to the doctors and looked at the ECGs and the test reports, because she was cool and logical and because her mother was frightened and hysterical. And early in the morning, rising from the bed that had been hers as a child, she went to the telephone and called the coronary care nurses, and brought the report of a good night in to her mother with coffee.

During the week, she visited him daily, sometimes with Lara, sitting by his bed, making small conversation, wondering if the slur in his voice had always been there, doing small things for him that he once did for her—tucking in his blankets, trimming his fingernails, fixing his pillows.

Sophie pulled herself together as Lou's condition improved. He'll be home in a couple of weeks, she told Ellin, and then maybe we'll go somewhere in the sun and rest. Your nagging, that will have to stop, Ellin said, and Sophie laughed: Then he'll really think he's going to die, she said.

The night Ellin came back to the brownstone for good, she realized again that it was she, not Lou, for whom she had been frightened. Now I can worry about me, she thought, now I have time. Now my father is going to live, and Sophie will manage, and now I don't need to be frightened any more. I will survive. I am an adult. And she knew that even in the early hours of the morning, the rehearsals would not return.

SIXTEEN

The staff meeting broke up at eleven-thirty, and, as was their custom, Cass and Amelia walked a few blocks uptown to Amelia's club, and played a fast set of racquetball that left Cass breathless and sweaty. Amelia, though nearly thirty years Cass's senior, was a strong, smart player. 'It's not safe to jog on these streets, and the private exercise classes with Pilates cost a fortune. I need competition to exercise, anyway,' Amelia told her. The club had all the facilities Amelia required, and after showering and changing back into street clothes, they met again in the Library for lunch.

The waiter brought Amelia's Perrier and Cass's Bloody Mary. Ordinarily, she did not drink at lunch, but she was nervous this afternoon: Amelia, with her customary sharpness, noticed but said nothing. They filled their plates from the buffet and discussed the staff meeting. Over coffee, Cass told Amelia about Grey Tucker's offer.

Amelia was not surprised. 'Grey has a sense about people,' she said. 'He can spot talent. It's his marketing background; the best CEOs have come up that route, although the financial wizards are beginning to take over. It's an interesting offer.'

'Well? Do you think I should consider it?' Cass asked.

'Do you want my advice or my blessing?' Amelia looked at Cass fondly.

'Both, I guess.' She touched Amelia's hand shyly. 'Amelia, I only got this far because of you. I like it at the agency. I enjoy being associated with the quality of

Amelia Jordan's firm; being associated with you. I have no complaints, none at all. I'm paid very generously, treated wonderfully, and I've never even thought of looking elsewhere.'

Amelia was sceptical. 'But surely the headhunters have been after you?'

'Well, yes. But I haven't ever followed them up. All they had to offer were agency jobs, and if I stayed in advertising, there's no other agency in the city I'd be interested in.'

'That's very kind of you to say—no,' she added, as Cass began to interrupt. 'I know you mean it, and I'm touched. Of course I don't want to lose you; it simply will not be as pleasant at the office without you. I've come to depend on you a great deal, you know that. But I've also considered the future, as you should. I'm certain Grey told you that you can't go much higher as long as I own the agency, didn't he?'

Cass nodded.

'Well, he's right,' Amelia said. 'I couldn't turn my baby over to anyone. Yet I don't want to work forever. I think I might like to enjoy some years of being a rich old lady. So the question becomes, do I sell out, or do I become chairman of the board and let someone else make the important decisions?' She smiled disarmingly. 'Fat chance. I'm much too much of a busybody. That would not be a sweetheart deal for the person who was named president; not with me on the sidelines, second-guessing every decision. A person cannot grow in a post that way. If I sold the agency, I'd have more than enough money for the rest of my life, and Natalie, of course, would be well provided for.'

'Are you considering selling?'

'Not unless someone makes exactly the right offer. And I'm not sure yet what that would be. Oh, there have been feelers, the ones you'd expect. Bates, and O & M, and Interpublic.'

'On what terms?'

'Variable. Essentially, they'd keep the agency the way it is. They've offered me management contracts, of course, but I don't believe I'd like that. I only want to manage what I own. The offers are intriguing. The best one includes a seat on the board of the purchasing agency, and an opportunity in the international division. Chances to travel, do a bit of selling, some consulting, and excellent fringe attractions. I could work only as hard as I wanted to.' She paused, and looked at Cass. 'I want you to know, Cassandra, that if I decide to do that, and you want to stay with the agency, I would insist on a management contract for you, and a generous deal on the stock options.'

Cass was grateful. 'I know that, Amelia, and I appreciate it. But that possibility—selling the agency—changes things for me somewhat.'

'It shouldn't. You should evaluate the AI offer on its merits, realizing, of course, that I'm evaluating the agency purchase offers exactly that way: what's best for me. I do not want you to stay at the agency out of loyalty. Particularly not corporate loyalty. Believe me, the big corporations don't expect that, and they shouldn't. On the other hand, personal loyalty . . . that's what Grey Tucker is buying from you. There's no telling how long he'll stay at Amagansett. If it suits his need to leave, he will. Perhaps he'll take you with him, but he might not. You can't exist in a corporation without a rabbi—a mentor. Grey Tucker is precisely the sort of businessman who'll eventually be called to Washington. Grey hankers for that kind of respectability. But that's quite a way off. I don't think it should be your primary concern just yet.'

'What do you think should be?'

Amelia frowned. 'Well, it doesn't sound exactly solid. As you've outlined the terms, it's rather like being a Cabinet member, isn't it? I mean, you serve at the discretion—the whim, even—of the chief. I think you certainly should have a contract, one that spells out your responsibilities and position quite clearly.'

'Maybe you're right,' said Cass. 'But PAs don't ordinarily have that.'

'Male PAs don't, Cassandra,' Amelia reminded her. 'Most women with that title, after all, are just glorified secretaries. You'll need one. And you should realize, if you haven't already, what an easy target you'll be. For anyone—the wife of a member of the board, the man on the executive committee who's jealous of you, people whose turf is threatened by your presence.'

'But that's just politics,' Cass protested. 'Anyone in a viable position, anyone with authority, has to deal with that.'

'True,' Amelia said thoughtfully, 'But "anyone" is not usually a young, attractive, single woman, personal assistant to a handsome, charismatic, youngish man who also happens to be divorced. People will talk.'

'Oh, hell.' Cass was impatient. 'Let them. This is today, Amelia. There are women executives everywhere you look, in big corporations.'

'And most of them have the same problems. Except that their positions are more precisely defined than yours seems to be, and clearer to the rest of the players. The only person who knows exactly what you'll be doing is Tucker; the job is all in his mind, not on paper,' Amelia said. 'Also, he's made a few enemies on his way to where he is; do you want to fight them, too? Or give them ammunition to use against him?'

Cass shrugged. 'I think perhaps in this instance you're being too cautious, Amelia, if you don't mind my saying so. I've never been discriminated against because I'm a woman. I guess I'd expect that at some levels of business, but not this high up. There are women vice presidents of plenty of corporations.'

'A few,' Amelia conceded. But most of them are good, grey old gals, either too old for scandal or safely married. They could travel with their bosses and people would believe they shared suites with the men so they could save the corporation a few dollars.'

'I'm not planning to have a romance with Grey Tucker,' Cass said indignantly.

'It really doesn't matter if you are,' Amelia countered calmly. 'You know, my dear, you are somewhat naïve. It's one of the charming things about you, but not in this particular case. Simply because you've never been harassed or discriminated against doesn't mean those things don't exist. You've been schooled in a place and time that actually did you a disservice: it promised you could rise as high as a man and not pay any price. Which is fine rhetoric for the institutions of America, but, as my grandfather used to say, is pure Shinola.'

'I think maybe you're wrong about that, Amelia,' said Cass.

'Think what you like, my girl—fiddle deedee! I'm not saying it will happen; I'm saying you should be aware that it might. And get yourself a clever lawyer to negotiate an employment contract for you. Then go do a hell of a job. As long as you do, they'll only nip at your heels, and gossip.'

'Then you think I should take it?'

Amelia smiled. 'I'd be very disappointed in you if you didn't. Perhaps you're right, Cassandra; perhaps times have changed more than I realize. I don't want you to be hurt, dear girl. By the way, what does your friend Nicholas think of all this?'

Cass sighed. 'I haven't told him yet. I didn't want to make any decision before I consulted you. Not because you're my boss. But you've always been honest with me, completely so. And you know everything.'

'Not everything. Just enough to be cautious for you, and very, very proud. People aren't usually honest with women; they don't tell us what we need to know. It's important to find someone like that in Amagansett, and it might not be Tucker. An objective sounding board; someone who won't lie to you. I think you could be a very good manager, if you wanted to. You know how to let your people grow and develop. I'm a good manager, too; I know when to let my people go.' She changed the subject adroitly. 'When are you going to tell Nicholas?'

'Probably tonight. He's going back to California tomorrow. He wants me to come out in May and marry him.'

'And does he expect you to leave your job?' Amelia was suspicious.

'Not now, anyway. Of course, that was before—now, I don't know. He wants me to take a leave for a couple of months. Then, I guess, we'd have a sort of bicoastal marriage. He's in and out of New York a few times a month; more, when the new magazine is launched. But I don't know whether I can handle two big changes at once . . . marriage and a new job.'

'Has he met Grey Tucker?'

Cass was amused at the older woman's perspicacity. 'No, but Nick isn't the jealous type.'

'I didn't mean Nicholas, I meant Grey,' said Amelia. 'Grey is going to want you on call around the clock, you know. He's looking for a backup in his corner, and you'll be it. He'll want you to handle all the flak while he carries out his plans for Amagansett. I don't know exactly how well he'd take to this bicoastal arrangement of yours. Not very happily, I suspect.'

'Funny, I never even considered that,' said Cass.

'Well, you ought to,' Amelia replied tartly. She looked at her watch, a wafer-thin sliver of gold. 'Don't think you're going to slack off just because you're a short-timer now, Cassandra. Let's go back to work, shall we?'

'Okay.' Cass laughed as Amelia signed the bill. And they walked out into the suddenly bright sunshine of Park Avenue together.

Clio brought the AI file back to Cass, who re-read it. What she wanted was not to be found in files or reports; she put them aside and dialled a number from her personal address book.

Carla van Rijn was the former president of a shoe company owned by Amagansett Industries. She'd quit to have a baby, and was just beginning to talk about re-entering the business world. 'When Timmy's in school, maybe I'll do some consulting,' she had said when he was two. That was a long time ago, Cass thought; the brownstone provided her with all the companionship she required, and she had let many of her other friendships wither away. She was vaguely regretful. It was like being in a relationship with a man: you let everyone else go, until one day you wake up and there's no one there except him.

Cass knew several women who had stepped away from successful careers, like Carla, and now called themselves consultants. Certainly a few managed the transition brilliantly; they chose only the most interesting projects, charged very high fees, and planned their work to complement their personal lives instead of the other way around.

But they were exceptions. Being a 'consultant' was also a way for a woman to save face, to avoid announcing—or even accepting—the real truth: that the zest was gone from her job and also from her life. 'I'm having a case of premature evaluation,' Carla told Cass after they exchanged greetings. 'Wondering, is this all there is? But then I think about working again and break out in hives.' She chuckled. 'Jack says I'm disgustingly domestic, and he's right. I lounge around, I play with Timmy, I putter around the house. And I love it. God, by the time I quit, I couldn't remember the last time I had sex in the morning on a weekday. Certainly not since my last job.'

That gave Cass the opening she needed.

'What do you know about Grey Tucker?' she asked Carla. 'I mean personally.'

'Facts or speculation?'

'Both.'

Carla laughed softly. 'Is he taking the Amagansett business elsewhere?' she asked. Carla always knew the story behind the story; the price of her knowledge was a confidence returned, and she knew when to keep her mouth shut.

'No, as a matter of fact, he's given us most of it by now,' said Cass. 'I'm thinking of going to work for him.'

'Well, I have nothing to report from my own experience,' Carla told her, in a voice that implied that she had additional information. 'He's a fair boss, doesn't surround himself with too many idiots, doesn't pinch ass, and when he says he admires your work it doesn't mean he wants to sleep with you.' She went on, warming to her tale; there was nothing Carla enjoyed as much as gossip. 'There was a rumour that he was having an affair with a certain TV star and pulled out of it when they cancelled her contract. Of course, you know how he got into Amagansett in the first place, by marrying the owner's daughter, don't you?'

Cass didn't. She pressed Carla for details.

'Her father owned the Rutledge stores and brought Tucker in to get rid of the losers. First Grey married her, and then he sold her Daddy's stores. Daddy was thrilled; Grey made a lot of money for him, and he was about ready to retire. With, I might add, a new wife who was about the same age as the daughter.'

'What happened to her?'

'She got bored. Said Grey was a workaholic and went back to Texas, where I hear she still gives tailgate parties at the UT home games. She married some oil man and still controls a big block of Amagansett stock. Daddy's new wife was apparently *tant* pissed when Daddy passed away and left the little woman out in the cold. Well, hardly, considering the furs and the jewels and the houses in Acapulco and Tortola, not to mention the little spread in Texas. But no, the daughter, Grey's ex-wife, got the stock. Of course, Grey still votes it all for her: I think her exact words were "If he gave me a tenth of the attention he gave the bottom line, we'd still be married, but since we're not, he might as well be making money for me." '

'Realistic,' Cass commented.

'For sure,' Carla told her. 'Personally, I think he's rather a cold fish. Clever, no doubt about that, but not what you'd call distractable. Not much of a jet setter, but he gets around. I know a few women who've dated him.'

'And?' Cass asked.

'To quote one, who shall remain nameless, the days were boring, but the nights were very hot. Surprised me. I wouldn't have figured him for a great lover. Too absorbed in the company. Goal-oriented. A Type A, I'd say. But you never can tell.'

Another woman Cass knew, a business writer from *Fortune,* had told much the same story, in similar terms. 'He uses people, you know?' Selma Friberg told Cass when she called. 'I did a piece on him for the magazine, and he got more out of me than I did out of him. I ended up telling him everything about a perfume company I'd heard was on the block, and a few weeks later he bought it. Meanwhile he'd taken me to lunch after the story ran, and kind of hinted around about seeing me again. There I was, wrestling with professional ethics—do you sleep with your sources?—and I never got to see which won, my lust or my ethics. He never called me again; zip, nothing. He's a tough one. Why do you want to know?'

Selma wasn't Carla, she was a blabbermouth, so Cass told her she was writing a speech for an agency client, and rang off.

What she'd learned about Grey Tucker was only a bit more than she'd known before, but it was a useful piece of the puzzle. She speculated on Carla's words—'I hear the days were boring, but the nights were very hot'—and squirmed. She was suddenly hungry for sex; should she tell Nick that she was taking the AI job before or after they made love?

Her mind was practically made up. Now all that remained was to explain it to Nick and still get exactly what she wanted; the job, him, and what Carla would call a very hot night. She was to meet him at seven; it would be at least ten by the time they got anywhere near bed, and she had a breakfast meeting the following morning. I haven't made love in the morning in ages, she realized. Not since I've been working for Amelia.

Nick was late as usual, but for once Cass wasn't even slightly annoyed. She was grateful for the extra time; she had a lot on her mind. She relaxed back into the soft leather booth at the Café des Artistes and sipped her wine.

The Café was crowded; she saw familiar faces among the well-dressed, attractive people whose modulated, accentless voices as well as their bland good looks identified them as television personalities. Geraldo Rivera sat at a table beneath a Howard Christy mural of a proud, naked woman with a lush body and a hint of shyness in her hazily defined eyes. David Susskind occupied a banquette nearby. Several networks and local channels had production facilities and studios in the neighbourhood.

The Café had a romantic, shabby elegance; the vitality in the room was provided by its clientele, overwhelmingly confident, supremely assured. There was a time when being alone in a fashionable restaurant like this one would have intimidated Cass; when she felt like an intruder, unsure of her response if someone—the maître d', perhaps—questioned her right to be there. Not now. The Café no longer seemed like a party to which she had come uninvited. The waiter who brought her a fresh *kir* addressed her by name, and enquired after Nick.

She was beginning to get annoyed at Nick's tardiness; she was working up to righteous anger when she caught sight of him at the far end of the room. He had stopped to talk to a couple she recognized—a former senator and his wife. They owned an apartment in Des Artistes, above the restaurant; once Nick had taken her there, to a dinner party. The apartment, like the couple, was slick and cool and full of glossy surfaces that were icy to the touch, and reflected multiple images. They served very dry white wine and spare, fresh food, small portions on translucent plates. Cass had not liked them very much, and was bored almost to somnolence during the evening.

Nick caught sight of her and waved, but as he moved toward her, others stopped him, reaching out to touch his sleeve, catch his attention. She sighed; it would be ten minutes before he got to her.

She enjoyed watching him take over a room as he was doing now, liked the characteristic jabs and gestures of his body that punctuated his conversation. The women in the room were drawn to him, too; she anticipated the moment when their heads would turn and follow his progress to her table. Would they wonder who she was, and why he had bestowed his attention on her?

Sometimes she enjoyed that kind of speculation. Often it was obvious why two people were drawn to one another. Her friends Holly and Paul, for instance: they were a couple who made sense. Both of them were misfits who could never be part of any group; once they found each other, they had no need to. Or Marissa, a model she knew, and Jean Paul, her photographer lover: they were both beautiful, and equally boring, but they spent their time admiring themselves, and so were not bored.

Nick was stopped again by someone as he threaded his way toward her. Cass felt a rush of attraction for him; what was it? she wondered. Men did not excite her with their looks. First came their words, their style, even before she noticed their physical appearance. Handsome was extra, and not always worth what came with it; cleverness counted more. Nick was clever; she liked his quick, agile mind, enjoyed the sparring and parrying; as accomplished as she was at it, she appreciated a man who challenged her.

Quiet men had interested her at one time; she remained interested until she learned whether the silence meant shyness or passivity—most of her difficulties with men came from misjudging that. The Marlboro Man, Paula teased her; she said Cass's fantasies were titillated by the sort of media campaigns she herself excelled at producing. 'Of course,' Cass told her. 'That's exactly why I'm good at them. I'm in touch with the sexual fantasies of my customer. You want someone to understand that even though the spot on your face is six inches in diameter and pulsing, *he's* not going to notice? Well, I *am* that customer. Give me your spot cream account, and I'll give you the biggest share of the spot market.'

Cass liked men who were smart. She didn't think a great deal about what the clever words meant, about what they said of the man himself, of his values. Such things mattered a great deal more to Paula, who had crossed more than one man off her list because of an offhand remark that revealed him to be a civilized racist, or even a garden-variety bigot. Cass, however, was more lenient; she might forgive one casual reference to niggers, but was guarded thereafter.

Cass stopped musing; she saw that Nick had extricated himself from the man who had stopped him, and she smoothed her hair as he came toward her, conscious of the women who would inspect her to see whom Nick Pappas found attractive. She and Nick made an appropriate couple; few might wonder what he saw in her. We are a lot alike, she thought as she considered how best to bring up the Amagansett offer; he is enough like me to understand why I want to take this job.

She said that, when she told him about it. He nodded. 'That's right,' he said, 'we are alike. Ambitious.' She frowned, as he drank down the Stolichnaya martini that had materialized, unnoticed by her, at his elbow. Nick was the kind of man whose preferences were remembered, and probably recorded, by maîtres d'.

'I think you should take it,' he told her finally. 'It's a fantastic chance. You'd be stupid to turn it down.'

She was nonplussed; she had not expected this immediate capitulation.

'You mean you don't mind?'

'Of course I mind,' he said impatiently. 'You think I'm crazy about the fact that you're going to be so wrapped up in this big new job that you won't have any time for me?'

'Don't be silly, I'll have plenty of time for you,' she began, but he interrupted with a shake of his head.

'Come on, Cass, not for months, that's not the way it works, you know that.' Her face fell, and he reached for her hand. 'Honey, if I wanted a broad who waits up for me at night with nothing more on her agenda than whether I liked the dinner she spent all day cooking, I'd find one.' He grinned. 'I did once, as a matter of fact. Married her. Dull as Sundays.' Cass thought of what Nick had told her about Shirley, his ex-wife, and smiled back. 'Cass, when I'm tired out, the last thing I want is a dame who's waiting for me to make her day. I want one who's just as exhausted as I am.' Cass knew that wasn't true; Nick's seemingly inexhaustible energy never ceased to amaze her. He could work for hours at a stretch, and go from the magazine to dinner to a party and on to dance until close to dawn without flagging. A couple of hours of sleep, and he bounded out of bed again, annoyed that the rest of his world was barely waking up. 'Look, you'll be earning so much money you can fly out to the Coast on weekends. Or I'll come here. We'll manage, don't worry. Besides, I have plenty to do myself for the next few months, getting *Orange* launched right. Although I gotta tell you I've really been counting on that sail around Mexico.'

A sail, she thought. Not a honeymoon, a sail. Maybe the offer did expire at midnight, after all.

'I could take a couple of weeks off between leaving Amelia and starting at Amagansett,' she offered.

Nick shook his head. 'I can't get away until June.'

'And I can't take a new job and then leave for vacation a month later, either.'

'I know you can't. But don't sweat it, baby, the Pacific

will still be there when you've conquered the corporate world.'

But will you? Cass wondered. He didn't mention marriage, and neither did she. Instead, he ordered a bottle of champagne, and offered a toast to her new job. 'Go for it, Cass,' he told her, and she felt his sincerity. 'Knock 'em all on their asses!'

In the cab on the way to his apartment, awash in champagne and a feeling of sadness she couldn't identify, she snuggled close to him, fingering his chest lightly between the buttons of his shirt. That was not like her; Nick was surprised, and even more so when she put her head in his lap and pursed her lips against the bulge in his trousers, blowing the warm air of her mouth against him until he hardened.

'Easy, baby,' he whispered, 'we're almost home.' And he groaned softly with pleasure.

Once inside the apartment, she grasped him with an urgency that surprised them both; he took her there, on the cool tile of the entrance foyer, the first time. Later, in bed, they made love wildly; she was unaware of where she began and he left off, of whose touch made which of them sigh, cry, explode. She could not get enough of him; they teased, tasted, filled, engaged, surrounded, explored all apertures and surfaces with abandon unusual for her. She held nothing back, propelled by her desire to be inside of him, to be lost in his body; she came in overwhelming waves, in long, shuddering gasps, and he matched her desire with his own until finally, silently, they slept, exhausted by what they had not said.

SEVENTEEN

Cass threw herself into her work at the agency with renewed vigour; preparing to leave, she wanted everything in good order for whoever would succeed her. She and Amelia had decided to postpone the announcement of her departure; everyone knew something was afoot, but only Clio was let in on the secret. Cass thought her secretary's talents were wasted in her present job, and Amelia agreed; they offered the new position of director of project management to Clio, and she was delighted, accepting it on the spot.

'Look, it's just a fancy name for ratcheting the account groups, being a high-priced nag,' said Cass, amused. 'And you haven't even asked what kind of a raise you're getting.'

Clio grinned broadly, her teeth very white in her creamy, coffee-coloured skin. She was Jamaican by birth, one of the fortunate few whose family had migrated to New York, kept all seven children healthy, together, and out of trouble, and seen three of them go to college on scholarships and graduate with honours. Clio contributed to the education of her younger sisters and brothers, even on her modest salary. Cass knew that Clio supplemented her income with occasional modelling jobs; she was tall and exotic-looking, and could have earned much more if she devoted more time to it. 'It's no life for me,' she told Cass once. 'Oh, as a part-time gig, it's fine, but I can't see myself as a clotheshorse forever. And forever isn't very long for models, just until the years start showing.'

Clio was a smart, ambitious woman, frankly eager for as much responsibility as Cass offered her, but seemingly willing to take much less than her talents and education indicated she could do. 'You're entirely overqualified,' Cass had told her, scanning Clio's résumé. 'I'm afraid that right now, all I'm looking for is a secretary. Well, an executive assistant,' she amended, realizing that, in fact, she did need more. At that time she had just been made vice president and creative director; the personnel office sent up several women, but Cass was not satisfied with any of them. She had to dictate every word of every letter; none of the others seemed capable of much independent thought. By the time she finished explaining what she wanted, she might as well have done it herself. She knew she would not have to with Clio; still, she worried that the handsome young woman would soon grow bored, and quit.

'Ah, already you need more than a secretary,' Clio had said in her pleasant, lilting voice. 'And sometime you'll need more than that, and I'll be here.'

Cass hired her, apologizing for the ridiculously low salary, and realized quickly how lucky she was that Clio had accepted. She soon made herself indispensable, not only to Cass but to everyone at the agency.

'Can I borrow Clio for a few days in traffic? Margie's out sick, and it's a terrible mess over here,' the office manager implored. 'Production's all screwed up, the paste-up girl quit and I don't have time to show the new one around, could you send Clio over to get us organized?' pleaded the head of that department. Clio went, cheerfully, learning new skills each time, but never leaving until Cass's own needs were met. Cass and Amelia had been looking for the right job for Clio for some time; now that Cass was leaving, she wanted to do right by her efficient, clever assistant.

Clio obliged Cass by enquiring about the salary commensurate with her new duties, and rolled her eyes thankfully upward when she heard the figure. 'Goodbye, girdle catalogues,' she said, and Cass smiled. It pleased her to see Clio finally earn a respectable amount of money; she enjoyed being the one to tell her, and accepted the thanks that rightfully belonged to Amelia, who had tacked another two thousand dollars onto the figure that Cass had suggested.

'You're going to be earning every cent of it,' she told Clio. And Clio did, first finding Cass a competent if uninspired secretary from one of the account groups. Cass suggested that she find one for herself, too. 'You'll be needing her,' she warned. But one evening, when Cass was preparing to leave the agency, she found Clio retyping meeting reports, and chided her none too gently.

'You're not exploiting Marianne by asking her to do the work we pay her to do, you know,' she told Clio.

'But she knows I can do these quicker than she can, and face it, it's shit work anyway,' Clio replied.

'It's the same work you were doing until a week ago,' Cass reminded her. 'We hired Marianne because we needed you for other things, things that required different abilities. Did you think it was shit work when you were doing it for me?'

'Not always,' Clio said. 'But to tell you the truth, every once in a while, when I was typing these reports, I thought, I ought to be writing them, I'm as smart as she is.' She blushed; the wave of embarrassment tinted her cheeks a rosy brown. 'Well, not that smart. But I would forget that I was only a secretary, and I'd want to change the words, rearrange things, put my own stamp on them, just so you'd know I was able to. I felt like the housekeeper who is actually a princess, except, of course, I wasn't.'

Cass smiled at her. 'We noticed, Clio. That's why we gave you this job. Your innate talent showed right through the housekeeper drag. Maybe Marianne's will, too. Forget what you felt like when you were doing what she's supposed to be doing now—no, don't forget entirely, just don't obsess about it. You can't do your work efficiently if you're here typing until midnight, while she's hanging out by the water cooler all day with nothing to do. You have to learn how to supervise; that's important, too.'

Clio covered her typewriter. 'Good girl,' Cass said. 'God, I'm going to miss you at Amagansett. I wanted to take you, but Amelia wouldn't let me. I'm glad for you, but sorry for myself.'

'Why, thank you,' said Clio, beaming. 'Listen, would you like to . . . no, you're probably on your way somewhere fancy.'

'Not at all, and I'd love to go have a drink. Several, in fact,' Cass finished.

And they went to Charley O's, and forgot the agency, and talked about clothes and men and a play both of them had seen, and whether Manhattan was really falling apart or just looked that way, and why some women seemed to hate their mothers so passionately. Cass wanted to pick up the bill, but Clio stopped her. 'Let's split it,' she said, and Cass, seeing it was important to her, agreed.

Cass let herself into a silent house. Paula was in Cambridge with Jake, and when she phoned upstairs, she could hear the echo of the phone ringing in Ellin's empty apartment.

She shucked off her shoes, then stripped and stood under a hot shower for a long time, flexing and stretching her tired body. She washed the city grit from her hair, towelled it almost dry, and brushed it in long strokes, waving the blow drier around it, enjoying the tingling that overtook the beginnings of a headache, sending the nagging little ache back into the recesses of her brain. She got into jeans and a soft old challis shirt, realizing that it was only eight o'clock, and that a long evening stretched ahead of her. She had work to do, but she didn't want to do it; she was hungry, but she didn't feel like going out. There was a lamb chop in the refrigerator that would surely go bad if she didn't cook it tonight, though, and she couldn't bring herself to let it spoil; the waste appalled her. So, reluctantly, she put it under the grill and made a salad for herself, thinking about Paula, missing her.

Cass didn't approve of Jake; she did not trust him not to hurt Paula again. She never had, and she had been right not to, she thought. Even so, since his sudden reappearance in Paula's life, she had to admit that his conduct had been exemplary; according to Paula, he was considerate and loving as he had never been in the old days. And he had gone out of his way to be conciliatory to Cass.

Cass wasn't actually jealous of Jake. But always before, when either she or Paula was involved with a man, they talked to each other—endless discussions in which they mulled over previous affairs, analysed past behaviour, considered future possibilities. Cass and Paula had been speculating about men, and their relationships with men, for fifteen years. They knew each other's tendencies and weaknesses, and pointed them out, each to the other, with loving familiarity.

Cass always fell in love the same way; the patterns of her affairs unfolded inexorably. She kept a mental checklist of every lover's actions; if he behaves in this way, does that, doesn't ask this, insists on that, she thought, then he loves me. If a man acquired too many check marks against him, she proceeded to fall out of love in an equally ritualized fashion; she withdrew from him, bit by bit, until each new slight or disappointment did not trouble her as much as it confirmed her belief that he was, in fact, the wrong man. 'You're like a salmon swimming upstream,' Paula told her. 'Knowing you're going to fuck, and die, and doing it anyway.'

'And your trouble is that you never let go of men you once loved,' said Cass. 'Even after you see through them, or figure out why they're such bastards; you don't ever break it off completely. And after you fall out of love, you never even wonder what you saw in them to begin with. Maybe that's your trouble.'

'Oh, do I have trouble?' Paula was amused, tolerant, glowing, happy, and bursting with vigour; she was painting a vivid mural on her bedroom wall, in colours that made Cass shudder. She daubed a final bit of purple on the tail of an enormous bird; perched on a ladder, she waved the brush and Cass moved away from the threatening splatters.

'Uh huh,' said Cass. 'Your trouble is that you believe in first, true love.'

Paula didn't deny it. What was it Max had said? Only virgins and children believed in true love. Max, she thought sadly. I miss him. 'But that's still easier to find than what you're looking for,' she told Cass.

'Which is what?'

'Perfection,' said Paula. She jumped off the ladder and advanced on Cass, waving the paintbrush. A drop of purple paint dripped onto Cass's nose, right in its centre. Paula laughed, spinning Cass around to face the mirror. 'And now you have it!' she pronounced, and Cass giggled, too.

That was the last time, she reflected, that she'd felt really close to Paula. They had managed a brief lunch together earlier that week, but it was not very satisfying. Paula did all the right things, and said them, too; like Nick, she ordered champagne to toast Cass's new job, but part of her wasn't there; tuned out, Cass thought. The part of Paula that feels and cares and is sensitive isn't there anymore. She isn't as concerned about anyone as she used to be; not even about Ellin, who was going through a rocky time in the aftermath of her father's near-fatal heart attack. That Paula had barely noticed Ellin's unhappiness was final proof to Cass of her friend's defection into love. So she didn't broach the subject of her own misgivings about the new job, and her quandary about Nick; she didn't want to discover that perhaps she, too, had lost that caring part of Paula.

Cass knew vaguely the details of Jake's reappearance. Paula told her that a deal of some kind had been made—'Frankly, it's not entirely clear to me, either,' Paula said, which worried Cass; she hoped Paula wasn't compromising her own professional ethics for Jake. She knew that the original charges against Jake, the bombing charges, had been dropped or changed, though she did not know why, or how, and Paula was unspecific when Cass pressed her. He had been put on probation on a misdemeanour charge, for a six-month period; Cass learned that from *The New York Times,* which ran a small paragraph headlined 'Ex-Radical Returns, Is Released.' Now he was in Boston, studying both for his final exams at law school and the summer bar.

Cass was mystified. 'How did he ever talk them into letting him back into Harvard?' she asked Paula, who shrugged.

'It surprised me, too,' she admitted. 'But he had a perfect four point before he left, and there are some people in the administration at the Law school who still think highly of him. I believe the Dean said he thought it was worth it if he could rescue a formerly brilliant legal mind.'

'And how is he going to get past the bar admissions committee?'

Paula shrugged again. 'Beats the hell out of me,' she said. 'He told me not to worry about it. Although I do, of course. But he's pulled rabbits out of hats before.'

And wool over your eyes, too, Cass thought, though, for once, she did not say it. Paula went on. 'He has a job lined up in Boston as soon as he takes his exams. Consumer advocacy. Not much money, but a good opportunity.'

Not as good as the opportunity you're giving him, Cass said silently.

Both Cass and Paula were right in their assessments of each other. Cass was beginning to make mental checks against Nick; he had not called her for several days, and the longing she felt for him was hardening into resentment.

Nor had Paula changed; she loved Jake as passionately now as she had in the old days, she realized, as she opened layers of herself to him, first tentatively, then completely, that spring. She forgot the promise of grief; almost, but not completely. Sometimes, after they made love, in the shabby furnished room with the cheap, thin mattress on the ugly iron bed, the frayed rag rug and the one reading chair with stuffing bursting through its worn upholstery, she remembered. Sated, full of his juices, the warmth seeping through her body, lulling it to sleep, she thought: it will almost be a relief when he finally hurts me again.

No one heard her thoughts, but she knew that Cass knew them. She could feel Cass's understanding like a soft, warm sweater on a chilly morning. And she resented it, just as she had years before, when her mother warned her against sunburn, or rainstorms, or some other, predictable emergency for which ultimately she would not be properly prepared.

Cass ate her lamb chop and salad, and washed the dishes, putting her kitchen to rights. In the library, she opened her briefcase, taking out a draft of the press release announcing her new post with Amagansett. Someone from the company's public relations department had sent it over that morning, and she frowned as she read it; it seemed purposely vague and undefined.

'Ms Campbell will head a new marketing relations department, advising on consumer services for all Amagansett divisions,' it read. 'In this capacity, she will report to Peter Marks, Amagansett corporate marketing director.'

She scanned the remainder of the story, which cited the awards she had won at the agency, and ended with a brief statement from Tucker: 'Ms Campbell's experience and ability will be a significant asset in Amagansett's continued growth.'

She crossed out several lines in the release and rewrote the offending paragraph. When she was finished, she pulled out her old Olivetti and retyped the story. 'Cassandra Campbell joins Amagansett Industries as a special assistant to chief executive officer and president Grey Tucker. She heads a new marketing relations department which will evaluate acquisitions and supervise strategic planning for the corporation and its divisions and subsidiaries,' it now read. That will give Pete Marks an ulcer, she thought, but what the hell, we might as well start out with the game and the players understood and identified.

Her work done, she paced the apartment restlessly. She tried to call Nick in California; she got his answering machine, and hung up without leaving a message. She turned on the television set, switching channels at random; nothing appealed to her. She heard the front door of the brownstone open, and went to see who it was; she was glad to see Vic, and stood in front of her door, making small talk, looking him over. She did not realize she was flirting, inviting his attentions, until he eyed her just as frankly and suggested that she join him for a drink. A fantasy played briefly on the silent screen in her mind; she saw herself in bed with him, legs tangled together, his long, dark hair on her belly, his olive skin against her own fairness. He had brooding eyes and a full, sensual mouth; she imagined it at her breast, and a shiver of excitement went through her. She stopped it quickly. You're getting as shameless as Paula is—was, she corrected mentally, before Jake came back. That's all you need, screwing the hired help. She backed into her apartment. 'I . . . uh, I thought it was Ellin. We were supposed to see a movie tonight. Been planning it for ages.' Why was she babbling? All she had to do was say no; you've done it a million times, she told herself.

He shrugged. 'Sure,' he said, 'a movie. Well, if you change your mind, the offer is open.' And he disappeared down the stairs.

Later she heard the front door again and knew that it

must be Ellin. She felt a rush of sympathy for her housemate; her year in New York isn't getting off to such a great start, she thought, remembering her own first months in the city. That was bad luck, her father's heart attack. And Paula's off with Jake, I'm busy getting ready to start a new job. . . . Ellin must be lonely. She would go and suggest a movie, give truth to her lie to Vic. But maybe they could simply skip the movie, and talk. Cass wanted to talk to a woman friend tonight. About Nick, who was so oddly compliant, supportive in such an offhand way, and almost never in when she phoned him. About Grey, who was not surprised when she accepted his offer; he had had no doubt that she would say yes, although she waited longer than the deadline to inform him, and insisted on a negotiated employment contract. He accepted her demands calmly; whatever you want, Cass, he had said, and he was more than generous.

If she had her choice, she'd talk to Paula tonight, but Ellin would do. She'd pay some attention to her, cheer her up and listen to her troubles. And then she would tell Ellin hers.

It was not Ellin coming in—the sound of the door was Vic, leaving. Cass watched his broad back disappear down the steps of the brownstone from behind the curtain of the window in her living room, and frowned. She was drawn to Vic in a visceral way, but she could anticipate an awkward situation. He had the look of trouble. A brooder, she thought; the kind of man who offered little, gave less, seduced women with his passivity. She wondered if the woman he was going to meet—she knew it was a woman—knew that. And if she cared.

EIGHTEEN

Cass need not have worried about Ellin. Despite the unexpected jolt of Lou's heart attack, she was doing just fine. Certainly, her day was beginning beautifully. The roses were pale yellow, creamy at the edges. Their fragrance filled the air around Ellin as she lifted them by their long, thorny stems out of the crackly green tissue paper.

She ran her finger over the fine engraving on the card nestled among the flowers. '*Encore?*' it read, and was signed, simply, 'Philippe.'

She thought there was probably a Mrs Philippe, in Westport, perhaps, or Paris. He had made no reference to her, but he had a settled, well-cared-for air about him that made her think he was married. He was unspecific about his business, although he had mentioned frequent commuting via Concorde; his card indicated offices in Paris, London, and New York.

She would ask Martine about him—she had met him at one of Martine's dinner parties. 'Piss elegant' was the way Ellin described both Martine and her elaborately appointed Fifth Avenue apartment to Cass and Paula. Martine was a designer Ellin had met while doing a story for a women's magazine on careers in fashion. She was sophisticated and sharp-tongued, and she frowned when people laughed at her bilingual malapropisms; French was Martine's native language, but she adored American slang, and her efforts to combine the two were often unintentionally hilarious.

The walls of Martine's flat were upholstered in rich

brown patent leather; the floors were mirrored, accented here and there by colourful Moroccan rugs. The party at which Ellin met Philippe, the night before, was a small one: a dozen people reclined on butter-soft suede cushions around a long, low mahogany table, and were served couscous shish kebab by Martine's Algerian maid.

The man seated next to her was Philippe; they chatted amiably for the rest of the evening, and he brought her home in a chauffeured Bentley. He was charming, attentive, and a dozen years her senior; he was, he said seriously as he brought her to the door of the brownstone, 'captivated' by her.

The compliment lightened her steps as she made her way upstairs. In California, glamorous rooms crowded with people who looked and smelled secure and expensive intimidated her; in New York, they did not. She was good in settings like Martine's; she drew people out, talked with them easily, and was funny in a vaguely sarcastic way. She made people smile, and sometimes chuckle—men who appreciated her wit, and women who assumed that, like themselves, she was in charge of her own successful life.

She measured herself against them, and was pleased with her self-assessment. In California she had wondered, Am I as pretty, as young, as appealing as they are? In New York, those self-doubts rarely attacked her; she felt as alive, as interesting, as cosmopolitan as the people she met, and she looked forward to New York parties with none of the reservations she had always had about such events in Los Angeles.

She called Philippe to thank him for the roses, and in his rich, romantically accented voice he invited her to accompany him to the ballet that evening; he apologized for the short notice, but said that he had come into the tickets only that morning, and remembered that she had said she was fond of the ballet. She accepted with pleasure, revising her plans for the day; after her lunch with a magazine editor, she would go look for a blouse to wear with her grey moiré taffeta skirt. She'd received a cheque for three hundred dollars the day before, payment for the foreign rights to an article she'd written months ago. It was money she hadn't counted on, and it really should go to Lara's orthodontist. But she deserved a splurge, she told herself, and decided that today she would have one.

She studied the young woman who stood next to her in the elevator as covertly as she could. A model, she decided; the enormous duffel bag, in which jars and bottles rattled as the woman nervously picked it up and put it down again, was as much of a giveaway as the portfolio case she also carried. She was quite tall, and very thin. Ellin was not surprised when the woman got off with her on the ninth floor; a little makeup and a push-up bra and she could be the cover girl, she decided.

The magazine's offices were all blue-and-white chintz, with framed photostats of previous covers on the walls. Ellin was surrounded by cleavage, tousled hair, and glistening, seductively parted lips, not only in the reception area but in the empty office to which she was led by Pandora, the article editor.

'Here are the assignment books,' Pandora said. 'Pick out a few that interest you and we'll talk about them at lunch.'

Ellin leafed through the thick, loose-leaf notebooks, giggling as she read some of the assignment sheets. These probably represent every sexual fantasy the woman has had since she was *in utero,* she thought. 'Does Penis Size Increase Sexual Pleasure?' headlined one page, and Ellin laughed out loud as she read the editor's notes. 'This should be meaty, but not tacky,' she read. 'Perhaps we could get some Really Big Names to talk—suggest Liz Ashley, maybe Keaton or Taylor. We can always fall back on Margaret Trudeau. Also, need some experts—one of the celebrity shrinks, or maybe Joyce Brothers.'

There were pages and pages of story suggestions, many overwritten in a girlish hand with violet ink, circles over the *i*'s, and a lot of ellipses. Ellin passed over How the Stars Fight Acne, and Will an Affair Revive Your Marriage?, and selected three stories she thought were workable. Some of the magazines for which she free-lanced preferred writers to come up with their own story ideas; others, like this one, adhered to strict formats, and knew exactly what they wanted.

As usual, Pandora's ideas about what Ellin should write were different from her own. Ellin had completed four assignments for Pandora, each of which was offered to her with a flourish over an expensive, winey lunch at a different elegant restaurant. Pandora was in her early thirties, with a lush body and terrible skin. 'Why don't you do this piece for us on older women and younger men?' she suggested over blini and caviar at the Russian Tea Room. She did not look Ellin in the eye as she spoke; instead, she craned her neck to see any celebrities who might be in the plush, red-and-gold mirrored room. 'Isn't that Shelley Winters over there?' she asked, and Ellin dutifully looked around.

'Not unless she's lost twenty years and fifty pounds,' Ellin replied. 'Sure, older women, younger men . . . I can do that.'

'Good,' said Pandora happily, and for the next half hour, they discussed the assignment.

Ellin knew it meant that Pandora had a new lover—nineteen, probably. Pandora always suggested articles according to what was happening in her own life. 'Why don't you do a piece for us on casual sex?' she asked Ellin once. 'You know, one-night stands, weekend affairs, the problems and the payoffs.' And then, a few months later, 'Blue-collar men—is there a Mr Rough and Ready who's right for you? Aim it at the professional woman, the one who usually dates doctors and lawyers.' There was the piece on the new abstinence, the one on midlife crisis, the article about acupuncture face-lifts and another on clitoral orgasms. 'I'm expecting an assignment on bisexuality any day now,' Ellin told Cass and Paula.

Pandora talked deadlines and copy length but not money. That was fine with Ellin; like many women she knew, she was uncomfortable negotiating on her own behalf. That was why she had an agent; she could get the assignments herself, but she hated to ask for money. She was likely to accept whatever was offered her; her agent had no such liability, and Ellin was grateful to her for handling that onerous task, and glad to pay her 10 percent.

Ellin's magazine business had improved dramatically since her move to New York. Assignments came frequently; editors who saw her work in one magazine called to ask her to write for their own. Most of them considered her still a Californian, which gave her an extra edge over the New York writers. 'We get so tired of the Manhattan perspective,' said the articles editor from *Glamour*. 'It's refreshing to know what women are thinking about in the rest of the country,' said the woman from *McCall's*.

Ellin spent a good deal of her time cultivating editors; she enjoyed what she thought of as The Hustle. 'I get turned on just by talking to people in my business,' she told Cass and Paula. 'I'll come away from a lunch with one editor and be full of ideas—say, something I can write for her and use another way for someone else. I get energy here just from the streets.'

'Except you're not very disciplined about it,' said Cass. 'You told me yesterday you haven't written a word all week.'

'This week that's true,' said Ellin. 'But I've learned to trust it—when it's ready to happen, it happens. And I've never missed a deadline yet,' she added proudly.

That was true, but it was getting more difficult. The city was a distraction as the ocean outside her house in Malibu had never been. Just going out for the newspaper could take hours. A chance meeting with someone in a bookstore or on a bus; a little flirtation that turned into a cup of coffee, and maybe a friendship. She was by nature a reporter and observer; she was inquisitive, she talked to strangers, and people responded to her. She was friendly, if watchful; she approached, and was approachable. One day she walked downtown to the Staten Island ferry, and struck up a conversation with a crew member, who invited her up to the bridge. He introduced her to the captain, and she sat on a tall stool, riding back and forth across the Upper Bay, listening to anecdotes about ferry life. Her hosts pointed out all the landmarks, and when their shift was over, they invited her to join them for a beer. She had a wonderful time, and she sold a piece to *The Village Voice* based on her experiences of the day.

Pandora paid the bill with a flourish of her American Express gold card; she replaced it in her Vuitton handbag, and turned to Ellin expectantly. 'Well, tell me how life in the big city is going for you, hmm? Done anything glamorous or wonderful lately?'

I could tell her about Philippe, Ellin thought; that's what she means by glamorous and wonderful. Pandora was a voyeur; she thought that people actually lived the kind of lives she suggested her writers cover, lives in which the size of men's penises and the appearance of a wrinkle in one's face were of paramount importance. Perhaps they were—Ellin didn't really care, as long as she was well paid for writing about them in that breathless, girlish style to which Pandora's magazine was addicted.

'Well, I went to a fascinating lecture at the Jungian Institute last week,' she began, but Pandora began looking around the room again, so Ellin mentioned the delightful Frenchman who was taking her to the ballet that evening, and regained Pandora's attention.

After lunch, Ellin called her agent. 'I got a new assignment from Pandora,' she told her, and gave her the details.

'Terrific, but I'd be happier to hear more about the book.'

'Oh, the novel's coming along fine,' Ellin said. She thought guiltily that she had not actually written any new pages for two months; she was turning out magazine pieces in record time, because they were easy, and because she needed the money. She panicked for a few minutes after she replaced the phone in the booth in the restaurant. What if she couldn't actually finish the novel? That's ridiculous, she told herself; you always finish what you start. But what if you finish it and it stinks? said the nagging counterpoint voice in her head. Ellin decided not to think about that now; she would go to SoHo, maybe to Victoria Falls, and find a lacy, sheer, feminine blouse to wear with Philippe that evening. Maybe he wasn't married. Or maybe he was. So what? He wasn't her husband. Maybe an affair with her was just what the charming Frenchman needed to revive his marriage. Pandora would certainly think so. And Ellin, who knew already that Philippe might be a diversion but clearly not an obsession, didn't especially care.

She stopped in for a quick check on her parents before returning home to dress for the evening. It was not a pleasant visit. Now that Lou was assured of a complete recovery from his heart attack, Sophie was more demanding and neurotic than ever. Next to her, Ellin's father seemed small and diminished, and Sophie's high-pitched voice and obvious agitation made Ellin uneasy.

Sophie was fretting about money. She talked nonstop about how much the special nurses Lou had required right after his heart attack cost; about the high price of the apartment in Florida; about how expensive electricity was. Sophie had never worried about a Con Ed bill in her life; the bills had always gone to Lou's office, and Lou himself rarely refused Sophie anything she demanded.

Poor Sophie, Ellin thought. She never figured on having to take care of herself, much less an invalid husband. And she's pressuring Daddy too much, he can't take it, not with his heart. She told Sophie that, and got a baleful glare for her trouble. 'Look who's the expert on marriage,' she said. Ellin swallowed her retort; perhaps, after all, Sophie had a point.

She had a cup of tea with them in the den, and listened with half an ear to the bickering. It was sad to see what was happening to her parents' marriage. Theirs had been a relationship built on the most solid foundation—that Lou would take care of Sophie, and she would not ever have to worry that he could not. Ellin knew what was eating her mother; fears about money, about money and old age and inflation and sickness. She even suggested, when Lou stepped out of the room, that Sophie ask him exactly what state his finances were in; she shouldn't have to worry about a light bill, for God's sake. Lou probably had plenty stashed away. He was the kind of man who took out insurance, paid his bills promptly, and had undoubtedly made ample provisions for contingencies.

'He doesn't want me to know,' Sophie told Ellin.

'So?' Ellin demanded. 'You're entitled to know. It's not unreasonable, given the circumstances. Just so you can stop going around the apartment turning off the lights all the time.'

That was a new habit, which Sophie acquired after Lou got sick. That, and her constant nagging about money. Lou, too, was slightly irascible; his usual good humour was evaporating as the intensity of Sophie's concern with economic security increased. He was bitter and sarcastic; Ellin had never heard him be that way before.

He's worried, too, she thought. To be a man meant to Lou that his family would never need to be concerned with money; he was raised in a time and a class that defined a man that way, a *mensch*. Ellin thought it sad that her parents could not be truthful with one another, could not talk about what was bothering them both. Even after Lou's official retirement, he had worked from time to time; a month before his heart attack, he'd rushed off to Boston to fix up the book of a show that was in previews there. Not anymore, said his doctor; a man with his heart couldn't take that kind of pressure, those crazy hours.

Ellin thought the life was dwindling out of her father, as the fear and bitterness seeped in. The rock on which Lou and Sophie had built their marriage was crumbling, and Ellin could do nothing to stop it. Certainly, Sophie wouldn't listen to her.

'If he wanted me to know his business, he'd tell me,' she told Ellin firmly.

'If you have to know, if you need to know, why don't you ask?' Ellin replied.

'Because I don't want to know,' Sophie told her.

'I don't understand,' said Ellin.

'Exactly!' said Sophie, triumphant. There the conversation stopped; Lou came back into the room, and they talked of other things.

Ellin's worries about her parents troubled her. What if they get a divorce? she wondered. After all, other parents did. People the same age as Sophie and Lou. Ellin was aghast at the thought of it. Not her parents! Had Lara ever reacted that way? Of course not; Lara was only a baby when Tony left. She wasn't used to a family where the parents lived together, as Ellin herself was. Lara probably barely remembered any other kind of family than the one-parent kind she'd grown up in. But Ellin couldn't imagine Sophie and Lou any way except together.

She was still fretting about her parents when she came home; they were among the few certainties in Ellin's life, the fixed points on her emotional compass. However, she reasoned, while she could for the moment do nothing to ameliorate that situation, she could clean up some of her own messes, like her apartment. Philippe would see it this evening for the first time when he arrived to pick her up, and perhaps later, too, if he came in for a drink. If she invited him. If she wanted to sleep with him. If he wanted to sleep with her.

Even if the answer is none of the above, she thought,

I can't live in this room for another day without cleaning it.

The focal point of the room was her bed, which was also her couch, usually her desk, and often her dining table. She wrinkled her nose in distaste as she gathered up the crumpled pieces of manuscript, emptied the ashtrays, and shook out the covers. She had designed the bed herself; she had fantasized about one like it for years. She had traced it onto drafting paper, measured dimensions carefully, and explained it thoroughly to the cabinet-maker she found through an ad in the *Voice.*

Her vision was clearly thought out; she'd refined it during years of living in unsuitable spaces. Spaces where her work was not immediately accessible when she wanted it to be. Spaces where the king-size bed she'd shared with Tony seemed accusingly lonely, driving her to sleep in the twin bed in Lara's room or on cushions piled in front of the fireplace in the beach house. The bed/couch in Ellin's apartment was her refuge, her retreat, her office, and her sanctuary.

Ellin was an essentially sedentary woman. 'You spend a lot of your life horizontal,' Cass commented.

'I'm not sleeping, I'm working,' she replied. Why, Ellin wondered, did she always feel slightly defensive with Cass? That day, her room had looked much as it did now. There were pages of typescript strewn around the platform bed, which was upholstered on its three raised sides, the corners softened with bolsters and pillows. One of the sides was a cleverly hinged piece that flipped up and over and accommodated Ellin's typewriter. She worked sitting up in bed, with the bolsters supporting her back.

She composed on the typewriter; she needed to see the words printed neatly and evenly on the page, in order to know whether they worked. With her legs tucked under her on the king-size mattress, she had everything she needed within reach; drawers built into the platform contained paper, ribbons, notebooks, index cards, all the paraphernalia of her trade.

The mattress, like the sides of the couch, was upholstered in soft grey flannel. She tossed the afghan and pillows off the bed onto the bleached wood floors, which were warmed by thick grey-and-white-striped Guatemalan rugs.

On the bed were remnants of her midnight meal—a slice of apple, some Brie that had crusted on the plate. A pile of manuscript pages was held down by a science fiction paperback; her place in a recent best seller was marked by an alligator clip from which protruded a partially smoked joint.

She shook out a mohair rug; it was sticky from a spilled can of diet soda, and she tossed it in a big straw basket that served as a hamper. She cleared the low Parsons table in front of the bed of overflowing ashtrays, old newspapers, a cup of cold grey coffee, and the telephone. She opened the glass doors to the terrace, feeling the cold air sweep the room clean of old problems, old smells. She checked the refrigerator for something to offer Philippe, and shook her head.

Ellin's refrigerator was nearly empty. There were a few cans of Tab, some juice, and a half bottle of wine. The shelves below the top one held a carton of leftover Chinese food, a plastic tub of chicken salad from the delicatessen, and a piece of stale Cheddar cheese. Ellin cooked as rarely as she could; all the years of preparing dull, balanced, wholesome meals for Lara stretched behind her. She was eating more lightly than ever; she thought it was because she was never bored as she had been in California most of the time. Most of the last ten years, certainly.

She hardly ever thought about food now. It was not only because she was active and busy—the presence in New York of hundreds of attractive, well-turned-out women her own age was a spur to Ellin's own efforts to look as good as she could. She did not diet obsessively, but often she ate only fruit and cottage cheese. When she was not horizontal—Cass was right about that, she thought ruefully—she was out walking the city. It was her only form of exercise, but it was regular, brisk, and prolonged. Sometimes she walked ten miles a day, prowling the neighbourhoods, delighting in their differences, discovering their uniqueness. Occasionally she stopped to browse in a store, sip coffee in a café, eavesdrop on a conversation. Sometimes she was so overstimulated by her peregrinations that she stayed in bed for a whole day, allowing the images and sounds to fade until she could hear herself think again.

There were so many sounds! A boisterous exchange between a jaywalker and an irate cabbie. The clang of traffic on the broad avenues, and the sudden quietude of a tree-shaded street between them. The excesses of the city continued to surprise her. There was so much of everything . . . thousand-dollar briefcases and tacky two-buck souvenirs, rare antiques and outlandishly dyed furs. Carcasses that hung in the windows of butcher shops, and cream puffs and napoleons arranged in even lines in a baker's display case. On almost every sidewalk, there was a fruit stand or a flower shop, tempting her as she strolled past. Plump orange nectarines, fat purple grapes; tall blue irises and pink-and-white-striped lilies. Improbably hued orchids, and mangoes and lichees. Gladioli and freesia and oddly shaped gourds she couldn't identify.

Occasionally it overwhelmed her; she was grateful to come home, shut her door, sprawl on her couch, and close her eyes. The couch was the centre of her life; when she came to it, and lay down, the cameras that took the city inside her stopped rolling, and she slept, soundlessly and dreamlessly. The next day, her mind was washed clean of what it had absorbed; it was ready for more.

She was wrapped in a big yellow bath towel, still wet from the shower, when there was a knock on the door. Damn; she'd forgotten about Vic. He was ready to install her bookshelves; she pulled on a robe and answered the door. She was conscious of being naked beneath the robe; there was something about Vic that made her conjure up sexual images whenever he was close to her. She was glad that the couch was decently made up, its grey flannel cover smoothly in place; why did she think of tangled sheets and pillows thrown on the floor in abandon when Vic came in?

He carried in the bookcases, and she watched for a moment as he began to set them up. Then she went into the bedroom to dress. That room had been her own at first; she felt lonely and closed-in within it, and decided to move into the front room, with its light, its fireplace, the view from its expanse of glass.

In what Ellin called the spare room were white pine twin beds, covered in a bold Marimekko print fabric. Cheerful rag rugs dotted the floor, and against one wall stood a small rolltop desk, which held Ellin's files and reference materials. The runnelled oak top slid back to reveal a tiny colour television set, which Ellin rarely used; when Lara was in residence, it was always on. Lara's own art work decorated the walls; Ellin had framed her daughter's seascapes of the California shore, which were misty, evocative, and surprisingly well done, in an effort to make it seem like Lara's own room.

Behind the mirrored closets were double-hung rows of Ellin's out-of-season clothes, and some of Lara's things. Late-afternoon sun streamed in through the window, making puddles of burnished gold on the wide oak floor boards. There were clean linens on the bed, current magazines and books on the night table, and pots of ferns and ivy hanging near the windows. The room looked fresh and expectant; although Ellin preferred not to live in it, she occasionally had guests, who were delighted by its warmth and charm. And of course there was Lara, who, as Ellin did, called it the spare room, despite Ellin's attempts to make it her daughter's own.

There had always been a spare room in every home and apartment Ellin lived in after college. When she was a child, hers was the room from which the owner was banished when company came for the weekend. Sometimes she didn't mind that very much; when her uncle Buddy came to visit Lou and Sophie, for instance, he would whistle her awake early, and they'd go off to the bakery for bagels and sweet rolls before anyone else in the house stirred. But often she minded quite a bit, and since childhood she had always had a spare room.

In California, it was the den, and friends came to live in it for a time, a time that had a beginning, a middle, and an end, all of which were determined, more or less, from the start. She liked it that the careful and difficult fitting together of two different ways of being and doing which bound or burdened more permanent arrangements—like marriage—was not part of those temporary cohabitations; it was her house, after all, so those delicate questions of turf and territory rarely intruded.

She had lost count of the number of keys she had the locksmiths in Los Angeles copy for those who came to her spare room at the beginning of an adventure or at its end; before Allen left for his sojourn in Mexico, after Carol came back from the temporary job with Indian Legal Services at Wounded Knee, when Peggy sold her house and had to wait until spring for the sailboat she bought to cruise the South Seas in its stead. Ellin's friends stopped in her spare room between homes, between planes, between jobs, and, most often, between lovers.

'George Washington must have slept here one night when he and Martha had a fight,' Paula remarked before leaving the den in California once, helping Ellin change the bed and freshen the room for the next person in the seemingly endless stream of the temporarily uncoupled who came to Ellin's spare room to catch their breath and begin to begin again.

Often the postman came to her door with a letter mailed to Ellin's house, but not to her. Her answering service operator relayed her daily messages and enquired tentatively after a new guest: would he or she be at this number very long? Sometimes, and sometimes not: sometimes Ellin's doorbell in Malibu rang after midnight, and she answered it, then retreated to the privacy of her own room, knowing that in the morning she would find the extra key on the hall table, the hastily written note of thanks and apology, the spare room vacant again.

Her friends were the family she chose for herself, particularly since she was a continent away, then, from the one into which she was born. Years before, in a time when 'happily' was not as important as 'ever after', she chose those friends and they chose her. They were both case load and caseworker to one another; that was a definition of friendship she treasured.

Sometimes her patience wore thin, though not as thin, it often seemed, as the ties that bound some of her friends to their mates. She wondered when they came to her spare room at how quickly love seemed to vanish, like a stone sinking into a pond, leaving only ripples that disappeared instantly from the surface. She marvelled at the way her friends moved in and out of liaisons, relationships, marriages. She was not surprised—she knew the statistics of divorce as well as anyone else—but she was dismayed. One never knew the texture and shape of any marriage except one's own, and hers had ended years ago, so perhaps she was no judge. But it was neither boredom nor restlessness that finished hers, as it admittedly did for so many of them; she counted her own pain greatest, after all. She came to think of them as consumers of commitments; they abandoned one for another, for a better, newer, bigger version. Nothing, they told her, lasts forever, and she agreed, sitting up with them until late into the night.

But some things did—or should. Sophie and Lou, for instance—their marriage was a noisy one, and not all of the sounds were laughter, and there were splintered edges to it that troubled her, but still it endured.

Since she had moved to New York, people still came to

Ellin's spare room—not as often, but more dramatically. 'I had to get as far away from that bastard as I could without leaving the country, my passsport's out of date,' said Bobbie from Bel Air, unloading four pieces of perfectly matched luggage on one of the twin beds. 'And I thought, Why, how marvellous, I'll come to New York. Darling, we miss you dreadfully at home!' They dropped in for a few days, rarely more, and Ellin enjoyed them. And as they complained and explained, she heard Sophie's voice saying, as she did so often, 'Happy? Who said you're supposed to be happy?'

Whoever, indeed. Few of the friends who moved in and out of Ellin's spare rooms were achingly, painfully unhappy; mostly, they thought they might be happier with someone else, if not now, then sometime. Not would be, not could be, not even should be . . . just might be. Ellin never pointed that out. She changed the linens, and put newer magazines on the night table, and fresher flowers on the desk. The room was there for her to offer them what they needed. Because that's what friends, and spare rooms, were for.

She lingered over her dressing, acutely aware of Vic in the next room, hearing him move about, considering him even as she prepared for the evening with Philippe. She knew barely more about Vic now than when she met him, despite his presence in the brownstone. Some days she never saw him, only noted his presence by the mail delivered to her door, the light bulb replaced in the hallway, the front stairs swept clean and the tiny garden raked and cleared. Occasionally she bumped into him at the Lion, where he still worked, and sometimes she exchanged a few words with him inside the foyer of the brownstone.

One night she went to the Lion, not because she needed a drink but because she was tired of being in her apartment and simply wanted to be somewhere else. She wasn't lonely, and she didn't feel like a movie, or even like browsing in a bookstore; the impulse that drives city dwellers into the streets for no purpose other than being out of the small spaces they call home sent her walking down Christopher Street.

The bar was nearly empty, and Vic brought her a beer. She made small talk, trying to draw him out.

'How's your book coming?' she enquired.

He shrugged his shoulders. 'On and off,' he said. Perhaps he didn't want to talk about his work with her—not that she was a big-deal writer, but she had had a book published, and she sold articles with regularity. She supported herself through her writing, and he did not. That was no gulf for her, but she thought it might be for him, so she changed the subject.

'How long have you worked here?'

'A couple of years.'

'And before that?'

He polished a glass, twirling the rag around and around it until it gleamed. 'Drove a cab, worked construction, was a fire watch in a national park, fished a few seasons . . . odds and ends.'

She was intrigued. He looked and sounded as though there was another earlier life besides the peripatetic one he described.

'And before that?'

He laughed, not unkindly. 'Is that what being a journalist is all about?' he asked. 'Gives you licence to poke around in people's lives?'

She was stung. She was just making conversation, after all. And hadn't it been Ellin herself who got him into the brownstone to begin with? Not a bad way to live, changing a few light bulbs, tending a patch of bleak earth that would never, no matter how much care was lavished on it, be a real garden. And rent-free, to boot, with plenty of time and space to write. If that's what he was doing, anyway; she knew a lot of people who said they wrote when what they really meant was, I play at writing so it doesn't seem like I'm just a bum. Or, I talk about it, I don't do it. Maybe Vic was one of those.

'Hey, look, I'm sorry,' he said hurriedly, seeing her reaction. 'Most of the time in here, I listen to other people's life stories, not tell my own. Oh, they ask, but they don't really want to know, they just want to tell you their troubles.'

'Sorry I don't have any to pour out to your sympathetic ear,' she said, not totally mollified.

'I got out of college, I went to business school, I had a bellyful of that bullshit after a couple of years with Citibank, and I went to Nam.'

'And then?'

He smiled again. 'You don't give up, do you? And then I put on my blue-striped suit again, got a job and a wife and a place in Co-op City, and then I cashed it all in and tried to write a book about . . . well, I tried to write a book. And stay alive while I did it, any way I could.'

'Any way?'

'Any way that's honest . . . I got a brother who's a cop, he keeps me in line.'

'Is the wife still in Co-op City?'

He put down the polished glass. Ellin could see her reflection in it.

'Damned if I know. Last time I saw her, she was looking for the American dream. She thought she found it in me, but it didn't work out that way.'

'Have you? Found it, I mean.' What the hell, he was talking, anyway, she might as well keep at it. Besides, she was interested. She liked encapsulated versions of people's histories; sometimes, she preferred it to the complete story. She liked imagining the rest, filling in the details herself.

He laughed shortly. 'Let's say I'm dreaming my own.' And then a customer signalled from the other end of the bar, and he left her to wait on him.

Could she do that? she wondered. Could she want to write so desperately—or do anything with that kind of perseverance? She imagined that the wife in Co-op City had grown tired of waiting for Vic to fulfill his promise, tireder still of living on such a precarious financial edge, bored sitting at home while he laboured away in another room, a lifetime and an obsession away from her.

She didn't think she'd ever had a goal as firmly fixed in her consciousness as Vic's seemed to be. She wrote because it was not difficult, because it paid well, provided her with a certain mobility and independence of life-style, and because people praised her efforts. It was a living, it was a craft, and, sometimes, it was totally absorbing, a way to put real life at a distance. On some rare occasions, the first few months with the novel, for instance, it was completely fulfilling and more fun than anything—chocolate, or even sex. For Vic, it seemed to be an obsession. The only other time they discussed it, he told her, 'I write to get it out of my head—Viet Nam, the war, the ugliness. Just to get it out of my fucking head.'

Ellin speculated about Vic as she finished dressing. He was very sexy, she thought; she had a thing for big, slow-talking, heavy-eyed men who seemed to know something about her, some secret, that she did not even know herself. She fantasized about having sex with him; smoothing her skirt over her hips, touching her breasts with dabs of Bellodgia, she felt sexy herself. She decided that Vic was not especially interested in her—or in any of the women in the brownstone, as far as she knew—but her escort for the evening certainly seemed to be. Were Frenchmen all fabulous lovers, she wondered, or was that only a myth, like the size of black men's cocks?

Jesus, one lunch with Pandora and I'm beginning to think like her. She laughed at herself. Perhaps she'd find out about Frenchmen for herself tonight.

And she floated out to the big room, moving in that way that suggests a woman's sexuality, languorous, gliding, humming to herself, a smile playing around her mouth.

'Nice,' said Vic from the ladder. He was wearing a plaid flannel shirt and jeans, a carpenter's apron tied around his hips. He looked big, and friendly, and pretty sexy himself, and she wiggled her hips a bare fraction more than usual as she walked to the kitchen to check on the ice and find that extra bottle of wine she knew she'd put somewhere.

NINETEEN

Paula saw Max Morton again on a June afternoon in the rotunda of the Federal Plaza Building in lower Manhattan.

She didn't remember later who caught whose eye first, but she felt a surge of happiness at the sight of him. He was stuffing a tie into his pocket; he looked up and wiped his brow with evident relief, then saw her, and a smile creased his face. She smiled back; they stood there grinning at each other while the crush of bodies that separated them passed.

Paula had left several messages with Max's secretary before she realized that he was not going to call her back. She had let him down—there was no question about it. It wasn't just breaking a date without notice—it was walking out on a friend who needed her. Who'd never let her down, because that's the kind of friends they were.

After the initial euphoria of Jake's return had worn off, she put her life back in order, stretching it in places to accommodate Jake's new presence in her life. That spring, Paula marked time by the completion of tasks—a brief finished, a segment of work on the abortion case done, a week ended and another begun as she boarded the Boston shuttle. The brownstone, her office, and Jake's furnished rooms in Cambridge—these became the points of the triangle that was her life.

Most of the time Jake hardly seemed to notice her presence. He had taken his law school exams and was studying for the July bar, working as a summer intern in a Boston legal collective.

She arrived on Friday evenings, laden with gifts and delicacies—a fan for his stuffy flat, a transistorized cassette player with headphones, so he could tune out the street noises while studying, herring fillets from Russ's, candied apricots from Balducci's.

He barely looked up when she came in; she kissed him lightly and put her things away, then rummaged in the Pullman kitchen, taking inventory. She went out and bought provisions for the next week, and did not disturb Jake until dinner was ready. Sometimes he went back to his books until she cleared away the dishes, and other times he was restless; he wanted to make love immediately, or go out to a coffeehouse or bar where people who knew him from the old days, and newer friends, too, gathered. Most of the latter were women, Paula noted, the kind of wide-eyed groupies who'd followed him everywhere ten years before.

Occasionally she was able to drag him out of the flat or away from the library; one day when the temperature hit 93 she could stand it no longer, and made him come with her to Lynn, where they swam in the ocean, and to Gloucester, where they ate lobsters. They came home sunburned and tired, and made love gently so they would not hurt their tender skin.

She wanted to help him with his studies, but he refused.

'For Christ's sake, Paula, quit it!' he told her angrily once. 'I know *you* know this stuff.' He threw a law book across the room and it landed with a thud, scattering dust motes in the still room. 'You've got a ten-year head start on me, don't rub it in!'

He's jealous, she realized; he knows if things had been different, he'd be where I am. They had always been competitive in law school; she too made *Law Review*, and their grades were only a few fractions distant. Law was a touchy subject between them now, and so, it seemed, was politics; for all his grandiose goals, the ones he brought back with him from his decade underground, he didn't appear to care very much about the rights of the disadvantaged. He had complaints about the part-time job, too. 'Why are you doing it, then?' Paula asked him. 'Because you have to lick them before you can join them,' he replied.

'Join them? What are you talking about?' Jake didn't reply. 'Did you bring me any of those grapes from the fruit stand on Seventh Avenue?' he asked instead.

'Over there, in the net bag,' Paula replied absently. She knew the collective Jake was working for; one of its most effective attorneys had been hired away by a big chemical company whose dumping of noxious poisons into an upstate lake had brought it into court on a class action suit filed by that same lawyer.

'You mean like Wally Sams?'

'Not exactly,' said Jake, but he would not elaborate, and resisted Paula's efforts to carry that conversation any further with the same simple, effective tool he used whenever he wanted to put her off: He quieted her talk with kisses, drowned out her questions with her own passion.

In bed, Paula thought, their communion was most complete. Only there did she have his full attention; only there was the desire, and the need, equal.

But suddenly that changed, too. One Friday night Jake wasn't home when she arrived at the flat, and he did not come home until very late. He looked haggard, spoke little, and moved as if he were underwater. She smelled no alcohol on his breath when he undressed, slowly, and lay down next to her.

'What's the matter?' she asked. She sat up in bed, snapped on the light, and looked at him. 'You look like you've been on a week-long bender, or a cocaine high.'

'Christ, Paula, lay off,' he said, and made no move to touch her. He lay there in the dark, after turning off the light, and stared up at the ceiling. He brooded silently, and she grew nervous, then frightened.

Finally she spoke to him. 'Is it something I did? Are you angry at me for some reason?'

He laughed shortly. 'Why do you always think it has something to do with you?'

She sighed. Jake would tell her when he was ready. She reached out for him and ran her fingers over his body, but he turned away from her and feigned sleep.

She took ten days off to spend with him early in June, and they made love only twice. One night, when she fondled him invitingly he snapped at her. 'Would you just lay off!' he said angrily, and she retreated to her side of the bed, recoiling in disappointment, waiting for his apology. But it did not come, and finally she fell into a restless sleep.

She made excuses for him. He's working too hard, she told herself. He's going through a very difficult time. He needs to lean on me. Afterward—when he's passed the bar, when he's settled—then he'll make it up to me.

'Is there something going on that I should know about?' she asked him finally. He shot her a glance; she saw something in it that looked like fear, and wondered.

'No, of course not, why should there be, what are you talking about?' He rushed his words together; a sure sign, she knew, that he was covering up.

'Oh, no reason,' said Paula casually. 'You seem . . . distracted, that's all. Sometimes I talk to you and it's like I'm not even here.' Sometimes I talk about later, after, whenever, and that glazed look comes over your eyes, and it makes me nervous, she thought, but Jake grinned at her in the old way and took her in his arms. It didn't work; that night he was first impotent, then apologetic, and finally, after she told him several times that it didn't matter, he was angry.

That was how things were between her and Jake the day she bumped into Max Morton. She hadn't known what to do about Max; finally, she concluded sadly that he might no longer wish to see her at all, and she wrote him a long letter explaining exactly what had happened that night she was to have met him and in the following weeks. 'I know I hurt you,' she wrote. 'I didn't do it on purpose, but that doesn't make it any better. I hope when you forgive me, you'll get in touch.'

That had been some weeks before. Now here he was, and Paula did not know what to say to him.

'I tried to . . . I'm sorry . . . oh, shit, Max, I'm so glad to see you!' she finally managed.

He hugged her then, and she exhaled in relief. He held her away from him and looked at her. 'I'm sorry, too,' he said. 'I behaved like an ass. Stubborn, carrying a grudge. When I read your letter, I understood. I was planning to call you today, before I left—I just came in yesterday for a meeting. Do you believe that?'

'Yes, I do,' she said simply, saying a silent prayer of thanks to the judge who had refused to put the case over to Monday for final arguments, and kept her from the Boston shuttle she would otherwise have been on at this moment. On her way to Jake. She pushed that thought away; Jake would probably not notice her absence until he got hungry. He could fix his own supper. She'd go up the next day instead.

'Do you have to be anywhere . . . I mean, probably you have plans for tonight, but if you don't, we could . . .' she floundered.

'I don't have any plans, and we could. We will.' He threw an arm over her shoulders. 'Let's get out of this place.'

They walked uptown slowly, through the narrow streets of Chinatown, across Little Italy to SoHo, and through the park at Washington Square. Max explained the complications of the development deal that had brought him to New York, the public offering he was supervising, the film itself, the problems with the producer who always went over budget, the director who was sleeping with the star, and the star who was trying to shed her husband the agent. 'And of course, they're all my clients, all nutsos, because I'm putting the whole thing together,' he finished. 'Some days I wonder why I didn't go into something simple, like my father's business.'

'Because you wanted to work with creative people,' said Paula. 'Remember?'

'You know too much about me.' He smiled. 'At least I get paid to take this *mishegas*—I take it from my family for nothing.'

He asked her about her work; unlike Jake, who wasn't the least interested, he was genuinely pleased to hear about her progress on the abortion case, the argument she had delivered that afternoon, a new client she'd recently taken on.

They were still talking shop when they arrived at home, and she led him through the hall to the backyard patio they all shared. Vic had fastened a hammock between two cherry trees that had lost their blossoms but not their leaves; she settled Max there while she went to fetch wine and glasses and ice. She joined him outside, and they gossiped and brought each other up to date on the details of their lives while the blue of late afternoon deepened into twilight as the sun moved west, beyond the Village, across the Hudson, and down over the horizon, somewhere past New Jersey.

The conversation dwindled; they had exhausted the safe topics. Paula brought it up first.

'So much for the easy stuff,' she said. 'Max, is it okay between us? Really okay?'

He reached for her hand. 'I guess it is.' He avoided her direct gaze as he spoke; he talked over her head, to a point behind and beyond her. 'I was counting on you to make the pain go away, Paula. It was the first time I ever said "I need you" to anyone. I never even said it to my wife when she left me. I couldn't. I toughed it out—I was a rational man in those days.

'You know, it never would have worked, Susan and me. I saw it coming from the beginning; I told you that, didn't I?' Paula nodded, and he went on; she wasn't sure he noticed. 'There was twenty years between us—an important twenty. She didn't want what I wanted. She wanted to be free. She was like a . . . a butterfly. I couldn't keep her. I probably wouldn't have wanted her if I could.' He sighed.

'You . . . you're not a butterfly. Anyway, I didn't think so. You were solid. Reliable. You cared in a deep, honest way. And then . . . you didn't.'

Tears collected in Paula's eyes, but she willed them back. Take it, Paula, you deserve it, she told herself harshly. One tear escaped, and dribbled down her cheek. Max noticed it.

'Oh, Paula, I'm sorry, of course you did . . . do. I overreacted. I'd been hurt, and I wanted to lash out and hurt somebody else and you were a convenient target. I couldn't let go of my anger until I understood that. I wallowed in self-pity for a long time before I did.' He wiped the tear from her face. 'Don't cry, please, okay?' She sniffed and nodded. 'I've been thinking about you for these last few weeks, wondering how I could say all that to you,' he said.

'You just did,' Paula replied quietly. She squeezed his hand and he squeezed hers back. 'Thank you. I'm sorry. I won't ever do that to you again.'

'I know you won't.'

When it was fully dark, they put some coals in the little hibachi and lit them, then walked over to Sixth Avenue and purchased steaks and wine. By the time they returned to the brownstone, the coals were ready and they cooked the steaks and drank the wine.

'You happy, Paula?' Max asked her later.

'Happy?' She shrugged. 'It's not a great time with Jake just now. We're kind of . . . on hold.'

'Are you getting what you need from him?'

'Sometimes,' she said. 'Not always.'

Max refilled their wineglasses. 'You know, when I told you about Susan, last fall, you never told me what I knew you were thinking.'

'Why should I have? Would it have made a difference? Would you have heard me?'

'Probably not,' Max admitted. 'Of course, you and Jake . . . it's a different situation. There seem to be a lot of . . . loopholes, if you know what I mean. Have you made any marriage plans?'

'Not exactly,' Paula answered. 'But it's . . . I mean . . . we go back a long way, Jake and I. One thing hasn't changed about him—he still has to think everything is his idea. When he has his life together, we'll get around to making some definite plans.' She wasn't entirely sure she believed that, but she would not confess her doubts to Max, not after the way she'd treated him because of Jake. 'And who says I want to get married, anyway?'

'Come off it, Paula. This is me, Max, remember? And that's what all this is about, right? The happy ending. Under the *chupa*, into the house, the law degree hanging over the baby's crib, lighting the Shabbas candles . . . am I wrong?'

'You make it sound like the wet dream of a liberated Jap,' said Paula amiably.

'Mutually exclusive—there's no such thing as a liberated Jewish American princess,' Max said. Maybe he was right. Some women merely needed to prove they could exist without a man, and that was the extent of their ambition. Max's sister Amy was one of them. 'Twelve years of training and the day she passes the boards in medicine, she gets married, nine months later she has a kid, and now she spends her days in Central Park or shopping at Bloomingdale's. If somebody yelled "Is there a doctor in the house?" she'd look around for one; she's completely forgotten she is one,' Max said.

'Oh, Amy will go back to work after the baby's in school.'

'Oh, yeah?' Max was sceptical.

'Well, she's earned the right,' Paula said. 'She delayed gratification for a long time, and why should she do it any longer?' And why should I? she thought. Once her big project was finished, Paula, too, would make a more complete life for herself. And in a few years—after the children she sometimes dreamed about were old enough, those children she could hear and touch and smell but not quite see, even in dreams where every other detail was sharp—she would get back on track.

'Amy's not the issue, she's made her choice. You're sidestepping it.'

'You're right,' she told him. 'I do want the whole thing—I want it all. With Jake? I think so . . . but I'm not sure. Not sure if he does, not sure if we could . . .' Her voice trailed off. Max was pushing her, making her confront the questions she tried, unsuccessfully, not to ask herself.

'I suppose you have to play it out, though,' Max said. 'Like me with Susan. Even if there's no light at the end of the tunnel.'

'Uh huh . . . you still have to get to the end of the tunnel,' Paula replied.

A breeze had finally come up, and it grew chilly on the patio. They sprinkled water on the coals and did the dinner dishes together.

Max looked at his watch. 'I have to go,' he said. 'An early plane tomorrow.'

'Sure,' she said. She didn't want Max to leave, she realized; she wanted him to stay. She remembered that she had never called Jake; let him deal with it, she thought tiredly. She moved closer to Max, and put her arms around him.

'Want to stay?' she whispered.

'I'm not the bionic man, of course I want to stay,' he said. 'But I'm still the same old Max. Not into being one among many.'

'There aren't so many anymore,' she said.

'No, but there's one,' Max replied gently. 'Even if he's not the right one.'

She looked up at him. 'You really don't think he is, do you?'

'That's not my decision, Paula,' he replied. 'When you make it . . . be sure to let me know.'

She studied him with affection and respect. Most men would have said yes; Max's values were different. Better than mine, she thought. Not quite so . . . situational.

'Thanks, Max,' she murmured against his shoulder. 'Thanks for not letting me use you.'

He kissed her on the forehead. 'You wouldn't have unless I wanted you to,' he said. 'I don't know what's going to be between us, Paula. Right now, being friends again, loving each other, trusting each other—that's what I want.'

'Me, too,' she told him. 'I'm glad for tonight, Max. You'll keep in touch?'

'I've got a dozen postcards I've been saving for you,' Max said. 'I knew I couldn't hold a grudge against you forever.'

'Thank God,' said Paula. 'I really missed those postcards.'

She went to Cambridge the next day; Jake did not ask why she was late, and she offered no explanation. He was still moody and withdrawn. They made love in the middle of the night, without speaking; later, she came into the bathroom and found Jake studying the little card with her birth control pills encased in individual plastic bubbles. He flushed when she caught him at it; he mumbled some excuse—'I was looking for an aspirin'—and pushed past her, back into the bedroom.

'What will we do when it's over?' she asked him later, idly tracing the line of his jaw with her fingertips.

'When what's over?' he said sleepily.

'Oh, when you pass the bar, start practising,' she replied. 'What happens then?'

She felt his body tense. 'Shit, that's months away. We'll do whatever . . . whatever makes us happy.'

It wasn't enough, but she did not push it. She knew what she would do. She would marry him, and she would get pregnant. Jake knew that, too, but he didn't want to talk about it now. She could understand that; he had a great deal on his mind. All right, Paula, she told herself. Not now. Later. You've waited ten years, a few more months won't kill you.

In the fall, she thought, we'll make some plans.

And the long days of summer crept past, moving so slowly that Paula, if she wished, could have measured each hour.

TWENTY

Cass was running when she hit the deck from her first day at Amagansett. She worked harder than she ever had, trying to absorb it all, trying to learn enough so that she wouldn't sound like a complete idiot when she opened her mouth at the regular management committee meetings. She was out of the brownstone by seven-thirty every morning, and rarely home from the office before eight at night. When she fell into bed, near midnight, she was asleep almost instantly. She barely had time to miss Nick; she flew to Los Angeles for the opening party marking the first issue of *Orange*, but returned to New York on the red-eye that same night; it was in the middle of the week, after all.

Nick's first-issue fete was an extravaganza every inch of the way, from the flower-decked launches that ferried the guests to a cruise ship moored offshore to the four bands, the sumptuous buffet, and unlimited quantities of champagne that awaited the guests—tanned, jewelled women and men whose improbably white teeth smiled at Cass over black ties or gold chains.

At ten-thirty, just before the fireworks display, Cass had to leave; she could not find Nick, and she ran through the ship, sneaking looks at her watch. Finally, she found him, and pulled him into a cabin for a brief goodbye.

'I'm sorry I have to go,' she told him. He smiled past her, to where his guests waited, drinking and dancing and chatting about tennis matches, turnarounds, points, and real estate.

'Well, you have to do what you have to do,' he said, not sadly but softly.

'I wish I didn't have to leave,' she said. He frowned. 'You're going to knock them dead, Nicky. You, and *Orange.*' She hugged him, and he returned her embrace.

'So are you, baby. You and the Big Apple. East takes east and west takes west and . . .' His voice trailed off.

'And?' she whispered.

He tipped up her chin, 'And someday soon, the twain shall meet, and take each other.'

'Promise?'

'Promise. Fourth of July, five days in East Hampton.'

'With a cast of thousands?' she asked. 'Parties and tennis and business and . . .'

'None of that,' Nick promised. 'A very private party. Just you and me.'

'I'll hold you to it.' She smiled. 'I love you.'

'Of course you do—you're a broad with great taste. If memory serves,' he added, and she felt guilty. They hadn't made love on this brief trip; her period had come on unexpectedly, and Cass was fastidious before she was abandoned.

'Has it been that long?' she asked.

'Only if you're counting, and who's counting?' He touched his lips to hers—they were cool, and she sensed his withdrawal.

The helicopter flew over the hotel en route to the airport. She touched her mouth with her fingers, feeling the last trace of Nick's kiss, and she was sad.

There was time before she boarded the red-eye to change clothes in the ladies' room. She stuffed her evening pyjamas and high-heeled sandals into her carry-on bag, and donned a jersey wraparound dress. She washed off her party makeup, dusted blusher on her cheeks, and freshened her lipstick. She took low-heeled pumps from her bag and shook the wrinkles out of a linen blazer. Checking her reflection in the mirror, she went to catch her flight. She had, she estimated, less than half an hour after landing before she was due at a meeting with Grey Tucker, a banker from Texas, two tax lawyers, and Dollie Shariff, the owner of a western-wear company Tucker was thinking of acquiring for Amagansett. In her briefcase she had the all-but-completed report she had written on the firm, its operations, performance, and possible place in the Amagansett marketing mix.

After the seat-belt sign went off, Cass asked the stewardess for a cup of coffee, and snapped on the light above her seat. Taking out her briefcase, she set to work. But not until she had deftly and firmly fielded the attentions of her seat mate, a portly salesman who insisted on knowing 'What a cute little gal like you is doing chewing the end of a pencil instead of . . .' He groped for the words, but he and Cass both knew what he meant. Resisting an urge to spill her water on his lap, she smiled sweetly and replied, 'I work for the Internal Revenue Service. I specialise in expense account cheaters.'

He blanched, and she controlled her impulse to laugh. After a time, he got up and changed his seat; the 747 was half empty, especially in first class.

They were flying into the sunrise; the rays of gold beaming in on her through the porthole wakened Cass. Guiltily, she rubbed her eyes; she still had a final paragraph to write. And they were less than an hour out of Kennedy.

She yawned . . . she was exhausted. She rummaged in her purse for the Preludin she knew was there—it was left over from an old prescription, two years before, when she had wanted to lose a few pounds and wheedled it out of her doctor. What she really needed, she thought, was some coke; she had had some early the previous evening, with Nick, while they were dressing for the party. If she took the Preludin, she'd never sleep that night, unless she took some Valium. And if she took the Valium she'd never wake up the next morning, when there was another meeting, and another report due.

She left the pill where it was, and caught the

stewardess's attention. A few minutes later, with a steaming cup of coffee at her elbow, munching a protein bar she kept in the pocket of her carry-on bag, she bent over her work, and wrote steadily until the flashing light and the voice over the plane's intercom told her to put her seat in an upright position, and fold away all lap trays.

It was done; she closed the briefcase and leaned her head back, feeling the kinks in her neck and shoulders. For the moment, it was done, and Cass exhaled deeply, and closed her eyes.

TWENTY-ONE

Ellin kicked off her high heels and wiggled her toes in the limousine's thick carpeting. She'd already been in Detroit, Milwaukee, Richmond, and Philadelphia that week. The first time, when her book was published, it was different, and fun: Chicago one day, Atlanta the next, television talk shows and radio interviews and signing her books in stores and talking to journalists. She couldn't understand why writers complained about taking their books on the road. Then she began to notice the depressing similarity of the shows and the stores and the hotel rooms and especially the interviewers. On the 9 a.m. local talk shows they were all alike, seemingly cloned from the same mould: a genial, folksy man who made bad jokes and a smarter, unthreateningly pretty woman who tried to seem as though she was just Mrs Averagewoman, not a bit different from the housewives in her audience, except luckier, of course.

But Ellin's book, *Movement Women,* had been issued in paperback that month, just as another radical from the sixties surfaced after several years underground. That incident created a flurry of interest to which her publisher responded with a hastily arranged mini-tour.

'Back to the hotel now, miss?' asked the Capitol Limousine Service driver.

'No, I think I'd like to stop at the East Wing before my next appointment,' Ellin replied.

'Very good, miss.'

The events calendar in the *Post* had mentioned a show

of Impressionist paintings in the stunning new addition to the Smithsonian, and on this slightly rainy, fragrant day, Impressionists suited her mood. She spent a blissful hour with the yellows and golds, the cool depths and wavy light of Renoir, Monet, and Pissarro, and then she made her way through the museum to a terrace café.

She saw him there first; they stood side by side, waiting for a hostess to approach them, but none materialized. They smiled tentatively at each other, acknowledging their mutual difficulty.

'Maybe we should find our own table,' the man suggested in a friendly fashion, and Ellin was about to agree when the hostess appeared.

'Smoking or no smoking?' she asked brusquely.

'Smoking,' said Ellin.

'Nonsmoking,' said the man simultaneously. The hostess led him away. Cigarettes are not only bad for my health, they'll kill me in the man department, too, Ellin thought grouchily.

She saw him after lunch, in the rotunda, under the enormous Calder mobile that dominated the space. She looked at her watch; she would be late for her interview if she didn't leave now.

She went out to Arlington, to a newspaper office, and talked and smiled and had her picture taken. The limousine driver dropped her at the gate to the Eastern shuttle at National Airport, where she caught sight of the man from the museum waiting in line for the five o'clock plane.

He preceded her onto the plane; when she moved down the aisle, he smiled at her in recognition, and patted the empty seat next to him. Without hesitating, she sat down.

They were still talking when the plane landed. She was doing most of the talking, she noticed, responding to his interested questions, editing the outline of her life she gave to strangers, tucking it in there a bit, twisting it here a smidge, noticing his responses, tailoring hers to fit. He was faintly attractive, with fair, straight hair that framed eyes that were deep-set and seemed to glow as if lit from behind. His face was craggy with dents and what might have been scars, or lines, or years. He was about her age, and wore no wedding ring.

He suggested that they share a cab from La Guardia—he lived in TriBeCa, he told her, which was generally in her direction. She would have agreed even if she had been going to New Jersey. The taxi dropped her off first, and he asked if he could call her.

'I'd like that,' she said, giving him one of her business cards. And in the one week, two days, and twelve hours before he did call her, she thought of little else.

Later, she tried to figure out why she fell so quickly and recklessly in love with him. Perhaps it was inevitable. She felt happy, free of responsibilities, confident, and strong. She had made her New York fantasy happen—at least, the first part of it. Perhaps he would be the other, unspoken, even undreamed-of part.

There was nothing about him to warrant the obsession that soon occupied her every hour. He was a rather ordinary man: intelligent, attractive, curious, well mannered, but she knew many men with those qualities. He seemed very interested in her, which was a great deal of his charm. Ellin had plenty of dates in New York—someone was always coming through town, introducing her to a friend, inviting her to a party. She rarely saw many of the men more than a few times; there was a brief, mutual sizing-up on the first or second date, and if no spark flared they did not call again, or if they did she put them off.

New York was full of possibilities; there was romance and adventure on every corner, and Ellin could make a fine life for herself out of bits and pieces of time and people. But she felt left out when Cass and Paula talked about Nick and Jake. She had friends and dates; they had relationships. Not necessarily perfect ones—but still, they came first with a man, and Ellin wanted to, too.

She was emotional about Gregory, the man she had met on the plane. She felt the tension of her longing when she was with him. At the end of an evening she was drained, exhausted; she replenished herself until he called again, and then the anticipation was almost too much to bear.

It went on for six weeks or so. He seemed to be testing whether love was appropriate for them; she was frustrated because he gave her no indication of his own feelings except by continuing to call her.

She felt him peeling back the layers of herself, and imagined she was performing the same deft strokes on him. He moved slowly on her sexually; it was two weeks before he kissed her, and they were agonizing weeks. She fantasized endlessly about sleeping with him. She could not concentrate on her work; she wandered around the city dreamily and smiled often to herself.

Then he stopped calling. She reached for the telephone several times a day, and restrained herself. What she liked best about Gregory—what she needed most—was that he wanted her.

Had wanted her. That was clear as the days passed with no word from him. Finally she phoned him at the office; she had rehearsed her words and, she hoped, the tone of her voice.

'Is there something intentional about your silence, or are you just busy living your life?' she asked him as lightly as she could.

He said nothing for what seemed like an eternity. 'I've been away,' he managed.

'Oh?'

She heard him sigh. 'I seem to be caught up in a whirlwind romance,' he said finally. 'I met this woman . . . it just happened.'

She said nothing, and he rushed to fill the silence. 'I'd like to see you—keep seeing you, I mean,' he said. 'I want us to be friends. You're an extraordinary woman; I admire you very much.'

'That's good,' she said. She wanted to slam down the phone. But she also wanted to keep hearing his voice despite the pain of his words. 'Let's have lunch,' she got out as casually as she was able. The great nullifier—let's have lunch.

'I'm glad you understand,' Gregory said. 'I'll call you.'

He did call, a few weeks later. Their lunch was strained and awkward. She had too much to drink, asked him gaily how his whirlwind affair was progressing, heard with petty satisfaction that it was not love, after all, just a case of spring fever, and had another drink.

He kissed her on the cheek when they parted. 'It was good seeing you,' he said, with what she recognized as finality.

'I'm glad you fell in love for a while,' she told him. 'I wish it could have been with me.' And she turned and walked away quickly, sorry that she had said that, sorry she had bestowed that gift on him, but glad to be free of the feeling she'd carried within her since he first disappointed her—the feeling that at any moment she might dissolve in tears.

The pain caught her unawares; she had forgotten how much it hurt to love and not be loved back. Over and over she replayed, in her mind, the words they had said to each other. She analysed the gestures he made toward and away from her, the meanings and the subtexts in the ambiguous phrases he had directed at her. Eventually Gregory disappeared beneath the complex layers of her mind, and who he was, or had been, was completely obscured. She counted it a good day when she only cried about him once.

It disturbed her that she could not regain her emotional equilibrium immediately. She could not write, either. So she consulted a psychiatrist; Ellin had an almost blind faith in the power of understanding to ease, or at least catalogue, her disappointments.

'I didn't realize how vulnerable I was,' she said to the analyst. He was not just any psychiatrist, but one who specialized in the emotional problems of single professional women. Ellin trusted experts; she met any crisis by arming herself with information, and as a journalist, she knew where to find it—the best doctor, the right dentist, the connection to the source.

The psychiatrist wanted her to talk about Sophie and Lou and Tony, not Gregory. 'I've already dealt with that,' she told him, and he smiled tolerantly. 'I want to talk about what's happening now. About why I hurt so much.'

'Then you tell me,' he said, lighting his pipe.

'There was a point in time,' she began, 'only a few weeks ago, isn't that funny, it seems like history now.'

'What point was that?' he nudged her.

She spoke as if recounting a dream. 'I was running,' she told him. 'On the West Side Highway. It was beautiful out—balmy, you could smell the river, the sun was hot, the running wasn't hurting, it was that time when you don't notice picking up your feet and putting them down, you just do it. I must have been smiling . . . other runners who saw me smiled at me. I was thinking how good I felt.'

'Why did you feel good?'

'Because . . . my work was going well. Lara's safe and happy. I love the brownstone. Cass and Paula . . . I love them, too. New York. Being here. All of it.'

'And?'

'And I was falling in love—I was in love—with this marvellous, sensitive, available, wonderful man, who seemed to be ready to fall in love with me. And I thought, if I could freeze one moment in time, one perfect moment, this would be it, this moment of . . .' She hesitated.

'Yes?'

'This moment of . . . balance.'

'I see,' the analyst said.

'And then it melted.' She felt herself drowning in misery, deluged by her tears, drenched and suffocating.

'Tell me about your father,' he said.

Her sessions with the analyst were frustrating, and finally she stopped going. 'He thinks every woman with a career has an unresolved Electra complex,' she told Cass. 'I've already dealt with that.'

She had over the years consulted several therapists, beginning with the marriage counsellor she and Tony saw together for a time. After the divorce, she drifted into the human potential network and flailed around in it for a while—a Gestalt group, a bioenergetics group, some marathons, a psychodrama week at Esalen, even a few hours of Rolfing. 'Sometimes I think my whole life is little piles of unfinished business,' Ellin said.

'Nonsense,' Cass told her. 'You just ran into a loser. What you need is a new man.'

Having delivered herself of a prescription, Cass proceeded to fill it. She paraded men through Ellin's nights; she had them for drinks in her apartment, or gave them Ellin's phone number.

'Your supply is inexhaustible,' Ellin told her. She was grateful for Cass's efforts, although she felt a debt was accruing, one that might be called at some time, in a currency she wouldn't have. 'But you have terrific hand-me-downs,' she added.

'They're not that, exactly. When Nick and I started being a couple, they just kind of fell away,' Cass explained.

Ellin thought she and Cass were so different that none of the men Cass brought around would be interested in her. But some were.

Henry was quick, with a mind that darted rather than probed; her dates with him were astringent and asexual. He was a well-regarded director at Playwrights Horizons and other off-Broadway theatres; Ellin liked his friends more than she liked him. But she spent a weekend with him in Connecticut, where he was doing a play at the O'Neill. She encountered some theatre friends from years before, when she was with Tony, and they did not recognize her at first.

Jay was a clown. He was a friend of Cass's from the agency who took nothing seriously except not taking anything seriously. He could not stand to hear anything sad, that he could not joke about, so Ellin could not really talk to him; instead, she was an audience for his frequently funny stories, and sometimes a participant in his gags and setups.

Martin was a business school dropout, a buddy from Cass's graduate school days. Martin looked like he was stuck in the Sixties; he wore embroidered Mexican shirts with faded blue jeans and taught junior high school in Bedford-Stuyvesant. He had been, he told Ellin, hopelessly in love with Cass for years, but it did not keep him from enjoying himself. 'I am a lover of women,' he said with a disarming grin: and it was true. Ellin sensed no threat from him—he was safe, so she relaxed, and they had a good time together. He gave her sensuous massages, and brought her flowers and joints and took her to the trashy movies she loved. They told each other their whole romantic histories, and drifted into bed in a haze of marijuana smoke. He was an enthusiastic and talented lover who seemed not to want anything in return except Ellin's occasional presence next to him in the big bed, beneath its summer slipcovers of pinstriped denim. 'You are proof that if God exists, She's a woman,' Ellin told Martin when he showed up at her door late one night with a chocolate malted from the Gem Spa. 'I live to please.' He grinned, and he went down on her for what seemed hours, licking ice cream from her cunt in playful laps. She had made love with a woman, once, in Los Angeles; sex with Martin was like that.

Summer went on, and Lara came east. She was sullen and withdrawn. She did not want to see any of her friends from previous summers at Sophie and Lou's beach house; she pronounced them boring, and Ellin could not prevail on her to change out of her torn jeans into anything other than a frayed bathing suit that barely covered her blooming body. Sophie nagged, too, but Lara ignored her as she did Ellin. When she talked, she talked about people Ellin didn't know, including, incessantly, Jessica, a new woman in Tony's life. 'Intentionally,' Cass said after dining with Ellin and Lara. 'She was baiting you all night. Why do you let her get away with that?'

'Do I have a choice?' Ellin said wearily. 'She's going through a stage. If you ever have a teenage daughter, she'll go through it, too, Cass.'

'Not if she wants to live with me she won't,' Cass said with grim determination.

It was true: Lara did seem to be intentionally goading Ellin. She knew which buttons to push, and she pushed them. Ellin tried to control her anger; she went to a psychiatrist again, a different one this time, a woman who dealt with adolescents' parents, not teenagers themselves. 'She's paying you back for leaving her,' the doctor said.

'Leaving her? Hell, she left me,' Ellin said ruefully. 'She was the one who suggested it in the first place, living with her father.'

Dr Horner sighed. 'Rationally, that's true, but she's not thinking rationally. She doesn't want to take the responsibility for leaving you, so she's displacing it.'

'So what do I do?'

'Don't get caught up in it, let her play her drama out, lay off. Enjoy her if you can, detach from it if you can't. It's situational. It'll pass. Want some Valium?'

Ellin felt better. This woman seemed to understand, and she relaxed a little.

'Did Dad tell you I got suspended from school for a week for smoking pot?' Lara asked Ellin, knowing perfectly well he had not. That was the deal with Tony; he never told her if he and Lara were having problems, unless it was a medical issue; whenever Lara had a cold or a bug or, as once happened, a little accident, Tony called Ellin immediately. Mostly he carried on about how close the two of them were, how much he was enjoying being a father. He had not wanted to send Lara east. 'I have a lot of lost time to make up for,' he said. Lara had not wanted to come, either, and, in fact, Ellin could have done without the visit herself; she was just climbing out of her own depression. 'But what kind of mother doesn't see her daughter for months on end?' Sophie scolded when Ellin mentioned that Lara might not come. She doesn't want to see you, either, Ellin thought spitefully; 'Oh, Mother, do we *have* to go to Sophie's, she's such a pain in the ass since Papa had his heart attack,' Lara had wailed, and it was true, Sophie was.

But Ellin had wheedled two weeks out of Tony and Lara, and cleared her calendar for the time. Lara didn't seem to appreciate Ellin's efforts, she complained to Dr Horner before they left for the beach.

'She still needs you, and she doesn't want to. Don't expect too much. Let her be. Love her and be tolerant. Don't get caught up in her drama. It will pass.'

Ellin took her advice; if the opinions of her experts matched her own, and if she trusted them, she always did.

When Lara told her about being suspended from school, she did not overreact.

'No, as a matter of fact he didn't,' Ellin said. 'How did that make you feel, getting suspended?'

Lara snorted in disgust. 'Oh, gawd, Mother, you're psychobabbling again. You must have a new shrink.'

'I do,' said Ellin mildly.

'Well, I don't need a shrink anymore,' Lara pronounced triumphantly. 'I've got Dad now. And you, of course,' she added.

'Of course,' Ellin said drily.

'You're not into being a mother these days, are you?' Lara asked.

'What makes you say that?' Ellin countered, startled; it was precisely what she had been thinking; she'd talk that over with Dr Horner at her next appointment.

'Oh, you hardly said anything about me getting busted. You don't bug me very much anymore.'

Ellin felt pleased; she was handling Lara better, thanks to Dr Horner. 'What good has bugging you ever done?' she asked.

'Not much,' admitted Lara. 'It just makes me stubborner.'

'More stubborn,' Ellin corrected out of habit. 'I guess I've decided that you're old enough to be responsible for some things, like what you eat, and wear.'

'How about what I do?'

'I care very much about what you do, baby. But I'm not in a position to influence that, not on a day-to-day basis anyway.' At some point, a mother has to say, There, I've taught her what I can, I hope it's enough, Ellin thought. From there on, it's mostly a matter of luck. But she didn't say that to her daughter.

'Oh,' said Lara. 'Hey, you want to play some backgammon?'

Ellin went into the city for a few days, leaving Lara at Sophie's. She had some appointments, an assignment to turn in, an hour with Dr Horner. When she went back out to the beach, Sophie reported that Lara seemed listless. 'She just hangs around.' Sophie sniffed. 'Sleeps until noon every day, goes off to the beach, comes home alone, and stays in her room all night, playing music. Reading those awful horror novels. It's not natural.'

'Sure it is. Remember when you were fourteen?'

'Of course not, do you?'

Ellin did. What she remembered most about being fourteen was thinking that her mother was a terrible bitch, a hateful enemy, nosy and overprotective and always snooping through her drawers. She remembered promising herself then that if and when she had children, she would be a much better mother than Sophie.

She thought she was, but needed to have it confirmed. 'I'm not making the same mistakes with Lara that Sophie made with me,' she told Dr Horner. 'I'm probably just making different ones.'

'Probably, but certainly not any worse. And you survived.'

'True, but it was a very painful growing up.'

The psychiatrist shrugged. 'The one thing you cannot

do for a child—for Lara—is prevent her from feeling pain. If she can't feel that, she can't feel anything else.'

'I'm not sure that's such a terrible burden,' said Ellin glumly.

'Oh, my, we *are* feeling sorry for ourselves today, aren't we?'

Ellin laughed. She liked Ruth Horner, enjoyed her frank, forthright manner and her sensible judgment. She was a woman about her own age; how could she be so wise? Ellin wondered.

'Do you have any children of your own?' she suddenly asked the psychiatrist.

'If I did, would you have greater confidence in me?' she parried. 'No, that's not meant to be an analytic put-off. Yes, I do—I have two sons, a few years younger than Lara. Twins.'

Ellin looked at her watch; her hour was almost up. 'Do you make mistakes with them?' she asked.

'Not the ones I know about. The others . . . I'm not sure. Would you like to make another appointment?'

Ellin thought about it. She felt happier than she had in a while. The sadness of Gregory was gone, and a week at the beach had renewed her physically. She was beginning to think life might be worth living again. And Lara was returning to California in a few days, leaving her free once more.

'Not now,' she told Dr Horner. 'But can I call you if I need you?'

The woman smiled. 'Sure you can. Even if you don't.'

TWENTY-TWO

Paula's frequent absences from the brownstone annoyed Cass. There were endless house chores that required her presence, Cass reminded her, but Paula procrastinated and finally refused.

'I didn't spend all this money to tie myself down to a house every weekend,' she protested. 'Besides, you have it all figured out—the garden, the fence, the patio. You want to do it, you do it. I think the patio is fine the way it is.'

'How do you know? You're never here,' Cass replied, accurately, for Paula was in Cambridge with Jake nearly as frequently as she was at home on Twelfth Street. Despite her own heavily scheduled days and weekends, Cass found energy for the tasks and chores that would turn the brownstone into the elegant, comfortable home she had pictured in her mind the first time she saw it. Ellin was glad to help; she liked puttering in the tiny yard on sunny afternoons. It made the house more her own. As she prepared the ground for the fruit trees and flowering shrubs that would bloom the following year and turn the small patch of earth behind the house into a green bower, she felt herself putting down roots, too. She was sorry Paula wasn't there to share the pleasure she felt, but did not resent her absence the way Cass did.

Paula was working whenever she wasn't with Jake—the brownstone was merely a place to change her clothes and sleep that summer. Before the Court's fall session began she had to complete a brief and a reply, which required frequent meetings with legal scholars and cooperating attorneys from organizations which planned to file *amicus* briefs. She delegated some sections of research to people whose expertise in a particular area was greater than her own, but the final responsibility was hers. So was the burden of reconciling the political differences among the members of her legal team; they debated strategy for hours at a stretch, and a consensus was not easily reached.

The case was a class action filed by doctors who protested that a state law that required notifying the husbands of women who wanted abortions abridged privacy rights which the Court had previously affirmed, beginning with the landmark *Roe v. Wade* decision. The decision favouring the plaintiffs was upheld and then reversed; the issue of constitutionality made it all but certain that the Supreme Court would hear the case. 'The issue isn't if, but when,' Paula said.

Cass was beginning to adapt to the rigorous demands of her new job. Grey Tucker was a challenging taskmaster, and Cass worked hard, not only because Tucker demanded it, but because she was fascinated with Al's agency. She had taken over supervising all Amagansett advertising, to the chagrin of Pete Marks. He was barely civil to Cass; try as she might, she could not charm him.

She was nervous and apprehensive the first time she had to turn down a campaign that Amelia presented. But Amelia seemed to have accepted the change in their status more gracefully than Cass. And after every meeting, Cass and Amelia managed a racquetball game and a leisurely lunch.

It was at one of those lunches that Cass asked after Amelia's daughter. 'Oh, we're estranged again,' Amelia told her airily. 'Natalie didn't like what I found out about her young man.'

Cass raised her eyebrows questioningly.

'Yes, he turned out to be a poseur. He seems to have

had two wives, both of whom were wealthy when he married them, and somewhat poorer afterward. Not that Natalie is exactly an heiress, but still . . . he simply wasn't suitable.'

Cass wondered if Amelia should have checked up on him, but Amelia herself seemed to have no qualms about her actions.

'It was my duty,' she said. 'Although Natalie didn't see it that way, of course. Oh, well, in ancient times they beheaded the bearer of bad news. And I haven't been beheaded, only dismissed.' She snapped her fingers. 'Like that!'

She made light of it, and would not accept Cass's sympathy. 'I made her who she is, you see . . . independent and self-reliant, that's what I tried to do. So it's my own monster that's devouring me.'

That was all she would say on the subject. But whenever Cass mentioned combining marriage and a career, much less a career and motherhood, Amelia shook her head. 'I didn't make sacrifices, I made choices,' she said. 'And by and large, they'll do.'

'Do you think she ever wanted a child?' Ellin asked Cass. Ellin was fascinated by Cass's stories about Amelia. She hoped she would get to meet the woman someday.

'At some time, she must have,' Cass said. She knew more about Amelia's early years now; since leaving Amelia's employ, they had grown closer. Professionally they were more equal now, and a different kind of friendship had emerged, in which they shared more of their personal selves.

Amelia had blocked out most of the memories of her early life, between girlhood and divorce. She grew up in Brooklyn, in a terrace house that was only steps away from a slum. Her father was boisterous and sometimes melancholy; he seemed to have given up on life when the Army refused to allow him to enlist in the war against the Germans because he had a perforated eardrum. Patrick

Brannigan saw the war as an opportunity to get away from his quiet, pious wife, his four squalling children, and Father O'Donnell, the parish priest, who was revered by Amelia's mother. Instead, he lived until just after V-J Day, and then he collapsed on a scrawny patch of grass behind the house on a hot August afternoon in 1945.

Amelia was in her early twenties then, going to City College at night, working at a department store in Manhattan during the day, and giving her mother half of her weekly pay-cheque.

When Patrick died, his widow used his insurance money to buy their house. She enlisted her sons in its renovation, turned it into a rooming house, and became a landlady. She hardly noticed when Amelia moved out.

Kevin Jordan was the store's advertising manager, and Amelia married him soon after they met. His dream was hers: that he would be a tremendous success in business, and they would settle happily in Larchmont or New Rochelle or perhaps even Westport, where they would raise a family.

Natalie was a difficult child, who could be teased out of colic or a temper tantrum only by her father. Kevin didn't mind; his career wasn't going anywhere. He lost a few jobs, and announced finally that he was going to open an agency of his own. 'Of course, I might as well work out of the house until the business is established,' he told Amelia.

She took a part-time job in the city, until that was assured—the commuting was difficult but they needed the money. And he was better with Natalie than she was; he could make the baby eat her vegetables, or stop screaming, or even smile.

When Amelia was offered full-time work, she accepted it without consulting Kevin. She didn't consult him before she filed for divorce, either, although when she did, he tried to convince her that Natalie would be better off with him. Kathleen Brannigan told Amelia exactly what Father O'Donnell thought about that. 'Your child is a gift from

God,' she chided. 'What kind of terrible hellfires are hot enough for a woman who says "No, thank you, God, it isn't convenient for me to have a little one just now"?' Kathleen's normally pinched face contorted even more. 'You might just as well have committed the mortal sin of aborting the babe as killing her now by leaving her. Not that divorce is to be taken lightly, of course, but abandoning your child—that's as bad as murder!'

She couldn't leave Natalie with Kevin; it wouldn't be right. So she took her with her into the city, into a world of strange babysitters and schools to which she had to be escorted, and into the nooks and crannies of Amelia's own new and busy life. And Natalie hated it.

Amelia loved Natalie, but she did not understand her child's simple yearning for what had been taken from her: her own house, her familiar surroundings, her wonderful father and her mother the way they used to be, always home when she returned from school, not tired and dragged out from working all day.

'I'll never be like you, never!' she shouted at Amelia once. Amelia realized then how much her daughter hated her.

Amelia never gave up on Natalie. She fully expected that if her daughter survived adolescence, she would do exactly the opposite of Amelia. She'll probably have nine children, get fat and sloppy, and live in a dirty old barn somewhere in the country, Amelia thought.

It surprised her that, finally, after a series of false starts, Natalie seemed to have made a career for herself. She was said to be smart and clever and ambitious; Amelia had sources in Paris who passed that information on to her. But they never say she's happy, Amelia thought sadly. And for that, she felt herself undoubtedly to blame.

Cass gave Ellin an edited version of Amelia's story, and Ellin thought Amelia was probably at fault, the agent of Natalie's problems; she had the self-righteousness of a single parent who shoulders her emotional responsibilities to her child despite her own needs. Ellin bristled at Cass's suggestion that there were similarities between her and Amelia. 'The cases are entirely different,' she said defensively. 'Lara went to Tony's because she wanted to. Even her psychiatrist agreed that it was the best thing for everyone. I would never put my career ahead of my child.'

'You don't have to,' Cass said complacently. 'You haven't had to make that choice—not yet, anyway.'

After Lara left, Ellin's spirits improved. She was getting over Gregory, and enjoying the slower pace of the city in summer. And the new men Cass introduced her to brightened her evenings considerably.

Paula smiled complacently at Cass's efforts. 'You're certainly a great matchmaker,' she said once as Ellin left for the theatre with Henry. 'How's your own love life?'

'Nonexistent,' said Cass. 'Don't ask.' And to her chagrin, Paula didn't.

That was just before the Fourth of July; Cass's planned break shrank to two days, and by the time she arrived in East Hampton to meet Nick, he had filled the void created by her absence. He had reconvened his old New York set; there were parties and tennis matches and an endless influx of people. Just as she knew there would be, she thought. She and Nick found little time to be alone, and when they were, he did not bring up the subject of marriage.

She planned to stay a few days longer, but Grey called and demanded that she return. 'We have deals that can't wait on your social schedule,' he told her, pleasantly enough. But there was a warning in his tone, and she heeded it.

Nick seemed to understand. The night before she left, he made love to her as ardently as ever; still, she sensed his moving away from her.

It was Cass who was doing the moving, establishing the distance between Nick and herself. But she did not tell that to Paula, who was in any case so preoccupied with her own life that she didn't hear what Cass did not say.

TWENTY-THREE

Ellin was going to Los Angeles to do a television talk show. As she packed for the trip home—funny how she still thought of California as home, she thought—she was excited. She was eager to see her friends, get back in touch with them, catch up with people she had missed in her eight months in New York.

She declined the invitation to stay at the rented house where Lara lived with Tony. She was keenly interested in observing how they lived, but there was no sense picking at an old scab.

It was scar tissue now, she thought; Tony's generosity toward Lara had planed its edges.

'I don't see how you can be so nice about that bum because out of the clear blue he suddenly decided to shoulder his responsibilities,' Sophie criticized Ellin. 'After all he did to you, and deserting Lara, he suddenly becomes a *mensch* and you act like he's God!'

Ellin was exasperated. 'Look, Ma, I don't care why he's doing it, and I don't think he's God. I'm grateful that he came through when I really needed him, that's all.'

'Oh, you didn't need him when Lara was little?' Sophie pounced. 'Not even once when Lara told us you were getting food stamps and we had to give you money? You didn't need him then?'

Ellin sighed. 'Sure, I needed him, but we survived, didn't we? We made it, right? Why should I carry a grudge? Everybody's fine now. We're all happy. Lara's happy, Tony's happy, I'm happy.'

'Happy?' said Sophie in amazement. 'Whoever said you're supposed to be happy?'

Whoever said you're not? Ellin thought resentfully. Sophie would never forgive Tony for what he'd done to her. She'd never forgiven Ellin for marrying him in the first place.

'An actor?' she shrieked. 'You're marrying an actor? You haven't seen enough *meshugena* actors all these years Lou's in the theatre, and you're marrying one? I wash my hands of you!'

Tony had confirmed Sophie's worst fears. He lived in a stage world, regardless of whether he was on a set. He approached marriage and parenthood the way he would approach a role, but he could not live up to the contract. That Ellin had kept him to it as long as she did surprised her more than it disappointed her; she'd gone into that marriage with her eyes open, prepared to pay. She just hadn't expected the price to be as high as it was.

As the plane chased the sun west, she worried about Lara. There had been a calm interval between the time her daughter mastered the rudimentary skills of survival, like crossing the street alone, and now, when the dangers were less obvious but equally threatening. All I ask, God, is no fluky stuff, like earthquakes or leukaemia, and please keep her away from fast cars and hard drugs, she prayed. Ellin always talked to God on aeroplanes; He seemed nearer then, so much more in charge of her fate.

And then she turned to pleasanter thoughts. Her friends at home. The way the dark gold of late afternoon turned the Pacific a deep teal blue. The scent of eucalyptus. Dinner at Musso's. Dace's new job and Allan's new house and Anne's party and Pepper's wedding, and Carol's new baby. And when the plane landed and she came out of the terminal and breathed in the warm, slightly muggy, flowery air of home, she was glad to be back.

Kate was at work, but she'd left Ellin the key, and a note. 'Welcome home,' it read. 'My house is your house.

I'll be back by seven; everyone's called to make dates with you, save me some time. I love you.' There was a sheet attached with messages, and Ellin scanned them happily. All her favourite people, the ones she'd kept in touch with since moving to New York. That was the nice thing about the move; it delineated all the marginal people in her life, the ones she knew and saw occasionally, but didn't really care about—the fillers. In her hand she had the ones who counted—the ones she'd missed.

She called Lara.

'Hi, sweetie, how are you?' She'd seen her a month before, but they change so quickly, Ellin thought.

Lara was monosyllabic. 'Okay.' 'Not much.' 'Just hanging out' she said, in response to Ellin's questions about her health, her habits, her plans. 'Daddy wants to talk to you.'

He was breezy, friendly, enquired about her trip, her health, her plans. 'When are you doing the Griffin show?' he asked.

'We tape tomorrow morning at eleven,' she said.

'Look, I've got to be near the studio around then,' he said. 'I want to talk to you. Let's have a cup of coffee—no, let's have breakfast. The Polo Lounge at eight?'

'Well, okay, but I was planning to see Lara tomorrow night, maybe bring her back here to Kate's with me. Can we talk then?'

Tony was impatient. 'No, this is something else, I'd rather have breakfast.'

That was just like Tony. Things went according to his schedule, or not at all. Whenever anyone said, 'I want to talk to you,' Ellin always felt a little bit sick to the stomach. It meant that she was going to be criticized, found out, confronted, exposed . . . it rarely meant anything good. But she wasn't worried about Tony; he had little power left over her emotions now. He probably just wanted to tell her what a hotshot parent he was, and how well he and Lara were doing together. Or perhaps he had found another woman, and was getting married again.

She was unmoved by the prospect; of course, maybe that wasn't what was happening at all. If a woman would make Tony happy—and she doubted that any one woman could, for very long—let him find one. Let him be well and happy and love Lara and want her with him and he could have any woman he wanted. Or man or dog or jackrabbit, for that matter. She knew Tony had had some homosexual experiences before they were married, and she suspected that he might have had some since. Not around Lara, she hoped, but other than that, she didn't care. Tony was pansexual—she had once accused him of being able to stick it into anyone, anything, even, anytime. That was when he wasn't doing it to her, as she recalled with a grimace.

She rose early the next morning and had tea with Kate before they both departed in different directions.

'Are you nervous about seeing Tony?' Kate asked her.

'No, I'm nervous about doing the show,' Ellin replied, twisting tendrils of her hair in her fingers. 'I wish it was over with. I wish I were twenty pounds thinner. I wish I'd had my hair done.'

Kate laughed. 'You're good on television. What's to worry?'

'It's my first national show, that's what,' Ellin said. 'What if I can't think of anything to say? What if my double chins show?'

'Not once in the ten years I've known you have you ever been tongue-tied,' Kate said. She was a psychoanalyst who specialized in treating anorectics. She was thirty-six, and had never married; she had some unsuitable suitors, and a rambling, comfortable house in Beverly Glen Canyon, and a clumsy golden retriever named Freud. She was patient, kind, and loving, and seemed to carry a secret about herself around in her head; Ellin treasured her for her good sense, elegant wit, and apparent distance from the turmoil that marked the lives and psyches of her other friends. 'If you keep talking, your chins won't show. Now go and be fabulous,' she said, pushing Ellin out the door.

Tony was late, as usual; heads turned when she came into the pink-and-green Polo Lounge, and quickly turned away. Don't bother, I'm not anybody important, I can't finance your movie or get an option on your script or find you an agent, Ellin thought. Credentials were important—she felt less naked now in Los Angeles than she once had, because people could introduce her with some qualifying statement—'This is Ellin Barnett, who did that book on . . .'

She was drinking her second cup of coffee when Tony arrived. A tiny thrill shot through her when he leaned down to peck her on the cheek; he smelled of Canoe—he wore the same after-shave her father did, a connection she'd never made before—and sunshine and that English toothpaste he was addicted to, and he was still an exceedingly handsome man. Silvering now at the temples, he was a graceful combination of size and sleekness, broad-shouldered and slim-hipped, casually but carefully dressed in a grey linen jacket, well-pressed khakis, and an Egyptian cotton polo shirt. There were new creases around his eyes, but he looked vital and healthy. She'd met a number of handsome men, some outstandingly beautiful, but no other man's looks ever pleased her as much as Tony's had. She'd always felt like the grey wren when she was with him; she was glad, today, that she had dressed and made up for the television show before meeting him.

They exchanged small talk, and then Tony dropped his bombshell. 'I'm going to Africa next month to make a film,' he said. Before she could interrupt, he told her all about the new Coppola movie in which he had been offered a leading role. He was glowing with enthusiasm; it was a role actors had been fighting for for months, and winning it was a great achievement. He went on and on about the location, the preproduction arrangements, his billing, his salary, and Ellin's vague sickness of the morning returned with a wave of nausea which she had to bite her lip to keep down.

'What about Lara?' she asked, already knowing the answer.

'Well . . .' Tony was vague. 'Of course, Africa's no place for a kid—'

'Take her with you,' Ellin interrupted calmly. 'It will be a marvellous experience for her. She can get assignments from her teachers, take her books, write papers—it's six months, you said. One school term. It'll be a great education.'

Tony frowned. 'No, it won't. They say six months, but you know how locations are, they always run over schedule. And we'll be in tents in the middle of the jungle, for Christ's sake. It could be dangerous . . . wild animals.'

She laughed shortly. 'You won't be in any danger, Tony, and neither will she. The only hazard is too many gin-and-oranges. You'll have a fabulous hotel room, or a big trailer, or a base camp in the Kenya Hilton or something. You'll land up on the comfortable side, I'm sure.'

Tony did have a taste for good living, and Ellin knew the housing situation wasn't really an issue. She wouldn't be put off that easily.

'Besides, what about this great father-daughter relationship you've developed?' she asked. 'You can't just drop in on her life and then drop out again because it's convenient. That's not what being a parent is all about.'

'You did it, didn't you?'

Ellin was angry. 'Goddamn you, Tony, I did no such thing. You're the one who came around and said, Let me play Daddy for this period. I was toughing it out with Lara . . . I didn't go to New York until she was all settled with you. Don't you dare talk to me about dropping out—you dropped out for ten fucking years!'

She was furious, upset, worried. What would she do with Lara in New York? How would they manage? Would she have to come back to California? What if her tenants wouldn't leave? How would she find another place to live in LA? Why should she? The memories of the last year with Lara were strong in her mind—the slammed doors, the screaming, the headaches, the worry. Not that again; she couldn't take it. She was just beginning to recover from the last time.

She didn't hate Lara. She loved her. In the past year, she'd missed her almost desperately sometimes, and when she longed for the sound of her daughter's voice, she called her. The conversations were usually one-way; Lara's monosyllabic responses had not changed much, she thought. But they were warmer lately; Ellin and Lara loved each other more when there was distance between them.

Phone calls and weekends and vacations had little to do with full-time parenthood, which Ellin was not ready for. She wondered if she ever would be again. She had put in her time, she thought ruefully, all those years when Lara's welfare always came first. Tony had rescued Ellin from those years, and now he was taking the life-preserver away.

They argued back and forth, but Ellin knew it was useless. Maybe she and Lara could live together, but not in the brownstone; her apartment was too small. Closed into that space together, they would kill each other.

Ellin felt sick at the thought of leaving the brownstone. She was happier there, with Paula and Cass, than she had been in a long time. They had become her family, even though Lara had a prior claim. They told each other everything; they knew the most minute details of one another's lives. They treated each other to presents; they applauded their own successes and sympathized with the failures, or even just the blues. They hugged each other a lot; they were like sisters.

The brownstone was the centre around which their lives revolved, a place where Cass could always count on feeling loved, where Paula had people who worried if she was sick or missed her when she was away, where Ellin lived without the loneliness she'd known since Tony left her.

Now all of that seemed snatched from Ellin's reach by Tony's abrupt decision to abandon Lara again and take off for Africa. Lara would upset the equation in the brownstone; Ellin knew it would never work.

'What about boarding school?' Tony suggested. He added hurriedly, 'I'll be glad to split the cost with you.' When Tony had money, he was not ungenerous. And after all he'd told her about the money he was receiving for the work, he'd better not be.

'That's still four thousand or so left for me to pay, plus clothes and expenses,' she said. She might guilt-trip him into picking up the whole bill. That, she knew, would be the easiest negotiation; Tony still felt shame about not having made enough money to contribute much to Lara's support when she was a child.

'Okay, I'll pay for it all.' He gave in easily, relieved that the decision was made and his conscience assuaged. Easy for you, Ellin thought resentfully—just write a cheque. Leave me with the hard part—convincing Lara.

'Have you told Lara yet?' she asked, and Tony fidgeted. 'Not exactly,' he replied. 'I thought maybe you could tell her and then we'd . . . work it out together or something.'

'Oh, no, you don't,' Ellin said. 'You tell her, and you convince her. This time you're not leaving me with the bad news to pass on. You did that once.'

She remembered how difficult it had been when Tony left. 'Where's Daddy gone?' Lara had whined in her childish voice. 'Mommy, why Daddy go away? Was Mommy mean to Daddy?' She wasn't going through that again, not any version of it.

The discussion over, Tony paid the bill and she walked out of the restaurant with him. People watched them as they passed; they were probably wondering who that dumpy old woman with Tony Devlin was, thought Ellin. Of course, they all knew him; word of his role in the

Coppola film buzzed around the room of powermongers, an almost audible hum.

He waited with her until the attendant brought her car. 'Listen, do a terrific job with Griffin,' Tony said brightly. 'And I'll tell Lara today.'

Oh, Jesus, she'd forgotten the show. Trust Tony to dump something like this on her just before an event in which she'd need all of her wits and self-confidence about her, not to mention her mind. She hoped Tony would be in Africa before today's show was broadcast. She hoped Lara would be in boarding school. And she hoped she'd be back in the brownstone.

The logistics were horrendous. Of course, Lara balked at boarding school. She threatened to run away. She cried and told them she felt rejected. She used all the buzz words, pushed all the buttons. And worst of all, Ellin was the one to tell her; as usual, Tony had opted out of the hardest part.

It was dangerously close to the start of school. Lara's grades were not high, and her record of expulsion the previous spring for smoking marijuana was attached to her applications. Ellin made a number of phone calls. Astrea, an *Apple* writer who was an ex-girlfriend of Nick's, had once done a feature on prep schools, and she expressed it to Ellin in California. Ellin brought the *Handbook of Private Schools* to Tony's house, and the two of them pored through it while Lara sulked in a corner. Tony convinced Lara it would be a great adventure, promising to bring her to Africa at the end of the filming. He flew back to the East Coast with her for interviews and tests at the schools that seemed the most likely choices.

'It's got to have horseback riding, and a ceramics class, and be coed, or I won't go,' said Lara. She had a whole list of other demands, too, and Ellin let her fight them out with Tony. I might as well use him while he's here, she thought.

It surprised Ellin that Lara was so vehemently opposed

to living in New York. She had held that option out to Lara—she could not bring herself to say, I don't want to share my daily life with you, to reject her so blatantly. But to her relief, Lara refused to consider it. 'I hate the city,' she said. 'Oh, it's okay once in a while, especially when we go to the theatre and stuff like that, but I couldn't live there. You can't even see the sun, and the air tastes terrible. Besides,' she added spitefully, 'I don't want to live with either of my parents, since both of them have deserted me.'

'That's enough!' said Tony. 'Neither your mother nor I are deserting you, young lady. The world simply cannot always run according to your whims, and you'll have to learn that.'

'Why not?' enquired Lara, not innocently. 'You seem to make it run according to yours.'

Touché, Ellin thought, that's telling him. Lara had said what she already knew: at least until this volatile time in Lara's life was passed, she and Ellin could not live together. Her daughter was wise enough to know that, she reflected sadly; at least I didn't have to say it.

'And I'm not going to one of those tacky preppy schools where there are rules and uniforms and creepos, either,' Lara added.

'Highly unlikely that they'd want you,' said Tony, and they glared at each other. So much for daughter-and-daddy bliss, mused Ellin with a certain feeling of satisfaction. Lara wasn't making it easy for Tony, and she was perversely pleased. All those years I got it all, all the shit, she thought—it's time you had a taste of it yourself.

They settled on a school. In spite of herself, Lara was excited. She and Tony arrived back in New York at the brownstone the day after Ellin returned from Los Angeles. They would fly west the next day, and one week later, Lara would return to start school. Tony was cheerfully paying all the bills, including Lara's air fare.

'He's doing everything he can,' Ellin told Dr Horner. 'Except keep her with him,' she added. 'I still resent that.'

'Of course you do,' said the psychiatrist. 'But don't blame Lara for that.'

Tony asked Ellin if he could stay at the apartment for the night. 'It's too late to find a hotel room, and we're leaving early in the morning.'

Ellin agreed. 'You can have the spare room, Lara will sleep with me.'

'I will not,' Lara said. 'You snore. And you kick. I won't close my eyes all night. You can sleep with each other . . . unless, of course, it's too utterly painful.' And she flounced off to her room.

'Look, if it's too much trouble,' Tony began, and Ellin shushed him.

'We're adults, Tony,' she said reasonably. 'We've slept together plenty without . . . without . . .' she faltered. Too many times, she thought. Too many times.

In the middle of the night he rolled over onto her, and she accepted his body soundlessly, pretending sleep at first so she could enjoy him without taking responsibility for it. She never could resist Tony when he wanted her. Their sex was familiar; she knew the rhythms of his body as well as she knew her own.

Later they shared a cigarette in the darkness. 'It wasn't all bad, was it, Ellin?' Tony asked suddenly. 'We had some good times together, didn't we?'

Ellin nodded; she was feeling that way herself, pleasantly nostalgic. 'And it wasn't for nothing, either,' Tony added. 'You've done a great job with her.' He indicated the spare room, where Lara was sleeping.

Ellin was strangely touched. She was glad that Tony thought she'd done right by Lara, grateful for the acknowledgement. 'We divorced each other, but not her,' Ellin said. She felt more comfortable with Tony than she had in a long time; she did not even mind that he could still awaken the old passion in her. She felt their shared history; they had come through the worst of it somewhere, to some place, some dimension in which the old hurts were healed and time blurred the sharp edges of pain. They caressed each other gently. Maybe love is just a place you have to get through to get to somewhere else, she thought as she fell asleep in Tony's arms.

They were both dressed and her bed was restored to its pristine singleness by the time Lara awakened. They breakfasted together, and Ellin kissed them both when they left.

'Thanks a lot,' she told Tony.

'I mean it . . . I'm in this to stay,' he told her. 'When I get back from Africa, Lara can live with me again if she wants to.'

'Good,' said Ellin gratefully. 'Make a great movie.'

She told Dr Horner about it the next day. 'He's not going to desert her again,' she said. 'I believe that now.'

'Good. Then you can finish letting go.'

'I thought that's what I had been doing,' Ellin told her.

'I didn't mean Lara, I mean Tony,' said the psychiatrist.

TWENTY-FOUR

Before Cass even walked through the smoked glass doors of the Amagansett building, she was already running behind. The entire day was like that, just enough out of synch so that she never quite caught up with it.

Nick had turned off her alarm clock without telling her, so when he woke her, his body urgent and his hands teasing her out of sleep, it was nearly nine o'clock.

'Oh, Goddamn,' she groaned, catching a glimpse of the clock over his shoulder.

He murmured happily into her neck, assuming her sigh was one of assent, and tightened his arms around her.

'Oh, Nick, Jesus,' she said, 'Look what time it is. I have to—I can't—' She pushed him off of her, exasperated, and he rolled over on his back, muttering a Greek oath she had heard often recently. It suggested that she do something improbable with a goat, and she hesitated before heading for the bathroom; she really should stop and make it up to him. But she did not; standing under the stream of hot water, she decided there wasn't enough time to go into it. What was wrong with the water pressure, anyway; why hadn't Vic fixed it? she wondered as the stream slowed to a trickle and she squeezed what she hoped was the last trace of shampoo from her hair. Had she told him to? No, she'd meant to, or at least to ask Paula or Ellin to remind him, but she hadn't gotten around to it before she left on the last business trip, and she was only home for two days before the week in Florida, and then there were the meetings with the underwriters about the new stock offering, and she just forgot about it. And then there was Nick.

God, I look awful, she told her reflection as she patted concealer over the lines beneath her eyes. She stopped squinting, but the lines remained. Happy birthday, you old bag. She was thirty-five this day, and when she opened the door of the bathroom, she saw Nick balancing a breakfast tray, croissants and juice, and an armful of gift-wrapped packages.

'I called your gal and told her you'd be late,' Nick said, as she stood there, overwhelmed by mixed emotions. She had another meeting with the underwriters at ten, and lunch with the management committee, and a stack of paper work and unreturned memos and messages waiting for her at the office, plus whatever else had accumulated in her absence. And Nick, who waited impatiently for her to clap her hands with delight, express her appreciation for his thoughtfulness. For a moment, she fought the desire to run back to the bathroom, lock the door behind her, and stay there until this day was over. But it was too late.

'She's not my gal, she's my secretary,' she said automatically, and then, seeing Nick's face, she fixed a smile on her own and moved forward.

It had not been a good time for Nick. The final figures for the first two quarters of *Orange* weren't in yet, but the signs that the magazine would not meet Nick's optimistic projections for immediate success were unmistakable. *Orange* hadn't managed to attract the subscribers or advertisers he'd counted on. The direct-mail campaign aimed at charter subscribers was a dismal failure, and newsstand sales were far below expectations. Worse, the start-up costs and promotion had escalated to nearly twice the original budget, which was much higher than even Nick's closest colleagues and staunchest supporters on the magazine's board of directors thought reasonable. The rumble of discontent from *Apple*'s stockholders grew louder; Nick heard them, even from California, but paid no attention; he was trying to keep *Orange* alive long enough to justify his judgement. It was brought home to him forcibly by a financial reporter from the *Times* that Hans Krugger, a German publisher whose empire extended from the biggest mass-circulation tabloid in Hamburg to a glossy women's magazine in Toronto, had convinced enough of Nick's *Apple* partners to accept an inflated offer for their stock. The threat to Nick's continued position as publisher and editor in chief of both *Apple* and *Orange* was serious.

By the time Nick realized it, it was too late. Miles Aldrich was firm. 'This time you went too far,' he told Nick bluntly. 'Krugger has enough new capital to get that pipe dream of yours in shape—decent enough so we can unload it, anyway. He has good systems people as well. They'll streamline *Apple*, make it more profitable.' He puffed on a briarwood pipe, which aggravated Nick even more. 'Of course, you'll still run the magazines,' he told Nick. 'You're the reason Krugger wants us. Your ideas, your style, your vision—'

'You can take your vision and shove it up your grey flannel ass!' yelled Nick. 'I wouldn't work for that fat Kraut if he owned the goddamned *New York Times!*'

'Perhaps he will, one day,' said Aldrich patiently. 'I hear he's been . . . looking into that situation.'

'Raiding, you mean?' said Nick. 'He'll never get to first base. Too bad. It's time the Sulzbergers and Ochses got out. But not *Apple*. Not my magazine. And not *Orange*, either!'

'That's what we've been trying to tell you, Pappas,' said Charlie Dahlstrom, echoing Aldrich's words like the bootlicking asshole Nick knew he was. 'It's not your magazine anymore.'

'Not unless you can meet Krugger's terms, or make us a better offer,' said Miles with infuriating calm.

Nick talked to his lawyer. 'You have thirty days to respond to Krugger's offer,' Hal Dent told him, and Nick went into a four-week marathon, shuttling between both coasts, trying to raise the money. In California, Bob Treat was apologetic, but adamant.

'Sorry, Nick,' he said. 'The loan for *Orange* just cleaned me out. I've invested pretty heavily in this movie, you know. Sure, I'm sitting on all my stock in Treat Industries. But I can't touch that. The old man would kill me. I might be able to do it in a few months, but not now. Everything else is tied up with the movie deal.'

Nick didn't have a few months, and his attempts to raise enough money to meet Krugger's offer for the stock failed. He knew he was losing the little influence he had left. Armies of sombre, florid-faced men with perpetually damp skin took over more and more desks at *Apple*, examining books and systems and asking questions of everyone, from the receptionist to the art director. They wrote the answers down with old-fashioned ink pens. The sale was inevitable. The final insult came when the board voted to take over Nick's apartment—part of his compensation in the early days before they had a dollar for salaries—for the magazine.

'You may still be the president,' Miles Aldrich informed him when he arrived back at the town house after a futile trip to Chicago in search of new capital, 'but this isn't the White House, you know. The board voted to pay your moving and storage costs, but it can't happen too soon. The magazine is growing so fast we need the space. We can't justify this extravagance any longer.'

'That's just about it, isn't it, Miles?' asked Nick. The movers suggested politely that he get out of the way; they were moving the huge rosewood-and-chrome dining table that had been the feature of *Apple*'s private dining room.

Aldrich shrugged noncommittally. 'Not completely,' he told Nick. 'It seems that we're getting complaints from some of our biggest advertisers. They're very upset about what they call your hatchet job on the city. That article on the power of the unions, and one on the increase in assaults on tourists, and the muck about all those French restaurants paying off city health inspectors.'

'We've been hearing from those bastards since the first issue,' said Nick, dismissing Aldrich's words with a gesture of contempt. 'So what else is new?'

'Tom Hobart,' said Aldrich.

'What about him?' Hobart was the editor of *Weekend*, a flourishing Long Island paper.

'The board thinks that since you're spending so much time in California with *Orange*, we need an editor in chief here at *Apple*. Someone who can give the job the attention it deserves.'

'Oh, is that what the board thinks?' Nick enquired, too sweetly.

Aldrich nodded in agreement. 'Of course, you'll still be publisher. Hobart's a good editor. You can work with him. You'll find him very amenable.'

'You'll find me that way, too,' said Nick. 'Amenable.' He tossed a key on the huge table as a husky blond man in coveralls negotiated one end of it past Nick and Miles. 'Talk to Hal Dent about my contract,' he said, and pushed past the movers, jamming his hat on his head and crushing it down savagely.

'I should have seen it coming,' he said angrily to Cass that night. 'Those fucking accountants, not enough imagination between them to invent the wheel, let alone run my magazine. *My* magazine!' he repeated for emphasis. He refilled his glass from the bottle of Glenlivet Scotch, and pushed away the ice Cass proffered. 'Here I am with a million bucks, more or less, when Dent works out the details of the severance pay, my contract, and my shares in *Apple*. And not even a place to hang my hat. Christ, out on the street again.'

'Not exactly broke,' Cass said. 'Or homeless, either. You can move in here, you know.'

Nick managed a grin. 'A househusband?' he said. 'Not exactly my style. I can't even get rid of yellow waxy buildup.'

Cass covered her glass when Nick picked up the Scotch.

'No, no more. I have to be at the airport in a couple of hours.' She looked at her watch. 'Nobody said househusband, Nick,' she said. 'I said roommate, houseguest, whatever.'

'Whatever,' said Nick. 'I like the sound of that. Ms Cass Campbell, rising young corporate executive, was seen attending the Paris collections with Nick Pappas, ex-magazine publisher, currently Ms Campbell's whatever.'

Cass giggled. 'I don't think Amagansett encourages the presence of whatevers on business trips.' She laughed. 'But I have some time between the openings in Milan and the Paris meetings. Why don't you come and meet me over there? We'll go to Corfu . . . remember what a wonderful time we had there a few years ago? And then when you come back, you'll have decided what to do next.'

'Not this time, sweets,' said Nick. 'I've got to get me a place to live, and a job. *Apple*'s gone, and they're going to fold *Orange*. I'm not entirely without resources, you know. I've got meetings, lunches, drinks all over town this week. And a few ideas. By the time you get back from this trip, I'll have something lined up.'

'Of course you will,' said Cass, reassuringly, and Nick's temper flared, fuelled by the three quarters of a bottle of Glenlivet he had consumed.

'Don't you patronize me, Cass,' he said. 'Don't you goddamn patronize me. The bastards may have dealt me out of this hand, but I'm not out of the game. Not by a long shot!'

'I wasn't patronizing you. Don't get mad, Nick.'

'Mad is a luxury I can't afford,' Nick replied. 'I don't get mad, I get even.'

They agreed that Nick would leave most of his belongings in storage, and move into Cass's apartment.

'Just until I figure out what's next,' he said, and she agreed 'I'm pretty old-fashioned, underneath this modern exterior,' he told her. 'Being a kept man isn't exactly my thing.'

Cass was too tired to argue. 'Semantics,' she said. 'If

it'll make you happy, you can make my mortgage payments. And have your own phone put in, and use the library as your office, too.'

'I already rented an office,' said Nick. 'And hired a secretary. Maybe I'll start a new magazine. The *Apple* writers walked out on Krugger yesterday. They don't want to work for the Kraut. They want to work for me.'

'Will they stick it out?'

'Who knows?' Nick shrugged. 'I appreciate the gesture, but they have families and bills and mortgages to meet, too.'

'Why'd you take offices, and where?' Cass wanted to know.

'Some space over on Eighth Avenue. Because a guy without an office and a secretary is a guy without a job. Appearances are important in this town.'

'Okay, forget the library and the telephones,' Cass said. 'Here.' She took a key from her purse and gave it to him. 'I had this made for you today.'

The head of the key was gold. Nick took it, turning it over. He squinted, trying to read the inscription. It had been engraved that morning at Tiffany; ordinarily, engraving required several days, but the salesman, who knew Cass as a frequent customer, had rushed the order through.

'My house is your house,' Nick read. 'Who writes your lines, Campbell?'

She shrugged. 'Not very original, I guess.'

He knocked over their glasses as he pulled her up from the chair. 'It's the thought that counts,' he said. 'You know I love you?'

'I know,' she said, hugging him back. 'Me too you. I cleared out a couple of closets for you, and some drawers in the bedroom. Make yourself at home.' She heard the door buzzer sound. 'That's the limo,' she told Nick. 'Tell him I'll be right out, will you?' She gathered her briefcase and checked in it for her tickets and passport.

'Whatever Madame desires,' he said, and she gave him a sharp look.

'Only kidding,' he assured her. 'You know, I could probably get used to being a kept man. Not a very demanding job, but the benefits are good.'

He opened the door, expecting to see the uniformed limousine driver. Grey Tucker stood there instead, and Cass held her breath as the two men inspected each other warily. Like a couple of male dogs, she thought.

'I didn't expect you,' she said to Grey as she made introductions. He looked at Nick, who was showing the effects of too much alcohol, and was half dressed besides.

'Obviously,' Tucker said coolly. 'Are you ready? The plane won't wait, you know.'

'I'm ready,' she said, and hurriedly picked up her travelling things. Tucker preceded her out the door, taking her suitcase, and she turned to Nick. 'I love you,' she whispered. 'I'll call you this weekend. You'll be here?'

He chucked her under the chin. 'Sure will,' he said. 'Just me and the girls in the dorm. Fly high, baby.'

'Just keep your hands off the dorm girls,' she told him. 'They're my friends, Nicky.'

'No problem,' he assured her. 'Tucker looks like a stuffed shirt, but you keep your hands off him, too.'

'No problem,' she said, kissing him quickly. 'Bye.'

On the plane, she replayed Nick's words. It was true, sometimes Grey did seem like a stuffed shirt. But not when they were really working together, cooking on their own energy, sparking ideas, plans, words off of one another. Those were the best times, times when she was consumed by her job to the exclusion of everything else, and loved it passionately.

But there were other times when it was painfully obvious that Tucker was not her colleague, but her boss. For instance, when they were alone together, she called him Grey; he made it known that in the presence of others he preferred a more formal mode of address. Always, he called her Cass.

He kept her off guard; she was not sure how she should be with him. She settled, finally, for a sort of breezy respectfulness.

Grey rarely resonated to her feelings, and gave her few opportunities to probe his own. He was emotionally inarticulate; he told her what he thought, and from that she had to infer what he felt. She had occasional sexual fantasies about him, as she told Paula.

'Yes, but do you *like* him?' Paula asked. Cass couldn't answer. Grey fascinated her; she did not know his vulnerabilities yet. She respected him. He was smart; not smarter than Nick, but smart in another way. Like him? That had nothing to do with it.

TWENTY-FIVE

It was cold, grey, and damp in Milan. The weather did nothing to dampen the enthusiasm of the half-a-hundred Italian designers who were determined to challenge Paris for dominance in the ready-to-wear market. The collections had opened a couple of days before; only because Cass had made two trips to Milan in the previous three months, tipping lavishly and generously, was she able to ensure rooms in a first-class hotel and the services of a chauffeur, which Grey insisted upon; he was not going to risk his neck in cabs driven by crazy Italians, he told her. Cass didn't see that much difference between cabs and limos, since the drivers were equally crazy, and equally Italian, but she made the reservations anyway.

The hotels, restaurants, and streets of Milan were jammed with photographers, journalists, buyers, mannequins and clothes watchers from all over the globe. They streamed out of the Milan Trade Fair Centre late each day, after ten hours of showings, speeches, and elaborate lunches. Each night the leading fashion houses hosted dinners, dances, parties, and extravagant entertainments.

Grey thought the whole experience extraordinary. 'Who is *that*?' he whispered from behind his programme to Cass, as a woman wearing a bizarre headdress of fishnet, seaweed, and shellfish sat down on a gilt chair in front of them, cutting off their view of the runway.

'One of the dragons. French *Vogue,* I think,' Cass told him.

'Dragons?' Grey was amused.

'Fashion journalists,' Cass translated. 'The first year I came to the collections, she wore an even crazier hat, wild flowers and moss and birds. Incredible. But it's a nice change from some of them, though; for women who cover fashion, they're pretty much a frumpy lot.' She lowered her voice as the stocky woman with close-cropped, greying hair who was covering the collections for the *Times* took a seat next to her.

From Missoni to Versace, Biagiotti to Krizia, the displays went on. One day was plenty for Cass, but Grey, diverted by the spectacle, was tireless.

She dragged him away from the Trade Fair Centre to visit the factory of the Italian knitwear manufacturer whose company she hoped AI would acquire, and to meetings with the firm's principals, a middle-aged couple who had resisted previous attempts by American companies to acquire their old, family-owned business. She went with Grey to lunch with the accountants, dinner with the chief designer, and breakfast with the sales representatives. In the limousine, on the way to the villa where Signor Montelli and his wife would finally, she hoped, agree to terms of the purchase, she went over the figures with Grey one last time.

'But don't some of their clothes look a little, well, overdone for us?' Grey asked. They had watched the Montelli collection that afternoon, from the best front-row seats, ruffling a few dragon feathers in the process; the *International Herald Tribune* reporter and her colleague from *Women's Wear Daily* had given up their seats to Grey and Cass, but not at all happily.

'A lot of what comes down the runway never makes it to the retail rack,' Cass explained. 'It's just for the fashion books. The Montellis have no intention of making everything they showed us today.'

'I hope not,' Grey said. 'Somehow I don't see our lady at Blythe's snapping up that number with the feather halter and the see-through riding pants.'

'The jodhpurs, you mean?' Cass laughed. 'No, that's

just Mario's bagatelle. It'll get him a good mention in the process though. And someone might order it. I saw Princess Caroline giving it the once-over today.'

'Do you suppose she'll be there tonight?'

'God, I hope not,' said Cass. 'The Montellis promised it would be a small group this evening. They know we're leaving tomorrow.'

She had noticed how easily Grey was impressed by titles; it diminished him somewhat in her eyes. She could, however, understand it. In the first few years of her career, she'd been that way, too. He confessed his awe with a boyish embarrassment she found appealing. 'Pretty heady stuff for a kid from Memphis,' he told her after he was introduced to a member of the British royal family, a princess whose ample figure did not make the most of the clothes she ordered in huge quantities each day.

The Montellis, too, had noticed Tucker's inclination, and the small dinner party they had promised included only twenty people besides themselves. 'And two titles per person,' Cass whispered to Grey after all the introductions were accomplished. Dinner was not served until after ten, and the effect of several round-the-clock days and too much wine made Cass sleepy. Finally it was over. People were beginning to leave, saying their good-nights and urging their thanks on the Signora. Cass could not find Grey.

'He is with my husband. They are—how do you Americans say it—closing the deal?' the thin-faced, sharp-eyed woman told her.

Cass was dismayed. 'But they can't—I have the papers here—' She looked around for her briefcase, which she had surrendered along with her coat when she and Tucker arrived at the villa.

'Oh, do not worry, Signorina Campbell,' said the Montelli woman. 'It is the figures, the bargains, the negotiating, for the men, not for us women, no?'

'No,' said Cass, more sharply than she had intended. Her fatigue was gone; her mind was clear and alert. 'It's my deal. I put it together. I—' She stopped, considering the effect of her words on the older woman.

'You young American girls, you are all alike, wanting to be like the men, making the deals,' said her hostess, a woman Cass knew to be, herself, an extremely skilled and adept negotiator. 'Better you should let him do that, and you go home to the hotel and get your beauty sleep. I can tell it is going to be a long night, my husband and your Mr Tucker. I will go and see that your chauffeur is called.' In spite of Cass's protests, she turned and left the room. Cass waited impatiently for a few moments, and then moved toward the stairs. She knew that Signor Montelli must have a study somewhere in the villa, and asked a maid who was emptying the ashtrays where it might be.

'In there, signorina,' the maid said, gesturing up the stairs. 'But Signor Montelli, he is in there with an American gentleman, he wants not to be disturbed. Signorina, I really don't think you should—' But Cass paid her no mind, and pushed open the thick, ornately carved mahogany door the maid had indicated.

Grey and Montelli were bent over an ivory chessboard. A decanter of brandy was next to the table. The cigar smoke was thick in the air, and both men were in shirt sleeves.

Tucker looked up from the game. There was a look of disapproval on his face, but Cass ignored it.

'Oh, signorina, my apologies, did not my wife tell you we were having a little game? She was to have called your chauffeur when it was time, but no matter, I will ring for him—'

Cass closed the door behind her. 'I thought perhaps we would discuss our business, Signor Montelli. As you know, we leave tomorrow, and the papers are ready, the letters of intent—'

'Cass, we'll take care of the papers, don't worry,' Grey interrupted. 'Why don't you just run along back to the hotel, and I'll see you in the morning.'

She ignored his look of warning. 'Grey, as I told you, there are still a couple of clauses in the agreement that need discussion before we come to—'

'Clauses, we will work them out, don't you have a care, signorina,' said Montelli. 'Now that you have so kindly introduced me to Mr Tucker, of your great Amagansett Industries, he and I will sit down, like two men, over some brandy and perhaps a wager on our game of chess, at which he, of course, is certainly much better than I, and we will work it out, like men, men who make the business together, and you will go and get the sleep to keep your very great beauty, and like that, it will all be done!' He snapped his fingers enthusiastically. 'Ah, here is my dear wife, with your most lovely wrap. I see your Mr Tucker already is a man of taste—'

Signora Montelli was holding out the Fendi mink jacket on which she had finally made the last payment at Bergdorf's.

Cass was furious. Montelli had negotiated every step of the agreement with her, over countless bargaining sessions during which each clause and sentence of the initial intent-to-purchase letter had been cagily fought over. To be dismissed now as window dressing made her furious; not only that, but Montelli's presumption that Grey had given Cass the fur which was such a symbol to her of her independence was an even greater insult; it made her anger of the dismissal from the bargaining table pale by comparison. With great effort, she contained herself, and simply nodded to the two men.

'Very well,' she said. 'Thank you for the lovely party, Signor Montelli. I look forward to seeing you in New York when you come to conclude the contract. And to working closely with you in the future. I'm glad that our meetings in the past several months seem to be coming to such a promising conclusion.'

There, she thought, as she finally slammed the door of her hotel room behind her, and sent the chauffeur back to the villa to wait for Grey. Just so the little son of a bitch remembers who bought him all that lousy, fucking brandy!

She raged around the room, waiting for Grey to return, cursing men; Italian men, American men, stupid men, rude men, ungrateful men, and all businessmen. Finally, she swallowed a Valium and went to bed, falling into a restless sleep.

She was groggy on the flight to Paris, and sniffling from the cold she had picked up in Milan. Her head felt feverish, and she wanted nothing more than to ignore Grey and sleep. But he was in high spirits, pleased at the outcome of his meeting with Montelli, full of enthusiasm for the deal.

'You did a terrific job, Cass,' he told her as the stewardess poured his coffee and offered him the morning newspapers. She filled Cass's cup, too, and held out a handful of fashion magazines. Annoyed, Cass refused them, and purposefully took out her briefcase. The stewardess missed the gesture; she had turned away to another passenger.

'I'm so glad you're pleased,' she said, with a faint hint of irony which Grey noticed. It amused him.

'Look. European men are that way,' he said, placating her. 'Montelli insisted that we meet together. He said some very complimentary things about you, by the way.'

'Did he ask how much you paid for my fur coat?' she asked, unmollified.

Grey laughed, and patted her arm. 'We really are touchy today, aren't we?'

The cutting response already framing itself in Cass's mouth was interrupted by a sneeze, and then another. Grey was solicitous, which did nothing to improve her mood. You're looking for a fight, she told herself, and you can't win it, so shut up.

Cass was not unclever; she knew when the wisest move was to back down, and bruised feelings were barely worth opening a discussion she knew would make no sense at all to Grey. She chose her disputatious moments carefully, and this was certainly an inappropriate one. There were three days in Paris ahead of them, three days before this gruelling trip was over, and if she got through them, she promised herself, she would take an entire week off.

The three days stretched into six. Although the meetings scheduled for the Paris trip were over, the collections were still going on, and Grey was enjoying the round of parties and fetes. On their final afternoon, leaving a showing at St Laurent, he informed her that he had rearranged their return reservations so that they could attend a lavish ball at the Elysée Palace, being given by the French government in honour of a Japanese syndicate which had recently purchased one of the great fashion houses. By then, Cass was thoroughly sick; her cold had turned into real flu, and none of the medicines prescribed by the doctor called by the hotel concierge had had any palliative effect. Not did she have an appropriate ball gown in her travelling wardrobe, she informed Tucker.

'Well, hell, we're in the fashion capital of the world, aren't we?' he demanded. 'Go and buy yourself one!'

She mentally calculated the cost of such a dress, and resigned herself to a major—and nontax-deductible—expenditure. She couldn't tell Grey that she was living very close to the financial edge; in spite of the high salary she was earning, her expenses were much higher than they had been at the agency. And there was the new boiler the brownstone was definitely going to require soon—had Vic said three thousand dollars?

'I've got to see some people from the trades,' Grey told her. 'The invitation says nine, so please be on time.'

She nodded and he left. A quick look through St Laurent and three other salons convinced her that a designer gown would certainly mean a season without hot water in the brownstone, even if she didn't pay her American Express bill that month. But American Express wouldn't carry accounts over thirty days, and she was already dangerously in arrears. Frustrated, she stopped for a coffee at a sidewalk café, and waved hello to an American model she knew from New York. Dorinda waved back, and came over to Cass's table.

'What are you doing here?' she asked, and Cass told her. The tall, green-eyed mannequin eyed Cass thoughtfully. 'I don't have anything that would fit you,' she said, 'but surely if you talked to one of the managers at a salon, you could get a discount. Amagansett is a big buyer. They'd probably give you something free.'

Cass shook her head. 'No, I don't want to do that,' she said. 'Look, aren't there any little boutiques around here that might have something more reasonable?'

Dorinda's eyes gleamed. 'There's a funky little place over on the Left Bank where all the rich Frenchwomen take their old Diors and Balenciagas,' she said. 'After they've worn them twice. Some terrific bargains. Come on, I'll show you.' Cass paid for her coffee, and followed Dorinda down the street, where they got a taxi.

True to her word, the shop was open, and in minutes, Cass had found a black lace-and-chiffon dress that bared her shoulders and set off her breasts. Dorinda looked at the discreet white ticket, and spoke to the proprietress in rapid French. Cass was already taking out her purse, but Dorinda wouldn't allow her to purchase the gown until she had bargained the woman down.

Cass was embarrassed; she hated haggling, even when it was customary and accepted. Although she was careful with her money, she always preferred paying to arguing, but Dorinda insisted. Moments later, they left the shop, Cass's new dress carefully boxed and carried under her arm. Translating francs into dollars, she realised that Dorinda's negotiations had saved her almost a hundred dollars, and she was grateful. 'But I don't know how you can do it,' Cass said as they walked. 'I couldn't, not for the life of me. In a bazaar or a souk, or a market in Mexico, maybe, but in a store in Paris?'

Dorinda laughed. 'They speak dollars here just like everyone else does,' she said. 'If I didn't haggle, I couldn't pay my bills. How do you think people like me live in France?'

Cass didn't know, and fervently hoped she would never have to find out. Dorinda had been a successful model in New York. Unfortunately, her all-American looks were not much in demand in Manhattan lately; photographers and fashion editors currently wanted exotic, dark-skinned types. So she had come to Europe to freelance the collections.

'Perhaps I can find some work for you in one of our divisions,' said Cass. 'At least I can put you in touch with the right people.'

'I'd appreciate that,' the tall girl said pleasantly. 'Us working gals have to stick together.'

'Without you, I'd be in an awful mess tonight,' Cass said. 'Give me a call when you get back into the city, and I'll see what I can do.' She gave Dorinda her card, and thanked her again.

The encounter cheered her. A brief nap and a long, hot tub soothed her body, and her stuffy head seemed to be clearing at last. When she met Grey in the lobby of the hotel, she looked rested and fresh, and he admired her dress and décolletage. 'You're gorgeous,' he told her frankly. 'Nothing like a new dress to cheer a woman up, right?'

She regarded him levelly. 'Wrong, Grey. It's a new hat that's supposed to do that, don't you know?'

'Maybe it's a dress that brings the sense of humour back,' he parried. 'Isn't that a St Laurent?'

'It is,' she said. From about five years back, but a St Laurent nonetheless, she did not add.

He shook his head in admiration. 'With your salary, and no family to support, I guess you can afford it.'

Wrong tactic for someone who needs a raise, she thought, smiling back at him automatically. I should have worn my tweed suit.

The evening was magical from the moment they stepped out of the limousine. The handsome rooms of the stately, elegant palace were dressed with beautiful people; liveried footmen offered champagne from silver trays to men in evening clothes who all looked handsome above their black ties and crisp white collars, and women in their finest ball gowns who seemed like flowers in a garden riotously planted, from a balcony where Cass, with Grey, looked down on them. At midnight a lavish buffet was served; Bocuse himself had planned and executed it, a German countess told Cass. She was glad that she had come; her bone-tiredness floated away with the lilting music, as she and Grey danced the evening away. His prowess surprised and pleased her; he was an excellent dancer, uncharacteristically relaxed, lithe and sure, bending her body into his own as they waltzed and spun and dipped. They left the palace at dawn together just before the sun lightened the sky.

Grey asked the chauffeur to stop the limousine near the river and opened the car door himself to help her out. He took her hand and led her out to smell the freshness of the early morning air and watch the lights of Paris flicker off and out in the aluminium-coloured dawn.

'Romantic, isn't it?' asked Grey. She nodded, and his hand tightened on hers in its grasp. He noticed her shiver; he took off his jacket and placed it around her shoulders, brushing her bare skin. She felt another kind of shiver, deeper inside her body, and then her surprise melted into pleasure as Grey took her in his arms and bent his head to hers.

It was a moment before the warning bells went off inside her head—a moment when he found her lips with his tongue, tracing their outline and opening them to his own as easily as if they were a lock to which he had the only key.

Perhaps his own alarm had sounded; he stepped away from her quickly, and said, 'That's what one does at dawn by the Seine, correct? One kisses a pretty girl, and—'

'And a photographer takes his picture,' Cass interrupted, gesturing toward a tall, stoop-shouldered journalist she had met during the collections. The *Trib*, she knew, and the next day, when she saw the picture of Grey and herself in the newspaper provided on their flight home by the Air France stewardess, she shuddered.

'Amagansett Industries chieftain Grey Tucker and his constant companion, personal assistant Cass Campbell, play tourists as the sun rises over the Seine. The sun also rises in Manhattan, where they live,' she read. Grey looked over her shoulder.

'Nice shot,' he said. 'I particularly like the shadows there,' and he pointed to her prominently displayed decolletage.

'Oh, they'll love it back in New York,' she sighed, disgusted.

He shrugged. 'You don't think I want them to know I really chose you for your brains, do you?'

She crumpled the paper and pulled a blanket around her. 'You know, sometimes you are a total blockhead,' she said, and snapped out the light above her seat before he could reply.

She tried to sleep, but she kept remembering his searching, insisting, exploring kiss, and the leer on the face of the photographer, and long before they landed at JFK, she had given up. Staring aimlessly out the window, she wondered what she could possibly tell Nick.

TWENTY-SIX

'Take tomorrow off, Cass,' said Grey as the limousine pulled up in front of his apartment building, the Olympic Tower. 'You look done in. Jet lag, probably. And that cold you picked up in Italy. This pace is tough on a woman.'

He looked fresh and ready for a business meeting; it made her angry. But she was too tired to deny his words. 'I can't,' she said. 'The report on the Montelli deal—we need it for the management committee meeting Monday.'

'That's right, we do.' He frowned. 'Look, why don't we move that off the agenda this week? We'll take it up next meeting. Besides, you're making a presentation of the new market research plan Monday, aren't you?'

She nodded. The presentation that was still in pieces, on index cards and bits of paper, hastily scribbled notes, ideas written down on the back of staff reports. The presentation that represented her first major responsibility at AI. She groaned silently. If she worked at home all day tomorrow and Saturday, she could finish it by Sunday and get it typed Monday morning. If she could get the fellows in the art department to work over the weekend on the charts and illustrations, and if she didn't stop to sleep or eat or . . .

'I'll come in and dictate the report on the Montelli acquisition in the morning, Grey,' she said wearily, 'and then put the finishing touches on the market research plan.'

He brightened. 'Atta girl. I knew you could handle it.

Most women would collapse under this kind of pressure, but you just take it all in stride. You're tough.'

Tough, she thought, resting her head back against the plush velour interior of the limo. Just what I always wanted to be, right? She could still laugh at herself, which was a good sign; she was not completely dead yet. She managed to keep awake until the car pulled up next to the brownstone. My own bed, she thought. My own bathtub. A cup of my own spice tea in my own big cup, and maybe a slug of my own brandy, and then sleep—blessed, wonderful sleep.

As soon as she opened the door of her apartment, she knew it was not to be. Nick was there—oh, God, she'd forgotten about Nick—and the living room was thick with the acrid odour of cigars. Three *Apple* writers were with him, including Astrea, a woman Cass especially disliked. The feeling was mutual; before Cass, Astrea had been Nick's constant companion. She was a brilliant writer, one of the reasons for the magazine's initial success, and Cass detested her. The affair between Astrea and Nick was over before Cass and Nick met, but it was Nick, not Astrea, who ended it, and Cass knew that until Astrea was happily coupled with someone else, she would still desire him and hate her.

'Hi, sweets, how was the trip?' Nick waved to her from the couch, and she took in the scene with one despairing, angry look. There were overflowing ashtrays everywhere, and newspapers and magazines piled untidily in corners of the room. Nick's clothes were scattered all over, and Cass's plants were brown and withered. The room was littered with coffee cups and glasses; she looked into one and saw a shredded cigarette floating in the scum of cold brown liquid. She grimaced.

Nick got up and came to her, his arms outstretched. She collapsed into them gratefully.

'Sunrise over the Seine—pretty glamorous, I guess,' said Astrea cattily, and Cass bristled in Nick's arms.

Greetings from the others in the room covered the awkward silence, and Cass whispered against Nick's ear, 'Get that bitch out of here, Nicky, please.'

'Oh, come on, Cass, that's just Astrea, she doesn't mean anything.'

'Maybe not to you, but she means poison to me. Nick, I'm dead on my feet. Exhausted. Please, let me get into bed. I'll tell you about that picture tomorrow, it's nothing.'

'Yeah, I know. Don't worry about it. Come on, I'll take your things in. We'll wrap this up soon.'

She managed to be civil to his guests, and dragged her weary body to the kitchen to put the water on to boil. The top of the tea canister had been left off; the few leaves still in the bottom were old and stale. The aspirin bottle was empty, and there were no clean towels in the linen closet. The bedroom was a mess, too; she was too tired to care, and she fell into bed. But the noise from the living room disturbed her, and she tossed and turned in the rumpled bed, wracked by spasms of coughing, unable to rest. She turned over on her back, and lay in the stuffy, dark room. Only the cool tears on her face told her she was crying, and she could not have told anyone, least of all Nick, why.

It was close to midnight when she heard the door to the hall close and the noise ceased. She waited for Nick to come to bed, but he did not, so eventually she pulled on a robe and went out. He was not there; evidently they had gone in search of food, since there was nothing to eat in the apartment. She stifled an urge to put the night bolt on, and surveyed the wreckage of her house. Her fatigue lifted; she began straightening up the room, carrying cups and plates and ashtrays into the kitchen, leaving them to soak in sudsy water in the sink. A strange euphoria overtook her as she cleaned; she opened windows and piled up the newspapers and debris near the door. The room looked better; she watered her plants and threw out a couple that were beyond help, and began to vacuum. When she came out into the hall, on her way to the garbage cans, she met Paula.

There wasn't a great deal of privacy in the brownstone. Despite what everyone said about pre-war buildings, the walls and floors weren't that thick, and it was smaller than many other, similar houses that had been converted into apartment buildings. It had originally been built for a family, and in many ways, the three women kept it that way. Cass and Paula had always been the custodians of each other's life; that had not changed. And Ellin, freed of that role without Lara, liked the unusual proximity of the apartments, and the women, to each other. She was alone, working, on the top floor, while Cass and Paula were at offices; she was always happy to hear them come in.

Privacy had not been an issue between Cass and Paula, either. There was little they did not tell one another, almost nothing too intimate to be shared. Ellin kept a bit more to herself, and they respected her vague limits—well, Paula did. But between Paula and Cass there were no limits.

'I heard the vacuum going, and I knew it couldn't be Nick,' Paula said. She looked beyond Cass to the living room. 'Cleaning the house at midnight? Either you're demented, about to give birth, or compulsive.'

Cass began coughing again, and Paula led her back inside. 'All three, I guess—well, maybe not pregnant.' She sat Cass down on the sofa, and looked around.

'I don't know which looks worse, you or this place,' she said, and Cass laughed weakly. 'Sit down, stay where you are, I'll finish it. Wait, I'll make you something for your throat.'

She mixed hot water, honey, lemon juice, and brandy, and brought it to Cass in a clean mug. 'My *bubbe*'s favourite remedy for everything,' she said, picking up the bags of garbage. 'I'll take these downstairs, and clean up the bedroom. No, sit, you look awful.'

I must, Cass thought, sipping the toddy. You're the

third person to tell me that tonight. She could not move; Paula wouldn't let her, anyway. She went upstairs to her own apartment, and came back with an armful of clean towels and linens. 'Looks like a fraternity house in here,' she commented. 'Doesn't Nick know how to make a bed?'

'I doubt it,' Cass replied. 'He always had some woman to do that for him, or a maid.'

'Aren't we all?' Paula laughed. 'Jake is worse. God, men are slobs.'

She changed the bed, and made Cass come back and get into it. 'Want a back rub?'

'Oh, I think I've died and gone to heaven,' said Cass happily, turning over. She relaxed as Paula's strong hands kneaded her tired muscles, and murmured something indistinguishable into the pillow.

'What did you say?' Paula asked.

'I said I loved you best in all the world,' Cass replied.

'Me too you,' said Paula. 'Cass, you're killing yourself with this job, you know. You haven't had a day off or even a weekend in months. With Nick here, you're responsible for a household as well as a company. Not to mention that Ellin and I haven't seen you forever. You can't keep this up.'

Cass turned over with a sigh and sat up against the pillows. 'It's not going to be forever. Just another few weeks and then I can slow down a little.'

'What happens in a few weeks?'

'Performance review. And then maybe a vice presidency.'

'If you live that long,' said Paula. 'It's not worth killing yourself for, Cassie.'

'I'm not killing myself, just pushing harder than usual. I really want that title, Paula. I need it to do what I want to do. Until I have it, I can get pushed around by people like Pete Marks, by all of them. Once I get past them . . .' Her voice trailed off.

'Then what?' asked Paula. 'I'll tell you what. They'll just throw a whole pile of other shit at you. Meanwhile, you have no life. What are you giving up to get it—to get power, turf, titles?'

'I'm not giving anything up,' said Cass wearily. 'Just putting a few things on hold temporarily, that's all.'

Paula pushed an errant strand of hair out of Cass's eyes. 'Okay, I won't nag. If there's anything I can do, let me know.'

'You did it, tonight,' She looked around the tidy, clean-smelling bedroom, and up at Paula. 'That's true love . . . someone who takes out your garbage at midnight.'

'You'd take out mine.' It was a statement, not a question.

'Damn straight,' said Cass, and they began laughing. When Nick came in fifteen minutes later, they were collapsed with giggles.

'The dying swan recovers, huh?' he said. He tossed his hat on the bed. 'Hi, Paula.'

'Hello, Nick,' she said. 'I just came down to welcome Cass home. See you.'

She kissed Cass and left. Before she did, she said, 'Dinner tomorrow night? Just you and me and Ellin?'

'Agreed,' Cass told her. 'See you, love . . . and thanks.'

Nick undressed and joined her in bed. 'Feeling better?'

'Much,' said Cass. She was not warm toward him; her temporary burst of energy had subsided, draining her of affection, or even the strength to talk to him. He was perceptive; he put his arms lightly around her, but did not signal any desire to make love. Cass was too tired to care. The picture in the newspaper, she thought; he's probably angry about that.

Resentment rose in her, hot and sharp. She remembered the way Grey had patronized her in front of the Montellis and once again she was mad. She was mad at the way Nick had made a mess of her home, too. She knew he was waiting for her to say something, to explain the picture of her and Tucker which had been picked up by the *Daily News* that night. I'll be damned if I'm going to explain it to him now, she thought. Instead, she set the alarm clock and moved it ostentatiously to her side of the bed, and turned over and went to sleep.

TWENTY-SEVEN

The Christmas parties began in early December; the city's seasonal frenzy mounted as the month wore on.

Paula made gifts for everyone: a red velvet waistcoat edged with antique buttons for Cass, a soft-sculpture muse to hang over Ellin's daybed, a purple patchwork skirt for Lara, a silk shirt embroidered with stars and a moon for Jake.

Jake had not heard from the admissions committee yet, and his edginess made him even more difficult than usual. He called Paula whenever she wasn't in Cambridge, wheedling, whining, complaining.

'It's very cold and lonesome here,' he said; Paula was working late at the office. The argument was now scheduled for mid-February, and her case load at the office was heavier than usual, too. 'Why don't you come up and spend the night?'

'Jake, I can't, I have so much to do, I'm getting a cold, I—'

'I need you, Paula, I really need you,' he said, and she weakened. Poor man, the waiting is awful, she thought, it's the least I can do.

'Well. . .' she temporized, 'if I came back in the morning I suppose I could—'

'Great,' said Jake. 'As long as you're coming, would you pick me up some of those candied apricots, you know the ones, and I think I left my running shoes in your closet, and . . .'Paula scribbled notes to herself as he talked, and promised to catch the eight o'clock plane.

'Atta girl, I knew you wouldn't let me down,' Jake said happily. But she missed the flight; she got to Boston after midnight, fighting for a taxi in the blinding snowstorm that had delayed all air traffic into Logan. She was red-faced and sneezing. When she woke Jake, he was cranky. 'It took me forever to fall asleep, and then you get into bed all cold and freezing,' he complained, but in minutes he had rolled over and was snoring heavily.

What am I doing here? Paula wondered. Jake shifted irritably when she sneezed. What the fuck am I doing here?

Ellin would have preferred to forget Christmas, though the festivities in the city assaulted her with the season. She had too many memories of unpleasant holidays with Tony, and without him. Still, she went with Cass and Paula and Vic to select a tree, and helped them drag it home through snow-slick cobblestone streets.

Cass was happily preoccupied with the house party she planned the week before Christmas. Ellin and Paula had invited their friends, too, and Amelia was coming, and Grey.

The housemates spent a stoned, happy afternoon readying the brownstone for the party, hanging wreaths and making hors d'oeuvres. They set up bars on each floor, and decorated platters of cheeses and fruitcake and pâtés. That night they were an attractive trio, greeting their guests at the front door. Cass was brilliant in red taffeta; Ellin was elegant in velvet knickers, a creamy satin shirt, and a gardenia pinned in her hair. And Paula vibrated in a rich-green brocaded cheongsam she had found in a thrift store, with gaudy jewelled chopsticks tucked into the curls piled atop her head.

Their friends brought ornaments to trim the tree, and music and laughter drifted through the brownstone.

Amelia was one of the earliest arrivals, and Cass introduced her proudly to Ellin and Paula.

'We should have lunch,' Amelia said. 'I hear Pete Marks has his knives out for you.'

Cass wasn't worried. 'Just corporate politics,' she told Amelia.

'Even so, I think you should take Marks seriously,' Amelia warned her.

'Oh, Amelia, you worry so,' Cass said lovingly. 'If I didn't know—if it didn't come from you, I wouldn't give it a second thought.'

'That's a mistake in judgement,' Amelia said tartly. 'You should listen to anyone who wants to tell you something for your own good, and only trust half of it.'

'Anything from you I trust entirely,' Cass said. 'Are you happy these days, Amelia?'

'Oh, one gets through as well as one can,' said Amelia lightly, and Cass felt a pang of regret for the older woman. She ought to be surrounded by a loving family at Christmas, Cass thought, and she's really lonely. She has her apartment, and her agency, and that awful daughter of hers. That cunt. Cunt was a word Cass hardly ever thought, much less used, but Natalie certainly seemed to merit it.

'Where is that lovely young man of yours, Cassandra?'

'Nick? He's probably on the phone to the Coast; that's where he is most of the time these days. He's a great fan of yours, you know.' Nick admired Amelia. 'She's straight as a die and twice as tough,' he often said, and while Cass did not agree with the second half of his assessment, she didn't correct him.

'As I am of his,' Amelia said. 'That magazine has simply gone to tatters without him. Has he found something else yet?'

'Not yet. Some things are pending, but nothing's definite. He isn't taking to enforced idleness very well.'

That was, if anything, an understatement: Nick was seriously depressed. He hung around the apartment waiting for the phone to ring; he went out infrequently, except for meetings with potential backers or partners. And he returned from those dark-faced and drunk.

Cass and Nick snapped at each other, though she did try to keep her temper in check. The apartment, more than big enough for Cass alone, seemed cramped with Nick there. He had all but taken over the library, so that Cass often stayed late at her office, and came home in Grey's limousine. When Nick saw the long automobile pull up in front of the brownstone, he sulked. When she talked about Amagansett, he seemed to fasten on whatever she said about Grey, and file it away in a list of grievances he was compiling. Whether his animosity toward Tucker was jealousy of his success with Amagansett or with Cass was unclear, but it was obvious. He was uncharacteristically rude to Grey when he arrived at the party; when Nick saw him come in, he closeted himself in the library.

'You never seem to want to fuck any more,' he complained often to Cass. It was true, she could contain her anger at Nick outside of bed, but she could not do so in the act of love. It had been a few weeks since Nick approached her sexually: 'I got the message,' he said the last time she refused him. She thought he might be sleeping with Astrea again; he came in one night reeking of an unfamiliar perfume.

Cass chose not to confront him. Perhaps in the holiday week ahead, things would get better. Perhaps the spirit of the season would help them through. They had been through difficult times together in the past, though he had not needed as much from her then. And now she felt that what she had to give him was not enough.

Cass thought Nick's need was demeaning. He seemed to have lost his ambition, his energy, his confidence. He came out poorly compared to Grey; it was an unfair comparison, given the differences in their professional situations, but Cass could not help making it. Nor could she tell Nick that the reason she did not want to make love with him lately was because, when she did, she also could not help fantasizing that it was Grey, not Nick, who was touching her.

Nick found Cass in the kitchen, where she and Paula and Ellin were refilling trays and ice buckets. 'What assaults on the citadels of power are you broads planning now, huh?' he asked.

He was more than a little drunk; Cass and Paula exchanged meaningful looks.

'Nick, there are some extra boxes of ornaments in the hall closet,' Paula said. 'Would you be a doll and bring them out for me?'

He complied, and ambled out of the room. Cass exhaled and went into the bathroom to make sure there were clean guest towels.

'She acts like he doesn't exist,' said Ellin to Paula when Cass left. 'When she talks to him, she patronizes him.'

'Poor Nick,' Paula said. 'It's not easy being number two.'

'Not when Cass so clearly enjoys being number one,' Ellin remarked. 'It seems to me that Nick is very needy right now.'

'Cass doesn't like to be needed, not by a man. It makes her think less of him,' Paula began, but her words were lost in the sound of a crash from the foyer. They rushed out to see what had happened, and found the huge blue spruce tree fallen over on its side. Ellin felt glass ornament fragments being crushed under her feet; Paula tried to get through the knot of people who blocked her path.

Nick was balanced precariously on a ladder, clutching a glass star he had been attempting to position on top of the tree. He had a drink in one hand, and the star in the other. He ignored Cass's plea that he descend the ladder before he fell off.

'Come on, old man, let's get down from there and put this tree back up right.' It was Grey, standing next to Cass, motioning Nick to come down.

Nick waved him away. 'Don't worry, I have it all under control,' he said, slurring his words. 'S'all right, all right.'

The ladder wobbled dangerously as Nick waved his glass; Tucker moved forward to steady it, and grasped Nick around the leg. Nick kicked his hand away.

'Get your fucking hands off me, Tucker, I don't need your help!' he said angrily. Suddenly the convivial tone of the party changed; people stood motionless, aware that something more than a minor accident was occurring. Cass's sharp intake of breath was clearly audible in the hush.

'You got my girl, whassa matter, isn't that enough?' Nick said, his tone hostile. Cass looked at him with disgust; Nick caught her glance, and seemed to sober up instantly. His face crumpled, and Paula thought he was going to cry.

She rushed forward to make peace. 'Nick, you promised to get those ornaments for us, come on,' she said. She took one step up the ladder, and helped him down. Then she led him away, through the expectant throng. Cass busied herself rearranging the tree, and the tension in the room dissolved like air being released from a balloon. But not before Ellin noticed the look that passed between Cass and Grey—a look of understanding and tacit acceptance that was more intimate than any word or touch she had seen Cass and Nick exchange for weeks.

Grey cornered Cass later. 'Merry Christmas,' he said, handing her a tell-tale blue velvet box. Cass opened it eagerly; her favourite presents came from Tiffany.

She gasped delightedly; inside the box was a slim gold watch, costly and beautiful. In the silk folds of the box a card nestled. 'To Cass,' she read. 'May you always be in the right place at the right time.'

'You shouldn't have,' she began, but Grey laughed, and so she did, too.

'Of course I should have,' he said, 'so I did.'

'I'm sorry about the scene with Nick. He's going through a difficult time.' She hated apologizing for him, especially to Grey, but she felt that an explanation was called for.

'I can't fault the man for telling the truth.'

Cass didn't know how to respond to that. She took Grey's hands in hers. 'I'm glad you came tonight,' she said. 'And the watch . . . it's beautiful.'

'So it is,' he agreed. 'And so are you.'

She didn't know what to say, which made him laugh out loud.

'I like it when you're speechless,' he told her. 'I think I'm onto the secret of Cass Campbell . . . just keep her off balance.' And with that, he kissed her lightly on the forehead and departed, hatless, into the wintry night.

TWENTY-EIGHT

On the day before Christmas, Jake was notified that his application to the bar had been approved. Paula was thrilled and delighted; she grabbed him by the hands and danced him around her living room.

'I'm so happy,' she trilled. 'I really didn't know . . . I wasn't sure they'd do it!' She hugged him, beaming. 'Now it's really over,' she said. 'Now we can move on to the next event!'

She ran to the refrigerator and pulled out a bottle of champagne she'd been saving for a special occasion. This was it: the day she'd been waiting for. That it was Christmas Eve seemed fitting to her; Jake's surprise was the present she wanted most.

'What next event?' he asked, and she turned sharply to see if he was kidding.

'Why, the rest of our lives, silly!' said Paula. She nuzzled him. 'Merry Christmas, darling.'

He kissed her absently; he was unresponsive. She was disappointed, but hid it; this is too much for him to take in, she thought. He hasn't really integrated it; he knows, but he doesn't know. He's still stunned.

'Uh . . . what time is Cass planning her big dinner tomorrow?' he asked.

'Around three o'clock. She's been baking and stuffing and shopping for this dinner for weeks. And trying not to kick Nick in the ass. She doesn't want a big blow-up with him now; she just wants dinner to be the way she's planned it. You'd think it was the Last Supper.' She kissed him again; she couldn't keep her hands off him. Maybe they'd get married in the spring, after the Court argument, she thought. 'Why?'

'Well, I have to get a seven o'clock flight. From Kennedy.'

She was confused. 'Flight? Where are you going? The shuttle leaves from La Guardia, honey, not Kennedy.' She popped the cork on the champagne bottle. It hit a mobile of shiny fish hanging from the light fixture in the centre of the room, and sent the silver figures spinning wildly. 'But you said you had this week off, Jake.'

She was hurt; she had planned a whole week around Jake's presence in the city. She had thought they might go to Hartford for a day or two; her parents knew that she was serious about Jake again. 'Mixed up with that wild man, eh, Paulie?' her father had asked her only a few months ago. 'You be careful now . . . he was mean to you before. A man doesn't turn from a mad bomber to a *mensch* overnight, you know.'

'Oh, Pa, don't worry, he's not a wild man any more. He's grown up,' she reassured him. 'Like we all have.' Of course, her father didn't know the half of it; he didn't know about the abortion, so long ago; he didn't know that she had helped Jake do a deal with Chris Carey. And he wouldn't, if she could help it. Her father was liberal enough, and he had faith in her judgement, but some things were too hard for a man his age to take. And her mother . . . Paula had tuned her mother out years ago. She was a good enough woman, but it was to Isaac Gabriel that Paula looked—had always looked—for approval.

Clearly, they were not going to Hartford; Jake seemed to have made other plans. Well, she could be flexible; perhaps he wanted time to let the good news sink in. Or had other ideas about celebrating it.

'Well, I do. Have this week off, I mean,' Jake began. 'But something's come up . . . wait, let me tell you,' he said, hurriedly, sensing her confusion and disappointment. 'It's just that . . . well, my pals from the farm, they're mostly in California now, and I told them the news, and they've planned this huge celebration. And I really should go . . .'

'If Cass would serve dinner just a little earlier, we could probably make that plane,' Paula interrupted him. 'Just think—California! Sunshine, hot weather, nothing to do but relax. It sounds fabulous! Besides, there's not really that much to do this week, the whole team is taking the holidays off. I can probably get away . . .' Her words trailed off. An unpleasant thought occurred to her. 'Or doesn't this trip include me?'

Jake would not meet her eyes. 'Well, actually . . . I mean, they're all strangers to you after all, Paula. You know how it is . . . we went through a lot together . . .'

'No, as a matter of fact, I *don't* know how it is,' she said slowly. 'Just how is it, Jake?'

He backed off. 'Forget it, baby, I won't go. It's no big deal, they'll understand. I can finesse it. Maybe after the first of the year I can get out there and . . . Never mind.' He smiled winningly. 'Let me make a few phone calls, and we'll go out and celebrate, okay?'

Relieved, she ran her hand inside his shirt. 'Why don't we stay in and celebrate instead?' she suggested. She poured them both champagne and ran her hands suggestively over his body. The threat of his leaving was withdrawn; she felt suddenly sexual. She looked into his eyes, and saw warmth there, and affection, but something was missing, and she knew what it was: desire.

She ignored it; she grasped him with an intensity she felt, but could not explain if he had asked her to. She pulled him down on the floor, on top of her; she felt the cold edge on her back where her shirt separated from her jeans, and tasted the champagne on his lips.

She was insistent, demanding, voracious. She worked on him until he was aroused; it seemed to take forever, despite the feverish frenzy of her mouth, her hands, her breasts. She could wait no longer; she climbed on top of him and thrust him inside her, riding him harder and harder, deeper inside of her, until she came. He was still hard; she took him in her mouth, and finally tasted the salty fluid of his release, and was satisfied.

She fell asleep; when she woke a while later he was no longer on the floor next to her, covered with the afghan she had pulled over both of them. She heard him in the bedroom on the telephone; he seemed to her, in her sleepy daze, to be pleading with someone, or perhaps explaining, and she heard that familiar, wheedling tone of his voice with a dullness that set up an unidentifiable ache in her own head.

Christmas dinner was a constrained affair that bore only surface resemblance to the close, warm, familial, and festive occasion of Cass's fantasy. Nick was almost desperately high-spirited, trying to please Cass and ease the tension between them.

Paula was high-strung and edgy. Sometimes she prodded at Jake, seeming almost to taunt him; alternately, she could not keep her hands off of him. 'Paula, you're *flouncing!*' Cass rebuked her, exasperated. Jake seemed to be humouring Paula; he is not part of her act today, Cass thought.

Nick and Jake refrained from their usual habit of baiting each other; Nick thought Jake's politics were hashed-over idealism from the sixties, tempered with more than a little self-interest, and Jake thought Nick was an arriviste and an elitist. Cass would have preferred a political shouting match to their strained politeness. It was almost as if the two men had made an agreement to keep things safely smoothed over. 'Like two bad boys trying to charm their mothers out of being mad,' Cass said privately to Paula.

Between Cass and Nick there was an unspoken truce. After the tree-trimming party, he was apologetic and contrite. Cass knew she should not let his behaviour go unremarked upon, but she chose to ignore it for the moment. After the holidays, she told herself, then I'll deal with it. We'll deal with it. But not now.

She wanted no contention, no arguments at Christmastime; she loved the season, and she wanted to wrap herself in the comfortable, warm blanket of her home, her friends, and her lover. She would shut out anything that might disturb those feelings. So she accepted Nick's apology, and went out of her way to be nice to him. To Paula and Ellin, though, she had vented her resentment.

'He'd better get his act together in a hurry,' she fumed to them. 'I care a great deal about Nick, but I'm not going to let him trample over my life—my personal life *and* my career—the way he did at my party.'

'Maybe he needs some understanding right now,' ventured Ellin.

Cass snapped at her. 'What about what I need? Don't I get a ration of holiday understanding, too?' She warmed to her indignation. 'Here I am, working my tail off, trying to succeed at a job Nick himself urged me to take, and what do I get for it?' She stomped dramatically around the room. 'I'll tell you what I get, I get shit, that's what! I get Cass, pick up my suit at the cleaners, Cass, how come we're out of chutney, Cass, why are you going out of town with Tucker again, Cass, why don't you want to have sex with me, Cass . . .' She buried her face in her hands.

Paula rolled her eyes upward; she'd been through scenes like this with Cass before. 'Shit, Cass, stop playing the martyr. You have everything you want and sometimes you have to stretch yourself pretty thin to keep it—we all do. That's the way life is in the world of grown-ups. Right now, Nick needs you more than he ever has, and you're not—'

Cass broke in angrily. 'And I'm not what?' she demanded. 'I'm not right there, cosseting him, building him up, telling him how great he is, being the supportive little wifey? Damn right I'm not! Because he's lying around every day, can't get up and go out, all his ambition gone, turning into a lush, while I . . . while I . . .'

'While you what, Cass?' Ellin asked the question—Ellin,

who was always ready to make allowances for a man, and rarely for herself. 'While you break your own neck for a job—and his heart for a man who's more successful?'

Cass turned to Paula. 'Is that what *you* think?'

'No, no, of course that's not what we think,' she said soothingly. She glared at Ellin warningly: don't push her, the look seemed to say.

'Oh, hell,' Cass said tiredly. 'Paula the peacemaker, thank God for you. I'm going to bed. The two of you can rearrange my life for me so it works.' She smiled, taking the edge off her words. 'In fact, I wish you would,' she added. 'My God, I wish *somebody* would!'

Today, only Ellin seemed removed; the currents of resentment and discomfort in the room flowed around her, but did not touch her. She was detached; she watched herself watching her friends, making note of the changes in their tone, the nuances of the conversation. Lara sat next to her, and Vic faced her across the table; she fancied the three of them as the neutral hosts, keeping the talk moving lightly, steering it to safer topics if any words seemed to threaten emotional response. Any feeling could be dangerous in that room. There was the palpable sense that anything at all might happen, and things were just not going to be the same afterwards if something did, though even Ellin could not have said how they would be different.

Finally they got up from the table. The women cleared the dishes away and made coffee, Jake, Nick, and Vic turned on the television set in the library. Loud groans of disgust and occasional cheers came in bursts from the room, and Cass wrinkled her nose. 'Is this liberation?' she asked. 'Pardon me, but what are we doing in the kitchen while they're parking their butts in front of the football game?'

Ellin and Paula burst into laughter, and for the first time that day, Cass felt the connections of love she had missed. They left the dishes in the sink and flopped on

Cass's bed, sharing a joint produced by Ellin. Lara, who had been watching television with the men, wandered into the room, sniffed, and eyed them suspiciously.

'Pardon me,' she said with exaggerated disdain, 'but aren't you the people my mother warned me against?'

They all howled. Ellin was proud of Lara—proud of her freshness, and sparkle, and appeal. Boarding school had been good for her; Ellin could see the difference in her daughter. She thought Lara was weathering the change well; she could almost see her sifting values, responding with alacrity to new people and challenges, and growing up.

'Lara, I have something for you,' Cass said, getting up from the bed. 'No, not Christmas presents, just some clothes I thought you could use.' From the closet she took a box of skirts, shirts, and sweaters. 'You're about my size, and if you don't want them, give them to Goodwill or trade them with your friends.' She turned to Paula. 'Remember when we used to swap clothes at school?'

'Uh huh, until you lost weight and I gained it,' Paula replied. Ellin felt the habit of years pass between the two other women; she felt sad that she had not known them then. And a little excluded; whenever Cass brought up the old days, the days when she and Paula first knew each other, Ellin felt left out of a whole host of little unimportant things that added up to a bond that had nothing to do with her.

The feeling went away; Lara was beaming, and she insisted on trying on each garment.

'This needs to be taken up here,' said Paula, fingering a skirt. 'Take it off, I'll do it for you.' She rummaged in Cass's drawer for the sewing basket, with easy familiarity which Ellin envied, and found the needle, thread, and scissors.

'You know, I've been thinking about cutting my hair again,' said Cass. 'How do you like it like this?' She stood before them, pushing her hair away from her face.

'If you do that, you'll have to make up your eyes differently . . . here, like this,' said Ellin, handing Cass an eyebrow pencil from the dressing table.

For nearly two hours, they tried on clothes, gossiped, told stories, giggled, and laughed. It was a warm, companionable interval—women without men, loving each other, 'validating each other,' said Cass in a serious moment. It seemed to her that her life was in balance again; often what she really needed was what she got from Ellin and Paula, but often too, she mistook that need for a different kind of love, and never understood why what she received instead left her empty.

Later, after the dishes were done and the fire burned down to white embers, Lara and Ellin and Vic went out for a walk. It was a clear, cold night, and they walked comfortably together down the nearly deserted streets of the Village. Vic stopped to buy a paper from a news dealer.

'Cass and Paula didn't seem real happy tonight,' said Lara, and Ellin was surprised by her perceptiveness.

'Why do you say that?' She was curious.

'Oh, I just thought it,' Lara replied. 'Are they having trouble with their boyfriends?'

'Why do you think so?' Ellin responded. 'Why couldn't Cass be having some problems with her job, or Paula with her own career? Why are you sure it's man trouble?'

'Because they're good at their jobs,' Lara said. 'You said so. So did they, tonight. It seems like they get what they need from their work. It makes them happy. But they don't seem to be that happy with Nick and Jake.' She squeezed Ellin's hand. 'Sometimes I'm glad you don't have a boyfriend, like a regular one, you know?'

Ellin pulled Lara close to her. 'Sometimes I'm glad I don't too.'

'Don't what?' Vic asked, re-joining them.

Ellin and Lara exchanged conspiratorial looks. 'Oh, nothing,' said Lara airily. 'Hey, Vic, want to get some ice cream?'

'Lawdy, the girl has a stomach like a bottomless pit,' said Vic good-naturedly, and they followed his brisk stride down the neon-lighted jumble of West Fourth Street.

Paula was in the bathtub trying to smooth out the jagged edges of the day when she heard the phone ring. Jake must have picked it up; it stopped abruptly. She lay back in the warm, soapy bubbles.

When she came out of the bathroom, wrapped in a towel, Jake was gathering his keys and change from the bureau, and pulling on a sweater.

'Going somewhere?' she asked in surprise.

'Yeah,' said Jake. 'Some friends of mine are in town. I thought I'd meet them for a drink at their hotel.'

Paula eyed him suspiciously. 'What friends?' she said.

'Look, I don't have to account to you for every—' Jake began, and Paula interrupted him.

'No, you don't Jake, you goddamned well do not!' She marched past him, and snatched her house keys away from him. 'You can go wherever the hell you want, whenever the hell you want, and I don't give a shit if you never come back!'

She flung herself on the bed, sobbing. Jake approached her; he began to say something, but stopped. Abruptly, he gathered his coat and went out of the room; she heard the front door close, and his steps descending the stairs. He did not slam the door, she thought later; he had not responded to her anger the way he sometimes did. There was a chilling sense of finality about his departure; she had the first presentiments of abandonment, and she cried and cried, alone in her bedroom, but he did not come back that night.

Ellin opened the front door. It was quiet in the house. She and Lara went upstairs, but there was something ominous about the silence in the brownstone. Lara did not feel it; within minutes, she was asleep in the spare room.

Ellin was strangely disquieted. She went downstairs, noting that Paula's door was closed, and that Cass's apartment was dark. She went down to the basement and tapped lightly on Vic's door.

He seemed glad to see her. 'Come on in, I'll make coffee,' he said. 'Hey, you want to play some Scrabble?'

She agreed. They played a hard-fought game; they were evenly matched, and he won by less than 20 points.

'You're pretty good,' she said.

'So are you,' he told her. 'Usually I hate playing games with women; even if they're better than you are, they let you win.'

'My mother once told me that boys didn't like girls who hit home runs,' Ellin said. 'I remember it clearly. I was in sixth grade, and I had a huge crush on a boy. David Carlson . . . I still know his name. Anyway, I won the game for our team, he was on it, and he walked another girl home from school. I was brokenhearted, I went home and told Sophie all about it, and she just said I had to learn to bunt.'

'You didn't take her advice?'

'I certainly did.' Ellin smiled ruefully. 'For years I let boys win. But not for a long time now.'

'That's good,' said Vic. 'You shouldn't have to.'

They put the board and tiles away, and sprawled casually on the couch, listening to Billie Holiday on Vic's tape deck. They talked about other Christmases; he told her a little more about himself.

He said he had been a restless, difficult teenager. He described a passionate affair when he was seventeen, which resulted in his girl friend's unwanted pregnancy. He had to tell his father to get money for the abortion; his family practically disowned him afterward. He quit school and joined the Marines, then passed his high school equivalency test and worked his way through college, and then business school. The rest she knew about; he had re-enlisted, found himself drawn to the horror and agony of war, and since then tried to write about it.

She told him about herself, too—about Tony, and the years in California. He put his arm around her, and they shared a joint.

She felt sexually stirred, and she moved her body closer to his, trying to get a message through to him. He kissed her without passion, a firm, friendly enough kiss through closed lips. Abruptly, he got up from the couch.

He was ill at ease; she did not know what to say to him, so she said nothing.

'I'm, uh, you might say, kind of turned off lately. Not very tuned into my body. I guess you should know I'm . . . I'm not feeling very sexual these days.'

She was embarrassed. He came over and sat beside her, taking her hand in his. 'Believe me, it has nothing to do with you, Ellin,' he said. 'I . . . I think my systems are sort of shut down. Not functioning very well . . . I mean, physically I'm okay, but the rest of it, all those lover kinds of ways, I don't seem to have it.' He was stumbling, hesitating, groping for words—was he telling her he was impotent? Couldn't get it up? Or was he really saying that she was not attractive to him; that he did not want her?

She felt humiliated, but she tried to finesse the situation, dispel the embarrassment they both felt.

'I'm in no hurry for that,' she told him, although it was not true; she wanted him very much. 'I like going slowly,' she said. 'I like touching people I like. I don't mean to be putting sexual pressure on you.'

'Oh, you're not,' he reassured her, but she didn't believe him. The spell of closeness was broken, and Ellin left as soon as she decently could.

She did not want sexual tension between her and Vic. She would have slept with him gladly if he'd wanted her; the fact that he knew that, that he felt the clarity of her desire, demeaned her. She did not believe that it really had nothing to do with her; she felt old, tired, used up, rejected. And later, under her grey flannel covers, alone in her bed, she was dry to her own touch; even her body refused to succour her.

Ellin and Lara and Vic and Cass and Nick were away from the brownstone three days later when Jake came back. Only Paula was at home; she had not left her apartment since Jake walked out on Christmas night.

She opened the door at his buzz; she knew it was him. He came in; he looked tired, she thought.

She herself was red-eyed and distraught. She had tried calling him in Cambridge, but there had been no answer at his apartment. She had called the friends of his she knew; they had no idea where he might be. She thought of him lying dead under the wheels of a careless taxi; she even called the hospitals and made discreet enquiries. It was the longest three days of her life, days in which the angry words she had flung at him rang in her ears.

She was contrite, ready to apologize, but Jake gave her no opportunity. With his opening words, she was jolted out of her carefully ordered reality.

'I'm leaving, Paula,' he told her. 'I'm getting married.' He did not wait for her reaction; he rushed on, his words tumbling over each other in his haste to get them out before she began to scream, or cry, or deny.

'I'm marrying Beth . . . you remember, the woman from the farm?'

She nodded in disbelief—he kept talking.

'We have a child, Beth and I . . . a daughter. She's five months old.'

Paula was hastily adding and subtracting times, months, years in her head. Five months? Then the woman had been pregnant when Jake came back to her, when he appeared in that taxi outside her office, almost a year before.

'She told me she was going to have an abortion. In California,' Jake went on. 'She and Sharon were making it then—they were heading down the Coast together, going to try to live as a couple.'

Paula put her hands over her ears, but Jake kept on talking. She could not block out his words; she could not, either, turn the clock back, only ten minutes, before he walked in the door.

'She said she was tired of trying to deal with men; she said she was going to have a real, sharing, loving relationship with a woman. Sharon had been coming on to her all those last months at the farm. So she left with her. I wanted . . . she said she wouldn't have the kid, and I believed her.'

'And when did you find out she'd had the baby?' Paula demanded. Perhaps he hadn't known . . . he'd been trapped. She'd helped him out of one trap; she could get him out of this one. But she knew she could not; and that even if she could, he wouldn't let her.

Jake looked uneasy. 'She wrote me a letter right after the baby was born. This summer. Just before I took the bar.'

Somehow, Paula kept functioning. Her mind was racing, back and forth; she careened wildly between anger and disbelief.

'So you've known all along? After the bar, when we went on vacation?'

He nodded.

'And not said one fucking word to me?' Her voice was shrill, and getting louder. She threw herself around the room, raising clouds of dust in her wake. 'You just pretended everything was perfect? Just waited until you got what you wanted?' Jake said nothing, and Paula began to shriek.

'And now it's zap, so long baby, I'm going to shoulder my responsibilities to my family?' Paula was mortally wounded; she was totally out of control, and she didn't care. 'And now you and that dyke and your baby set up housekeeping?'

Jake defended the woman. 'She's no dyke, she just

thought power struggles didn't happen between women, and she wanted to have a, well, a father for the baby.' He buried his own face in his hands, then faced her. 'Look, Paula, I didn't mean for it to happen this way, I swear I didn't! I didn't expect Beth to come here, or to bring the baby . . . I never planned that. I never planned any of this.'

'What the hell *did* you plan?' Paula screamed. 'Were you ever planning to tell me? Or were you just going to wait until I said Jake, let's get married, and *then* spring it on me?' She ran to him and beat at his chest with her fists. Her face purpled in rage. 'Or were you just waiting until everything fell into place, the bar exam and the admissions committee, and the job—everything I got for you? Were you just going to wait for all that, and then tell me?' She collapsed, crying, on the floor. Jake tried to pat her shoulder, tried to comfort her.

'Don't touch me!' she hissed through clenched teeth. 'Don't you ever touch me again! Get out of here, you bastard, and don't you ever come near me again!'

TWENTY-NINE

'Have you ever seen her this way?' Ellin asked Cass.

'Never. Not even in law school when Jake skipped, when she had . . .' Cass's voice trailed off. She didn't know if Paula had ever told Ellin about it.

'. . . the abortion,' Ellin finished, and Cass nodded. They were both very frightened for Paula.

She lay curled in her bed for days on end, wrapped carelessly in a tatty flannel robe. Her eyes were puffy from crying; there seemed no end to the tears that welled up in them and dripped heedlessly down her cheeks. Her hair was lank and lifeless; her apartment began to smell as if someone had recently died in it.

'I wish he had,' Cass said bitterly to Ellin. 'I wish she'd stabbed the rotten son of a bitch.'

Ellin methodically cleaned the apartment. She brought Paula nourishing soups, and spoon-fed her. She pushed her into the shower and demanded that Paula clean herself. She answered her telephone and made excuses for her absence. Even the pleas of her colleagues from the Centre did not stir Paula.

'Are you going to let that despicable bastard take everything away from you?' Ellin finally cried in desperation. 'Everything you've worked for for ten whole years?'

Paula didn't answer, and Ellin screamed at her, uncharacteristically. She hated scenes, but she had to shock Paula out of her lethargy. 'Well, if you don't care about yourself, then think about them! About all those poor women who are going to get hurt worse than you've been! Nothing for them but life sentences, because the government will force them to have the babies they can't feed, or love, or raise!' Her voice rose to a pleading crescendo. 'Think about them, damn you, Paula, think about them!'

That was the only time she lost her temper with Paula. Mostly, she cared for her, listened to her cry, held her when Paula would allow it, and helped her move through the days.

Cass did not know how to help Paula. She had no experience with this kind of betrayal. So instead, she bought Paula presents—silly toys that would have made her giggle before: fresh croissants from the bakery, a pot of fragrant hyacinths. Presents spelled love, and she loved Paula. But her own life went on, and she hurried to catch up with it.

Occasionally in the weeks after Jake left, Paula threw on jeans and an old flannel shirt and went to the movies in Times Square in the middle of the day. She ate chocolate bars compulsively through double showings of the films. At least twice, she seriously considered suicide.

Cass lost patience with her, finally. 'Will you at least see a psychiatrist?' she demanded, but Paula refused.

'Goddamn it, Paula, you are being one selfish, self-centred bitch, wallowing in your own self-pity while people are counting on you!' Cass raged.

She had tried to distract Paula with her own tales of woe about Nick, and reports of the continued pressure she was under at Amagansett. But Paula didn't care; she didn't even make an attempt at listening. And when Cass blew up at her, she blew right back.

'Why is it okay for you to make your life one continuing melodrama, and not okay for me to have a crisis once in my life?' Paula cried. 'It's not as if I don't have enough reason to be miserable, you know!'

Cass stormed out, too furious to reply to Paula's charges. Paula turned to Ellin and complained in a whining, bitchy voice that Ellin had never heard her use before.

'Isn't it just too bad that it isn't convenient for Cass to have me upset and unhappy right now?' she said bitterly. 'Ordinarily, we'd all be rallying around her, sympathizing while she tries to dump Nick and get Grey Tucker. While she tries to win over the fucking Amagansett corporate office. Only this time she can't have a crisis, because I'm having one!'

Ellin tried to soothe her. 'Oh, come on, Paula, that's not fair, Cass loves you, you know that—' but Paula cut her off.

'I know, I know. What you don't know is that Cass loves me because I'm always the one who does the understanding, I'm always the responsible one, I always listen to her little troubles and handle my own. Only I'm not doing either now—I can't stand to hear her whine about nothing, and I can't get a grip on my own life!' She burst into tears for the third time that day. 'Well, I don't want to listen! I don't want to sympathize while Cass wallows in her same old shit. And that's all it is, you know, the same old shit! Cass is having sexual problems with Nick because she's got the hots for Grey, that's all. Cass is having business problems because she's a woman and she thinks men are putting her down. Well, you know what? I'm sick of Cass's problems!'

'You *are* feeling sorry for yourself, aren't you?' Ellin asked. She was being sympathetic, not sarcastic, and Paula knew it.

'Fucking right!' she answered. 'Wouldn't you—in my place?'

Ellin could only nod in agreement. Appeased for the moment, Paula looked around her squalid apartment. 'God, this place is a dump, isn't it?'

It was true. They set to work, cleaning and shaking and dusting and polishing, with a frenzy that surprised them both. After it was done, Paula fell onto the freshly made-up bed. 'Let's go see a really shitty ten-handkerchief picture, okay?'

'Sure,' said Ellin. Anything was better than waiting around for Paula's next onslaught of tears. 'They'll hardly notice you sniffling in the audience.'

Both of them cried copious tears during the movie. Afterward, they gorged themselves on chocolate rum cake at Rumbul's. It was snowing lightly when they came out of the café, and Paula looked better. 'God, I'm glad it's not spring,' she said. 'I can't stand being miserable when it's spring.'

Six weeks after Jake's betrayal, Paula pulled herself together. Despite her sorrow, she could no longer ignore the greatest challenge of her professional life. She was grateful for the pressure; without it she would have stayed trapped in the mire of her depression, like a victim of quicksand.

The Supreme Court argument was scheduled for the second Wednesday in February. Paula checked into the Mayflower on Sunday night; for two days she wrote and scratched out and started again. The team of lawyers and researchers who had worked on the argument with her were scattered around the city; she met with them in offices, at the Library, in the living room of her hotel suite.

She did her homework. She tried to anticipate everything the justices might ask her; she outlined her answers on long sheets of lined yellow paper, and codified them on index cards. She added any other relevant arguments that might be woven into her responses. She looked for opportunities; she made her game plan. She would not be taken by surprise—that was her skill as a litigator.

The night before the argument, she went to the Court with what she called 'my seconds'. They were the best legal minds she knew. They were her colleagues from the Centre: Dave from the ACLU; two highly respected, seasoned litigators who had argued before the Court before; Geoffrey, one of the first blacks to clerk for a justice; and the dozen or so others with whom she had written, rewritten, argued, and reargued the fine points of the case. The teamwork of the past few days reached its peak at the traditional dress rehearsal. They sat in the justices' seats and tested her, forcing her to think quickly, to shape what she knew in her head and her gut into a cohesive whole.

Stan Wilkie, a veteran Court litigator, put his arm around her as they walked out of the building, close to midnight. 'When you get up there, in front of them, all this grandeur fades away,' he said, pointing to the awesome building behind them. 'It's really very relaxed. You don't raise your voice above what would be a normal conversational level. It's not all that dramatic in there; there are no grandstand plays. There's no one there, as far as you are aware, except you and the nine of them. You know the basic law of the courtroom: never argue in an argument. It's even more applicable in there. Be helpful, not contentious. And remember that we're all there behind the railing, pulling for you.' He kissed her cheek briefly, and was gone.

He left her alone on the wide marble steps of the Court. It was a cold, unusually clear night; the stars overhead were sparkling, icy flickers in the sky. The remnants of an earlier snowfall outlined the chiselled letters above the majestic Corinthian columns: EQUAL JUSTICE UNDER LAW. She stood and looked at it for a long time. She remembered the young girl who had read the Constitution, and marvelled at the beauty and simplicity and strength of the words in that worn red book. And she remembered her determination to make a difference, some day, in the rights of human beings to exist equally and happily under that document. And then she went back to her hotel room, and slept.

She stood as the justices entered the courtroom from behind the bench. It was a room to inspire the awe she felt: twenty-four marble columns rising to a sculptured marble panel, dark wine-red draperies framing the scene like a stage. She felt the attention of the entire room, which was packed with supporters and opponents, with court reporters from all the media, with her friends and colleagues. The justices arranged themselves in high-backed black leather chairs, and at the proper moment she stepped forward to the podium. The clerk and the marshall flanked her. She stood in a marble throne room, facing the bench, a half hexagon of gleaming mahogany. Above the bench were sculptured marble panels, depicting the Majesty of the Law, and the power of Government. Between them was a tableau of the Ten Commandments. Paula took a deep breath, and began.

Oral arguments, she knew, won a case before this court only infrequently. More often, awkward or poorly presented arguments lost cases that were, on the merits of the brief, solidly researched and lucidly prepared.

The justices questioned her at length; while she responded with alacrity, her mind leapt ahead, anticipating where the questions were leading. She saw her yellow sheets of paper in her mind, her strong block printing.

She parried well; she was excited, she was on, she was deft and prepared and she was enjoying it hugely, she realized, a brief second between the conclusion to one question and the start of another.

The questions finally trickled out, and it was time to stop. 'We submit that this court should fully, explicitly, decisively, and definitely uphold the position taken in *Roe v Wade,*' she finished and bowed her head briefly to indicate that her argument was completed.

She listened intently to opposing counsel; she knew him, both through the replies he had written in response to her own briefs, and also from law school; he had been on *Law Review* with her, and was now the attorney general of the state in which the original case was filed. She'd always known Larry Keyes would have a career in politics; even in law school, he had that sheen, that ambition.

He was good, predictably so. He always had been. But so had she, she knew.

She handled the rebuttal easily. When the chief justice ended the session with the traditional words, 'The case is submitted,' she was exhilarated. For the first time since Jake left her, she felt like laughing and leaping. She had done her best, and she knew that her best was very good indeed. The small, only partially silenced voice that had nagged at her since her first appearance in a courtroom —the voice that asked, Are you good enough?—was stilled. She knew the answer. This was the final test, and she had passed it. She did not have to wait the long weeks for the Court's decision. She knew how good she was, and she had prevailed. No matter what they decide, she said to herself, they can't take this away from me.

The justices dismissed counsel, and she walked out of the courtroom, outwardly calm, but inwardly floating several feet off the ground. She saw her friends' smiles, and returned them; even her opponents and their supporters nodded their respect to her. Her father was seated prominently in front of the public section, he made a victory sign, which she returned with a wink.

She went through the massive oak doors into the Great Hall, past the busts of the great chief justices of the past, which were set in niches along the side walls. She walked out through the bronze doors and into the grey February day. There were court reporters; she spoke into microphones, and posed for pictures. Flashbulbs snapped all around her; the CBS cameraman, an old friend from her Washington days, called, 'This way, Paula, please.'

There were endless questions, and many hugs and kisses. Stan Wilkie pumped her arm rhythmically; to stop him, she kissed him smack on the lips. 'You were absolutely right on, Gabriel, you were extraordinary!' he pronounced, and kissed her back; she snuggled into his camel-hair coat, and hugged him.

Her tears and laughter were mingled; an icy drizzle was falling, and no one knew the difference. Finally it was over, and people began departing. Again she was alone on the wide marble steps. This is it, kid, she told herself; this is the payoff. Suddenly a great wave of exhaustion and loneliness overcame her. Jake, you should have been here, she thought—without you, the trumpets and bugles don't play as long as they should. Without you, it is so quickly over.

If only she could hate him as passionately as she had loved him, she wondered, would the loneliness be easier to bear?

She went to a celebration that night at the Georgetown home of Stan Wilkie. She saw her team members there, and they exchanged postmortems, congratulations, speculations, and appreciations. The champagne flowed, the fires burned in the tiled hearths, and Chris Carey came to kiss her on the cheek.

He was handsome in his evening clothes. He was on his way to a diplomatic reception. 'I stopped in to congratulate you,' he told her. 'I was in the Court today—you were magnificent.'

She acknowledged his compliments with a smile; he was, after all, her teacher. He had shaped her passion for the law into the instrument she had become; it was through him that she had arrived at this place, at this time. He had been her professor, her mentor, friend, and lover, and she felt nostalgically glad to see him there.

She had not seen him since that night at Sonya's, almost a year before, except briefly on business concerning his ill-fated bid for the nomination; it died, prematurely, before the first ballot.

Chris was not faring well in the new, Republican-controlled Senate. 'The winds are shifting at home, too,' he told her. 'The conservative tide is sweeping over the country. It's like trying to stop a natural phenomenon.'

He added philosophically, 'But at least I'll have a clear alternative to offer the voters next time around.'

He looked around the room. 'I don't see Jake Stern, by the way. Is he here celebrating with you tonight?'

'Uh, no, he's not,' said Paula. She knew Chris didn't know of Jake's abandonment, of his duplicity.

'Why not?' Chris was taking an almost paternal interest. He sensed that Paula had been hurt by Jake again. He knew the signs, he'd seen them ten years before.

She told him, sketchily, and Chris's face darkened. 'That thoroughly unprincipled son of a bitch,' he cursed quietly, with uncharacteristic venom. 'The rotten little blackmailer. I'm sorry I ever lifted a finger to help, sorry for you, sorry for me . . . Christ, I'm sorry for the law!'

'Why did you, Chris?' she asked. 'Why did you help him?' She was curious in a detached sort of way; she had worried about that at first, wondering what kind of negotiations there had been between Jake and Chris, but she had not thought about it in some time, not since Jake had been permitted to register for the bar exam.

Chris backed away. 'Oh, an old political debt, nothing important,' he said, but she knew he was lying.

'I need to know,' she said. 'I need to know exactly what happened between the two of you.' She needed to know exactly how much Jake Stern had cost her; she had an intuition that she had paid much, much more than she thought.

Chris steered her away from the living room, into a small library at the back of the house. He was an old friend of Stan's; the prominent civil libertarian was one of Chris's earliest and most influential power brokers in Washington.

He poured her a brandy from the bar, and sat down across from her in a comfortable old leather chesterfield chair. He beckoned to another one like it, and placed his drink on the richly burnished table between them.

'Did he blackmail you over me?' she asked him. 'I didn't realize he lied about that, too.'

'No,' said Chris. 'He had something else on me. It would have finished me politically—he would have destroyed me if it were known.' He smiled oddly. 'Although, come to think of it, in this political climate, it might have helped.'

He looked at her wryly. 'Which would you rather have it be, Paula? What kind of turpitude? Sexual? Moral? Political? Ethical?' He waved his brandy glass; she realized he was slightly drunk. 'Just take your pick.'

Sometimes when Paula was in a taxi, she had a terrible fear that she would not have enough cash in her wallet to pay the driver. She counted and recounted the bills, watching the meter click with dread. She had that feeling now.

'Do you really want to know, Paula?' Chris asked her. 'Are you tough enough to take it?'

Was she tough enough to take Jake's blackmail? For that it had clearly been. Was she strong enough to acknowledge her own responsibility in it? For she knew where the responsibility lay. She had stilled her own doubts about the transaction between Chris and Jake—she knew then that she was accruing a debt of dishonour, but she would not recognize it then for what it was. Now the bill was coming due.

'Tell me, Chris.' For she knew he would, knew he had a need to unburden his own soul to her, to make his crime her own.

'For two years, I gave information to the CIA about the Scholars Committee for Asian Peace,' Chris said calmly. 'I was a conduit. I never gave them anything important—at least, I didn't think it was. Until Gibbons was murdered in Thailand. I told them about his meeting in Hanoi, and they killed him before he could see his North Vietnamese friends. And maybe stop the bloodshed, the torture . . . the war.'

Gibbons was a Yale professor, a key spokesman for the Committee, an early, powerful, and important voice in the American antiwar movement. SCAP was active on every campus from Berkeley to Cambridge in the Viet Nam years; it dominated the movement. And Chris was one of the Committee's most prominent members who rose with the help of its supporters into the Senate. It was his political base.

The meeting between Gibbons and important members of the ruling North Vietnamese government was highly secret; only the leaders of the Committee, of which Chris was one, knew of it in advance. After Gibbons' murder, rumours abounded that he had been killed by the CIA.

With that opportunity destroyed, the government paid increased attention to SCAP, none of it welcome. Pressure was applied in unsubtle ways. Federal grants were withheld, tenure was jeopardized. The IRS audited the tax returns of Committee members.

The pressure did not destroy the Committee, but it weakened its effectiveness. And the murder of Charles Gibbons left a widow with five children to raise alone.

Chris went on. 'Jake knew about it, and he had irrefutable proof. He had tapes of my conversations with my contacts in the CIA. Photographs of secret meetings with them. Copies of Agency memos about the information I gave them. It would have destroyed me.'

Paula was truly stunned; she was speechless. Chris, working for the Agency? Chris, selling out his friends, his colleagues, his principles? Chris, making an innocent man a target for treachery and death?

She shuddered. 'Why, Chris? Why did you do it?'

'I thought there might be factions in the Agency that could be reached, influenced, modified,' he began, but then he stopped. 'No, to be perfectly honest—and I am being perfectly honest, by the way—I did it for my own selfish reasons. I thought what I could do here was important enough to do almost anything to get here. I took campaign money from people connected with the Agency. I had rumours planted about my opponents. I had strings pulled for me. And that was just to get to the Senate.' He looked directly at her, intent on his words.

'I'd do a lot worse to get to the White House, and tell myself all the way that the end justifies the means. And I don't know a man in the Senate who wouldn't say the same thing—hell, not even in the House.'

He sipped his drink. 'Crude, but true. You don't have that lust, do you, Paula? Not many of you women do. Too bad; you'll never get anywhere without it.'

Oh, but he was wrong; she had that lust. Not for power, but for love. For Jake; to help him. To bind her to him with ties of gratitude, appreciation, loyalty. To keep him, she'd perverted the principles she believed in—equality under law. To make her girlish fantasy come true, she'd sold out, too. She had known it all along, she thought dully; the truth had been staring her in the face, and she'd ignored it. She hadn't really believed Jake when he told her there was no blackmail involved, but she accepted his statement without checking it; unthinkable for someone as skilled and experienced and, yes, principled as she was.

Chris seemed to echo her thoughts. 'You knew something like this was involved all along, Paula. But you wouldn't face it. Because you loved him, I suppose. That's what separates you from me—women from men. You think with your heart, with your feelings; we don't let them distract us from our goals quite that easily.' He laughed shortly. 'Hardly at all, in fact.'

Paula murmured something half to herself. ' "The last temptation is the greatest treason . . ." ' and Chris finished the quotation.

'Yes, I know,' he said. ' "To do the right deed for the wrong reason." The reasons were wrong, yours and mine—self-interest is rarely noble. But the deed? I think not. Getting Jake off . . . what purpose would it have served to send him to jail for his protest, an act he thought was morally right?'

Paula was confused. Was Chris sticking up for Jake? Did all men rationalize their most heinous crimes this way? Jake had perverted the law to serve the law—just as she had, she realized sadly. And Chris . . . well, she would not be his judge. She could not be. She had no right.

She felt no anger at him, and only a vague disappointment. Did that mean she didn't care any more—about ethics, or morals, or justice? She had that day served the law she loved with every fibre of her being, but the taste of victory was bitter in her mouth; her professional life was a lie.

Evil, she thought, comes in many shades of grey. She was no longer stunned: she had lost the capacity to be surprised by betrayal. The men she loved most were exposed as morally hollow—straw men, empty men. And she was no better than they were.

THIRTY

'Nick's moving to California,' Cass announced calmly to Paula. 'He's going to make deals.'

'Deals?' Paula echoed. 'What do you mean, deals?'

Cass inspected herself idly in a full-length mirror. 'Who knows?' she said. 'He's going to make a million dollars in the movie business. Looking for properties. Buying options. Packaging talent. Maybe try to buy *Orange* back, revamp it. Try something new. He found a sublet in Laurel Canyon. He's leaving in a few weeks.'

She delivered her news in a flat, unemotional tone, and Paula followed her lead.

'How do you feel about that?' she asked carefully. She hoped Cass was not going to indulge in histrionics; she could not take that just now. Her wounds were still fresh, as yet unhealed; any outburst might make them bleed again.

She need not have worried. Cass flopped on the bed and rummaged in Paula's night table drawer for an emery board. She filed her nails diligently, holding each one up and checking it for a flaw, concentrating on her task.

'Relieved, if you want the truth,' she replied. 'He's been impossible lately. It's like living with a full-grown child. He bitches if I'm not home for dinner—can you imagine? And he complains all the time. He says I'm cold.'

'Are you?' In spite of herself, Paula was interested.

'Probably,' Cass admitted. 'I don't have much patience. I'm no good at being the loyal, supportive, encouraging little woman. It's not me—not my role, you know?' Paula nodded; she did know. 'He turned down a couple of terrific jobs here. Said he couldn't work for anyone else. So he's going west to make his fortune.'

'Did he ask you to come?'

'Let's say Nick let me know he'd welcome the company,' Cass replied. 'But he didn't ask me directly. He wouldn't. Not until he's on his feet again. He's too Greek for that—too proud.'

'He needs you,' Paula said simply.

'I know. But I can't just pack up and go. What about my job? What about the house? Paula, what about my life?'

'You can get another job. And the house—we bought it as an investment. You could rent your apartment until . . .'

'Until what? Until I figure out that this is where I really want to be, right here, in New York, doing what I'm doing? I already know that.'

'Do you love him?'

Cass sighed. 'Love? I guess so. I'm not very turned on by him right now, though. He's changed.'

'Maybe you have, too.'

'Maybe I have,' Cass conceded. 'That's what life's about, right? Change. Growth. New horizons.'

'Change, yes,' said Paula. 'Growth? I dunno. You're pretty blasé about a relationship of four years' standing.'

'Oh, shit, Paula, what can I say? It's just not there for me with him any more. Maybe it'll come back. Maybe after he leaves I'll realize I really don't want to live without him. Maybe I'll see the light.'

'What if he doesn't see the same light?'

She shrugged. 'That's the chance I'm taking. Grey says relationships based on dependency are sick.'

'Since when is he the big expert on love?' Paula asked.

'Oh, since never. I told him what was going on. I don't usually do that, take my personal life to the office. But Grey's different. He's understanding.'

'Is he why you're not upset about Nick leaving?'

'No,' said Cass. 'Grey's not like that—he doesn't need me.'

'But Nick does.'

'Maybe I just don't want to be needed,' said Cass. She loved Nick, but she did not want to be loving to him. When she was, he was penitent, which she hated. He did not enquire deeply into her feelings, for which she was grateful. They had existed since Christmas in a stasis with which both of them felt uneasy, but which neither wanted, dared to disturb. Toward the end, they were excessively polite to one another. They told the lists and details of what they had done, whom they had seen, where they had been, as if that would substitute for the intimacy they had not shared for several months.

Ellin thought it was the coolest finale to a long relationship she had ever witnessed. 'Not a scene, not a sob, not even a tear,' she told Paula.

'That's Cass,' Paula responded. 'She only cries when they leave her. It was over when he started needing her.'

'I'm tired of thinking about it,' Cass said to Paula, effectively ending that discussion. 'What about you? Are you still miserable because of Jake, or did the case shake you out of it?'

'Somewhat,' said Paula. 'There are some days I don't even mind waking up any more.'

'I'm certainly glad to hear that.' She inspected Paula critically. 'You know, sweetie, you look like hell.'

Paula suppressed the desire to tell Cass to go away; she knew she was right. She had paid scant attention to very much recently except the oral argument and her own unhappiness. Her skin was sallow, and her body flabby; the lack of interest in food which marked the first several days after Jake's departure had been replaced for a longer period by a compulsive desire to eat, and her clothes, she noticed, were tight. She was bored with them, too; it was that time of the year when she was sick of her winter wardrobe, but felt too fat and unattractive for anything new.

'Aren't you going to California next week for that women's law conference?' Cass asked. Paula nodded. 'Well, I have to be in LA on business then, too. I don't want to come right back; I don't particularly want to be here while Nick's moving out. So why don't we go to La Costa for a few days?' She jumped up enthusiastically. 'Oh, Paula, it's just what you need. Me, too! Pampering ourselves, getting rubbed and creamed and exercised and beautified! Let's do it!'

Cass always felt better when she knew she looked good. At the end of a relationship, she usually let herself go, until she was bored with that kind of statement and ready for the next romantic event. She did not go from lover to lover without a suitable period of mourning or anger—whichever was appropriate, given the circumstances of the breakup. Her special light dimmed during that interim; it grew brighter again as she came closer to a new love.

Paula had her doubts about La Costa. 'A spa for people who can't be too thin or too rich,' she said disdainfully. But she let Cass talk her into it.

'Think of it as an anthropological experience—Margaret Mead with the Kwakiutl,' said Cass. 'That ought to ease your social conscience.'

They stayed at the spa for five days, and Paula, to her own surprise, enjoyed it thoroughly. 'Decadence,' she said as a slim man named Bob sloshed her body with coarse salt and buffed her with a loofah sponge. 'Bizarre,' she commented when someone else stuck her under a needle shower. 'Ridiculous,' she said, giggling, when a pretty woman named Nora wrapped her in herb-saturated sheets. 'Too impossible,' she muttered when a lithe, pliant yoga instructress commanded her to contort her body into bizarre positions.

'Amazing,' Cass said when they checked out. 'You look like a whole different person.' She was relaxed and buffed to a healthy sun-tanned gloss, but Paula was striking. Her hair had been cut so the curly tendrils at her temples and nape made her look younger and at the same time much more sophisticated. Her new makeup was becoming; her eyelashes had been dyed an even blacker black than they were, and her eyes looked huge and thickly fringed. Freed of her frizzy, flyaway mane, her features asserted themselves, especially her fine high cheekbones. She decided to buy some new clothes to go with her new look; for once, on the short flight from San Diego to Los Angeles, she accepted the fashion magazines offered by the flight attendant and pored over them with Cass.

'What do you think of this?' she asked, studying a stark, elegant, and expensive black dress in *Vogue.*

'It looks very, very,' Cass said, and Paula agreed.

'I think that's going to be the new Paula,' she said. 'The very, very Paula.'

Cass grinned. 'Decadence can be very addictive.'

The new Paula—the very Paula—inspected herself in the hotel room's full-length mirror. She was pleased with her reflected image. Just before she checked out of the spa, she called Max in Los Angeles. He was delighted to hear from her—of course she must come to LA before she went east.

After the Court argument, he had sent flowers—two dozen long-stemmed roses, beautiful white blooms. She found them waiting when she returned to the brownstone from Washington. Dear Max, she thought, you really are a friend. Still, she could not call him then. She had been through so much since she'd last seen Max: the numbing shock of Jake's deception, the weeks of depression after he left, the surge of energy before the argument, the elation that followed it, and then the final blow—Chris's revelation about Jake's blackmail and his own betrayal. Paula could not dissemble with Max; if she talked to him she would have to tell him everything, and at that time she could not. Instead she wrote a note to thank him for the flowers, mentioning that she would be in touch with him soon.

The five days at La Costa cleansed her mind as well as her body. The tension seeped out of her muscles under the soothing hands of the masseuse; she washed away her pain in the needle showers. She cried her last tears in the steam room. And she rethought her own role in Jake's treachery.

She knew she was not innocent of complicity. She had sensed from the beginning that Jake was not being entirely truthful with her. She would have probed more deeply with a client; she would have refused to help one who would not tell her everything. She had an unerring radar for evasion or dishonesty; it failed her with Jake, because she loved him so much that she ignored it.

Why had she allowed herself to be taken in by him? Why had she rationalized away his moods, his deceptions, his petty cruelties?

Before she left for the spa, she spent a long evening talking to Ellin about it. Ellin thought there was a pattern in everything, and that logic would reveal it. She analyzed herself at regular intervals the way some women weigh themselves, and she observed and analyzed her friends the same way.

Like Paula, Ellin believed in causality. But unlike Paula, she always considered, before she acted, what the worst thing was that could possibly happen. If Paula stopped first to think of the probable outcome, her vision was always rosy, a vision of the best possible future.

Ellin's analysis of Paula's pattern was lucid, and informed by her knowledge of psychology and human behaviour. 'You triumphed in the Oedipal struggle,' Ellin told her, 'and you felt guilty about that. But it set up a whole script about needing a man's approval to feel good about yourself.'

'You mean Jake and Chris were father substitutes?'

'Sort of,' Ellin replied. 'You told me yourself, from the time you could read, your father was yours.' That was true, every achievement made Isaac Gabriel love Paula more. When Paula was thirteen her mother told her that she and Isaac had not shared the same bed since Paula's birth. 'You ripped me apart, with such a big head,' she said. Sex was still mysterious to Paula then; she felt only the vaguest sense of responsibility for the twin beds in her parents' room.

'But my mother always complained about his snoring, so I really didn't think it was such an awful thing,' she told Ellin.

'Yes, but there was guilt,' Ellin said firmly; she was a great believer in guilt as a motivator. It didn't always get desired results, but it made people act in understandable ways. 'And of course, you couldn't actually play out the drama . . . you couldn't sleep with your father. You could with Jake, though, and he was like your father. Perform, make me proud, or I'll withhold my love from you.'

It made sense to Paula when she thought about it later. Never again, she told herself. I'll never be so desperate for a man's approval that I sacrifice my self-respect again. And if there are no ties, no commitments, I won't be. And then she picked up her shawl, and went to meet Max.

Over margaritas at El Adobe, she brought Max up to date on her life. She did not repeat what Chris had told her; she owed him loyalty despite his betrayal. But she did not spare any of the other details, including her resolve never to be beholden again to the approval, or love, of any man.

'And what about the white picket fence and the *chupa* and that whole enchilada?' Max asked, mildly amused.

'Not for this kid,' said Paula firmly. 'You can't have it all, you know. You make a choice—a woman has to. A career or a life. And so far, I seem to have chosen a career.'

'Or the wrong guy. Maybe the career is winning by default.'

'That could be,' said Paula. 'But right now, I need a

new goal. Something I can get myself. Something I don't need a man for.'

'A new job, you mean?'

'A job, a project, a case . . . something. I'm in a good position for it. Maybe the right one will find me. I have a good reputation, a solid foundation—in spite of everything else, at least I've accomplished that.'

'You have indeed,' he said. 'And then what? Party time again?'

She coloured. 'Well, maybe not quite that bad. But I'm not going to just sit around, either. I'll probably start seeing men again. There's no reason not to. But I can feel another kind of change coming. I can smell it, feel it . . . I just can't see it yet. It won't happen immediately. Meanwhile, I'm not bereft. I have Cass, and Ellin, and the house . . . God, I'm glad I bought the house. I let Cass talk me into it because I couldn't think of a reason not to, and it was the best decision I ever made. It's home now—it's my home, I get a good deal of comfort in Casita Rosita. I miss it when I'm not there—it's become a refuge. A family. Cass and Ellin love me.'

'They're not the only ones,' said Max.

Paula smiled. 'Oh, Max, you're wonderful,' she told him. 'You're probably my best man friend in the world. If I only had you in New York, I wouldn't need anything else.'

'And what about me?' he countered.

'Oh, I suppose after a time some sweet young thing would come and take you away, but you'd still be special to me,' she said. 'We'll always be special, no matter what, won't we?'

'Absolutely,' he promised. 'Special. No matter what.'

They put down the top of his convertible and drove up and down the winding roads of the city, stopping at the crest of Mulholland Drive, where the lights of the valley spread out below them like a sparkling necklace. On the way back to the hotel, they sang at the top of their lungs—old Beatles songs, Dylan tunes, music from their youth. She was in high spirits when they stopped in front of the hotel.

'When are you coming east again?'

'A month or so,' he replied. 'Save me a line on your dance card.'

'You can have a whole page,' she promised him.

'Hey, Paula?'

She was out of the car, leaning into the driver's window for a last kiss good-bye. 'Hmm?'

'You can have it all,' he told her. 'The trick is, you really have to want it all.' And he patted her cheek, and pulled away before she could reply.

THIRTY-ONE

Even after a year in the executive offices of Amagansett, Cass had made little headway with some of her colleagues, most notably Pete Marks. He was barely civil to her: he resented her growing power in the corporation, envied Grey's increasing reliance on her judgment. Pete was popular at Amagansett. He had come up through the ranks in sales, and his cronies were scattered through most of AI's divisions and subsidiaries. He was an easy-going manager, unlike Cass: her style was more direct, brusque, and confronting. She was less inclined than she had been in her first months at AI to persuade by charm and nicety. She was impatient with the necessary charade; she had proved her worth to Grey Tucker, and that was what counted. Trying to please others was time-consuming, and her current project was demanding most of her time.

She had broached her idea to Grey that spring. 'Go ahead, look into it,' he told her after he read her lengthy memorandum. She was already overcommitted with planning, acquisitions, and ongoing tasks; she kept the research and reports and figures and notes on what she had come to think of as her own project separate from her other work; at night, on weekends, in moments snatched from her regular duties, she planned and revised and rewrote. She hoped—she knew—her project would be an important new direction for Amagansett, and she intended to use it to get the vice presidency Grey had airily promised her back at that breakfast meeting at the

Plaza. She couldn't win Pete Marks over, so she didn't try. Others in the highest level of AI management were loyal to him out of what she assumed was simply corporate male bonding. Grey himself looked with cool amusement as Cass and Marks, in meetings and memos, jockeyed for turf.

'Competition's good for the company,' he commented after a bitter argument in one of those meetings. 'Pete hasn't worked this hard in years—you're keeping him on his toes.'

'Is that where his brains are?' Cass asked sarcastically. 'Really, Grey, when he suggested that maybe it was "one of those days" for me, and that's why I lost my temper at him, I almost threw something at him.'

'Come on, Cass, you know better. Marks just isn't used to dealing with strong women, that's all.'

'And I'm not used to dealing with idiots!' she said hotly.

Her efforts to balance the scales depended on Sarah Kaiser, a former business-school classmate she had brought to Grey's attention. Grey was impressed and hired Sarah for the corporate finance group. 'Maybe with two of us in there fighting, some attitudes will change around here,' she said to Sarah, who was unenthusiastic.

'Then they'll just have two targets instead of one,' Sarah told her. 'All you can do is ignore Marks, Cass.'

In fact, Sarah may have been her natural ally, but in terms of the corporation, Pete Marks was closer to Cass's point of view. There was a new trend coming in company management: the money people were beginning to mind the store, and financial managers were supplanting marketers and merchandisers. Financial strategizing was coming into its own; it had been left to the accountants for too long. Cass and Sarah argued about it over lunch. 'You can't run a business like this strictly on the numbers,' she told Sarah, who disagreed.

'Using capital to reduce costs makes as much sense as using it to buy new companies. I haven't forgotten who got me in the door at Amagansett, Cass, but that doesn't mean I think you're always right.'

The first test of wills between Cass and Sarah came when Cass presented her major marketing proposal at a management committee meeting. She prepared as carefully and thoroughly for the presentation as she ever had, at AI or even at the agency. She took the group through the proposal, one step at a time, until finally she pulled back the conference room curtain and revealed a complete, outsized mock-up of the catalogue she had conceived, a catalogue as rich and elegant as any mail-order book in existence. All the merchandise, she explained, would come from present or anticipated AI companies, divisions, and subsidiaries: the most beautiful, expensive, top-of-the-line offerings, from luggage to lingerie. The cover was a hazy outline of Blythe's, Amagansett's flagship store, with its famous bronze doors die-cut into the cover of the catalogue and opening into the book itself.

She explained it all—the costs, the expected profits, the market research that proved women would buy from the catalogue—even Blythe's old-line, conservative customers. 'They'll buy because they trust our name, our quality, our taste,' she said. 'They don't even know that many of these items are already manufactured by us—that's the beauty of it.' She turned to Grey. 'We've talked endlessly about giving the corporation an identity, an image that could apply to every one of our companies, everywhere we have them. This does that. It also absorbs our less successful products; it strengthens them simply by positioning them with the stronger ones. It's as if our customer had Blythe's—a new, updated, contemporary, high-fashion Blythe's—in her mailbox. And, more important, it moves Amagansett into an entire new field, one in which the potential is enormous.'

The field, she explained, was publishing. She pointed to the success of many new magazines. 'Despite rising mailing costs, these are making it,' she said, tossing copies of *Savvy, Self,* and other publications on the table. She went on, speaking of the proposed acquisitions that fitted with her presentation. 'Synergism,' she said, flipping through her beautifully inked flip charts . . . the direct-mail marketing company in Boulder, the paper firm in Oregon. And on and on.

Finally, she took her seat, offering copies of her proposal around the table. She had given them the sizzle, she thought; they would have to chew on the steak themselves, as Amelia would have said.

Grey complimented her on her thoroughness. 'I think we all need time to study it before we make a decision,' he said.

He adjourned the meeting; Cass heard him ask Sarah, who was studying the figures attached to the proposal, to step into his office. And there, for several weeks, her proposal rested.

As Amelia had predicted, Grey was exactly what the new administration was seeking: a successful, respected business executive with good connections and reliable, conservative politics. He was offered a sub-Cabinet post early on; he declined, but he did agree to serve on a Presidential-level advisory commission on productivity. He was often in Washington, and often Cass was with him. She sat in hearing rooms while he testified before congressional committees considering tax reform; she went to a reception in the White House with him one evening. The invitation was addressed to Grey Tucker and guest, she noted; she did not receive her own heavy, square white card.

She accompanied Grey to a dinner at the home of the French ambassador before an opening of the Comédie Française at the Kennedy Centre. The *Post* ran a picture of them captioned, 'Amagansett CEO Grey Tucker and favourite lady exec Cassandra Campbell.'

Gossip flourishes in the world of the corporation as it does everywhere else, and Cass and Grey were a photogenic couple. But their romance was only a media fantasy. Since that dawn kiss in Paris, Grey had not been anything other than correct; even, perhaps, a bit more removed from her than usual.

The affair with Nick had ended, suitably analyzed and dissected by Cass. 'It's like *Rashomon,* the difference between her version and his,' Ellin said to Paula. Nick came to New York occasionally; Ellin bumped into him at Elaine's one night, surprised that he was in town. Cass hadn't mentioned it. Nick was boozily philosophical.

'You want us to be emotional,' he told Ellin. 'You want us to be sensitive, you want us to be open, you dames want us to share our innermost feelings with you, you want us to be goddamned fucking vulnerable, isn't that it? Isn't it? Well, isn't it?' He was getting belligerent; Ellin patted his arm soothingly. But people were used to scenes at Elaine's—Norman Mailer was making a louder one at the other end of the room.

'Well, I'm here to tell you that's bullshit!' he went on. 'You don't want the bad feelings, you only want the good feelings. You don't want to find out we're only human, just like you are, and sometimes we're scared. Oh, no, you don't want that!'

'What do we want, Nick?' she asked him.

'Oh, shit, you want to find out that we're perfect so you don't have to be,' he said. 'You want to find out that you're the most important thing in our lives.'

'Is that so terrible?'

'Fucking A it is!' he said, slapping the table so emphatically that his drink tipped over. He paid no attention as it dripped into his lap. 'A man's got to do what he's got to do, that's all.' His words trailed off, and she steered the talk to a safer subject.

Cass saw it differently, of course. 'He didn't call for two weeks after he left,' she told Ellin. 'He forgot our anniversary. He's been fucking Astrea; he says that has nothing to do with me, but that's ridiculous, he knows I detest her. He promised to come Easter weekend, but he went fishing in Cabo san Lucas with Bob Treat instead. He says he loves me, but he's obviously lying. After all, he's the one who moved out.'

Yes, but only after you made it impossible for him to stay, Ellin thought. She didn't say it. As far as Cass was concerned, the discussion was closed. Nick was gone, out of her life. And if she missed him, she did it privately.

She didn't date other men very often; she was sexually abstinent, which was entirely satisfactory. There was no lover to distract her from her purpose; she concentrated on her work, fighting for every advantage, playing the power games more skilfully, searching for ways to put her abilities where people could see them, and approve. Especially Tucker.

She felt lean, hard, and healthy. She pared her life down to essentials: her work, Paula and Ellin, the house. She had enormous energy; only occasionally did her strength and her concentration falter. She called in a decorator to finish the apartment; she gave him clear instructions, approved some samples, and happily paid the bills, just so she didn't have to do it herself. It would be years before she realized she hated the colours he'd chosen for the spare room, and got rid of the andirons he picked out for the fireplace.

She spent a great deal of thought on Grey Tucker. He stymied her; she could not believe that he was not falling in love with her, but he gave no sign. She did not love him; she wanted him to be in love with her. Yet she made no move, created no openings, in case he rejected her. She would wait. It would be up to him to make the initial moves.

It happened finally after the management committee voted against her project. They took Sarah's side of the argument; they said the initial investment was too costly, and required diversion of money from acquisitions and expenditures of greater value to the bottom line. They said her proposal would put Amagansett at a disadvantage in a new area, one in which the corporation lacked management depth; the long-term benefits were there, they agreed, but they would take too long to realize.

Grey summarized the official position; he used Sarah's words. Strangely, only Pete Marks supported Cass's project; he had missed a political advantage, aligning himself with the majority, but he was a marketing expert—he saw the value in Cass's ideas. Perhaps she had ignored a valuable ally, she thought; she had assumed he was so personally antagonistic toward her that it would weight his judgement of her efforts. But it was too late.

Grey took her to dinner at Nicola's, and he was sympathetic. That undid her; she felt the tears well up in her eyes, and bit her lip to stop herself from crying. Months of work that had come to nothing. The vice presidency still tantalizingly out of reach. For a moment, she missed Nick. And then the rich, heavy food rumbled threateningly in her stomach, and the wine made her head swim, and she felt the sick sweet taste of bile in her throat.

She threw up her dinner in the ladies' room, and sat on the cool tile floor, feeling the nausea recede. She washed her face, rinsed her mouth, and applied fresh makeup. When she returned to the table, her face was composed, and she smiled brightly up at Grey.

'I've had enough business for one night,' she said. 'Let's go dancing!'

In the crowded disco she pressed herself against Grey, as if by accident; she smiled at him continuously, and laughed at his jokes. She saw a phony Italian countess she knew, and dragged Grey over to introduce them. In the taxi on the way home, she pretended to be a bit more intoxicated than she was, and leaned her head lightly on Grey's shoulder.

She fumbled for her keys, until he took them from her and unlocked the door. He followed her into the apartment, and she led him into the library. She waved in the direction of the brandy, and suggested that he pour them some. And she went into her bedroom.

When she returned, she was wearing a high-necked silk dressing gown of deep turquoise, fitted closely to her breasts and waist, flaring gracefully around her body. Her hair was loosened from the chignon into which she pinned it at the office. She was regal and beautiful, and she moved close to him. She said nothing.

He considered her thoughtfully. He smiled with his thin lips, but his eyes gave no clue to his feelings. After a long moment, he set down his glass.

He touched her hair, feeling its soft, burnished mass. Carefully, deliberately, he unfastened the tiny pearl buttons on her gown. The rustle of silk was the only sound in the room.

He uncovered her breast, and took it in his hand, noting its heft, squeezing her nipple, watching it harden as he squeezed it softly between his thumb and forefinger. He traced a line on her body, along the soft, pale down, below her navel, to the thicket of hair below. With his finger, long and slender, he sought her opening; he touched her there so lightly she could barely feel him. When he thrust his knee between her legs, she made room for him, standing on tiptoe, lowering herself onto him. He pumped her rhythmically, and when her moistness darkened the fabric of his trousers, and her breath came in short gasps, he spun her gently around and followed her into the bedroom.

THIRTY-TWO

The brownstone was lonely without Paula and Cass. Ellin hadn't taken a real vacation in years, one that was not a research trip or a book tour or a family visit. She envied her housemates the freedom to indulge themselves; she felt burdened with responsibilities.

She almost went to the spa with them. But Lara had spring vacation from boarding school, and she couldn't just dump her on Sophie and Lou. She'd secretly hoped Lara would make just one close friend at school, one friend who would invite her home to spend spring break with her. But it hadn't happened. Lara didn't mind school, although she complained that she missed the beach, that her classmates were nerds, that Ellin didn't write often enough or come to visit her. Guiltily, Ellin sent her presents: clothes, books, a box of candy from Sweet Temptation. On Lara's sixteenth birthday she drove up to the school, five hours from New York, in a rented car, and took Lara and a half dozen of her friends out to dinner. She tried to make it a festive occasion; Lara wasn't cooperating. Ellin didn't feel all that cheerful, either; Vermont was not where she wanted to be.

She spent the night at an inn near the school, and the next morning she and Lara had breakfast together in the almost deserted dining room.

'When Daddy comes back, I'm going back to California to live with him,' Lara said. Location filming on the movie was running behind schedule, as Tony had said it would; he expected to remain in Africa for several months longer than he had anticipated. Ellin didn't argue. She tried not to take it personally; Lara was not so much rejecting her as she was choosing to live another kind of way. It was her right, after all. It was a choice she had exercised once before, and after the first pangs of guilt and sadness, Ellin had acquiesced in it. So perhaps she had lost the right to interfere in Lara's plans for her life now.

Ellin had really let go of Lara when she went to live with her father. It was no orderly leave-taking, not a long visitation according to decrees and orders, dispositions signed a decade before, but an angry and awkward departure from the family Ellin had constructed as well as she could with the leftovers of her marriage.

Her daughter had left her to live with Tony; futility and rage had thinned and shredded the ties of love between her and her daughter, whose tormented adolescence had trapped them both.

Lara had gone to live with her father, a childish fantasy Ellin thought had been abandoned long ago, with the stuffed animals and lacing shoe, the picture books and the toy box. The small framed photograph of Tony had disappeared from Lara's room years before, without mention, after the birthdays that passed without cards or gifts, the phone calls that were never returned, the promises that were not kept.

But the last call had been answered, the one Ellin dialled out of desperation. For nothing else worked, not since Lara's waist slimmed and her breasts budded, her braids disappeared into a halo of chestnut curls. The limits Ellin set for Lara were ignored, and her daughter's defiance was open and shouted. Lara was obstreperous and arrogant in school, constantly in small troubles that might have been overlooked if she were at least using her intelligence in ways that tests or teachers could determine. Lara tried Ellin's patience, and that of her friends, her teachers, her mother's friends. She was most difficult at home—prodding, pushing, taunting, testing, flaying Ellin with the edges of her anger. And Ellin was tired to her bones, trying to juggle Lara's needs with her own work, her life, her lovers.

Her daughter had left her to live with her father; by then, Ellin was relieved to let go. For ten years Lara had consumed her—'She's sucking the lifeblood out of me!' she raged once to her friend Kate, who murmured sympathetically and prescribed Librium for Ellin's anxiety. Lara had consumed her just as Tony had, but the letting go of her daughter was at first much more difficult than detaching herself from her husband had been.

The last few days before Lara left to live with Tony were heavy with silence, a silence so intense that it resonated. She had washed and folded Lara's clothes, darned holes in her sweaters, consumed hours in the small but seemingly final tasks.

The night before what Lara by then was happily calling 'the big switcheroo', mother and daughter retired to their separate rooms, with the tension of unsaid words between them, heavy like thunder-clouds. In the middle of the night, Ellin heard Lara vomiting in the bathroom; she clenched her hands but did not go to her. This is for her to face alone, Ellin thought. For all her bravado, Lara was scared, frightened of the father she barely remembered. And Ellin could not tell Lara what he might be like now; she did not remember, either, though in the darkness she tried to call him up, recall the qualities she had loved in him, take some comfort in the good memories—Tony, who are you now? she silently implored—and blot out the others.

They saw each other on weekends before Ellin moved to New York, but she and Lara were strangers, withdrawn from their anger and withdrawn, too, from the painful love between them, the resentments and recriminations. There was one brief, happy weekend; it was the first time Lara began menstruating, and Ellin was glad it had happened then, when she could smile at her daughter tenderly, help her with the strange belt and pads, enjoy the unexpected wash of tenderness and pleasure that swept over her. The next day, she took Lara to lunch at an elegant restaurant in Beverly Hills, and bought her a small pearl ring to mark the occasion, and when she drove Lara to Tony's that night, she kissed her goodbye with a love she had not felt in weeks.

At first, after Lara left, Ellin's relief was indistinguishable from her loneliness. There were no more tears; they collected, uncried, in the void Lara's departure had created. The space she had filled in Ellin was empty and accusing; not with blame or anger, only sorrow that what she had tried to give Lara was not enough. Her anger, muted though it was, was only for Tony—Tony, who, with the simple words, I want you, could do what Ellin, who had loved and wanted Lara and loved her still but wanted her no longer, could not.

Lara had left her to live with Tony. She was funny and kind and creative and generous; underneath the anger and apart from the treacherous hormones that had changed her from a laughing, loving child to a silent, surly teenager was a girl of quality. To uncover it, Lara had to leave her—to live with a half-remembered parent whose ways were strange to her, whose life had taken turns and taught him lessons unfathomable to Lara or Ellin. 'It's time I paid my dues,' Tony said when Ellin called him that last time. 'It's my turn to worry about her.' Ellin believed him because she had no choice. And the shrunken knot of her own pain, ten years dead, dead with her marriage, expanded and filled the void in her.

Ellin came back to the brownstone after the weekend at school with Lara and looked through the mail that had accumulated in her absence, grimacing as she saw the cellophane windows of what she knew could only be bills.

As usual, she was balanced precariously on the thin edge of financial disaster. It always threatened to topple her. Money never arrived when it was supposed to, and sometimes it never came at all. She was due fees for an assignment completed for a magazine that abruptly declared bankruptcy. Another assignment was rejected, and she could not sell the piece elsewhere. Her royalty statement had a negative balance; there had been heavy returns of the hardback edition of her book during that royalty period, in anticipation of the paperback release. The water main broke in the Malibu house; her tenants called to complain, and she told them to call a plumber. The bill was twelve hundred dollars.

Her editor was sympathetic, but firm: 'When we see more of the manuscript, perhaps we can give you something on the advance,' she said.

Ellin turned to magazine assignments; she even went back to see Pandora. 'I want a major Relationships piece, about five thousand words,' said the editor, beaming happily. She must have a new man in her life, Ellin thought sourly.

She was tired of writing about Relationships, tireder still of reading about them. For numerous articles, she had made up countless women who had only first names and lived in a geographically balanced selection of cities. There was Dorothy in Santa Barbara, who couldn't get rid of a man she'd outgrown—that was for *Glamour*. Or was it *Mademoiselle*? And Shirley in Hartford, who could never please her mother—was that for *Redbook*? There were real people, too: the women firefighters in Houston, the women's network in Portland, the single mothers in the support group in Atlanta. And there were the experts—on sexual dysfunction in Purdue, on assertiveness in women in Berkeley, on anorexia in Manhattan.

Ellin was bored with all of them. She wanted to finish her novel, but she couldn't afford to ignore the necessary revenue from magazines. She wanted to be at La Costa with Paula and Cass. She wanted almost anything except an assignment on Relationships from Pandora, but she took it. That would pay for the water main, her phone bill, and the new flute that was Lara's birthday present. It could be worse, she thought—I could be waiting tables to support my writing habit. Jesus, maybe Sophie was right. Maybe I should have gone to medical school.

She wrote the entire piece for Pandora from her big grey platform bed. She interviewed her sources by telephone, which was the only link between Ellin and the world that week. She sat up on the third floor, in her eyrie, and ordered in her life, occasionally descending to admit a messenger with dinner or materials sent over by the magazine or Chinese food and cigarettes and the newspaper.

She crafted the article together. Her facility pleased and disgusted her; it was glib, slick, really meaningless. But Pandora would love it, and if she was lucky, some of the foreign magazines might pick it up and pay her extra for it.

She finished it at ten o'clock at night, and it was quiet in the house. She wanted company. She walked over to Sheridan Square, and turned east toward the Lion. She felt at home there; she nodded to several regulars, who nodded back. There were some new dust jackets tacked up on the wall; they represented the published work of Lion habitués, and she wondered if she would ever see her own dust jackets displayed there.

Vic was at the bar; she nodded to him, and went into the back room. The waitress brought her stuffed clams and a salad; Ellin read a few pages of a paperback she'd tucked in her pocket. Later, she found a stool at the far end of the bar and sipped a cognac, watching Vic as he worked.

'Want to go over to Seventh Avenue later and hear some jazz?' he asked, wiping the counter in front of her. 'Some buddies of mine are playing after hours tonight.'

She'd been working steadily since that morning, but she wasn't tired; she was keyed up, the way she always was after she completed a piece of work, hungry for people and laughter. Vic was easy to be with; she had not completely gotten over the feeling of being rejected sexually she'd once felt, but she didn't dwell on it. He was friendly, but not at all romantic, and she supposed it was better that way. 'Sure,' she told him. 'Why not?'

They pulled a couple of extra chairs up to the small table and crowded in, close to the stage. Ellin was wedged between Vic and Donna Louise, a good old Texas girl she'd met before. Donna Louise was a dancer who waited tables at the Lion between gigs. She had come to New York ten years before, dreaming of being a Rockette; for the last three weeks, she told Ellin, she'd been delivering Dance-O-Grams.

'Dance-O-Grams?'

'Sure, honey, you know, liking singing telegrams. Your choice of ten minutes of tap, hula, or flamenco. I bring this darling little cassette player with me, snap on the music, and dance my tushie off.' She pronounced 'tushie' with four melodic syllables.

'Who sends Dance-O-Grams?' Ellin was disbelieving.

'Oh, cute little faggot boys send them to their lovers, mostly,' Donna Louise said airily. 'Hey, you all, this is Ellin, and Vic, you know him.' Someone brought them drinks, and the lights went down. The music came up: a trio who played the old standards, gently, sweetly. They were joined by a singer, a young black woman who looked and sounded achingly like the early Billie, and had a sad, husky contralto voice. The music made her nostalgic; it pierced the veil of memories, and made her soft inside. Vic draped an arm around her shoulders, and she settled into him, glad not to be alone.

When they came out of the club, the sky was washed with a translucent grey light; it was nearly dawn. They walked back to Twelfth Street, and Vic unlocked the door with his key.

'I enjoyed it,' she told him. 'Thanks.'

'So did I,' said Vic. He hesitated at the foot of the stairs; so did she. It was very quiet in the empty house. They were standing close; she could feel the exhalation of his breath on her face. He seemed to be waiting for something. She shifted her weight slightly, and he put his arms out as if to catch her, and then he was kissing her.

It was a long kiss, soft at first and then more insistent, his teeth catching her lower lip, nibbling it, his tongue seeking hers, tentatively and then demandingly. She breathed him into her; he sucked the air from her throat, from her lungs, and she felt the weight of him, felt him grow taut and hard against her.

She didn't remember, later, how they got upstairs or into the apartment. He entered her quickly the first time; he did not even undress her fully then.

It seemed to go on for hours; he brought her to climax again and again. Everywhere he touched her, she burned with heat; and he touched her everywhere, with his hands, his tongue, his fingers, his thick, strong, searching cock.

She thought she could take no more of him, finally, and rolled over on her belly, but he straddled her from behind and pushed himself slowly into her. She lifted her head from the pillow and made sounds of protest; her mouth was so dry that no words escaped her lips, and she could only shake her head—no, not there, please, no. He did not stop, but brought his hand to her mouth, and as she sucked her juice from his fingers he came the rest of the way into her, and she burned there, too, with pain that was indistinguishable from pleasure. He lifted her onto her knees, thrusting insistently in and out, in and out, filling her until there was no part of her he did not know, and own, until his thick, warm syrup poured into her and he collapsed heavily on top of her. Then there was only the long slide into nothingness, only the faint wail of a siren somewhere in the streets below them.

THIRTY-THREE

Movement Women made a brief appearance at the bottom of the *Times* mass market best-seller list; one of the book's subjects, a Weatherwoman, suddenly reappeared, guns blazing in a shoot-out with Brink's guards. A few weeks later the book sank out of sight again, but not before earning for Ellin the five-thousand-dollar bonus specified in her contract.

She put it in a money market fund, to earn the highest possible interest until she collected the second half of her advance on the novel and became a full partner in the brownstone. She had not made a final decision, but she was leaning that way.

To each of the women, Casita Rosita meant something different. It represented roots of her own to Cass—she would never have to leave it unless she wanted to. Paula thought of the house as a womb, where she was safe, protected, loved. For Ellin the brownstone filled in all the outlines of the second great fantasy of her life, gave it colour and texture. Tony was the first fantasy, but this was the one she had made happen; she thought of Tony as having happened to her, like a disease. And the house was tangible proof that Ellin had earned the privileges as well as the obligations of adulthood.

In Ellin's mind the line between fantasy and ambition was blurred; she never knew when one became the other. And even then, she would not have called what she wanted an ambition, because that seemed presumptuous, or a goal, because if she did not accomplish it, she would have to deal with her failure.

Ellin's writing was a portable skill, her ticket out of California. New York was the logical destination—she didn't think any place very interesting existed between the two coasts. She never considered a foreign city; without language, she was lost, and she was not fluent or even passable in French or Spanish or Italian, or anything else, for that matter. She did think fleetingly of London, but everyone she knew there was Tony's friend, or a connection through him, and she did not want to begin again in a place where she knew no one.

That moving to New York was a wise career decision became clear to her later, after she decided to do it, and realized that the truth—that she was bored—was not palatable to anyone. It seemed like a frivolous reason for such a momentous upheaval. Kate was quite huffy about it. 'Oh, you're bored with your friends, are you? Well, fuck you, too!' she said with unaccustomed indignation, and Ellin had to soothe her and say, Not you, Kate, don't be silly, I'm not bored with *you*.

So she told people she was going because it was good for her work—she wouldn't say, for her career, because that's not what it was, not then. It was simply the way she would survive, and pay her bills, as it had been, one way or another, all her adult life.

She had written more than her share of ads, brochures, press releases, and flyers, the lot of a freelancer's life. The journalism was an accident—she went out with a man who was trying to start a weekly paper to replace the *Free Press* in LA, and wrote a few pieces for the dummy he comped up for presentation to his backers. She found a new niche, and, eventually, what she was best at: talking to people, and writing about them, about the emotional quality of their lives, how they felt about themselves.

The book happened just as fortuitously. A friend who was an agent at ICM saw the potential in her series of newspaper interviews with radical women; he helped her write a proposal, and then sold it to a publisher.

After that, the assignments starting coming from national magazines, and then the contract for the novel she had wanted, for a long time, to write. The New York fantasy shimmered and grew clearer. The edges took shape, and the brownstone filled them in, like the pieces of a jigsaw puzzle—the brownstone, and Cass and Paula.

Ellin made friends easily in New York. Many of them, like her, were writers; she was delighted to know people whose hours were as erratic as her own, who would come out and play in the middle of the day, who would understand if she was immersed in her work and suddenly unavailable. Nick's ex-girlfriend Astrea was one of them; Ellin liked her tart manner and her wit, though she preferred seeing her away from the brownstone. There was no sense alienating Cass, after all.

Other people she met were in publishing, or the media. Through them she followed the trade gossip. She heard of fabulous sums paid for books. She knew which first novel by the daughter of a literary genius brought a six-figure advance on the basis of a single chapter. She heard which Hollywood starchild's lurid exposé of life with Father brought a million, and was then turned down by the reprint houses, to the embarrassment of the publisher who had committed a million dollars to it before finding someone to ghostwrite the drug-hazed details. And her own book—her novel—became important to her in a new and disturbing way.

At first the novel represented a good opportunity to learn another aspect of her craft, with someone else paying for her training. The longer she worked at it, and the more time she spent with people who wrote or published, or did both, the more the book had to accomplish. It had to make her rich or famous—in her fantasies, she preferred both. Fantasy, not ambition, she reminded herself, for she recognized it as a rather shallow, even a trashy goal. She knew it was all bullshit anyway, at least the famous part. The food at Elaine's wasn't any better in the back of the front room than it was in the front of the back room, the siberia to which the tourists, the bridge-and-tunnel crowd, were exiled. Ellin had no such compunctions about rich—she'd long since outgrown them. Still, rich wasn't a very worthwhile goal, either. But Ellin's fantasy stubbornly refused to stay that way; it inserted itself into her consciousness as if it had a life and momentum all its own, and she began to feel the first curling tentacles of fear. The New York disease—did she have it?

A lot was riding on the novel. She had upped the ante by moving east; she had taken what she belatedly realized was a big risk. She was aware of the narrow tightrope she was walking; beneath it was at the least economic chaos, and, even more important, her own identity. Because her work had become not only what she did, but who she was. It was New York, the brownstone, her friends, her life. In California, she thought, she'd had little to lose; here, now, everything was at stake.

The only one who understood how important the book was to Ellin was Vic. He did not mock her ambitions, but he named them. He had a different goal: to exorcise the horror of war by pulling it out of himself, one painful memory at a time. They never repeated that extraordinary night in bed; as if to make up for it, they showed each other their work in progress. It was, Ellin thought, a greater intimacy; in the pages Vic showed her, and in those she gave him, were the real secrets about each other.

At first it was difficult to criticize his writing; she was hesitant, careful with her choice of words, even ambiguous. Vic would not allow her to spare his feelings; he was a direct and even harsh critic from the outset, and he beamed when he elicited the same toughness from her.

It was a collegiality new to Ellin; the intimacy of it both attracted and repelled her. She knew she could not have that with him, and also the raging, animal-like sex that they had shared that once. She could not be hostage to that—to her own desire for it. If she gave herself up to that sexuality, there would be nothing left to fuel her work; not even her ambition would be strong enough to ignite it.

He made no sexual advances to her, and she was relieved. She had the part of him she needed; she could not tolerate more. He never brought up that night, nor did she. They never said it would not occur again; it simply did not. And they argued and talked and read and criticized and praised each other, and she was too far out on the tightrope to retrace her steps.

THIRTY-FOUR

Paula was not tired, but she had no energy. Her work was uninteresting, and she performed it without inspiration. Almost no one noticed. It was as if her triumph in court embalmed her in success; none of her colleagues expected her to be less than excellent, so did not see the difference.

Hugh Tierney did. He was the Establishment's favourite liberal; he had founded the firm back in the McCarthy era. Hugh's daughter, Moira, was Paula's age, but she was as lost to him in the labyrinth of sixties politics turned terrorist as she would have been if she'd died in the explosion in a Lower East Side loft—a bomb factory, the newspapers called it—that had killed most of her co-conspirators.

Hugh took Paula to lunch at his club, and amid the burnished leather and the smell of fine cigars, he talked to her.

'Paula,' he began, and hesitated. He had never interfered with Moira's choices—perhaps even if he had, he mused, nothing would have been any different. He knew something was troubling Paula, and she knew that he knew. She trusted Hugh; she felt his affection for her.

'Paula, my dear, I'm worried about you. Since the argument—since before that, really—you haven't been yourself. Is there anything I can do to help?'

She was grateful. She wanted to unburden her soul to him, tell him about the grievous hurts of the past winter. But she could not do that. It was only her professional dissatisfaction that she could share with him.

'I felt extraordinary after the Supreme Court,' she told him, 'but the feeling went away. I—there's a big hole where that excitement used to be, and nothing going on in the practice that I can get that charged up about. Hell, Hugh, I'm sick of it all. I'm sick of deals and bargains and judges being bought—you know that's true, don't deny it—and one standard for the rich, who are mostly our clients, and another for the poor, who I can't even get that worked up about any more. I'm tired of cynics and power brokers, and most of them seem to be lawyers. I don't want to be like them.'

He listened calmly. 'I would suggest a vacation, Paula, except that I know you took one recently—you look wonderful, I must say—so what's troubling you isn't going to be solved that easily.' He leaned back in his chair. 'You know, I've a son in the Church.' Paula nodded; Sean Tierney was going to be a bishop one of these days, maybe even Pope—he had his father's brains, and compassion, and the independent spirit his sister, Moira, had evidenced in such a radically different way. Hugh went on. 'Sean once shared with me a period in which he had what he called a failure of faith. He considered leaving the priesthood. He felt as though a basic premise of his entire life—as a priest, as a Catholic, as a man—was being called into question. He was, he said, bereft.'

Hugh patted Paula's arm. 'I think that's what you're going through, my dear—a failure of faith. Faith in the law—or even the practice of it—to sustain you in your work.' He smiled. 'It's an imperfect system, and justice often has little to do with it, but it's the one we have. Perhaps you need to step away from the practice, and see how you can change it. Or if you can.' He chuckled. 'Or if it matters.'

Paula considered Hugh's words. What he said rang true to her. He had succinctly summed up what she had been feeling, and offered her what could be the direction she sought.

'Oh, wise old Hugh.' She smiled at him. 'This must be

an old story to you—young lawyer gets his shield dented. Loses faith in the system. Gets cynical. Gives up and keeps bees in Dutchess County, like Leon.' Leon had been an associate in the firm who quit abruptly one day, announcing that one had to make a choice 'between this insane, inhumane rat race and inner tranquillity'. That was right after Leon lost a death penalty case—the day after his client was executed. Leon had a rich wife who did yoga and went to macrobiotic cooking classes and had been left a working farm, complete with restored farmhouse, an hour north of the city. Paula went there for dinner once; Leon had grown a beard and gained fifteen pounds and was 'into' Siva mind control. He said he didn't have nightmares about his executed client any more.

'Bees? Not you, Paula,' said Hugh. 'As for the practice, I can see that it's not challenging you. Oh, I've had no complaints from clients, don't worry,' he said, noticing her look of apprehension. 'It's just that I don't see you taking any joy in life these days. At least, not in your professional life.'

He gave her an opening there, but she did not respond. She thought he probably knew about Jake—gossip spread quickly throughout the office, and Hugh had friends in Cambridge and Boston—but he was kind enough not to mention it. And if he had ever known anything about her affair with Chris Carey, he was too much the gentleman to mention it.

'You're right,' she said glumly. 'I feel like I'm at some kind of crossroads, and I don't know where I'm going next. Maybe I wasn't cut out for private practice, or even litigation. I don't have any patience with people these days. If I have fantasies about what I'd like to be doing, it's studying. In a library. Consulting. Advising. About something that matters. It's still rather formless . . . I haven't set a goal.'

'Can you continue your search for a new direction and still satisfy the demands of your practice?' Hugh asked.

He was, after all, the senior partner of the firm as well as her friend and advisor.

Paula assured him that she could, and he seemed relieved. 'If there's anything I can do,' Hugh said again. 'I know some people, I hear of things . . . I'll keep my ears open.'

'And I'll keep my problems to myself,' Paula said gratefully. 'Thanks, Hugh. Your patience is—well, it's good of you to be concerned. I wish . . .' Her words trailed off. I wish your daughter would let you be a father to her, Paula thought, but I'm very grateful that you're taking such an interest in my own welfare.

Hugh seemed to know what she was thinking—he was a remarkably sensitive man—and he said nothing. He helped her on with her coat, and they left the restaurant and walked the few blocks back to their office, in companionable silence.

While she was wrestling with her professional dilemmas, Paula was also actively seeking the company of men; she relished the warm oblivion of casual sex, and even more casual friendships. She looked better than she ever had; there was a new edge to her attractiveness, a worldliness Ellin had not noticed before. Perhaps it was the week at La Costa, and, since then, the feverish exercise programme Paula had undertaken. She went to the gym every day after work, and at night she went out with one or another of the many men who were attracted to her.

She brought them home to the brownstone, slept with them, and rarely saw any of them more than twice. 'I don't want to get involved,' she told Cass and Ellin, and those of the men who persisted even when she made obvious excuses not to see them again. 'I feel like I'm on hold,' she told her housemates. 'Numb above the neck.'

'But obviously not below it,' said Cass critically.

'I don't want to be crazy in love again,' said Paula. 'I don't want to be either hailing or wailing. I just don't want to be horny, that's all.'

'Well, aren't you afraid you'll catch some kind of disease?' Cass asked.

Paula was unconcerned. 'For that, they have shots,' she replied.

She did not pick up men in bars; she didn't have to. She took up her old social whirl with intensity; she projected an abandoned sexuality to men, a female toughness that was inviting and did not seem to demand from them any intimacy they did not want to offer.

One man recognized Paula's act for what it was. 'Does someone write your lines for you, or do you just memorize old Joan Crawford movies?' he asked her when she told him that she would not see him again. 'Big, tough lady, sexy as hell and twice as independent, huh?' He didn't believe her, he said. 'You women that talk that kind of bullshit, I don't want any commitment, all I'm looking for is a good time, you're all full of it,' he said. 'What all of you want is the husband and the babies and someone to lean on, only you're so sure you'll never get it that you do everything you can to make sure you never will.'

Paula recognized the truth in the man's words—the partial truth, anyway. She was thinking about what he'd said the night she was raped in the West Fourth Street subway station.

Her attacker was a wiry Puerto Rican in his early twenties, who wore sharply creased dark-purple polyester slacks and a tight-fitting black turtleneck jersey.

She did not struggle in the dank half-light of the terminal; he had a knife, with a thin, long blade that mesmerized her when he brandished it, shoving her into the near darkness of a deserted platform.

She felt the tip of the blade a breath away from her heart as her attacker fumbled with the zipper of his trousers. She did exactly as he told her, lifting her skirt and allowing him to back her into the wall. As she cowered against it, concentrating on the knife to the exclusion of everything else, he pulled down her tights, cursing under his breath as the garment stuck to Paula's suddenly clammy belly and thighs.

'Shit!' he swore, and in one slashing movement cut the offending nylon away from her, down the front. She could feel the warm trickle of blood on her stomach and groin where he had nicked her, and though she flinched in pain, she made no sound.

His penis hung long and dark between his legs and his frustration grew as his member refused to. Paula, certain now that he would kill her, closed her eyes and tried to pray. She thought of people who might have helped her—her father, her friends, the man in the token booth at the lighted end of the platform, the people speeding heedlessly by as trains rumbled through the station.

The man beat at her with his limp penis, but it did no good; enraged, he yanked Paula down on her knees on the gritty concrete floor, shoving her by stepping on her shoulders.

'Suck it!' he commanded. He shoved himself toward her lips, but Paula could not open her mouth; an enormous scream blocked it, and she knew if she allowed it to escape, he would surely cut her throat. She tightened her jaw trying to hold back the scream, as he grazed the tip of her ear with his knife.

And then she vomited all over it, and him. She opened her mouth, and thirty dollars' worth of pasta Alfredo fed to her by the man who just an hour before had laughed at her and called her a liar and a phony spewed out onto her attacker's wretched little cock and his awful purple pants.

She began to keen hysterically, rocking back and forth; she had so surprised her tormentor that he jumped back from her and tried to clean himself, all the while brandishing his knife at her. His penis hung limp in his pants, dripping barely recognizable blobs of pasta and cheese.

Twice he kicked her in the ribs; he seemed to forget that he had a knife in his hands, and kicked her until she started to scream. And then he turned and ran away down the platform, into the dark recesses of the passageway.

She waited a few moments to be sure he was gone, and crept toward the stairs, wrapping her raincoat around her body. She climbed up to the street, biting her lip until it bled. She kept it clenched between her teeth, tasting the salt of her tears and her wounds as she made her painful way home. She passed St Vincent's—she did not even think of going there, into the bright, cold rooms, facing the bored aides in the emergency room, dealing with the supercilious doctors, the cynical police officers.

A police car passed her, and she shrank into the darkness, aching with pain from her attacker's beating. At the door of the brownstone she fumbled for her keys. She had lost her purse, she realized, and then she cried out, in loud, sobbing gulps, and beat her fists in frustration against the dusky-pink front door.

It was Vic who found her, moments later; he was coming home from the bar, and saw her huddled against the door.

'Oh, Jesus,' he said, and gathered her up in his arms. He unlocked the door; she buried her face in the cool leather of his jacket, and closed her eyes. She heard Cass's voice—'Paula, what happened?' —and the sudden intake of her friend's breath, and then her head swam with blackness and she passed out.

She came to on Cass's bed, surrounded by her housemates. She felt Ellin's long, warm hands on hers, and Cass's cool touch on her face, and smiled weakly. 'Down, but not out,' she said. 'It's all right, don't worry. Somebody just tried to rape me, that's all.'

They helped her peel off her filthy, vomit-stained clothes, and filled the tub with hot water and Vitabath. Ellin cleaned her gently, her face creasing with worry whenever Paula winced. Cass paced the small bathroom, fuming.

'My God, you know better than to take the subway at night,' she told Paula crossly. 'Cabs after dark aren't a luxury in this city, they're a necessity! Besides, I thought you had a date tonight.'

'I did,' said Paula weakly, 'only it turned into a disaster, so I left him in the restaurant and decided to come home.' She had heard Cass's lecture about the dangers of the subway before; Cass took only buses or taxis, and never walked alone at night even on the well-lighted streets near the brownstone.

'Would you just shut up about that and call a doctor?' Ellin replied over Paula's head. 'Hasn't she been through enough, without a lecture, too?' Sometimes Cass was so intent on proving herself right that she ignored the needs of others, and this, thought Ellin, was one of those times. What Paula needed was caring and comforting and medical attention. But Cass continued to scold Paula and went to the telephone.

'I don't need a doctor, I'm all right,' Paula said wearily. She wanted to slip beneath the water and wash it all away. 'He kicked me a little, and I think he cut me.' There was a thin line of blood coagulating in the water above her stomach; Ellin washed the cut carefully with pHisoHex, and helped Paula out of the bath, enfolding her in a huge towel. She dried the thin bloody line from Paula's navel to the thicket of her pubic hair, and applied first-aid cream to the shallow cut.

'Of course you need a doctor,' Cass said, carrying the phone into the steamy bathroom. 'You might have internal bleeding, or broken ribs.'

'Hardly, or I wouldn't have made it home,' said Paula. 'Look, I'll be fine. I'm just a little shaky.'

'Sure you are,' said Ellin sympathetically. 'Would you like us to call the police?'

'Of course she would,' said Cass. 'In fact, I will.' She was pleased to find a suitable action to take, but Paula stopped her.

'I don't want the police,' she said. 'I don't want a

doctor. I want some hot tea and . . .' She started to sob, and sank to her knees on the tile floor, hugging herself and rocking back and forth on her heels. She was shielding her body; trying to hold in the broken parts, Ellin thought.

Cass stood by helplessly; she was sorry for Paula, she felt terrible, but she did not know how to help her—as she had not known how to help her mother all those nights, years ago, when she would wake and hear the soft cries which, despite her efforts, Kathryn Campbell could not always contain. And Cass felt the same sense of frustration now as she had then.

It was Ellin who crouched down on the floor with Paula, Ellin who took her in her arms and rocked her, soothing her, as she had with Lara when her daughter was small and wounded. 'It's okay,' Ellin whispered to Paula. 'It's really okay, honey, it's all going to be okay.'

'Why won't you let me call the police?' Cass demanded. 'If it happened to me, I'd certainly want to see justice done.'

'There's no such thing,' said Paula, 'they'll never catch him, and besides I feel so . . . ashamed,' she finished in a weak, tiny voice.

'Ashamed? What have you got to be ashamed of?' Cass was furious: how dare Paula feel that way? 'You didn't ask that weirdo creep to rape you!'

'He didn't rape me, he just tried to rape me. That's a distinction. Legally it's a very important distinction . . .' Paula's voice trailed off again.

Over her head, Ellin made shushing, warning signs to Cass. Shut up, she begged her silently, mouthing the words. Don't ask her, don't call anybody, don't do anything, let her be. Cass, for once, did as she was told.

Cass checked on Paula in the morning; satisfied that she was sleeping, she went to the office, since Ellin promised to keep an eye on Paula during the day.

Paula confounded them both; early in the afternoon, she dressed and went to her own office. She had a hearing, she explained to Ellin; she couldn't ask for a continuance, it was important, she was the only one who could do it.

Cass was aghast. 'And you let her go?'

Ellin shrugged. 'I had no choice, and it probably wasn't such a bad idea. Paula is coping, in her own way.'

'What kind of way is that?' Cass was hysterical. 'She'll just bury it, let it eat her up inside! She has to confront it, deal with it, even go to the police. If it were me, I'd—'

'But it's not you,' said Ellin impatiently. 'It's Paula, Cass. She has to handle it her way.' She admired Paula's resilience—she thought her friend was probably taking care of herself the best way she knew how. 'She doesn't want us to treat her like she'll break. Paula's a survivor.'

Paula did not want to talk about the attempted rape, and eventually Cass stopped pressing her to do so. She kept taking subways at night, out of habit as well as a refusal to be kept from her routines by the threat of danger. But she moved more quickly through the terminals, hurrying toward the light as fast as she could, and it was weeks before she could look directly at any of her fellow passengers on the trains that rattled noisily through the city.

THIRTY-FIVE

'Your proposal is directly contrary to the strategy agreed upon by this same committee less than a year ago, at the instigation of its chief executive officer!' Cass said heatedly. Her disagreement with Sarah Kaiser's plan to sell off two of AI's money-losing divisions, a plan that struck at the very heart of Cass's marketing strategy, was couched in a carefully worded exchange which nevertheless left no doubt as to Cass's feelings. Sarah would not be put off, however, and she had the figures to back up her position. The woman Cass herself had brought to Amagansett's attention was undercutting her—worse, she was doing it successfully!

Cass could not believe her ears. Why hadn't she seen something like this coming off? The committee was listening carefully to Sarah; they were all worried by the dip in corporate earnings, and Cass could almost visualize the erosion of her power base, her turf, if Sarah's plan was approved.

She turned for support to the man who had hired her, the man who had backed her plan and given it his blessing from the beginning. Perhaps it would not hurt to remind the committee—and Sarah Kaiser—of that fact. 'Isn't that right, Grey?'

Before he had a chance to respond, Sarah spoke up.

'What I propose is completely in line with the direction agreed to by this very committee four months ago,' she said. 'To strengthen our balance sheet and use our capital—not just to bring non-revenue-producing divisions up to speed, and not to spend millions penetrating markets that are already well served by other, more successful manufacturers and distributors.'

'The rate of return a division must promise to justify our continued investment in it is unrealistic,' Cass replied vehemently. 'We decided a year ago—before you joined Amagansett, I might add—that the eventual value of these divisions is significant enough to exempt them from those kinds of hurdle tests, at least for eighteen months. You're looking so closely at the bottom line that you're being nearsighted!'

Both women turned to Grey from opposite sides of the long mahogany conference table. They began to speak at the same time. 'Grey, you said—' said Cass, as Sarah interrupted her. 'Grey, we discussed—' Sarah began.

Then Pete Marks stood up and interrupted them both with a genial wave of his hand. 'Now, ladies, let's just go a little slower here, what do you say?' he said amiably. 'A man sure enough likes to have the ladies fighting over him, but I don't think the conference room is exactly the right setting, do you?'

He sat down, grinning foolishly at his own inappropriate remark, and a few of the other members of the committee laughed. Cass was rigid with fury; how dare he make such an implication? Sarah, who controlled her anger better than Cass did—outwardly, at least—began to respond to Marks, but changed her mind. She swept her papers into her briefcase and satisfied herself with a venomous glare at him.

Grey pretended not to have heard the remark. 'Leave your memos on this with me after the meeting,' he said curtly. 'We'll postpone any decision on this for now.'

Cass sat in her office with the door closed and her shoes kicked off. She knew Sarah was winning the war on points, and that she was losing her ground. Her own function at Amagansett was taking a distant second place to the bottom line. More and more dollars were being diverted to take positions in companies that had little or nothing to add to AI's marketing mix. Cash flow was being tightened up; her own budget had been cut. And Grey was no help at all.

She no longer felt they were allies in wresting control of the corporation from the money-minders. She told him that; his answer was unsatisfactory as well as patronizing.

'It would be jim-dandy if we could fit everything around your marketing objectives, but it isn't quite that easy. If we manage our assets better, we can raise the dividend next quarter, which is what keeps stockholders happy and CEOs in business. You could take a few lessons from Sarah on that subject, Cass.'

'Sarah has vetoed every proposal I've made to the management committee in the last three months.'

'Can't we take this up another time?'

'Certainly we can,' Cass replied sweetly. 'We can take it up at dinner. We *are* having dinner together this evening, aren't we?'

Grey's eyes darkened into impenetrability, and she knew that he was angry; it was the only sign of change in emotion she had learned to identify in him.

'Not if you don't get out of here so I can finish my work we're not,' he said.

She marched out of the room and gave the door an emphatic push as she left. But it, too, foiled her; it coasted very, very slowly, and closed with an unsuitably muffled thud.

Cass considered Sarah Kaiser. Hoist on my own petard, she thought ruefully; if it wasn't for me, she wouldn't be here.

Sarah was every inch the professional executive. She looked severe; in business school, she had already evidenced that potential, though her youth softened her features. Not now; she looked as brusque and impersonal as she acted. Except with Grey, Cass thought; with Grey, Sarah seemed more yielding, more pliant, more feminine.

Was Sarah supplanting Cass in Grey's affections as well as in the corporation?

Not that his affections were anything to write home about, she said to herself. She had not found Grey's soft spot, his vulnerable area. She had begun to doubt that he had one; he was the only lover she ever had who had not revealed it to her. She did not think Grey would allow her to become any more important to him than she was, however much that might be. He has me checkmated, she thought.

Sarah, though . . . she didn't know about Sarah. She didn't know if Sarah was out for Grey—she might just be doing her job. She could confront Sarah, she supposed, and find out. And before she could rethink the wisdom of that option, she decided to do it.

She set the scene as carefully as she might have for a rendezvous with a man. She invited Sarah to brunch at the brownstone, on a weekend morning. She outdid herself, with delicate slivers of smoked salmon, an omelette of herbs grown in her window boxes, and mimosa served in her crystal champagne glasses. There was a fruit salad heavy with raspberries and melon balls, and sweet coffee cake from the Italian bakery, and an apricot tart from Miss Grimble. Cass brought the conversation around to Amagansett, attempting to show Sarah why her approach was wrong for the company.

'It isn't just me, Cass,' said Sarah. 'It's the way business is going today. The accountants are taking over; you're absolutely right about that. Grey is not going to buck that trend, not in this economy. Not if he wants to go any higher.'

'He's already CEO,' said Cass. 'How much higher is there?'

Sarah laughed shortly. 'How about CEO of a huge, highly diversified multinational corporation? How about making AI so financially attractive to, say, W. R. Grace or Westinghouse that they can't resist it? And how about a seat on the board of that multinational, and a major role in its management?' She helped herself to another slice of apricot tart. 'You can't think AI is big enough to hold Grey Tucker for long.'

That had never occurred to Cass. It had to Amelia though—she remembered Amelia saying something like that, long before, when she discussed Tucker's offer with her.

Cass looked at Sarah with renewed respect. Sarah Kaiser knew Grey better than she did; she didn't allow her vision to be clouded by her feelings for the man—if she had any. Tucker did not exist for her that way.

'Do you remember at B school they taught us that what we can do together is greater than what we can accomplish alone?' Cass said. 'That even though two managers are competing, they need each other?'

'What I remember about B school is that you saw every woman in our class as a competitor—as a sexual threat,' said Sarah calmly and unemotionally. 'You put the competition on that level, Cass—with our classmates, with our professors, even with the Dean. You're still doing it. That's what we learned when we were growing up. But it doesn't have to be that way, unless you do it.'

'I didn't do that, they set it up that way,' Cass protested. 'They always have.'

'Sure,' said Sarah. 'So what else is new? Men make us think like that; they set us against each other, and wait for the claws to come out. Some of us act predictably; you, for instance.' She folded her heavy linen napkin into a rectangle, and set it beside her plate. 'I don't know anything about AI that you don't know,' she said. 'But I will tell you this. I have nothing except a professional interest in Grey Tucker. Pete Marks and the rest of those idiots can think what they like, and they probably will. It's begging the question. I'll fight you to the bloody end because I think Amagansett's future lies in my direction. But as far as Tucker is concerned, I couldn't care less. I'm not letting them push me into a catfight with you either.'

She delivered her words with a tone of warning. Cass's anxiety about Grey and Sarah receded. The lines were drawn, and they were clear. Until she figured out how to win Grey over to her side in the management committee, that would just have to do.

A few days later, over lunch with Amelia, she related the scene in the conference room, and her discussion with Sarah. 'All I can advise you is, don't trust Sarah Kaiser,' said Amelia. 'She may be a thoroughly principled woman, but it is coming down to a battle between the two of you, and the issue of Tucker is simply a smoke screen . . . a diversion. Whether it's your diversion or hers, I'm not certain.' Amelia looked sideways at Cass. 'I'm not probing, my dear, but it appears to me that you are banking on your personal relationship with Grey Tucker to force him to make a choice between you and that woman. I don't believe he could or would decide things on that basis. Tucker is a man who plays both sides against the middle, when it's to his advantage. And if I were you, I'd look for stronger ammunition than sex appeal.' She sighed. 'I hate to say I told you so, and I shan't, but love and business don't always mix.'

She looked at her young protégée fondly. If only Natalie had turned out like this one; if only she had allowed Amelia to help her. But she never had. She was different from Cassandra, who was ambitious in a way that Natalie never had been. Cass was capable and smart and wanted success enough to make the required compromises. She's like me at that age, Amelia thought, without the conflicting demands of a difficult child. She shouldn't stay at Amagansett. She doesn't belong there. Grey Tucker will chew her up and spit her out in little pieces, love affair or not. Ah, well, she decided, Natalie may not want my help, but Cassandra does. And I shall give it to her; I have a few cards left to play in this rather interesting game.

THIRTY-SIX

New York is a small town, Cass reflected. She knew that everyone in the corporation, and some outside of it, had assumed all along that she and Grey were lovers. It did not perturb Cass; she had never paid attention to how her sexual behaviour looked to those who were not her intimates, because it never had had any consequence in her life. Now she saw that it did; she saw how people's perceptions of her relationship with Grey might be used to her advantage.

Paula disapproved of the affair; she thought that if and when Grey tired of Cass, he would discard her. Cass thought it would have exactly the opposite effect; she did not know that most men could not bear the sight of a woman they had tired of; they could not stand the guilt. She thought she would bind Grey closer to her; inasmuch as she could, Cass planned how things would end before she allowed them to begin.

After they became lovers, she and Grey continued much as they had before. Little changed. They dined together every few nights, and she never knew if he would suggest that he accompany her home. She never went to his apartment; he did not offer, and she did not ask.

She went everywhere else with him—to openings, benefits, theatres, dinner parties. Their companions on those occasions were generally dull—conservative, wealthy businessmen, often a Presidential advisor or someone from Commerce or Treasury. As the summer waned, and her status in the company began to slip, she looked for signs that Grey was losing interest in her; she did not find them, but that was hardly encouraging, since from the onset of their affair he had treated her no differently from before.

'He's not exactly warm, is he?' Paula commented. The previous night, Cass and Grey had stopped in at Paula's after a particularly deadly business dinner. Paula's apartment was full of people; after the rape, she never wanted to be alone. The gathering was lively and boisterous, and her guests, high on drugs and liquor, were noisy when Cass and Grey arrived.

Cass was eager to play; she wanted to dance to the loud, hot music. Grey held back, but she was insistent. 'I went with your friends, now you come with mine,' she bargained; reluctantly, he allowed himself to be pulled into the crowd.

A man Cass knew dragged her into a circle of writhing, bobbing bodies; as the music increased in tempo, she threw herself into it with abandon. The crowd parted to make room for Cass and the man who had spun her away from Grey, and she lost herself in the music; she was sinuous and feline, teasing and sexy, graceful and erotic. Soon they were the only two people in the cleared space at the end of Paula's living room, and when the music stopped, Cass collapsed, breathless and exhausted, against her partner.

Grey was angry; his eyes were dark and fathomless, but the tight white lines around his mouth gave him away.

'Loosen up,' she teased him, nibbling on his ear. 'It's just a party. Scott and I are old friends, we've been dancing together for years.'

Grey smiled insincerely. 'I'm not in the mood for this tonight,' he said. 'You stay—no, it's fine, I should be going anyway. I have work on that Chemcon problem.'

She sighed; she had work on the same problem, and Grey knew it. Reluctantly, she left the party with him.

He did not follow her downstairs. 'I really should go,' he said, kissing her coolly on the forehead, pushing her hands away.

She fumed after he departed. She had left her friends for him, and then he left her. The work was an excuse; they had completed almost everything for the upcoming meeting of the board of directors of Chemcon, a company Sarah was pushing Grey to buy. Grey left, she decided, because he didn't get his way; he was punishing her. He didn't need her; he didn't need to give in to her wishes if he didn't want to.

In fact, she mused, Grey Tucker, in the office and outside of it, was not behaving at all the way her lover should. It was not only that he had not declared his feelings, although that was part of it; ordinarily she had little use for such words, for she always knew when a man was in love with her. But she did not know that about Grey, and he gave no indication that he regarded her as more than a colleague, even in their most intimate moments—which, she thought, occurred more often in the boardroom than the bedroom.

He made few demands on her; he was who he always had been, cool, detached, maintaining a space around himself like an animal marking its territory, defining its turf. As Paula said, Grey was not warm. Not like Nick, certainly, whom Cass sometimes missed with what she recognized as heartache. She had basked in the aura of Nick's love for several years. She missed it; she was not used to being without a man's affection. She missed Nick's passion, his zest, his enthusiasm. When she had lacked her own, his had infused her, catching her up and making her feel alive.

With Grey, she was still hesitant, not confident, sometimes uneasy. Even in bed, he was detached and controlling; although he was not an inconsiderate lover, neither was he especially attentive or involved. Yet despite his detachment—or perhaps because of it—she was more sexually satisfied than she had ever been with any other man, even Nick. She had orgasms easily, which was unlike her; her lovers had to learn to please her, as Nick had.

Cass permitted this odd kind of half love, this unsatisfactory relationship to continue. She told herself she would let it go on until Grey yielded up himself to her, revealed his secret, even though she dimly suspected there was no secret, only what she already knew.

Because Grey's life was narrow and consumed by the corporation, hers became that way, too. Paula noted it first: Cass, she thought, was getting unpleasantly tough. She was quicker lately to size up people and judge them by standards Paula thought unimportant—position, wealth, and status, not generosity or intelligence or perceptiveness. She had always had that potential, but now it was more pronounced than ever. Paula thought Cass had begun to become her career. Paula's profession was important to her, too, but at that moment it was not a major part of her identity. On a good day, it represented skills that allowed her to effect her political beliefs; on a bad day, it was what stood between her and the hosiery counter at Macy's, as she was fond of saying. She thought that Cass was disappearing—the Cass she loved, from all those years, was hardening into this new person, 'buried alive under all that *Savvy* magazine bullshit, the executive woman,' she remarked to Ellin.

'Would you mind that—Cass being consumed by her work—if you thought it had redeeming social value?' Ellin questioned.

'Maybe not,' Paula admitted. 'Or if I thought it was making her happy.'

'If it doesn't, she'll figure it out and fix it so it does,' said Ellin. 'Cass gets what she wants. If she wants happiness more than success, she'll get that, too.'

'I think she thinks success *is* happiness,' Paula said darkly. Paula did not keep her opinion of Tucker to herself. Nor, characteristically, did she wait for Cass to solicit it.

'I think he's a limited man,' she told Cass. Since the rape, Paula had been mostly celibate, which she imagined gave her an objective perspective about men. She still dated, but only once did she bring a man home to bed, to prove to herself that she could, like a rider climbing back onto a horse that has thrown her.

'Limited by what?'

'By his lust for power,' Paula replied.

'That's ridiculous,' Cass said, effectively ending the conversation. Privately, Paula told Ellin that she thought Grey treated Cass dreadfully; 'Like shit,' she said with disgust.

'He's certainly not a very giving person,' Ellin agreed.

'Well, neither is Cass, unless it's convenient,' said Paula.

Paula, of course, was immune, safe from Cass's selfishness. And Ellin assumed that she was, too.

The summer wore on, and tempers grew short. A heat wave blanketed the city; the air conditioner in Cass's apartment shorted out. The electrician she consulted informed her that the wiring in the brownstone was inadequate to support the burden; the house would have to be rewired. They had known that was true when they bought the house, but they had gotten through the previous summer with no electrical failures, and had been able to postpone the rewiring. Cass was anxious to get on with it, and Paula had no objections. But Ellin was against the whole idea.

'I can't have my apartment invaded now,' she complained. 'The electricians have to crawl all over the roof, and do most of the work in here, ripping out these walls. I'm at a critical point in the novel. I can't be distracted like that. Besides, I don't think it's necessary. We made it through last year without rewiring; if we're careful not to overload the circuits, we can get through another year. Also, I simply can't afford it now. You said when I moved here that I'd be consulted about any major expenditures that would increase my costs if I decided to buy in.'

'Well, when are you going to decide?' Cass wanted to know.

'When I finish the book,' said Ellin.

'Which you can't do without interruption.'

'Which I can't do with that kind of distraction. Plus more financial pressure. I can't handle this right now.'

They were stalemated; Cass tried to persuade Paula to overrule Ellin, but Paula was reluctant. 'It's only a couple of months more,' she told Cass. 'Ellin really can't take that kind of stress.'

'And I can't stand this damn heat, or not knowing whether Ellin is really going to make a commitment to the house,' said Cass. 'To us,' she added; her tone made it plain that she considered Ellin's permission to go ahead with the rewiring a symbol of her fidelity to the brownstone and its inhabitants.

'To us' made Ellin angry; who was it, after all, that had pulled Paula through this dreadful year? She had never failed Paula, or Cass either, for that matter; she thought Cass was jealous of her closeness to Paula, threatened by the bonds between them that had grown stronger since she came to live in the house.

'For God's sake, Ellin,' said Cass in exasperation, 'you can write in my apartment if you have to. Of course, the air conditioner doesn't work, but it's not that bad.'

'You don't understand,' Ellin replied, in the same voice she used when reasoning with Lara. 'I can't just move my typewriter downstairs. I need to work in my own room, with my own things around me. In my own space. It's very important to me. I can't create anywhere else.'

Cass rolled her eyes. 'Oh, Lord, spare me the temperamental *artiste*! Can you tell me, at least, when it will be convenient to proceed with the rewiring?'

'When I finish the damn book!' Ellin snapped angrily. 'Unless you'd rather I just moved out now? If you want to find a new tenant, go right ahead. Just give me a few days to move, that's all!' Her work was not going well, her temper was short, and Cass, she thought, was being unreasonable.

'Oh, come now, nobody said anything about moving out,' Paula said in a conciliatory tone. Really, she thought, Cass was being a prima donna. So was Ellin, but Paula thought her justification was greater than Cass's. Cass was simply trying to push Ellin around.

If Paula hadn't been feeling so negative about Cass she might have stayed out of it, and let Cass and Ellin settle it by themselves. Instead, she took Ellin's side, and Cass saw it as disloyalty of the worst sort. She could not punish Paula for it; that would not help. She would have to find a way around both her and Ellin. But before she could formulate a plan, events transpired which made the whole issue of rewiring the brownstone at least temporarily insignificant.

Cass couldn't believe what she was reading. The advance copy of Monday's issue of *People* was on her desk; she had no idea how it got there until Clio called. 'A friend of mine is a researcher at the magazine,' she told Cass. 'He sneaked this over to me and I had it messengered to you as soon as I saw it. I thought you might want some warning.'

'Bless you,' said Cass. 'I don't know what I can do about it, but forewarned is better than being caught with a stupid grin on your face.'

Clio was sympathetic. 'Say, Cass, it's not as much fun around here without you. Why don't you tell Grey Tucker to drop dead and come back?'

'Is that a message from you, or Amelia?' Cass laughed with an amusement she did not feel. The story could not have been worse from her point of view. There were several photographs of Cass and Grey together, including that old one from Paris. 'Who's minding the store?' was the caption, and the first paragraph was enough to make Cass physically ill.

While Amagansett's quarterly earnings take a nose dive, conglomerate chief Grey Tucker has his own head in the clouds over his 'personal assistant' Cass Campbell. Some execs buy their lovers jewels from Tiffany. Not enough for Tucker, who in recent months has acquired an entire Italian atelier from Montelli—his inamorata's favourite designer—plus a beauty spa in California where she often drops in to shed the concerns of executive ladies. Could it be that Amagansett's limp fiscal performance is linked to its dashing CEO's distraction, the lovely Ms Campbell, or just to absentee management while the beautiful couple cavorts with the international jet set?

Cass didn't wait for Clio's reply; her secretary buzzed her. 'I can't locate Mr Tucker for you, Ms Campbell. He's somewhere in the building, but no one knows where. What shall I do?'

'Nothing,' said Cass. 'Just ring me as soon as he comes in. No, never mind, I'll find him myself.'

She tracked him down, finally, and handed him the magazine article. 'This is next Monday's issue,' she said. 'I thought you'd better see it now.'

Grey read it, his face darkening. 'Get Tom Brier in here,' he told his secretary. 'Where the hell did they get this?'

'Ask Tom,' Cass said bitterly. 'He's been talking for weeks about this rag. We've had interviewers and photographers around here for a month, and Tom told everyone to cooperate with them—he said it was a great opportunity for AI.'

When the public relations director came in, Grey handed him the article. 'Oh, Jesus, they really sandbagged us, didn't they?' His florid face was damp with perspiration, his usually genial smile crumpling into a pitiful mask.

'They certainly did,' Grey retorted. 'The question is, what are we going to do about it?'

'Well, you'll have to make some kind of a public statement, that's clear,' Tom said. He reached for a yellow pad, and began scribbling. 'We can explain the earnings drop—all the acquisitions last year, the overall marketing strategy, the way Montelli and the spa fit into it . . . let's see.' He wrote quickly, while Cass chewed her fingernails. Grey gave her a disapproving look; defiant, she stood and paced the room.

She listened while Tom read the press release he had quickly composed. The first part was fine—a description of the cash flow situation and the cost of acquisitions that accounted for the dip in earnings, and the corporate decision to cut the shareholders' dividend.

With reference to media speculation concerning the relationship between Amagansett's president, Grey Tucker, and Cassandra Campbell, his personal assistant, Mr Tucker stated that her position at AI has nothing to do with such a relationship, which he denied existed. Said Tucker, 'There are aspects of a corporate presidency that may seem unrelated to management because they are carried on outside of normal business hours and locations, but which are nonetheless important business relationships, in which the presence of my personal assistant, who bears significant responsibility for strategic planning, is both useful and necessary. Ms Campbell is a dedicated executive who has been promoted strictly on the basis of her talent and ability. The speculation that a personal relationship between us has in any way been disadvantageous to Amagansett, its companies, and stockholders is entirely without basis.

'Jesus, you have it both ways, don't you?' Cass asked bitterly when Brier left the room. 'Grey, you're wrong about this. I think your rebuttal ought to end with Tom's first paragraph. I don't want you to respond to that gossip at all; can't you see what a position that puts me in? First you deny that there's a relationship, then you say that if there is, it hasn't hurt Amagansett.'

'Isn't that true?' Grey said coldly.

'No, it's not. First of all, there *is* a relationship, right? It's one of those Do you still beat your wife? questions.

By responding to that publicity, you make it worse. And you certainly don't think anybody's going to believe it, do you?'

'It doesn't matter what they believe,' said Grey. 'You can't stop gossip. You can only advance your own story.'

Cass wasn't convinced. 'I don't want you to go public with anything about us at all. Let them talk. As soon as you descend to their level, we're both in the position of having to constantly deny it.'

'Why don't you let me worry about that?' said Grey. 'It seems to me that's my responsibility, not yours.'

She exploded angrily. 'But it's my reputation that's at stake here!' she shouted. 'You're lying, and getting me caught in your lies. You're telling them there's nothing going on between us—Jesus, Grey, that's so damn easy to disprove, they'll never believe anything you say!'

'Then what would you suggest?' he asked icily.

'I just told you,' she repeated. 'Keep me out of it. Just respond to that bit about the quarterly earnings, the way Tom wrote it. Right now, the rest is only rumour. If you answer it, you'll feed the rumour mill. Ignore it and it will go away.'

'I sincerely doubt that,' Grey said. 'I have a much better idea. I think you should take an extended trip. Go back to Italy—look over what's happening at Montelli. Go on a fact-finding mission—yes, that's exactly it. Get out of town for a few weeks. When you come back, it will all have blown over.'

'I think that's absolutely the last thing I ought to do,' Cass replied.

'Do you have a better idea?'

'As a matter of fact I do. I think if you won't ignore the innuendos about me, about us, we should come out fighting. I think this is the time to name me vice president!'

'What?' Grey was aghast. 'With this breaking next week? What on earth do you expect that to accomplish?'

'It will make it perfectly clear that merit, and nothing

else, is why I'm here,' Cass said, more calmly than she felt. 'Especially if you make the announcement today. It will make all the papers—it will get in tomorrow's editions. Besides, we have a board meeting this morning. You can make it official. By the time this rag hits the stands, it will be old news. *People* has a Friday closing; we might even get it pulled.'

Grey seemed to be considering her proposal. 'What about a vote of confidence from the board? Wouldn't that do just as well? This is no time to stir things up with a vice presidency.'

Cass was determined. 'That's exactly what you need to do. A vote of confidence alone means nothing. Not unless the board backs it up. That's why this is so important.' She paced the room, thinking aloud. 'The first woman to crack the ranks at Amagansett Industries—nobody would accuse you of anything except backing me—and your own judgement of me—a hundred percent.' She grimaced at her own words; the phrase was too reminiscent of a former political candidate ousted from the Vice Presidential race because of revelations about his unstable mental condition. Her own, she thought, was extraordinarily clear and lucid.

'I'll consider it,' Grey said. 'Right now I have to go into a board meeting and explain *this*.' He gestured to the article. 'I think you should make yourself scarce today.'

'No, I won't,' said Cass. 'And taking this trip is ridiculous. It makes it look worse than it is. I don't want you to say anything publicly about me, Grey—not unless it's an announcement about the vice presidency.'

'I know what you want, Cass,' Grey said wearily. 'We all know what you want. Let me talk to the board, and then we'll see what you can get.'

Unsatisfied, she left his office. What rotten timing this was! Her position at AI was tenuous enough, and the rest of her life wasn't in much better shape. Grey was not being supportive; he has his own skin to worry about, she thought. But she had expected more of him. What if she had to leave the company? What would she do about money? That's silly, she reassured herself; you won't have to leave. The worst that can happen is a little unpleasant publicity. It will go away. She was less certain about her relationship with Grey. About Grey himself, and her own feelings. She was confused—did she love him, or was she just enthralled by his aura of power? She was pretty sure Grey Tucker wasn't capable of love—not as she understood the word. Nor was her relationship with him uppermost now; for Cass, men had taken second place to her career for some time. And the battle in which she was presently engaged—the struggle to win—was far more important than ever Grey Tucker could be.

At six o'clock, the door to the boardroom was still forebodingly closed. 'They've been in there all day,' the secretary told her. 'They just sent out for sandwiches and coffee. Looks like it will be a marathon meeting.'

Cass waited until after seven and left a note on Grey's desk, telling him she'd be at home. Then she left.

She spent an agonizingly long evening waiting for the telephone to ring. Finally, it was not the phone which rang, but her doorbell, and it was Amelia.

She stormed into Cass's living room, angry and tense as Cass had never seen her. In her face, too, was something Cass couldn't identify, but which might have been sympathy.

'Cassandra, do you know what the Amagansett board did today?' Amelia demanded. Cass was confused; wasn't that exactly what she'd been waiting to find out? And how did Amelia know?

'I have my spies,' said Amelia, answering her unspoken question. Cass knew she meant Kelly Fletcher, Amelia's pipeline to the AI board. He had courted Amelia for years; he was responsible for bringing her agency to AI's attention long ago.

'Well, sit down, my dear,' said Amelia, and Cass was

alarmed. She allowed Amelia to lead her to the sofa, and with the older woman's next words, she sat mutely down.

'They named that woman, Sarah Kaiser, to a vice presidency,' Amelia reported. 'A senior vice presidency.' Cass was so stunned she barely heard Amelia's next words.

'Apparently,' Amelia went on, getting the distasteful task done as expeditiously as possible, 'apparently there's been some brouhaha about you and Tucker—terrible, these gossip rags.' Amelia tsk-tsked; her disapproval was evident in her every gesture. Her voice grew warmer. 'Clio showed me the *People* article. I understand she brought it to your attention this morning. Poor child . . . I am so sorry.'

Cass accepted Amelia's sympathy wordlessly. She detected no hint of reproach in the older woman's voice, only kindness.

'The board seems to have decided that the best way to prove that your relationship with Tucker has nothing to do with your position at Amagansett is to sidestep the issue by making this Kaiser woman the first female senior executive. The implication, of course, being that despite whatever is going on between you and Tucker, it has nothing to do with board decision-making.'

Cass was speechless. She could understand the strategy; it bore Grey's Machiavellian touch. Sarah Kaiser was above reproach in the gossip department. Not only that; at AI, she took pains to blend into the background, careful to avoid any situation in which her morals, or her reputation, might be compromised.

She had to admit it: Grey's stroke was masterful. With one play, he had diverted attention from his relationship with her, and made it clear that the corporation was not inhospitable to women in high positions. He had also picked up some badly needed points with his fiscally conservative board, which approved completely of Sarah Kaiser and her ways—because she was everything Cass was not, and because her approach to management of the company's assets was precisely congruent with their own.

Grey was publicly casting his lot with the board; Cass was abandoned, angry and humiliated. Only Amelia's kind words kept her from bursting into tears right then. She did not wonder why Grey hadn't called her after the meeting; she knew. Knew he was cutting her loose, and that her own position at the corporation was in grave jeopardy.

He never did call that night, or come to her apartment. Instead, he had his secretary schedule an appointment with her the next day; much more formal than his usual procedure, which was to ring her up at her desk or holler 'Cass, I need you in here!'

'There's only room for one woman at the top,' Grey said over Cass's protestations. 'Sarah is the logical candidate. There's no one else at her level who can touch her for ability, professionalism, the whole thing. The chief financial officer of the Company is retiring. She's absolutely right for the job, and the position has to carry a senior vice presidency. If I tried to give her the job without it, she'd probably run to the EEOC. I wouldn't blame her. But the board won't take two women senior vice presidents at once; not yet, anyway.'

He made no promises about when, if ever, the board would, Cass noted.

Cass swallowed her pride, and went back to her office. She had an even more difficult task ahead of her that week. Particularly with Sarah's new authority, Cass knew that she could not hope to win the biggest battle of all—the fight over Blythe's. Sarah's memo that morning told it all: on the agenda of the upcoming management committee meeting was her proposal to close Blythe's.

The store was not a heavy money-loser, but its drain on AI's balance sheet was a constant one. The store could be disposed of, at a price that would improve the bottom line significantly enough to allow a reasonable dividend the next quarter. Cass knew what the problems with Blythe's were. The store catered to a clientele that was getting older, and dowdier, every year. It had an image as a place where people's mothers and grandmothers and maiden aunts went to shop. The store management was equally greying and dowdy; it was out of touch with the market. Blythe's had been neglected for so long that it was a joke among city retailers. Yet it had a few loyal customers, a revered name, and a prime location. And Sarah wanted to sell it.

Cass tried to forestall such a drastic move. 'Grey, I don't belong in the corporate management, not doing what I'm doing now,' she told him. 'I'm a marketing person; you told me that yourself. And when you hired me, that's what you wanted me for. But we're moving completely away from that philosophy. All the pieces of our marketing strategy, our acquisitions, are getting chopped up and sold off. Let me take over Blythe's. I know I could make the store a money-maker. It wouldn't require that much capital investment to bring it into the black, just a strong head with a sense of the market, and a knowledge of merchandising. Which I have.'

Grey laughed unkindly. 'Who do you think you are, Geri Stutz?' he asked. 'Advertising director, maybe, but president of the store? Come on, Cass, be sensible.'

'What do you have to lose?' she pleaded. 'You can't unload it for very much, not with the figures we have now. Just give me a hand in restaffing it, and a year's grace. I know I can do it.'

'Out of the question,' he told her. 'What you should be doing is concentrating on the reorganization plan.'

'That's busywork,' she told him. 'And it's a lousy plan, anyway.'

'Then you'd better get busy on it, and make it a better one,' he replied coldly. 'I know you're upset about Sarah, and the vice presidency. But forget it. You women take everything too personally, that's your trouble. Now get out of here and let me get back to work.'

THIRTY-SEVEN

Paula's first impulse was to decline the invitation from Westwood Law School. Then she reconsidered; she knew that Hugh had some connection with the California school, and if he had recommended her to the search committee, which was likely, it would be impolite to ignore the feeler. Besides, Max lived near Westwood—she had not seen him in months.

'We welcome the opportunity to meet with you and discuss the challenges and rewards of leading Westwood Law School through the difficult years—and the years of opportunity—that lie ahead,' read the letter.

Difficult, thought Paula, my ass—that's an understatement. The eighties were not going to provide the best political climate for the survival of a public-interest law school, even one with Westwood's high reputation. There was not a great deal of opportunity for *pro bono* lawyers, and the school's endowment was negligible; its graduates rarely amassed enough money to increase it. Just keeping Westwood's doors open would be plenty of challenge.

On the other hand, she reasoned, was there a more deserving mission? Making realists out of idealists—preparing them to practise law in an environment hostile to their values—rather appealed to her. For months Paula had been searching for the right new career direction, one that offered her an opportunity to make a real impact, to make a difference in people's lives, and in the law she loved. She had always been happy in the academic milieu. She liked the sense of purpose, the calm, unhurried pace.

She had once considered teaching law—long ago, in Cambridge. It was a profession she thought could be combined with marriage and a family. But that was when she and Jake first met, she reminded herself. Now that didn't matter.

Since the Court argument, Paula had explored a number of job possibilities. There was a grant from a foundation to investigate the plea bargain system; there was an offer to associate on a major case that was almost certainly destined for another Supreme Court argument. There was a feeler about a job with the United Nations, which came to nothing: her politics were far too liberal for the present administration. Paula had talked to lawyers and scholars and policy-makers; she had long discussions with Stan Wilkie, and even Chris Carey. Nothing truly piqued her interest until the Westwood offer, and the more she thought about it, the more intrigued she became.

'I thought they'd get around to you,' Hugh Tierney told her. 'I didn't suggest your name immediately. Gave them time to get used to the idea of a woman dean—took some getting used to. I thought it was time, for the law school and for you.'

He cautioned Paula. 'They have some excellent candidates, you understand—you may not make it to the final cut. The fact that the abortion case went your way tipped the scales.'

Just before recessing for the term, the Court announced its decision. It was an anticlimactic moment for Paula. When she was good, she always knew it before anyone else did; she was not particularly surprised.

'Well, I'll go and let them have a look,' Paula told Hugh. 'I'm honoured to have been asked to compete. And who knows what else might turn up? I've always thought that where you are tomorrow depends on who you meet on your way to work today.' To herself she thought, Why not? It's an expense-paid trip to California, and a few days with Max—you can't die from that. It would be good to get away from the house for a while; Cass and Ellin were snapping at each other all the time, and she was tired of trying to make peace between them.

She flew to California in early July, and drove her rented car out to Westwood the next morning. It was not an especially beautiful place—not like Harvard, with the sense of history that permeated those ivy-covered buildings. Westwood was different: low, sprawling two-storey buildings, in an architectural style Paula thought of as California Brutal, glass and corrugated steel baking in a sun that turned the grounds sere and sepia. There were only a few students on campus; economics had forced Westwood to cut back its summer programme. But Harry McAllister, the head of the search committee, was sanguine and enthusiastic. 'In the fall, when the new semester begins, they come in here, full of spunk and determination,' he said. 'That changes the way everything looks.'

He led her into the administration building and she was introduced to the rest of the committee members. That afternoon, and all the next day, they grilled her. Paula went back painstakingly over what seemed like every hour of her professional life; they questioned her views on the theoretical and political underpinning of the law, on practical training, on the traditional case method of teaching, on curriculum reform and social engineering. It was, in a way, like being on trial.

'I think it went well,' she told Max when she saw him. They met for a drink late in the day; Max had other plans for the evening, he told Paula apologetically. 'But I'll cook you dinner tomorrow night,' he promised.

Paula wondered about Max's other plans. Was there a woman in his life these days? Probably—Max liked the company of women, and he was an attractive, eligible man. But she did not question him, and he volunteered no other information.

'Do you know who else is being interviewed?' he asked her.

'I've a fair idea,' she said. 'Tony Gomez—he clerked for

one of the justices, then ran a clinical law programme in Chicago. There's a retired appeals court judge from Missouri, Hugh told me, and a federal public defender who teaches at Georgetown and publishes frequently.'

'Any other women?'

'Not as far as I know.'

Max looked at his watch. 'I have to go,' he said, 'but I'll see you tomorrow. Did I give you directions to my house?'

'Mmm hmm.' She nodded, turning her cheek up for his kiss. 'Are you really going to cook for me?'

''Betcher ass,' he said with a grin. 'I'm a man of considerable hidden talents.'

The next evening she sat on a high stool in Max's gleaming kitchen, munching on celery as he chopped and sliced and sautéed. His fingers flew over the thin slivers of mushrooms, the medallions of beef, the precisely quartered tomatoes, the bunches of improbably green parsley and strips of red pepper. They chatted companionably while he tossed them lightly in oil in a wok, and uncovered a pot of steaming rice.

Paula carried their plates out to the patio; Max followed with wine and glasses. The night was hot and dry—bushfire weather, Max called it. The fragrance of gardenias was heavy in the still air, wafting from the opulent bushes that edged the yard.

'Do you want the job?'

'I don't know. It's a huge task. Revising the curriculum, raising money—a lot of it, and quickly, before they have to lay off faculty, cut down the student body. There's one professor who wouldn't be any loss, as far as I'm concerned; he seems to think he should inherit the position. He's the Assistant Dean. Didn't like me. Kept talking about "outsiders", like Harvard was a different country.' She was starved she realized, and made herself stop eating as if the food would be snatched away at any moment. Dinner was a feast for the eyes as well as the palate, and she was grateful for Max's effort. He'd worked all day, and then hurried home to have dinner ready when she arrived.

'They said they'd be in touch in a few weeks,' she told him. 'It may not come to anything, you know—Hugh says I shouldn't get my hopes up.'

'If they offer it, will you take it?'

'Who knows?' Paula speared another piece of beef on her chop sticks. 'I don't think they'll offer.'

'But if they do?' Max was persistent, but Paula just shrugged. She was determined not to think about that now; she would deal with the problem when and if it became one.

After dinner, they washed the dishes together. Paula liked the way Max did things—he was competent and thorough, but not obsessive. Most men who cooked did it showily, and left the cleaning up for someone else—a wife, a lover, the maid.

Max had completely remodelled the old farmhouse in the Valley he'd bought a few years before. He showed her through his wood-working shop in the garage, and she teased him gently. 'What's a nice Jewish boy doing in a place like this? You don't have the right genes for making things or fixing things.' Her words sounded familiar in her own ears—she'd said something like that to Jake, hadn't she, when he told her about building houses in Canada? She felt memory stir in her, but not desire—not even the old familiar ache, she realized. When had it left her? Where had it gone? She didn't know, and didn't care. She was here, with Max, and she felt only a sense of deep peace and contentment.

They settled in the living room; Max brought them tumblers of brandy, and she leaned back comfortably into the thick pillows of the couch and looked around. This was her first visit to Max's house, and she liked what she saw. It was furnished simply, but with taste. The wall behind her displayed a thoughtful collection of Pre-Columbian artifacts, and there was a small Nevelson frieze of polished black wood above the adobe-style white-plastered hearth. Navajo rugs covered the tiled floors, and rosewood-and-leather sling chairs flanked the buttery leather sofa on which she reclined, with her feet tucked warmly under Max's jeans-clad buttocks.

'What's going on at Casita Rosita?' Max asked.

'Oh, Cass and Ellin are bitching about rewiring the house—Ellin's trying to finish her book, and Cass wants to have her own way. As usual.'

'Would you leave the house if they offer you the job? Would you leave Cass, and Ellin—and New York?'

'It would be hard,' said Paula thoughtfully. 'Cass will think I'm crazy . . . I can hear her now.'

'I'd think she'd be very proud . . . a lot of ifs, I know, but even Cass can't deny that it's a tremendous opportunity.'

'The first woman who, and all that?'

Max nodded.

'Oh, she'll be pleased for me, I think, but she'll feel deserted. That's Cass. She sees everything in terms of how it affects her.'

'Don't we all?'

'Ultimately, I suppose.' Paula held out her glass for more brandy. 'I guess that's how I'll make my decision, if there's one to make.'

'Oh, I daresay there will be at least one,' Max said. 'And if there's one, perhaps another.'

What did he mean by that? Paula wondered. Was he talking about them—about Paula and Max? Or did she just think so, because her own thoughts, disturbingly enough, had been along very similar lines? One thing at a time, Paula, she told herself. Get one part of your fucking life together before you start messing around with the other.

THIRTY-EIGHT

Ellin waited while Lara went through customs, studying her tall, slender, surprisingly lovely daughter. Lara had become a beauty. When had that happened? She'd set off for Africa in June, just as Tony promised—a colt, tripping over her own long legs, over her camera bag, over her excitement and a bit unconvincingly concealed fear. She'd changed in two months—or had it happened gradually, and Ellin not noticed? She was lithe and supple like Tony, with his straight, dark hair and russet colouring. Her mouth was Ellin's, wide and generous, and the shape of her face was the same, except sculpted with the clear, firm lines of youth. She was graceful like a dancer, and her body curved, with no hint of excess.

Lara saw her, and waved wildly. Ellin felt a rush of love, like the wind on a warm night; she was so glad her daughter was safely home!

She was used to being separated from Lara in the summer; at first her daughter went to Lou and Sophie's, and later, to camp. Those were Ellin's only respites from the state of single parenthood, which, in the early years, she wore like a badge proclaiming her name. When Lara was in either of those places, Ellin didn't worry about her; she shed that skin of concern like a snake in August. When Lara was in the care of someone Ellin trusted, she relaxed. It was those few weeks she concentrated on with singular attention as Lara grew older, and more challenging—every year, around April, when Ellin thought she absolutely could not stand being a mother one more day, she thought of summer as a straggler in the desert conjures up visions of an oasis.

At first, when Lara was with Tony, Ellin was anxious. She wasn't that sure she could trust Tony. But she had come to understand that Tony loved Lara, too. As much as she did? Well, never mind, she told herself, as much as he can. And Lara might as well find out just how much that is.

Certainly, he had come through this time, and Lara looked as though she'd had a wonderful time. She was sun-bronzed and healthy, in jeans and a safari jacket, her camera bag casually slung over her shoulder, her duffel bag in the hands of a clean-cut young man in horn-rimmed glasses and jeans and a jacket like Lara's.

As soon as Lara cleared customs, she ran to Ellin, embracing her. 'Oh, Mom, I had the most fantastic time, I can't tell you, it was absolutely maximum!' she burbled, and Ellin tried not to cry with happiness at having her baby back in her arms again.

Lara dragged Ellin over to where her friend waited, hesitantly. 'Mom, this is Ian, Ian, my mom. Mom, we were together most of the trip, Ian's dad's the cinematographer, he goes to UCLA, he's going to be a director. . . .' The boy shook Ellin's hand, looking embarrassed, but Lara didn't notice, she was rattling on and on.

'Listen, do we have to go to Sophie's tonight, Mom, can we stay in the city for a day or two?' Lara's words ran together in her haste to be understood. 'The thing is, Ian's not going back to LA till Wednesday, we thought we'd hang out in New York, do some sight-seeing stuff. Mom, do you think we could?'

'Sure, I think that's a fine idea,' said Ellin as they walked out of the terminal with the luggage. She was in no hurry to go to Sophie's herself. She'd tell Sophie Lara had made other plans; she'd just have to accept it. Besides, her writing was progressing nicely; since Lara had a friend to keep her company, maybe Ellin could finish a chapter before the obligatory visit to Sophie.

As it turned out, she did almost no work for several days. The phone began ringing for Lara as soon as they arrived home at the brownstone; she had sent her school friends postcards from Africa, telling them the date of her return, and those who lived in the city came to the brownstone, two or three at a time. The apartment was noisy with the sound of young laughter and the omnipresent music from Ellin's tape deck, whose speakers shuddered at the unaccustomed volume.

'I've spent the last week refilling the refrigerator, cleaning up after them, and handing out twenty-dollar bills like they were jelly beans,' Ellin said to Paula one afternoon, after Lara and a group of her friends had left.

'I wanted to go with them,' Paula said. 'All that youth, all that energy—it makes me feel like a tired old chicken who's got maybe one little spark left. And inside of me, something keeps saying, go with them, Paula, you're still a kid, too, you ain't no middle-aged old lady—you're still a teenager!'

'Dick Clark thinks that way, too,' said Ellin wryly. 'But you're not ready for chicken stew yet, honey. God, you could practically feel the hormones surging in the air, couldn't you?'

'Mmm hmm. Did Cass talk to you about the wiring again?'

'She came up last night, when Lara was having a party, and asked rather pointedly if I didn't find it difficult to work in all the chaos, if that's what you mean.'

'That's what I mean,' Paula replied. 'Don't let her get to you. She's not in a very good place these days. Trouble at the office, Grey, that magazine article . . . you know how it is.'

'Cass is always having some kind of crisis,' Ellin replied, unmoved.

Paula began to try to explain Cass to Ellin, and thought

better of it. She thought she knew what was bothering Ellin.

'Cass certainly has been rather friendly to Vic lately, hasn't she?' Paula asked, not at all innocently.

Ellin picked at her cuticles. 'Has she?'

It was stupid to feel jealous, she told herself. Cass was just flirting, out of habit, she supposed, and Vic was simply flirting back. It was meaningless. She didn't own him, after all. They weren't having an affair. They were having a . . . well, a friendship. Ellin's logical, analytic mind told her that Cass was looking for strokes from a man because she wasn't getting them from Grey. Any man would do. Even Vic, whom Cass called, with what Ellin thought snobbery, their 'ladies' man'.

'I hadn't noticed,' she told Paula.

Paula didn't believe her. She knew Ellin had noticed—one could hardly not. Only yesterday she herself had warned Cass.

'Look, lay off of Vic, will you? You don't really give a rat's ass about him, and Ellin does,' Paula told her. 'That display last night was revolting.'

Paula, Cass, and Ellin had congregated in Cass's living room, where the brownstone's only operative air conditioner was struggling to provide relief from the sweltering heat. Vic had knocked at the door, with a quart of Häagen-Dazs he'd picked up on his way home from the Lion's Head. He offered it around, and after a while Cass turned on the radio. The Puerto Rican station was playing sultry, hot music, and Cass got up, moving her body to the beat. She was wearing a thin shift, a short nightgown which outlined her body as she danced. The music built to an erotic, pulsating climax, and so did Cass's performance. Vic was mesmerized by her; she seemed to be dancing only for him.

Paula had not been able to stand it. As soon as she finished the ice cream, she got up to leave. Ellin felt unseen—Vic was staring at Cass like the village idiot, she thought resentfully—and she left, too. And listened, once she was upstairs, for the sound of Cass's door opening and closing again. Only Lara's arrival finally moved Ellin from her perch at the top of the stairs. 'It's cooler out here than it is in the apartment,' she told Lara.

'It's cool at Cass's, too, and there's ice cream. Vic's down there,' she informed Ellin, who closed the door behind them with a resounding thwack.

'Evil is in the eye of the beholder,' Cass told Paula cattily. Paula sighed; sometimes Cass was impossible, and had a difficult time displacing herself from the centre of the universe long enough to be sensitive to someone else's feelings. Paula accepted that. She was accustomed to being Cass's friend; it was a difficult habit to break. Occasionally Paula caught a glimpse of the pure, loving, loyal Cass, and remembered why they had forged the bond between them years before. She knew why it did not weaken—shared history kept the two women close. Like spouses, they took each other's faults for granted; sometimes chafing, but knowing that that would change nothing.

Ellin might be hurt, or angry, but she wasn't going to show it. Ellin usually kept her feelings to herself; she was neutral, calm, at least on the outside. She rarely complained; she edited the tragedies of her life into an amusing tale of misadventures, and people came away thinking she was plucky, and wise. When she fooled them, sometimes she fooled herself for a time. It was a trick she had learned from one of her many therapists. Pretend that you're not depressed, and pretty soon you won't be, he had told her. Ellin thought it was a simple, even simpleminded idea, until she tried it. She was still surprised that it worked.

Paula changed the subject. 'Lara seems very grown-up these days,' she said.

'I know,' Ellin said. 'She catches me by surprise. It happens so quickly. . . .' She wondered what she had missed of Lara's maturation, in her eagerness to be free, to live her own life. Lara's childhood was a blur of endless but unremembered days and nights, and the pleasant camaraderie between them lately had erased the memory of the difficult time before she left for Tony's. 'Kids are really a terrible investment,' Ellin said. 'By the time they get old enough to be reasonably good company, they leave home.'

Lara was a delight to be around these days. Boarding school had opened up her mind; she was reading, she was thinking, she was soaking up new impressions and ideas and information as avidly as she had once absorbed the sun and scene in California. 'She spent the whole afternoon at the Met yesterday with Ian, and came home glowing. I wanted to fix them dinner, but she said she was too filled up with beauty to eat.'

'Fabulous,' Paula said. 'Maybe this is the payoff after all the years of shit. Maybe she'll get through the awful stage just high on art and beauty, and you'll never have another fight.'

'That's too much to hope for,' said Ellin, although she did, regularly and prayerfully.

'That boy of hers is very hunky,' Paula said. 'Do you suppose they're fucking?'

'I've wondered: they spend a lot of time closed in her room. He's a nice boy. If I were his mother, I'd make him cut his hair and change his clothes, but since I'm not, I can just enjoy him. He and Lara are very tender with each other. It's nice to watch them together. Fucking? I guess they could have. But I think I'd know.'

Paula hooted. 'It shows on your face, huh, the way we used to think it did?'

'No, no.' Ellin laughed. 'I just think I'd know.'

She felt a strong tie of love between herself and Lara, and a current of something akin to respect that seemed to strengthen it. Of course she would sense such a monumental event in Lara's life, wouldn't she? She hoped that she would, and feared that she might not; as they grew closer, they somehow became more separate. Now when she observed her daughter, she saw not just an extension of herself, but an almost fully formed adult; unique, apart from her. It was liberating and terrifying. Lara was like someone she had known intimately who had been to a remote place and returned changed in ways she could not wholly identify, more closed off from her and at the same time familiar and more accessible.

The telephone interrupted Ellin and Paula; Ellin reached for it with no sense of foreboding. She knew where everyone she loved was at this moment.

There was static on the line, and then the oddly accented voice of an overseas operator. 'Ellin Barnett? One moment, please; we have Nairobi on the line.'

'It must be Tony calling,' Ellin told Paula, 'he's—yes, this is Ellin Barnett, who . . . what . . .' And then, as she was walking away, into the kitchen to open another beer, Paula heard Ellin scream in a thin, high, keening voice that was like the scream of an animal in a forest.

At first Ellin thought she had not heard Todd correctly. She was surprised to hear from him; he was the unit publicist on this film, as he had been on several of Tony's earlier films. She made him repeat his words.

Tony was dead. Killed in a plane crash, Todd said, his familiar voice breaking, near tears as he relayed the news. A helicopter flying Tony and two members of the movie crew out of the base camp had crashed on take-off. There were no survivors. The pilot and the three passengers had burned to death in the explosion and fire.

Ellin heard the details numbly, repeating them as if they were instructions. Paula rushed to her side, and heard her words. 'All of them? No survivors? Was Tony . . . did he suffer, do you think?' Tony could not be dead; it was unthinkable. He was the most alive person she had ever known. All his energy, snuffed out so quickly, so arbitrarily, so unluckily . . . there had to be some mistake.

But there was not, and she knew it when she collapsed into Paula's outstretched arms. Tony was dead, and with him, half her life—twenty years gone, obliterated, ashes in the African bush.

That was the only time she cried for Tony; she felt his death as if from a vast distance. Her grief was tantalizingly out of her grasp, although she knew it was there, could feel its presence like an umbrella shielding her from a hailstorm. It was there, intermingled with the memory of a darkly handsome man with a ready smile and strong arms with ridged blue veins that stood out even against a perpetual tan. It was there with all the days and nights of her years with Tony—a movie playing over and over again in her head. There were gaps and splices in the movie; she was surprised at how little real detail she remembered of so many years. Her memory was in her blood, in her senses, not her mind. She had made those cuts and splices herself, long ago, edited the film of her time with him and shut it in a box and hid it behind a wall in her heart; it was the way she got through the pain of his leaving. She rarely went behind that wall; she imagined that time had turned the contents of the box into ashes, as the flames of the crash had done to Tony.

What was left of that heat, that passion? She felt no loss or grief for herself that day, beyond that first awful moment when she saw herself dying with him; she felt pain for Lara's pain. Behind her wall was a tiny ember of anger, an ember that licked at its edges. Tony had up and died on her just when she had begun to think again—to feel, again—that she could count on him.

'He always had a lousy sense of timing,' she told Paula, as she wiped her eyes. 'Not on stage, but in life. And death.'

They paced the apartment together, waiting for Lara's return. Ellin missed Tony's presence acutely—how could she tell Lara something this important alone?

'There isn't anybody else who'll ever have the same feeling for her, now, except me,' she said sadly to Paula. 'Nobody with the same emotional investment in her.'

'Are you sad about that for her, or for you?' Paula asked gently. She was trying to help Ellin in Ellin's way, analyze away the feelings, discharge them with understanding.

'Both, I guess,' Ellin sniffled. 'I'm sorry I'm still weepy, I just—'

'You just lost someone dear,' said Paula. 'Cry. It'll do you good.'

'I can't,' Ellin said, running her hands through her tangled hair. 'I have to be okay. For Lara.'

Paula respected that—Ellin had a job to do, telling Lara. Being a mother was a job, like being a lawyer, or a manager, or a writer. It was Ellin's job, and Paula held her and stroked her, lending her strength to help her do it.

'My father used to tell me nobody would ever love me as much as he did, and I thought it was a blessing,' Paula said softly. 'But it was a curse. I believed him, and sure enough, nobody ever has. Don't do that to Lara.'

Ellin didn't take offence; Paula was one of the two people who were allowed to give her advice about Lara. Kate was the other. Funny, she thought idly, since neither of them has children.

'I get the point,' she told Paula. 'But it's true, though—you'll see someday. Nobody ever does love you like your parents do. When you're a mother, you'll understand.'

She heard Sophie's voice saying those exact words, like an echo in her mind. When she was young, she was never sure precisely what it was that she would understand, especially since when Sophie said it, it seemed to be a non sequitur. It had always accompanied Sophie's denials of what Ellin considered the privileges of adolescence; no, she could not wear high heels, no, she could not go out with a certain boy, no, she could certainly not drive to Florida with her friends for spring vacation.

Sophie said it sometimes when her eyes misted over—when she was especially proud of Ellin, or angry, or frustrated by her. 'What *is* it that I'll understand?' she'd asked Sophie, who shrugged her shoulders evocatively, or shook her head.

Years later, when Ellin held Lara in her arms for the first time, she looked deep into her infant's impossibly bright blue eyes for the answer, but Lara only gurgled and sought her breast. Ellin thought the explanation might come in her milk, but it did not—not then. When she handed Lara over to Sophie the first time, there in the hospital, Sophie's eyes misted in a familiar way. 'Now what?' Ellin asked impatiently, but Sophie only smiled and replied, 'You'll understand when you're a grandmother.'

Ellin knew, now. Knew that motherhood conferred a treasure of great value—and for it, exacted an awesome and enormous price.

The price was the discovery of a door into the soul whose existence she had never dreamed of. Within was a capacity for love no other human connection could ever evoke or awaken. It wasn't like the love that had been between her and Tony—it was an emotion that subsumed her self.

Ellin thought it was like another human potential that didn't develop without a catalyst—like extra-sensory powers, or a quality of character manifested under extraordinary circumstances.

It was like no other commitment. Distance didn't weaken it. It was the most vulnerable to disappointment, and the most impregnable against the usual assaults on love—boredom, dishonesty, loss of spirit or will. Her child might, and probably would, anger, humiliate, exhaust, and defeat her, but she would love her nonetheless, and probably assume responsibility for her happiness long after she should, and feel guilt, deserved or not, for her failures.

Like Sophie, she thought. Except Sophie carried it to extremes; she was a caricature rooted in truth, for Ellin knew her mother's love for her sprang from the same pure source as hers for Lara. It was the same love, twisted cruelly in on itself, because it was the most dependent love, and Sophie had not willingly yielded to Ellin that autonomy which was necessary for her to survive. She hoped she would let go with more grace—had let go with more grace. For it was through Lara that she had learned—was learning—that extraordinary capacity for selfless love that would ennoble her long after Lara was full-grown and gone.

That, she knew, was the good part. But for such a gift, an equally great price had to be paid. By the time you get the bill, Ellin reflected, it's too late—and futile as well. For a time she had consoled herself by thinking that it wouldn't last forever. Someday Lara would be an adult, and Ellin would own her own soul again. Someday there would be an end to the denial of her own needs. Someday she might even be able to vacation on an island where there were no telephones. Someday Lara would be strong, self-reliant, independent, and Ellin would regain her freedom.

Except, she knew, that was not true. She would spend the rest of her life worrying every time Lara exercised the initiative and independence she wanted her to have. Ellin would never again reach with anticipation or delight for the telephone that rang in a darkened room. She would never ignore the ambulance that shrieked in the distance, not until she knew that Lara was safe, and accounted for. Ellin had ceased forever to be an entity unto herself; somewhere, out in the world or even asleep in the spare room, there was a part of her, and she would feel whole only when it was within range of her touch, her love, her protection.

Mothers got no windfalls of time, money, or pleasure that they did not automatically divide among themselves and their children. Mothers talked to God and bargained recklessly for their children's safety. Mothers had hostages to fortune; they were in thrall to fate forever. Friends and lovers, even husbands, came and went, but a child was for a lifetime—Ellin's. All of this, of course, she knew intellectually. But Sophie was right. There were some things you never really understood until you were a mother.

'Well, Lara still has you,' Paula said. 'You did it alone all these years. You'll do it this time, too.'

She was right—Ellin would. And she had, truly, forgiven Tony, because in giving himself to Lara, he had given Ellin back to herself, too. But there would be no further gift; there was finally and irrevocably only Ellin for Lara. In spite of the heat of the afternoon that coated the brownstone like a shawl, in spite of Paula's comforting arms around her, Ellin felt cold, chilled, and absolutely alone.

THIRTY-NINE

There were obvious indications that Cass's star was in the descendant at Amagansett. Grey's rejection of her proposal for Blythe's, and Sarah Kaiser's handsome new office, as big and as close to Grey's as her own, were danger signs. Then two members of Cass's staff were reassigned. 'We need them,' said Grey flatly when Cass complained. 'You have plenty of manpower for your needs.'

Cass's secretary was reassigned, too—to Sarah Kaiser. She was replaced by a young woman from the typing pool who could not spell—or even know when she had misspelled, unless Cass told her—and who spent much of her time filing her long, scarlet fingernails.

Finally, there was an acquisition Cass learned about first from an article in *The Wall Street Journal*.

'The worst of it is that I don't really give a damn,' she told Paula. 'I feel like I'm just punching in and punching out, and I don't care.'

She continued to lunch with Amelia, to whom she outlined the proposal she had made to Grey about taking over Blythe's. 'It's a stupid decision, selling it off,' she told Amelia. 'I know that store could be a money-maker.'

In the fall, Cass thought, she might look for another job, or at least put out some feelers. Cass knew it was time to leave; she always knew when that time occurred.

She and Paula talked at length about their mutual dissatisfaction with their careers. She admired the way

Paula was conducting her own search for something that would turn her on again.

She and Paula were getting along; the old closeness was back. Of course, Ellin was being impossible, but Cass tried to ignore that. She felt sympathy for Ellin—Tony's death had been an enormous shock to her. 'Intimations of mortality,' she characterized it to Paula. 'If Tony could die, she could, too.'

'It's not quite that simple,' said Paula. 'It's having Lara on her hands again, too.'

Lara was not, strictly speaking, on Ellin's hands. She was back at the boarding school in which she'd spent the previous year. There really was no choice. Ellin couldn't leave New York now. She had the book to finish. She had told Lara about Tony as gently as she could. The words were chillingly like those she'd spoken to her daughter years before, when she and Tony divorced.

'It's not your fault,' she said, hugging Lara close to her. 'It's not your fault! It had nothing to do with you. It was just an awful, terrible quirk of fate. If you'd been there, you couldn't have done anything.'

'I know!' Lara cried. 'But if I'd been there, he wouldn't have been all alone, he wouldn't—'

'He wasn't alone, darling girl, and he wouldn't have wanted you there. He wanted you to come back, to go to school, to grow up, to have a good life . . . he loved you so much,' she explained, and her own tears mingled with her daughter's.

They went to the beach for the rest of the week, and Sophie and Lou tried to help. Sophie even restrained herself from making any nasty remarks about Tony, for which Ellin was grateful; she could take that, was used to it, but Lara could not, and need not. Sophie did not sing Tony's praises—even Lara would have recognized that for the hypocrisy it was—but she was gentle and tender with her granddaughter.

It was decided: Ellin called the school; they were kind

in their expressions of condolences, and glad to make a place for Lara again. She had done well there, and besides, the class was not completely full.

But Paula was right—despite the distance that separated the brownstone from the boarding school, Ellin felt as though she had sole responsibility for Lara again. She wrote to her regularly, and called her often; Lara still answered her questions in monosyllables, but Ellin heard no complaints from her teachers or advisors, so she assumed Lara was coping, assimilating her father's death.

Ellin explained all the details of Tony's death to Lara as she understood them. 'Was there . . . will we . . . I mean, is there anything left of Daddy to bury?' Lara asked her, and Ellin ached for her.

'Todd said there were tests, autopsies I guess, being carried out. He said he'd tell me when he heard anything. I think there may be some, uh, remains, but I don't know. If there are, we'll have a funeral for Daddy, if you like.'

'I dunno,' said Lara. 'He wasn't much for church, was he?' So Ellin concentrated on the financial problems of Tony's untimely death. According to the lawyer for the movie production company, Tony had no heirs except Lara; since Ellin was Lara's legal guardian, it fell to her to settle Tony's rather jumbled financial affairs. The lawyer was attempting to locate his assets, if he had any; he asked Ellin for all kinds of documents, including back tax returns, insurance policies—though Ellin knew Tony had let them lapse long ago—and copies of their divorce papers.

Most of what was required was stored at the beach house; Ellin called her tenant and asked him to forward the marked file box to her. When it came, she read it all: the love letters; the photographs; the cracked, folded onionskin documents; the legal forms that all made Tony real to her again, and his dying even realer. She wondered where Tony's possessions were—what pictures and papers he had kept, what memories of their marriage he might have stored up or stowed away. She supposed she would find out; at some time, she would be told where Tony's things were, and she would go through them. Later. When she was more used to the idea.

Cass was bored and restless. A few days after Labor Day, on her way back to the office after lunch, she passed an airline ticket office. On an impulse, she went in and booked a ticket to Seattle. She had accumulated three weeks of unused vacation; she saw no reason not to take some of it.

'They'll hardly notice my absence,' she told Paula drily. 'By the time I come back, they'll probably have moved my desk to the mailroom.'

Grey was on a business trip with Sarah Kaiser when Cass left. She placed a report she'd been working on on his desk, and left her father's telephone number in Seattle in case he needed her. And then she boarded a plane, and flew west on a clear, full-mooned night in early September.

Her father was delighted to see her; she was glad to be home. She called a few old friends, including John McKay.

'You'll probably have quite a time tracking him down,' her father said. 'He's all over the state, campaigning.'

Cass was surprised; in his occasional letters to her, John had not mentioned that he was running for office.

'Attorney general,' her father told her. 'Always told you that boy would go far—he's his father's son, he is. Johnny's been involved in politics for a few years, you know. The good government boys've been all over him to run for something.'

When she saw him, John told her the same thing. 'They wanted an independent in the office. It's been too partisan and too politicized too long. They said they'd raise a campaign war chest, and they did, so I said yes.'

It was the week before the primary; John proudly took her along to meetings, banquets, even a picnic, and she watched him work the crowd. When he spoke, he seemed to be speaking to every person individually; he roused them to applause, and she saw his appeal. He has charisma, she thought, he's got it: I'll be damned, Johnny McKay is good!

The night he won the primary election, she celebrated with him. 'You never told me you had political ambitions,' she said, sitting with him on a log on the beach at Shilshole Bay, watching the moon go down. The tall masts of sailboats in the harbour were silvery in the light; the night was mild and balmy, a beautiful Indian summer evening.

'I never told you I had any ambitions at all,' he said amiably. 'As I recall, you once told me I didn't.'

Cass admitted it. 'You didn't. Not then. You were working in that law collective, and you and everybody else, including the secretary, were taking home a hundred dollars a week. Working for lost causes,' she added.

John curled her hair around his finger, an old habit since he'd done it to her pigtails. 'So? Do you like me better now that I'm ambitious for bigger things?'

'I liked you plenty before,' Cass said, and meant it.

'Well, that's a step in the right direction.' He skipped a stone into the water, and they watched the ripples disappear into the dark inkiness.

She brought him up to date on her life since the last time she'd seen him; almost two years, she realized. She told him about the brownstone, about Paula and Jake, and Paula's rape, and her search for a different job, and about Ellin, and her book, and Lara, and Tony dying.

'It sounds like Ellin's had a tough life.'

'Well, but she makes out. Her kid's practically grown up, and she has a decent career. Except she certainly is bitchy these days. I don't know how Paula stands her—I just keep my distance. I don't even know if I want her to buy into the house any more. I think she disapproves of me.'

'And you sound a little jealous of her friendship with

Paula.' Was there a question mark at the end of that sentence? Cass thought so.

'Jealous? Not really. Paula's just helping her through a bad spell. Nothing comes between me and Paula, you know that.'

'I know,' said John, 'believe me, I know.'

She told him about Nick, and about Amagansett, but she didn't mention Grey except in terms of her job.

She never told him she was lonely; she wouldn't have agreed that she was. But she knew she was playing for sympathy. Even so, she was surprised when he said, 'Why don't you pack it in and come home?'

'Home?' she said. 'This isn't home for me any more. What's here for me?'

'Me,' said John simply. He dribbled some sand through his fingers. 'There's me, and your family. There's me, and a different kind of family. Me, and maybe kids, and a pretty good life.' She didn't reply, so he went on. 'I've always been in love with you, Cass—you know that,' he said. It was true, and she knew it; she'd known it since she was sixteen, and hardly ever thought of it thereafter. She took it for granted; she always had. But John had never pressed himself on her. He had never talked about a future together, except in the most general terms. When she left Seattle for New York, he'd said to her, 'If we're old and grey and no one will have us, there's always each other,' and she'd nodded, not seriously considering that such a thing could happen—not to her, anyway. 'There's never been anyone else but you for me,' he finished.

'Oh, no?' she teased lightly. 'Last week's *P-I* called you one of Seattle's most eligible bachelors. My dad cut out the article and shoved it under my nose as soon as I came home.'

'They said it, I didn't. Besides, I don't want to be a bachelor. I want to be a husband. You ready to be a wife yet, Campbell?'

She realized that he wasn't kidding. He had waited for her with the kind of faithful loyalty no man had ever offered her. He'd always been there for her. He always would be.

'You really mean it, don't you?' she asked, and he nodded.

'Look,' she said after a time, 'I know it sounds ridiculous to say this is so sudden, but it is. I always thought you'd meet somebody, I'd meet somebody, we'd dance at each other's weddings. We wanted different things, you weren't—' She stumbled over her words, and stopped. You weren't anybody then, she thought. You weren't ever going to be anything but a medium-sized lawyer in a medium-sized town. You weren't going to win elections. You weren't going to make anything of yourself. Me, I was going to have A Career. And look what I have. A job I'm two steps away from losing. A best friend who's probably going to find a job in Timbuctoo or a husband who'll give her the babies she so desperately wants. A housemate who hates me. Plus a barn of a house with dangerous wiring and impossible taxes.

She looked at John, and smiled. 'We've never even . . . we haven't . . .' She hesitated, and he put his arms around her.

'We can remedy that pretty easily,' he told her.

He kissed her, gently at first, and then more urgently, his tongue searching out the delicate, tingly places, his hands caressing her under her thin blouse. She felt herself responding to him; it had been a long time, two months at least, since she'd slept with a man. And that was with Grey—cool, detached, in-control Grey.

She looked up and down the beach. There was no one in sight. She nodded yes, and John stood up.

'No,' she told him. 'Here. Now.'

They made love in the shadow of the seawall, their bodies sticky and cool with sand. She climaxed again and again, pulling him closer and deeper inside her with each spasm. At last she lay back on the sand, her head on his arm, exhausted and replete.

'God,' she whispered, 'who'd have thought it? All these

years and now . . . wow.' Her voice was dry and cracked, but he answered her with a soft, deep growl.

'Me,' he murmured against her neck, 'I knew. I always knew.'

She had only planned to stay a week; she called Grey and Paula, and was vaguely dissatisfied when both said to stay longer if she wished. 'There's nothing here that can't wait until you get back,' Grey said. 'Everything's running fine.'

I'll bet it is, she thought ruefully. Paula had little to report. Amelia had tried to reach Cass: she would be out of the country for a few days, but would call on her return. Ellin was holding her own, working hard and keeping to herself. Paula had a few job leads, but nothing definite. 'What's the big attraction in Seattle?' she wanted to know, but Cass made a vague story about beautiful fall weather, and going hiking with her brother, and seeing old friends, so Paula didn't push her.

She stayed another week, seeing John whenever she could, putting him off when he sought an answer to his proposal. In spite of the increasing pace of the campaign he found time to call her or see her every day. When she accompanied him, people murmured about what an attractive couple they were, and her father was impossibly smug.

For Cass, the days were a vacation. She basked in John's devotion; she pictured the elegant dinners she would give in the governor's mansion in Olympia—surely he wouldn't stop with the attorney general's office—and then . . . well, that was a long way off. In John's arms at night the fantasies were almost real.

The day before she left, John took her to see a house. It was a handsome Tudor, a block from the lake, surrounded by tall evergreens. It was the kind of house Cass had once imagined herself living in. As she walked through it with John, though, she knew that was a different Cass, the girl who dreamed those dreams. John loved her, and she was genuinely fond of him. But she knew that she would tire of him, of all of it. She knew that she would hurt him, and she did not want to. He—and the life he held out—were not enough.

After they made love that night, she told him. Told him in the safety of darkness, feeling like the worst kind of bitch. She wanted him to call her that; she wouldn't have minded, even, if he'd hit her. He did not, of course; that wasn't like John.

Instead, he said almost what Nick had said to her so long ago. 'The offer has no time limit,' he said. 'Don't say no now. Think about it. There's plenty of time. Go back to New York, and think about it. I'm not going anywhere.'

He did not blame her. It would have been easier if he had. But her father was not as understanding. 'You're a damn fool if you ask me,' he grumbled as he drove her to the airport. 'Finest kind of man, that Johnny McKay—as good a man as his father was. You couldn't do any better.' He sighed. 'I never figured you for stupid, Cass, but you're not getting any younger, and that lad's not going to wait forever. Some pretty little thing is going to come along and snap him up, and you'll be one sorry, lonesome lady.'

Sorry? Probably, she thought; not now, but perhaps later. Lonesome? Well, who knew? First there was her job to deal with. And Grey, she supposed. And the brownstone—Paula and Ellin. Maybe a new job. And maybe a new man. But not John. She could fool him for a time, but she couldn't fool herself. Once, maybe, it would have been enough. But now it wasn't, and there wasn't anything she could do about that.

FORTY

Paula went to California again early that fall; she was one of the top three finalists for the deanship. This time the interviews were, if anything, even more thorough. She met the entire faculty; she listened, and she talked, and at the end of two days her face was stiff from smiling. She and Max went to dinner with Hal and Betsy Morris; Hal was the senior partner in Max's firm, and his wife, Betsy, was a film maker. She was a few years older than Paula; she had recently given birth to the couple's first child.

'Don't you miss it?' Paula asked her after dinner, after admiring the sleeping infant. 'The excitement, the life?'

'Not really,' Betsy said. 'I'll go back to it in a few years. I quit while I was ahead. A movie is a three-year commitment—when I'm in the thick of it, there's no time for anything else. I bought myself this time, with a lot of hard work. Three years, I figured.'

'Three years?'

'Mmm. To find a man, get married, have a child.' She looked at Paula quizzically. 'How about you?'

Paula coloured. 'I had something like that in mind. It didn't work out.'

'That's not the way it looks to me. Max is beaming like a kid in love.'

'Max?' Paula laughed nervously. 'No, it wasn't Max. It isn't . . . I mean, Max and I are just good friends.'

That's all they were, she thought. But still, there was a kind of tension between them that hadn't been there before. Being at Hal and Betsy's underscored it: this could be us, Paula thought. Me and Max. Couldn't it?

The baby woke with a mewling cry, and Betsy went to him, unbuttoning her blouse. She put him to her breast, and Paula watched, feeling a stirring, tingling feeling in her own breasts. Then Hal came in and she watched the three of them together, a tableau of love and contentment. Max had to tell her twice that it was time they were leaving.

Two weeks later, she was in Los Angeles again, for the final meeting with the committee. Later, she went to Max's house in the Valley.

'So you've decided to take the job,' he said. It was a statement, not a question.

'It's everything I want,' she replied.

'It's an awesome job.'

'But a good life.'

'What's the goal, Paula?' Max asked her. 'Not just the job, but the life. What do you want?'

She shrugged. 'I want to make a difference.'

They walked outside, beyond the grove of lemon trees, to the Mexican hammock at the far end of Max's property. They lay in it together, enjoying the breeze, the rustle of the leaves. Above them the sky was a purple blanket, the stars like icy points in the moonless night. Max shifted to make more room in the hammock, and put his arm around Paula's shoulders. They lay side by side; his heavier body pulled her almost on top of him. Their faces were only inches apart; his breath was cool on her cheek.

'What else?' Max almost whispered. 'What else do you want?'

She shut her eyes and took a deep breath. Go for it, Paula, she urged herself, and felt her heart skip several beats. The whole world seemed hushed, waiting for her reply.

'You,' she whispered back. 'You and this and us and . . . everything.'

'Everything?' Max asked with a smile that was serious, and eyes that questioned hers—eyes that seemed to see into the depths of her own and beyond, beyond to her soul.

She nodded, and buried her face in his neck. Her heart restarted itself, thumping in short, anxious beats.

He lifted her face to his; his other arm encircled her, and their lips met. At first they were tentative; then their mouths opened wide, and in the airless void they breathed each other's breath so that there seemed just enough between them for one; they shared it, inhaling and exhaling it, until their tongues sought one another.

They kissed for a long time, devouring, searching, seeking out the hidden places, the hard ridges and the soft flesh. She fitted her body to his, and felt her nipples harden under her thin blouse. She ached for the touch of his fingers on them, his lips around them, his teeth biting them gently, but she could not take her mouth from his; time was slowing, was almost stopped, and she wanted it to go on that way forever.

Max's hand was cool on her leg, warmer as he stroked her thighs and belly. She touched his groin lightly; a soft moan escaped his lips, an exhalation of pleasure blown into the chamber of their mouths, and she took his hardness in her hand, feeling him taut and rising. Tiny pulses came alive through her body; there, at her neck where one hand caressed her, and there under the soft warmth of her inner thigh, and there, yes, there at its juncture with her groin, and oh, God, yes, there, in the centre of her, there, wet and slippery, leaping out of her skin to meet his questing touch.

She unzipped him, and his cock sprang into her hand, hard and hot, throbbing, demanding entrance. He pulled her on top of him and somehow her panties disappeared, and her skirt was spread around her, bunched up over her belly. He entered her, and she came with him almost immediately, in long, rolling surges that did not stop even after they tumbled out of the hammock onto the dew-damp grass. They chuckled, their mouths still fastened together, and he went on fucking her in slow, deep strokes until at last, exhausted, they rolled away from each other and lay on their backs, looking up at the moonless sky, slowing their breathing.

Presently they came together again, silent for the most part, occasionally murmuring little sounds that said nothing and meant everything. Paula fell asleep there; she did not wake until Max picked her up and carried her inside, where he laid her down on the bed and covered her with a blanket. He stood at the window, looking out at the night.

After a time Paula rose from the bed and went to him. Her head came just to the tip of his ear. She did not touch him. He turned toward her, his face dim in the shadowy light.

'Is it all right?' she whispered. 'Oh, Max, is it all right?'

He smiled, his teeth white in the darkness. He took her in his embrace and pressed her face to his cheek. 'It's fine, Paula,' he said. 'It's fine. Everything.'

'Everything,' she echoed, and he nodded. Then they went back to the bed, and undressed each other, and made love again, slowly this time. They discovered what made them groan, and cry, and shudder, and it was as if they had always known. And then they tumbled together off a mountain into a long expanse of cool green ocean, and finally, they slept.

FORTY-ONE

By the time Cass came back from her vacation, the flap about Sarah's vice presidency had quieted down. Even the *People* story was old news. Cass tried to reach Amelia; Clio told her she was in Europe.

'You've heard she's selling the agency, I suppose?' Clio asked, and Cass was startled.

'Of course not, I—oh, Clio, to whom? Tell all!' she urged.

Clio didn't have all the details, but enough to indicate to Cass that Amelia was following the plan she'd outlined to her as a possibility sometime before—before Cass had even joined Amagansett. Amelia had agreed on a price with a very big international agency, Young & Rubicam. As Clio understood it, Amelia got a huge chunk of stock, plenty of cash, and a seat on the Y & R board. She had a noncompete clause in the contract: she couldn't open another advertising agency for five years. As far as Clio knew, there wouldn't be any major personnel changes at Amelia Jordan, Inc.

'She told me not to worry about my job, she was insisting on a contract for me, can you imagine?' Clio was excited; that was validation of her worth to the agency, and Cass was pleased for her. There were contracts for all the senior executives, too. 'Of course, it won't be the same without Amelia here, but there's a management committee, I guess they'll report to Y & R, or we'll get a new president or something,' Clio said. 'Interested?'

Cass chuckled. 'Not that I know of, Clio. Look, tell

Amelia I called, and to call when she gets back, huh? Is she off looking for Natalie across the ocean again?'

'Beats me,' Clio said. 'Even the office grapevine doesn't know. She just up and went and said she'd be back when she got back.'

Cass smiled as she put down the phone. She hoped Amelia was having a holiday with a wonderful, romantic man—she'd been known to disappear like that, occasionally, in the years Cass had worked for her. But not to Europe—Amelia had a little house in Tortola, and spent frequent holidays there. Maybe Natalie was in some kind of trouble again; Cass hoped not. She thought Amelia had given up on her daughter after the last unpleasantness; at least, that was what Amelia led her to believe. 'I suppose she has decided to live her own life, and let me live mine, with as little contact between us as possible,' Amelia had told Cass a few months before. But perhaps Amelia was trying to effect another reconciliation. Cass didn't think it would work, however. Both Amelia and Natalie were similarly intransigent when they felt wronged. Maybe Amelia didn't feel that way, but she had been, Cass said to herself. And so, probably, had Natalie.

At Amagansett, Cass was clearly being stripped of her authority. Publicly, she still enjoyed Grey's confidence, though she brought nothing up at management committee meetings that he had not cleared in advance. She had no interest in challenging him. Besides, the signs that her influence was waning were clear—in meetings from which she was excluded, memos that no longer crossed her desk. Her opinion was sought infrequently; more often, people turned to Sarah for functions that had been Cass's.

Grey's personal response to Cass's return, and to the *People* story, was to redouble the amount of time they spent together, especially at business-related functions. They had fewer evenings alone, fewer events that were just personal. When they were out in public, he was attentive. One night, as they came out of a fashion gala at Lincoln Centre, he spotted the news cameras. He pulled Cass close to him and kissed her, murmuring, 'Give the paparazzi something to shoot at.' When she saw the picture in *Women's Wear Daily*, she winced.

That night they dined together at a charity party. He wanted to drop her off at the brownstone, but she insisted that he come in.

They had not had sex since her return from Seattle. And they did not that night, either; Grey said he would have a drink, and leave; he had an early meeting.

Cass poured them both brandy, and showed him the picture in the newspaper.

'Nice shot,' he said noncommittally.

Cass looked at him. 'Somehow I get the feeling that I'm being used,' she said. 'This won't hurt you—if anything, it will add some lustre to your reputation, don't you think?'

He said nothing, but she continued. 'I, however, am rapidly becoming known just as Grey Tucker's girlfriend. They don't even bother with my title any more.'

'Well, isn't that true?' He smiled lazily. 'Aren't you Grey Tucker's girl?'

She stood up and looked down at him. He was getting bald, she noticed: there was a definite hairless circle just behind the parting on his head.

'No,' she replied. 'No, I don't think I am any more.'

The breakup, when it came, was that simple. Though Cass herself said the final words, she had no other choice. She had not made that much of an impact on Grey; she had barely dented his facade. Nor had she ever felt the genuine caring for him that she once had for Nick. She was finished with Grey; it was simply a matter of time before she was finished with Amagansett as well.

Ellin re-read what she had written and ripped the offensive sheet out of the typewriter. She tossed it on the floor, an ocean littered like an ice field over which her daybed towered like an ominous grey glacier.

She was stuck, and she tried all her rituals for getting unstuck. She got stoned. She read half of a paperback book. She ate. She cursed her typewriter. And then she went in search of Vic. Sometimes he was very helpful at times like this.

He wasn't in his apartment; she called the Lion's Head. Paul, the relief bartender, answered the phone. 'He's not here, Ellin. He's off for the weekend. Said he was going fishing in Montauk.'

Shit. She had come to depend on Vic for a great deal. He had been with them all through so many crises—Paula's rape, Tony's death, the time the house was broken into and somebody cut all of Cass's underwear into shreds and wrote horrible things on her mirrors. With Paula, Vic was protective and brotherly; with Ellin he was supportive, critical, direct, and encouraging.

Ellin had not slept with Vic since that one night; still, there was sexual tension between them, and she fought her desire for him. She already felt vulnerable and exposed; in their long discussions of her book, especially the character whose experiences and feelings were virtually her own, she had revealed too much of herself to him. Sexual intimacy as well was frightening—it was too much to risk.

She didn't think she could write another word without talking to Vic. Or somebody. Maybe Paula was around.

She was. 'Want to go to a movie?' Paula suggested.

'Might as well, I can't work,' Ellin replied. 'Where's Cass?' Not that she cared; in fact, if Cass was coming, maybe she'd bow out. She wasn't so hot on Cass these days. Cass reminded her of Lara, of the way Lara used to play Ellin and Tony against each other. If she was Ellin, who was Tony in this triangle? she wondered, but she knew. Just the other day Cass had said, 'You know, it's Paula who suffered all through the summer with no air conditioning—it'll be too bad if she has no heat this winter, what with the rewiring so far behind schedule and all.' And later, 'Oh, Paula's got plenty of time for us now, but wait till she finds a man again, or starts a new job—then we'll probably never see her.'

Cass was getting to be a real pain in the neck, thought Ellin. But Paula's next words made her more of a nuisance than that.

'She's away,' said Paula. 'She said she was going fishing for the weekend. Do her good—she's finished with Grey, you know.'

Fishing? Cass hated fishing; Ellin could hear her words on the subject, spoken a few months before: 'It's hot, slimy, and boring.'

'Oh, where?' Ellin asked, as casually as she could.

'Montauk, I think. Want to see an early movie and eat later?'

Impossible, thought Ellin. Ridiculous. Cass and Vic . . . Cass would never. Or would she? Cass had told her at least once that she thought Vic was sexy. 'Not my type, but sexy'—those were her exact words. And Vic . . . he never talked about Cass. Suddenly Ellin remembered the way he'd watched Cass dancing that night in her apartment. The look he'd given Cass that Ellin couldn't decipher: desire, perhaps, or maybe only fascination. That was the way men always looked at Cass; Ellin never paid it much attention, except, perhaps, for an occasional pang of envy.

At first, when she made the connection, she was annoyed. Then she was hotly, jealously furious. Vic was hers, if he was anyone's—even Cass had acknowledged that. 'He spends more time upstairs than he does downstairs,' she said once to Ellin. 'Something going on there, hmm?'

Ellin hadn't replied; it was a few days after her one night in bed with Vic, a night about which she told no one, not even Paula. Still, both of her housemates knew there was something more than casual friendship between her and Vic. It was not anything Ellin could identify; it was unlike any relationship she had ever had with a man.

She did not articulate it; she could not. It was special, unique, and, to Ellin, not at all casual.

She fumed throughout the movie, and all the way home. Paula noticed. 'Something eating you?' she asked.

'As a matter of fact, yes. I think Cass went away with Vic for the weekend.'

'That's Cass,' said Paula blithely. 'Standard operating procedure. When a man drops her she makes herself feel better by finding some poor shnook to fall for her, and . . .' She stopped abruptly, tuning in to Ellin's anguish. 'Oh, fuck!' she cursed. 'Vic. Of course Vic. Why *not* Vic? Goddamn it, Cass is just . . . oh, Ellin, I'm sorry!'

She tried to soothe her but inwardly, she was seething. Not only at Cass, but at Vic. She'd seen the signs, long before that night Cass danced for them. Paula had seen Vic looking at Cass in a way that was all too familiar to her. Cass was aware of it, too. 'Frankly, I thought about it,' she confided once to Paula. 'Right after he moved in, Vic came on to me. But who is he, anyway? A bartender who lives in our basement and takes out our trash and pounds away at some novel he'll probably never finish. Oh, he's smart, and he's very sexy, but who needs him?'

Ellin had, Paula thought, and Cass had spoiled him for her. She knew Cass was not feeling that good about Ellin these days. She even knew why—Cass had been jealous of Paula's friends before. Cass probably didn't do it for that reason, Paula thought. Cass probably didn't give Ellin a second thought. Which, for Paula, was a far greater transgression.

Two days later, as the late afternoon darkened into dusk, Ellin heard Vic and Cass come in; she was heading down the stairs. Quickly, she moved up again; she could see them down the stairwell. They were carrying fishing tackle and overnight bags; Cass hung on to Vic's arm. She looked up and saw Ellin.

'Hi,' she called gaily. 'We caught an enormous mess

of blues, and we're cooking them for dinner. Come on down!'

Ellin shook her head and muttered something unintelligible. She fled back into the sanctuary of her apartment, her face burning. She felt betrayed, not by Vic, but by Cass. That bitch, she thought. That spoiled, rotten, manipulative bitch!

Cass acted as though nothing out of the ordinary had happened. She chattered brightly about her weekend. 'God, I needed that!' she told Ellin happily. 'Sun, salt air, and terrific sex. And the very same hired fellow, our ladies' man!'

She said almost the same thing to Paula. 'Just one of those things,' she said. 'The right time, the right place . . . chemistry.'

'Chemistry?' said Paula sarcastically. 'You've been living in the same house with him for two years, and all of a sudden there's chemistry? Come *on*, Cass. This is me, Paula, remember? Don't you realize what you've done to Ellin?'

Cass was honestly surprised. 'What I've done to Ellin? She and Vic are just friends, that's all. It's not like they were fucking or anything.'

'Does that matter? Is that your measure of whether a relationship between two people matters, for Christ's sake? Is that how you decide whether to plop yourself down in the middle of it? Or did you do it on purpose, to bug Ellin?'

'To bug Ellin? Are you crazy? Of course not! Ellin had nothing to do with it!'

'That's exactly my point, Cass,' said Paula. 'That's exactly the point. You weren't paying attention. You saw what you wanted, and you took it.'

Cass was thoughtful. 'Do you think I should apologize to her?'

'I think you better do something.'

But she didn't, because Ellin soon had something far more serious on her mind.

The headmaster of Lara's school phoned her at noon on Monday. 'Is Lara still with you, Ms Barnett?' he enquired.

'Why, no, she's not,' Ellin replied. Then she realized what he had said, and sat down, frightened. She listened to him explain.

'Lara signed out for the weekend,' the headmaster told her. 'She said she was coming to New York to see you. When she didn't return for her classes this morning, we were worried.'

'This morning?' Ellin was practically shouting; she was fighting to control her terror. 'Why didn't you call me last night? Why didn't you call me before she left? Why didn't—Have you talked to her friends? Was she in any kind of trouble? Was she sick? Why did you let her go?'

The headmaster interrupted her barrage of questions. 'Well, you did give Lara permission to visit you in New York,' he said, 'and she did it last year, of course, with no trouble. We haven't made any enquiries except of her roommate. The girl said Lara packed her bag and told her she'd see her on Sunday. That's all we've been able to determine.'

He tried to be reassuring. 'Perhaps she's just gone off to see a friend,' he said soothingly. 'A bending of the rules, true enough, but I'm certain nothing more than that. We will continue to ask questions, and be in touch with you as soon as we hear something.' Ellin was very, very frightened. There was an icy chill in the air; goose pimples clustered beneath her skin.

'I'll drive up there right now,' she said. 'I'll get a car. I'll be there before midnight.'

'I really don't think there's anything you could do at this point, Ms Barnett,' he said. 'Really, we're doing all that we can. This is a small village, you know; it's possible Lara took a bus or a train somewhere, and we'll ask immediately.'

The headmaster called again that evening. 'Well, we

have learned some things,' he told Ellin. She withdrew some money from her checking account—a couple of hundred dollars. She was seen on Friday boarding a New York-bound bus. She had been moody lately, according to her friends; her grades had slipped somewhat. She was not very communicative. Her housemother had urged her to see the school psychologist, but Lara had not kept the appointment. And they would, of course, keep her informed. They had, of course, notified the authorities. They were, of course, certain that no harm had befallen Lara.

Ellin remembered the talk she'd had with that same school psychologist when she drove Lara up to school two months before. 'It's a hard time for a young girl to lose her father,' the woman had said. 'She had no father at all for so many years, and finally her fantasy came true—he wanted her. And now he's gone. We'll try to get her to talk about it a bit; that sometimes eases the grief. But time, her friends, the routine here—they'll all be a help. And we'll keep a special eye on her.'

Ellin had taken Lara to a movie the night before she left for school. It was a comedy, and Ellin enjoyed it. On the way back to the brownstone, Lara turned on her.

'How could you sit there and laugh?' she demanded. 'Daddy just died, two weeks ago, and you sit in a movie theatre and laugh. How could you?'

Ellin didn't know what to say; she hadn't been able to reach Lara for the past weeks. Lara wouldn't talk about Tony; that she was able to that night, even if she was angry at Ellin, seemed a good sign. But Lara was worse than angry; she was spiteful. 'You really are a cold person, you know? Daddy always said that about you, and he was right!'

In the morning, of course, she'd apologized, and the ride back to school was uneventful. Driving down the long winding road away from the school, she'd been comforted by the psychologist's words. They'd keep a special eye on Lara.

And now this. She was angry—at the school, at Lara, at Tony for dying and leaving her with this to handle. But then her anger was gone, submerged in the anxiety she felt. She thought of the possibilities, all of them distasteful and most of them gruesome. Lara, a baby, really, just sixteen. Lara, somewhere in the city—no, she couldn't, mustn't think of that, of men lurking in doorways, psychopaths stalking the streets, cowboys in fancy pimp cars cruising the Port Authority, enticing young girls like Lara into awfulness she couldn't bear thinking about. There was bile in Ellin's mouth; she wanted to throw up.

There was no one she could call; she hadn't seen Vic, and didn't want to. Certainly she could never talk to Cass. Paula was out for the evening. She thought of calling her parents, and decided against it; she could not take Sophie, not tonight. And she was afraid of her father's heart condition; she could not tell him. She called Kate in California; the phone rang for a long time, but no one answered.

She took a hot bath and a Valium. But even so, she did not close her eyes all night.

There was no word from the school in the morning. Lara's friends had been canvassed; they knew nothing of her plans. But the withdrawal of money pointed to some kind of plan. Lara clearly had made one. She was not—she had not been—the victim of some senseless crime or accident. The images of crazed men lurking in alleys that plagued Ellin all through the night receded; they were replaced by pictures of Lara, suitcase in hand, destination in mind, boarding a bus to the city and then . . . and then. Ellin couldn't think past then; Lara might be somewhere in New York now. Maybe within a few miles of her. But where? She didn't know; she couldn't begin to guess.

There was no word of Lara the next day, or the day after that. Sophie called; she asked after her granddaughter in a way that indicated she knew nothing of Lara's disappearance. But the call did give Ellin an idea. Could Lara, perhaps, have gone to Sophie's summer house?

She was heading out the door when Vic came in. He knew about Lara's disappearance; everyone in the brownstone knew. 'Where are you going?' he asked.

Ellin told him. 'Wait a minute, I'll get the car, I'll drive you,' he said, and she did not object. They were silent on the ride out to the Island; she kept playing the radio, and Vic gave up trying to talk to her.

The house was closed and silent, as she had feared; it was clear that Lara had not been there.

Paula tried to help. She enlisted the aid of a detective, who went up to school to interview Lara's friends. He came back empty-handed. Lara's trail, after arriving in the city, at the bus terminal—that, at least, had been verified by the driver, who remembered the pretty young girl—was cold.

Cass tried to help, too. She pretended the incident with Vic had never happened; Ellin had her resentments, but they were submerged in the fear she felt for Lara. And Cass's attentions chafed her.

'I know she's trying to help, but does she have to preface everything by telling me she knows how *guilty* I must feel?' she complained to Paula. 'And I wish she'd stop telling me I'm being self-indulgent! She said I should let go of responsibility for Lara and get on with my life!' she added indignantly. 'Very easy for her to say. She assumes that Lara is punishing me for something . . . God, I wish I knew what it was!' Cass implied that Lara was deliberately trying to worry Ellin, and she criticized the girl without hesitation. 'You know how I feel about that,' Ellin told Paula, not at all apologetically.

Of course Paula knew. She had said as much to Cass when Ellin first moved into the brownstone. 'I've known Ellin since Lara was practically a baby, and I'll tell you this, she's very, very sensitive about her. Maybe it comes from being a single parent, I don't know. But you can't tell her anything about Lara, or criticize how she handles her. Not unless she asks you for advice, which she almost never does.'

Sometimes, in fact, Ellin did ask, but only Kate or Paula. She trusted their judgement, and knew that they both loved her, and Lara as well. She didn't feel that way about Cass, not now. But that didn't stop Cass. 'Lara had a plan, and she's over sixteen. She's well able to take care of herself—lots of kids her age are on the streets,' she said.

That was no consolation to Ellin, although Paula and Kate were reassuring. 'This isn't so uncommon,' said Kate, her friend the psychotherapist. 'Lots of kids run away. I did, a few times. Lara's smart and she's capable. I don't think she's in trouble, in any danger, or spaced out on drugs. She knows better than to get into cars with strangers, unless she's hitchhiking, and she has pretty good judgement. Perhaps she needed to go away to prove to herself that she could make it on her own.'

'But why should she have to?' Ellin cried. 'She has me. She doesn't *need* to make it on her own.'

Kate had no answer, and neither did Paula. The days took their toll on Ellin. 'I just see her out there, hungry and lonely and scared to come home . . . she's just a baby,' she sobbed one night. Cass shushed her.

'That's ridiculous,' she told Ellin brusquely. 'She's perfectly all right, you know she is. She just wants to make you suffer a little.'

'For what?' Ellin cried. Her tearful eyes flashed angrily at Cass. 'What makes you such a great authority on how a mother is supposed to feel, or even an unhappy kid, for that matter? Just because you sailed through adolescence, the belle of the ball, doesn't mean *everybody* does!' Her words and her vehemence surprised her; with the detached, observant part of her, Ellin wondered at it. Where did that come from? Was she that jealous of Cass, of all the years life had been so easy for her? She was momentarily ashamed. 'I'm sorry, Cass, I didn't mean that. I'm just at the end of my rope.'

'I'm at the end of mine, too,' said Cass. 'We can't talk about this without losing our tempers. So let's just not, huh? Let's go out to eat.'

'I'm not really hungry,' Ellin began, but Cass wouldn't hear it.

'Of course you are,' she said. 'You haven't eaten a thing all day. Now Paula and I are coming up to get you in fifteen minutes, so get dressed and wash your face, okay?'

'Okay,' said Ellin meekly. 'Okay.' It was easier to give in than resist. But she left the number of the restaurant with her answering service, just in case.

FORTY-TWO

Cass wasn't expecting Amelia's proposition. It was just a routine lunch at Amelia's club, after the obligatory game of racquetball. Amelia made Cass work for the points she won; somehow, the older woman seemed infused with new drive and energy. Her vacation must have done her some good, Cass thought, sitting across from her at lunch. I wonder if she went to that clinic in Switzerland, or had her face lifted? Amelia didn't say, and Cass didn't enquire. But there was excitement bubbling just under her words, which Cass heard with some confusion. She had her own agenda with Amelia this afternoon; she was going to sound her out about the sale of the agency, and see whether there was any role for her to play in it. She didn't suppose it was good form to ask for one's old job back, and she wouldn't put it that way, in any case. She would just casually enquire whether Amelia knew much about Y & R's management record with new acquisitions.

Before she had a chance, Amelia brought up the subject of Blythe's.

'Blythe's?' echoed Cass. 'Grey's selling it off, but I think it's a mistake. An infusion of new capital, a change in management—it could be solvent again. But the AI board isn't interested. They don't want to invest another dollar in it. Why?'

'Because I'm buying it,' said Amelia. 'You know I've sold the agency'—Cass nodded—'and so I have the capital. It's amazing how much Y & R wants my little shop, my dear. Even after Uncle Sam is finished, I'll still be a rich old lady.'

'Rich, maybe, but not old,' said Cass.

'Semantics,' said Amelia impatiently. 'The fact is, I am not really ready to retire · et. I'll have some duties on the Y & R board, but I can handle them easily. I will still have a great deal of time, and money, at my disposal.'

'Still, Amelia, AI won't sell Blythe's cheap. The real estate is worth millions.'

'I've been approached by an Arab syndicate—don't raise your eyebrows, Cassandra, it's bad for wrinkles. Anyway, Arabs have all the money these days, you know that. It just so happens that one of their wealthier number is an old, dear friend of mine. So money is no problem.' She sipped her Perrier and lime with delicacy. 'I know what's wrong with that old store, and so do you, if I taught you anything.'

Cass nodded. 'Bad management. Poor merchandising. Losing its loyal old customers to age and inflation. But Amelia, why you? It's very different from the agency business. I know, I worked in retailing for a few years before I came to you. It's backbreaking. Seven days a week—eight, on a week like Thanksgiving. If you're looking for excitement, why don't you start another agency? Or take up skydiving? It's safer.'

'You may not know it, but I began my own career in retailing, too,' Amelia replied. 'And that nice store in Seattle—they still think very highly of you.'

Cass laughed. 'Oh, sure, I could have been another Geri Stutz. That's what Grey accused me of when I asked him to let me take Blythe's over. He said I was overreaching myself.'

Amelia harrumphed. 'That man is not nearly as smart as I gave him credit for,' she said. Geri Stutz, the legendary president of Henri Bendel's, was the most famous woman in retailing. And she, too, had bought the store from its parent conglomerate, Cass recalled—with a Swiss syndicate behind her, if her memory was accurate.

'There's only one Geri Stutz,' said Amelia. 'And only one Amelia Jordan. And only one Cassandra Campbell. I'm going to buy Blythe's, and I'm going to be chairman of the board—oh, dear, I guess we'll have to make it chairwoman, these days, won't we? Such foolishness . . . anyway, you're going to be president, my dear—you're going to run it. And we're both going to have a wonderful, exciting, and exceedingly profitable time!'

Cass did not ask Grey about leaving Amagansett and moving to Blythe's—she told him, immediately after the sale of the store was completed. She laid the hateful reorganization plan that had been her particular cross for the last several months on his desk, and with it, her letter of resignation.

If Grey was sorry that she was leaving, he concealed it well. 'You and Amelia always did make a great team,' he said. 'She's exactly what you need—a firm hand on the reins and a careful eye on the bottom line.' He can't even mix a metaphor decently, Cass thought. He is an extraordinarily patronizing asshole. That realization astounded her, and she giggled in spite of herself. 'Women . . . Jesus, spare me,' Grey said. And a closet sexist, too, Cass added silently.

Grey leaned back in his chair and flexed his fingers into a triangle. 'Of course, you have my blessing, Cass.'

Not that I need it, she silently replied. 'You learned something here, from me,' he went on. 'It will stand you in good stead at Blythe's. The bottom line is still the name of the game, even there. Amelia will help you with that. But the marketing, the merchandising, the creativity—you have that in abundance. What you lack is an appreciation of the economics.'

She didn't remind him that she had assessed her own skills in almost those words at that breakfast with him at the Plaza. There was no sense alienating Grey Tucker; she might need him again.

Their parting was clean, clear, and without rancour.

'I'm too old for scenes,' Cass told Paula. 'We didn't really have a love affair. It hardly leaves a hole where he used to be.'

She shed a few tears; she thought she ought to. But she knew that for the self-indulgence it was. And she was too caught up in the details of her venture with Amelia to fret over Grey Tucker.

She spent hours with Amelia, planning the remodelling of the store, the changes she would make. Amelia watched her protégée with pride and offered enthusiastic encouragement. If I had a daughter, she thought, I'd want her to be just like this one. And then she realized that she did, indeed, have a daughter, and the old familiar ache clutched at her with such intensity that she grabbed her chest in a reflex action.

'What's the matter?' Cass asked with concern, looking up from the architects' drawings.

'Nothing,' said Amelia. 'Really, nothing at all.'

Paula made her own announcement at the dinner the three women had to celebrate Cass's news.

'I have something to share with you, too,' she said. 'I'm leaving the firm at the end of the year. I'm going to take a sabbatical for a few months.'

Oh, damn, thought Cass, just when I'm taking a big financial risk. If Ellin doesn't buy into the house, and Paula's not bringing in any money, we could run into trouble.

Paula ladled onion soup out of a turkey-shaped tureen, and handed bowls of the steaming liquid around the sawhorse-and-trestle dining-room table in her apartment. In the middle of the table was a papier-mâché model of Blythe's she had constructed, with a doll-like figure on top of its tall spire that looked almost like Cass. 'It's a Barbie doll dressed in Barbie Gets a Job clothes,' she had told Ellin. Ellin thought the centrepiece was a remarkable job, and the Barbie doll appropriate.

'And then I'm starting a new job in May,' Paula went

on. 'I'm going to be Dean of a law school. The first woman dean, by the way. I just thought I'd mention that.'

Ellin was thrilled for Paula. It was the perfect job for her. She knew Paula was bored with her practice and bothered by her increasing cynicism about the law itself; in a milieu of students uncorrupted by their own experience in the system, perhaps she could regain what the years of working within it had taken from her.

'That's fabulous!' said Ellin, and Paula, beaming, agreed.

'The dean of a major law school has some power,' she said. 'Power to change things—to influence how people practise and how justice is administered. I'm very excited.' She passed the salad bowl around. 'The academic calendar appeals to me, too,' she went on. 'It leaves room for a personal life. If I ever have one.'

'Oh, don't be ridiculous, Paula, of course you'll have one. Maybe you'll meet the prince at a faculty meeting,' Cass said.

'And maybe a change of scene will do me good, too,' said Paula.

'Change of scene?' Cass questioned. 'Just where is this law school, Paula?'

There was a moment of silence. Paula put down her spoon and looked directly at Cass.

'In California, Cass,' she said. 'I'm going to be Dean of Westwood Law School.'

Westwood. Cass took it in slowly. Paula was leaving her. Leaving the brownstone. She couldn't believe it. Helpless to stop the tears from collecting behind her eyes, she gave up, and they spilled heedlessly down her face.

Paula got up from the table and went to Cass, embracing her. God, she loved Cass, even if she could be an impossible bitch sometimes. And she knew Cass loved her, in her fashion.

'We knew it would come to this sometime,' Paula said.

Cass sniffed. 'Sometime,' she said, 'but not yet. I thought if one of us left, it would be, it was because . . .'

Paula finished her sentence. 'Because of a man. Yes, I know. I guess I did, too. It just didn't work out that way.'

'And I suppose you think you'll find the man in California, huh?' Cass said, wiping her eyes. 'And then you'll have it all, the job, the man, the family,'

Paula smiled. 'Hey, nobody's talking about a man. Although maybe if I make a place in my life for one, it'll happen. I never made a secret of that, Cass. I always said that's what I wanted.'

'So why are you moving three thousand miles away if it's not because of a man, huh? Tell me that!' Cass said sulkily.

'Would it be better, for you, if that's why I was leaving, Cassie?' she asked. 'Look, at Smith they told us to marry a lawyer. Then in the middle, they changed the rules—they said, be one. And ever since, we've all been conflicted about what our real roles are, or ought to be.'

'*I* haven't been.'

'No, maybe you haven't. If you wanted to be married, you'd be married by now. To Nick, or somebody like him. You know that.'

It was true; Cass had exactly what she wanted.

'But what makes you think you'll find Mr Wonderful in California?' Cass wailed.

'Let's say I have a few leads,' Paula smiled. 'But I can't build my life around waiting for a man. I have to do something that's challenging, that makes me happy, that's a step in building a life, that's all. This job offers me that, so I'm taking it. Life is what happens while you're making other plans.'

Cass saw that pouting would get her nowhere, so she stopped. She even managed a smile.

'It couldn't have happened to a better woman,' she said. 'Except . . .'

'Except you. Right?'

'Right,' said Cass. She went to her apartment, and found a magnum of champagne there, and brought it back to toast Paula's new job, and her own future, too. And Cass tried, really tried, to be happy for them both.

FORTY-THREE

When Paula told Ellin and Cass about the job, she purposely refrained from mentioning Max. She wasn't sure quite how she felt. Not about Max—she knew with a deep, steady sureness that she loved him. About the two of them as a couple, a unit, she was less certain. She did not want to hold her relationship with him up for inspection. Not to the light of Ellin's analysis, though she knew that it would be lucid and loving and explain why she and Max were suddenly . . . while she was strangely . . . why they both seemed to . . . She couldn't put it into words.

Ellin could, of course—that was her skill. But Paula kept her own counsel. Cass prodded her. 'Is there more out there than just the job?' she asked Paula. 'How much does Max Morton have to do with your decision?'

'Some,' she said evasively. 'He's not the main reason.' She mentioned casually that she would be staying with Max for a while—'until I get settled,' she said.

She did not want to tell Cass, either. For Cass would immediately expect Paula to clarify it, amplify it, and, especially, delineate the difference it might make; not to Paula alone, but to her, and to the brownstone. Then she could, perhaps, accept Paula's affair. Her relationship. Her 'thing.' And then she would insist on reviewing Paula's entire romantic history, from Jake to Chris to Jake to Max, and all the other men in between. The Israeli chargé d'affaires from the UN, the network producer, the writer from *Rolling Stone,* the endless insignificant 'things', some of them meaningless and brief, others dramatic and painful, others easily slipped away from. Sometimes Paula had seen the disasters coming—the man who wanted a mother, the one who couldn't handle her independence, the man whose politics were impossible, the one who just didn't, after all, really turn her on. But sometimes—with Jake, for instance—she hadn't. She didn't think it would be a disaster with Max, but until she was sure, she was keeping it to herself.

No, Paula didn't want to tell Cass. She wanted first to let go of her past, inasmuch as she was able. She wanted, she thought ruefully, to cleanse herself. For Max. She still went out with old friends, but they weren't really dates; she slept happily alone, and she held her secret close to herself, like a talisman.

Her life was busier than ever. Ten days a month she was in California with Max, and it kept getting better, fuller, more perfect. He committed none of the usual crimes of intimacy. His breath was sweet even in the mornings, he did not rush to fill her silences, he was not so cheerful that she felt graceless and ordinary. He was solid, reliable, strong, and not afraid to love her. And the more time they spent together, the more she knew he was exactly right for her.

Their differences masked their similarities; if they had known at the beginning how alike they were, it never would have happened. She still did not wholly trust it. Could this be love? There was no painful grinding down of small but precious private places—only a slow, sure blending of the two of them together. There was no drama—not even melodrama. It did not hurt; she was not certain it was real.

In New York, she wound up her work for the firm, reading old files, completing work on pending cases, transferring her clients to other attorneys. An announcement of her new position appeared in *Time.* She studied the photograph, an old one, taken in the days of the Carey committee hearings. Another magazine used a picture taken on the steps of the Supreme Court, right after the argument. Is that me? she wondered. God, what happened to the frizzy hair, the bizarre clothes, the boots and the miniskirts, the hippie lawyer? What happened to that Paula—to those Paulas? Where is the Paula that happened to me when I wasn't looking? And then she thought about the future, about the perfect, wonderful new job, and about Max—imperfect, wonderful, old, new Max—and said a silent little prayer of thanks, just in case God was listening.

She planned her departure from the firm, and the brownstone, carefully. She would divide her time between California and New York until Christmas. Then she and Max would take a holiday in Mexico. She would bring only the essentials to California; she would leave the rest, some things discarded, the remainder stored in the basement of Casita Rosita. She would retain her financial interest in it for now; Cass would handle subletting her apartment. For three years Cass would retain the right to buy Paula out—that was the duration of Paula's contract with Westwood. Renewable, if both parties wished.

'It will take that long to get a decent capital fund drive launched and the curriculum revised,' she told Max. 'And by then I'll know if I want to stay on, and they will know whether they want me to.'

'Is that a timetable for us, too?'

Paula smiled, a secret smile. She was still smiling it that night, when she returned from Los Angeles. Cass was suspicious.

'Something's going on, Gabriel,' she told Paula. 'This is me, Cass, remember? Is it you and Max? Well, *is* it?'

But Paula only smiled. 'I guess you could say we're in pre-love formation,' she told Cass, who repeated her words to Ellin.

'What does that mean?' Ellin asked, and Cass rolled her eyes upward.

'With Paula, God only knows.'

Paula felt no impatience with the pace of her love affair. By mutual but unspoken agreement she had made Max's home her own. He had cleared closets and bureau drawers for her; he gave her a set of house keys casually, and she accepted them with equal aplomb. 'You'll need these,' he said one day as she helped him pack for a two-day business trip. And when he went with her to buy a car—a sensible, well-maintained Japanese import with less than three thousand miles on the odometer—and she hesitated over the address on the registration papers, he took the pen from her and wrote down his own.

Like that, they moved into each other's life, a step at a time. Mostly Paula did the moving. She met more of Max's friends—she made a place for herself in his life. Sometimes they spent weekends touring the state. They went to the missions, the mountain lakes, the desert. Once they went to San Francisco to the wedding of an old friend of Max's. On the way home, they took the Seventeen Mile Drive between Carmel and Monterey. They stopped to listen to the seals barking from the rocks, and watch the cypress trees bend and sway in the wind like dancers.

'She seems like a nice person,' Paula said of the bride.

'Pete waited a long time for the right one,' Max said. 'He deserves to be happy.'

'Don't we all?' Paula asked lazily, liking the feel of the wind in her hair.

Max caressed the nape of her neck and she felt the beginnings of a stirring inside her. Max never failed to move her sexually—he was a beautiful lover, knowing and intuitive and passionate. They made love often; they could not get enough of each other.

Paula bent her head to Max's lap. She sucked him, gently at first, and then greedily. He rested his head on the back of the seat and groaned. 'If you don't stop that, I'm going to come,' he warned her.

She took her mouth from him for a moment. 'Come a little,' she said, 'but save some for me.' She took him between her lips again, flicking the tip of his cock with her tongue, finding the tiny hole, pressing on it with her finger inside her own mouth. She felt the short bursts from him, and rolled his sweet saltiness around in her cheeks and swallowed it. He pulled her on top of him, and lowered her onto him. He rocked her back and forth, burying his head in her breasts as he came in a last, long spasm.

She collapsed against him, and there was only the noise of the surf, louder than their breathing in the quiet night.

Much later, he looked down at her in the moonlight. She was drifting, half asleep, sated and languorous.

'We deserve to be happy, too, don't we?' he asked, and she remembered the conversation she had stopped with her lips. She thought for a long moment.

'Yes, I think we do,' she said. 'Do you think we will be?'

He pulled her against him and nuzzled her. 'I don't see any reason why not,' he said, and it made perfect sense to both of them.

•

She was packing, a few weeks later. 'Bring what you need to make you happy,' Max had told her. 'Leave everything else back there.' She sorted and sifted, eventually reducing her important possessions to a few cartons of books and several trunks of clothes, and a collage of photographs of her friends and family, of the brownstone and Ellin and Cass. Max called and she settled down on the sofa for a chat; she had seen him only three days before, but missed him terribly.

'I filled out change-of-address cards today,' she told him. The move was a month away. First the week in the Yucatan, then the beginning of a new life.

'Have you got everything?' he asked her.

'Everything I want.' They had spoken no formal words of commitment to each other; not yet. 'How about you?'

'What I want is what we have,' he told her. 'No

endings, just beginnings. Being. Sticking. Staying. Everything.'

'Everything?'

'Everything.'

She had voiced that same desire to him only four months before. Time had not changed that for her; if anything, it had intensified Paula's feeling of sureness, rightness. She did not dwell on it, but it stayed with her, became part of her. She waited, hopeful. Strong, knowing she could survive if she did not get everything. That was what made waiting and hoping possible, she thought. She felt certain, positive that it would work out. And if it didn't, what she already had was enough. *Dayenu,* that was what she used to say, to sing, at Passover seders—*dayenu.* Enough. What she already had would have been enough. But there was more, too, and she wanted that as well.

'Then that's what I want, too,' she told him, the long-distance wire quivering between them. 'Everything.'

Max laughed softly. She could imagine the corners of his mouth turn up, in her mind, as clearly as if he were standing next to her.

'It's very hard to do this traditionally,' he told her. 'Will you take it from me that I'm down on my knees, next to the phone, three thousand miles away?'

Paula's heart leapt wildly. 'Does that mean this is a proposal?' she asked. Please, God, oh, please, yes.

'That's what it means,' Max said. 'Will you marry me?'

She cried then, and Max teased her. 'Ridiculous, isn't it, the way these solid professional types take refuge in tears when they can't take the pressure?'

'Oh, Max,' she cried happily. 'Oh, Max. Yes. Yes.'

'I love you,' he breathed into the phone.

'I love you, too,' she said. 'Soon. As soon as I can. After I get my bearings at the law school. By this time next year. Or before.'

'Before,' he said firmly. 'Unless, of course, you're not sure.'

'Oh, I'm sure, Max,' she told him.

'Beyond a reasonable doubt?' he asked. 'It's an old standard, and imperfect, but it works, most of the time.'

'This time, too,' she said fiercely. She wouldn't have believed him, nor he her, if they had no doubts at all. They were both too old for that kind of innocence. But they were too young to give up on that dream entirely. Marriage was a risk—just living was a risk, Paula thought. But theirs, she was sure, would make it.

FORTY-FOUR

Lara had disappeared just before Halloween. Somehow Ellin got through the days, though there was never one in which she did not call up some image of her child, have the awful fears again, and then the chills. She let it get to her sometimes; sometimes she gave in to her enormous sense of guilt, and loss, and terror, and beat her fists on the smooth grey flannel cover of her bed, and soaked the pillow with her tears until, exhausted, she slept.

She went to the police several times, but they were of little use. They did not think Lara was in danger; they pointed to the withdrawal of funds from her checking account as an indication that the girl had planned her departure. The private detectives came up with few leads. They checked all of Lara's contacts in California—Ellin thought she might have gone there, but none of Lara's friends knew anything of her whereabouts and Tony's lawyer told her that his apartment had been sealed by the coroner after his death. 'Sometimes kids crash there, so we boarded it up, to protect his belongings,' he said. 'When you come to California to settle the estate, I'll give you the key.'

Paula thought work was the best thing for Ellin. Cass kept a respectful distance; she felt Ellin's coolness, and avoided anything more than an occasional overture—a gift of flowers, a call before coming home: 'Is there anything you need?' There was nothing, in any case, that Cass could have provided.

Mostly Ellin stayed home—she didn't want to be far from the phone, just in case. Occasionally Paula dragged her out. 'Look, that's what your answering service is being paid for,' she said. Once she went out with Paula and Cass, and had a reasonably pleasant time until she remembered that she had not thought about Lara for hours. Guiltily, she returned to the brownstone, where the phone waited, silent and accusing.

Finally it did ring, the day before Thanksgiving. It was the voice of a stranger who identified himself as a representative of a 'runaway hot line'.

'I'm calling on behalf of your daughter, Lara Devlin,' he told her, and Ellin's heart leapt.

'Where is she? Is she safe? Oh, where is my baby?'

'I can't tell you that,' he replied. 'In fact, I don't know. Lara called us and asked us to call you; she wouldn't say where she was. She wanted us to say—just a minute, I have it written down here—'Tell Mom I'm okay, and not to try to find me. I need to think things out for myself, and I'll call her as soon as I have.'

The call was not much, but it allayed the worst of Ellin's fears. 'At least she's alive,' she told Dr Horner. 'At least I know that much.'

'And aware of your pain and worry,' the psychiatrist said. 'She's a compassionate child—she's not doing this to hurt you. She needs to do it for herself, and you have no choice except to let her.'

'But what if . . . doesn't she know that . . .' Ellin's words trailed off, and Dr Horner patted her arm sympathetically.

'Of course she knows,' she told Ellin. 'There are some things she doesn't know—like how much she needs you. When she does, she'll come home.'

Work was the only surcease from the heavy burden Ellin carried within her. Oddly enough, she was writing better than she ever had; she could lose herself in the words as they appeared in the little plastic triangle above the ribbon, and joined the orderly rows of the others, on the orderly stack of pages that rested in the cardboard box next to her typewriter. Her deadline was two weeks before Christmas, and she knew she would make it. Christmas. She couldn't bear to think of that. She'd made reservations before, promised Lara they'd go home at Christmas. What would Christmas be without Lara? She felt herself slipping back into the whirlpool of fear and loneliness and grief, and willed herself out of it. Work. She could concentrate on work.

Kate came from California for a visit. She made Ellin go out at first, and then she just sat there with her, when Ellin's black periods came over her.

Ellin couldn't function very well in the present, so she spent a great deal of time ruminating over the past. Her book was done, finally; she turned it in to her editor in early December. She had reservations west on December 22—she wanted to leave earlier, but she kept hoping that Lara might turn up.

Paula was already gone, off to Mexico for a couple of weeks in the sun. 'Look, I can take this trip some other time,' Paula had told her before leaving. 'I'll be glad to stay around, if it will do any good.'

Ellin was grateful, but declined Paula's offer. 'It won't,' she said. 'I'll be okay. I wouldn't even go west myself, but I have some business of Tony's to settle, and Kate insists that I come. Besides, I feel closer to Lara in California. For a while I thought she might be out there, you know. I called some of her friends, and the tenants in my house, but they haven't seen her. So go. It's only two weeks until I leave myself.'

'And then?'

Ellin smiled sadly. 'And then I'll come back here, I guess, and start another book or something. And . . . wait.'

Paula didn't press her about the brownstone, but once she left, Ellin could not wait to get out of it. It was oppressive; she and Cass exchanged pleasantries, and even had dinner together occasionally, but without Paula, it was nothing like it had been. The subject of Vic was never brought up: Cass tried to say something once, but Ellin stopped her. 'I'd prefer not to talk about him,' she said. 'It's okay, Cass.'

It wasn't okay at all, but Ellin would not give Cass the satisfaction of telling her that. Vic acted as though nothing out of the ordinary had occurred; to see him with Cass, as Ellin did occasionally, was to know nothing of anything that had passed between them. Cass was as cool and detached from Vic as she had been before their weekend together. He had suited her purpose. And, as she told Paula, 'What do I do with him? Take him to parties and say, This is Vic, he's my handyman?'

Ellin didn't want a scene over Vic. She hated confrontations; she just wanted to be alone. She thought she might look for another apartment when she came back to New York after Christmas; with Paula leaving, she had no reason to stay in the brownstone. Even when Paula was there, it was not as it had been. And when she was not, Ellin wanted to get out of the house in the same way she had wanted to get out of that terrible apartment she lived in with Lara when she was a baby. She wanted out of Cass, too—without a scene, without words, without anything except her pride. Cass had not wounded her in quite the same way Tony had, but the disappointment was not entirely dissimilar. With Tony, too, she had wanted to make a life; she had invented one, and lived in it for a time, until it no longer worked, and then it was over. And that was the way she felt about the brownstone.

She packed a small bag for her trip west; she did not expect to be gone long. She took with her only a few clothes, and, on impulse, the small box, wrapped in heavy brown paper, that had come, finally, from Africa. Tony's remains. His remains. She shuddered—she would put them in the basement in her house for now.

Kate met her at the airport, and folded her into her

arms. Ellin couldn't help it—she began to cry. So Kate took her home, and fed her tea and brandy, and told her funny stories, and led her into the guest room, and Ellin slept.

She dreamt of Tony that night, and of Lara, and when she awakened the next day, she called the lawyer who was handling Tony's affairs, arranging to see him that afternoon. Borrowing Kate's car, she drove out to her house.

I miss this, she thought sadly; oh, how I miss it. All the days and nights that she had been unhappy there fled from her mind; she remembered only the good things.

'We certainly have enjoyed living here,' said her tenant. 'Going to be sorry to leave. I suppose you'll be moving back in then, this spring?'

'I don't know yet,' said Ellin. 'I just don't know.'

At the lawyer's office in Century City a pleasant-faced secretary offered her a cup of coffee and some magazines while she waited. Then she was ushered into his office.

It was a long meeting. There were papers to sign, and forms to go over. The lawyer had an inventory of Tony's assets, and gave her a copy.

'Some of his things are still in the house in Venice,' he said. 'Tony had prepaid his lease there until the end of the year. Here are the keys; I've been there, of course, but you might like to go out and look things over. There are some clothes, a few books, some pictures. You and your daughter should decide what to keep, and I'll be glad to handle disposal of the rest.' He took off his glasses and rubbed the bridge of his nose; he did not know about Lara's disappearance, Ellin realized.

'I can't tell you how sorry we all are about this,' he said to Ellin, not unkindly. 'He was a young man, so much to live for, and a great dramatic talent. We're all poorer for his passing.'

We certainly are, thought Ellin. We certainly are. She

took the keys, and copies of the documents, and left the office.

The telephone rang frequently on Christmas Eve at Kate's house—Kate's friends and her own. Paula called from Mexico, and Ellin was glad to hear from her. From Cass there was no word—Ellin had not expected it.

Every time the phone rang, she jumped. But it was never Lara. She had left Kate's number with her answering service, and she tried to control herself, but it was difficult. Lara loved Christmas; Ellin had had to steel herself to keep from buying gifts for her. But she could not—it was, she knew, a way of denying that Lara was gone.

Kate had a brunch on Christmas morning; Ellin fled the house, unable to bring herself to pretend a happiness she did not feel. Instead, she drove out to Venice, to Tony's house. I may as well get this over with, she thought, as she let herself into the place, a lower duplex a few blocks from the ocean.

Somebody's been crashing here, she thought, despite what the lawyer said about having the place sealed. None of the windows appeared to be broken; she couldn't imagine how anyone had gotten in. And there was no power—the electricity had been cut off weeks before. She pulled the heavy curtains away to let in some afternoon light, and picked up a towel from the floor. It was still damp. That's odd, she thought. In the bathroom, she found a bathing suit hanging on the towel bar. With a start, she recognized it as Lara's. It, too, was slightly damp.

A ray of hope leapt in her and she followed the trail of dirty clothes into the bedroom that had been Lara's. The bed was rumpled; it had recently been slept in. She sniffed at the pillows; the scent was salty, and fresh. Excited, she ran to the closet—she could not see in the dimness, but she stumbled on an overnight bag, the one she had given Lara when she went back to school in September.

Lara's here! she knew joyfully. Lara's here, and she's

safe! No matter what the lawyer said, she was. She must have been hiding out somewhere during the day, and sneaking in here at night. Lara must have found a way in—or did she still have her own, old set of keys? That could explain why there were no signs of break-in.

On a hunch, Ellin checked the hall closet, where she knew Lara kept her surfboard; it was missing, and Ellin was certain that Lara was at the beach. She hung up the damp towels, opened some windows, and settled down to wait for her daughter.

A pang of sadness stabbed her: Tony. Ellin went to his room and opened his bureau drawers. The scent of his cologne wafted up; the sight of his handkerchiefs, neatly arranged in tidy rows, moved her. She found a stack of letters in the top drawer, and turned them over thoughtfully. They were letters from her, letters and pictures, and she felt his absence like a sharp knife.

She was rereading the words of love she had written him so many years before when Lara came in. Mother and daughter looked at each other for a long moment, and then Ellin ran to her.

'You're safe!' she breathed into the girl's damp hair. 'Thank God, you're safe!' She cried then, and so did Lara; it was a long time before they sat on Tony's bed, facing each other.

'I'm not going back,' Lara said, a touch of defiance in her voice. 'I'm sixteen, and I'm not going to. You can't make me.'

'Did you hate it so much, then?' Ellin asked softly. 'Was it so awful?'

Lara rubbed her hair with a towel; she wore shorts and a T-shirt over her bathing suit, and Ellin thought she looked very thin. She must have been living on canned goods, she thought—she couldn't have been eating very well. She had no money.

'Not until . . . only after Daddy died,' the girl said. 'I was only doing it for you, for that one year. Daddy promised I could come back here after the movie was over. And then he—and then—' Her voice broke, and Ellin's heart cracked, too.

'Oh, baby, baby,' she said. 'You don't have to go back . . . nobody's making you. I promise . . . you don't have to go back.'

'I won't,' Lara said. 'I got a job, washing dishes at a place near here. And I can finish school, you know. I can get my GED once I'm eighteen.'

Ellin's head swam. Lara had a job. She was all right. She was going to finish school at night, she heard, as her daughter talked on and on. 'And you can go back to New York if you want to . . . I'll be just fine by myself.'

Her chin had a determined, stubborn lift to it; just like Tony, Ellin thought.

'New York? We'll talk about that later, baby—no, don't worry,' she added, as she saw Lara square her shoulders—so much like her father!—and begin to reply. 'I won't force you to come back, if you hate it that much. But night school and washing dishes . . . I don't know.'

She gathered Lara up in her arms. 'Look, let's take it one day at a time, darling . . . you'll come back to Kate's with me, and we'll talk about it, and decide . . .'

'I'll come to Kate's for a little while,' Lara said, 'but I'm staying here. The apartment's paid for until the thirty-first—Daddy left a copy of the receipt here, it says so.' She thrust out her chin. 'I'm staying until I have to leave.'

Poor orphaned baby, Ellin thought. She really doesn't have a home, not now. The beach house has strangers in it, and the brownstone . . . well, that was never her home, only mine. This is the only place she has . . . this is all she has left of her father.

'Okay,' she said. 'Just come let me feed you, all right?' And hug you and kiss you and hold you and understand that you're safe, she thought to herself. Only that.

FORTY-FIVE

Ellin stood in the centre of the living room and directed the movers. 'The bed,' she said, 'be careful with the bed.' It was the only piece of furniture she was shipping back to California; she had put the rest of the things she'd accumulated in her two years in the brownstone in storage, or at Sophie's. She and Lara would live at Kate's until April, when they would take back their own house.

There was no moving Lara, and Ellin accepted that. Not graciously—not at first. She had loved her life in New York, and she was not all that happy about returning to California.

'If I were you, I'd tell her she has no choice,' said Cass.

'Yes, but you're not me,' Ellin replied.

She didn't blame Cass; that was her way. She wasn't a mother, and Ellin secretly hoped she never would be. Some women shouldn't—Amelia was one, Cass herself often said, and admitted that she probably was, too.

Ellin didn't expect life to be easy with Lara. She was practically grown; she had demonstrated her ability to make her own way in the world, and Ellin couldn't take that away from her. She'd taken a Greyhound bus to California, Lara told her; saved the money from her bank account, let herself into Tony's apartment with her own key, and, as Ellin suspected, lived on what she found there until she got a job in a nearby restaurant. She hadn't seen any of her old friends; they, at least, were telling the truth when they told Ellin they hadn't seen Lara in months.

'I needed to be near Daddy,' she said simply. 'And the beach. That's where I feel most alive . . . the beach. Daddy and I had a boat, you know—a little Laser. I've been sailing it around the jetty by myself.'

She sailed it out of the small harbour the day she and Ellin buried Tony. They opened the paper-wrapped box, and lifted out the ashes. They were white, the colour of bone, Ellin saw, and shut her eyes as she scattered them over the side of the little boat. Maybe these are Tony's ashes and maybe they're somebody else's—she couldn't tell, and she didn't think they'd known for sure in Africa, either. They were small and sharp, like pebbles, although underneath they were just dust.

Lara took the box from her and scattered the rest, out over the Pacific. She dropped a white rose overboard, as did Ellin, and then she read the Twenty-third Psalm and Ellin read a passage from Ecclesiastes. They held each other, and watched the setting sun flame the edges of the roses before they disappeared under the water.

They went through Tony's things, and Lara picked out some remembrances—a watch, a bracelet, a picture of her as a baby, and Tony's scrapbook of clippings and reviews. She kept Ellin's love letters to him, too.

They closed the apartment, and moved into Kate's, and Lara started school. If she took courses in the summer, she would graduate with her class in a year and a half.

It's not so long, Ellin thought as she packed the last few things in the apartment. Lara's grown up a lot—maybe it won't be the way it was before.

'But why does it have to be *you* who makes the sacrifices?' Cass asked Ellin in exasperation when she told her about her plans. 'Doesn't she realize this is a very important year for you professionally and that personally you'll be bored to death in Los Angeles?'

'I guess she does,' Ellin said, 'and I guess that's probably true, but I guess it doesn't really change anything.'

She hadn't felt that way at first. At first, she raged to Kate, to Paula—but not to Cass. 'Where is it written that

I have to leave everything that stimulates me and feeds me and gives me pleasure and recognition and rewards?' she had cried to Kate, that day after Tony's funeral. 'Why did that son of a bitch have to die on me, anyway?'

Kate was sympathetic, but sensible. 'It's not forever,' she told Ellin. 'And as for where it's written—well, I always thought it came with the territory—with motherhood. Maybe that's why I take care of other people's daughters and don't have any of my own.'

'I'm not ready,' Ellin told Paula. 'I'm simply not ready to be a full-time mother again. Christ, what's the matter with me? I'm so damn ripe for a permanently empty nest I can't *tell* you!'

Paula didn't remind Ellin how frantic she had been when Lara was missing. She didn't have to; Ellin heard her own words, and shut up. But not that way, she cried inside; I didn't want it that way!

'And so guilty for wanting it,' Paula said sympathetically. 'I know, Ellin, I know. Shit, I'm not a mother, I can't tell you what to do. Only if it were me, I'd go back. It's like—you have a job to do, that's all.'

She was saying what Ellin already knew. She had Lara to finish raising—she owed it to her. And to herself, and, yes, to Tony.

She could come back when it was done. Come back, make a new home for herself after Lara was safely launched in the world.

She'd had two years; she was a better mother now, and Lara a better daughter, too, simply because she did not need Ellin as much as she had, not in the same dependent way. She had learned when Tony died that she would survive, and that when Ellin died, too, she would be all right.

On the way to the car, after the ritual on the boat, the goodbye to Tony, Lara turned to Ellin and hugged her fiercely. 'If you die on me, too. I'll *kill* you!' she whispered against Ellin's neck.

'I won't, love, I won't. But even if I do, you'll be okay. I promise you, you'll be okay.'

Cass insisted on hiring a limousine to take Ellin to the airport. They chatted about the house, Paula's love affair, Ellin's plans for a new novel. 'Look, about Vic,' Cass began, and Ellin hushed her.

'It wasn't about Vic,' she said.

'I know.' Cass looked ashamed. 'He was just . . . well, he was there. I guess I knew all along how you felt about him but I needed him. To make me feel better about Grey, probably.'

Probably, Ellin thought. If that hadn't been the reason, it would have been something else.

'We were really fighting over Paula, weren't we?' she said.

'Yes, I suppose we were.' Cass looked at Ellin hopefully. 'Look, when you come back . . . well, there'll always be an apartment for you in Casita Rosita . . . a place. Even if I have to kick someone out.'

'I know,' said Ellin. 'I know, Cass . . . and thank you.'

She hugged her quickly. 'I'd better go,' she said. 'I think they're announcing my flight.'

The limousine brought Cass back to Twelfth Street. When she closed the door of the brownstone behind her, it echoed hollowly. She was alone.

She dropped her things in the living room and climbed the steps slowly, taking inventory. The carpeting on the stairs was fraying already, she noted; she'd have to get that replaced. The light on the top floor landing was out, too; she'd mention it to Vic. She was maintaining a friendly distance from him; life, she thought, was complicated enough as it was.

Finished with her inspection, satisfied that her house was in order, she retraced her steps down to her own apartment. She called her answering service, and checked her mail.

Amelia had called, and Clio, and Grey Tucker—what was that about? she wondered. There was a message from a man she'd met a week before. He was pleasant and attractive, a banker from Texas—she supposed she would see him, when she had time. There was a bill for dues from the Women's Forum, and a letter from the vice-chairman of a corporate board; Amelia had mentioned that they were looking for a woman director. There was a bill from Con Ed, and a reminder from her dentist, and a bank statement. There was a postcard from John, with a picture of Mount Rainier that made her briefly homesick. Except that she was home, she reminded herself. Finally, there was a square, heavy card bearing the Presidential seal. It was an engraved invitation to a White House dinner honouring the women presidents of American companies—still a small enough number, Cass thought ruefully, to get us all in one room. In the space left for the name of the invitee, she noted, the beautifully calligraphed script read, 'Cassandra Campbell and guest.'

Perhaps she would ask the Texan to accompany her. Or maybe Grey Tucker. There was a touch of irony in that thought, as she remembered how her first and only invitation to dine with the President had been as Grey's guest. And it certainly would give people something to talk about, wouldn't it?

She set the invitation on her desk, and snapped on the reading lamp in the library. Then she took out her briefcase, and got down to work.